THE ENDLIGHT EVENT

by

John P. Cater

9-29-12

Jo Sharon, Mark & Kate —
Thanks for joining our
Tin-Jam. Hope to see you
back! Enjoy this first
tale of Mayan lore,
— John P. Cater

Endlight Event
Copyright 2008
John P Cater
All rights reserved
First Dailey Swan Printing
March 2008

ISBN 978-0-9815845-0-8

Written by John P. Cater

Published by Dailey Swan Publishing, Inc

Dailey Swan Publishing, Inc
2644 Appian Way #101
Pinole Ca 94564

www.Daileyswanpublishing.com

Also available From Dailey Swan Publishing

Confessions of a Virgin Sacrifice by Adrianne Ambrose	$12.95
Beyond the Fears of Tomorrow by Casey Robert Swanson	$9.95
Apers (2006 Golden Duck Winner) by Mark Jansen & Barbara Day Zinicola	$12.95
Revenge by JH Hardy	$12.95
The Lamp Post Motel by Joe Gold	$14.95
The Pub at the Center of the Universe by Dale Mettam	$14.95
Bones of the Homeless by Judy Jones	$15.95
Noggle Stones by Wil Radcliffe	$14.95
Black Beast of Algernon Woods Nickolas Cook	$14.95

www.daileyswanpublishing.com

Dedication:

To the one love of my life, Jaye. I could never
have done this without your unfading love
and support. Thank you for being on this
Earth during my lifetime and sharing your
love with me.

"Now, starflake frozen on the windowpane
All of a winter night, the open hearth
Blazing beyond Andromeda, the sea—
Anemone and the downward seed, O moment
Hastening, halting in the clockwise dust,
The time in all the hospitals is now,
Under the arc-lights where the sentry walks
His lonely wall it never moves from now,
The crying in the cell is also now,
And now is quiet in the tomb as now
Explodes inside the sun, and it is now
In the saddle of space, where argosies of dust
Sail outward blazing, and the mind of God,
The flash across the gap of being, thinks
In the instant absence of forever: now."

Howard Nemerov, 1920 from
Moment

Prologue

Once every thousand years or so celestial events occur that defy explanation, and sometimes, even belief. This story is about one of those events. It will come as certainly as a passing near-Earth comet or asteroid will eventually be pulled into our path by random gravitational forces. However, it will not be a violent rendering of the Solar System's third planet from the Sun, but instead a peaceful event, beautiful in its onset though just as devastating at its end, all the while reminding us just how vulnerable, and helpless, we are against the cosmos.

In all unexpected cosmic events we witness, a noted discoverer emerges. Halley is probably the most famous of all for his comet. A more recent comet, splitting and impacting Jupiter in the mid-nineties, was discovered by two newly-famous astronomers, Shoemaker and Levy. The Endlight Event also has a famous discoverer associated with it—Galileo. Not the Galileo of ancient astronomical fame but a new Galileo, destined to be placed at the same level in the annals of astronomy.

The new Galileo was born in the small Texas town of Fort Davis in early November 1975. Each cooling fall October day prior to his birth, his father Sid Pruitt would stand on the old porch of what was once his grandfather's home and stare in reverence at the gleaming white domes on the distant peak of Mt. Locke. He knew he would have a son and that this son would become a famous astronomer. He and his wife Beth had almost lost the family farm during recent droughts and they wanted better for their firstborn. On November 5th at 6:01 p.m. they named their new son Galileo Mason Pruitt in honor of the great seventeenth-century astronomer Galileo Galilei.

Galileo, or Galley as his folks called him, matured in the shadow of, at first, two observatories, then a third and much larger one being constructed as he started high school. As his father wished, Galley eventually did become interested in that beautiful night sky and what it held for him in its mysterious darkness.

He first became fascinated with comets and their beauty while reading about Halley's Comet in Ms. Roder's fifth-grade science class. He began counting down the days, one at a time, until he could visit the large observatory and actually have a chance to see it. Galley planned to watch and document it just like a real astronomer through the large McDonald telescope.

During summer breaks from school when all his friends were relaxing around the large spring-fed pool at Balmorhea or enjoying vacations to Indian Lodge and Big Bend, Galley frequented the large observatory. As he would sit thinking, on the lush grounds surrounding the immense domed white buildings, he imagined himself a famous astronomer with a comet named after him, like Mr. Halley. He *really* wanted that.

Galley saw all types of people enter and leave the big buildings. Some men had large beards, some small ones. The smarter the man, the larger the beard, he theorized. Galley was making plans to grow a beard—when it started growing, anyway. The women that entered and left mostly reminded him of variations on Ms. Roder, lean and athletic looking, but very tomboyish. They all reminded him of librarians, too.

Every minute that was not spent at football practice quarterbacking (everyone at Ft. Davis High played football, it was just the Texas small-town thing to do) was spent on Mt. Locke, out in the back yard gazing at the sky through his dad's hunting binoculars, or in his darkened room, examining the ceiling-projected star maps from his newly acquired Spitz planetarium. He had taken on a local newspaper delivery route just to buy the little mesmerizing blue ball with the light in it. It had so captivated his imagination since he first saw it in a mail order catalog that he had carried the dog-eared flyer with him everywhere he went until that monumentous day the large box arrived on the front porch.

Galley was thrilled to see his dreams of becoming an expert in astronomy begin to come true. He already knew more about the planets than anyone else in his new class, and he was even catching up to Ms. Roder's knowledge.

One spring afternoon in 1992, the year before his high-school graduation, Galley encountered a stately astronomer from the large observatory. Quietly immersed in a borrowed graduate astronomy textbook in the courtyard of the nearby observatory, Galley was startled as the scientist approached and began to speak. He introduced himself as Ian Arthur-Hyde, speaking

7

with a strangely chopped deep accent. "Don't remember seein' ya round these parts," he said. "Are ya from the UT grad school in Austin?"

Galley looked shyly back to the pages of his book. "No, sir. Not yet. I'm Galley Pruitt, a senior at Fort Davis High majoring in astronomy." He blushed at his awkward lie. He was neither a senior nor majoring in astronomy—it just made him feel more important in the stranger's eyes.

Arthur-Hyde smiled in return and squatted in the shady newly mown grass next to Galley. "Well Galley, do you mind if I rest here a moment?"

Galley's smile gleamed through his bookish stare. "No sir! Not at all."

Several minutes of silence passed before Galley spoke again. He raised his gaze from the printed words to the quiet stranger's face and paused. "Are you from Australia?"

"No, Galley. I'm from England. Have you ever been there?"

"No sir. Sorry, I haven't. Haven't even been very far out of West Texas, for that matter," Galley replied, looking back to his book.

"That's nothing to be ashamed of, Galley. I think this country is beautiful. So stark and rustic . . . I hear locals in town call it God's country . . . can't say I blame them either. The smell of spring thunderstorms with cedar and wildflowers in the air—there's nothing in my England like this any time of year."

Galley, not looking up, breathed in deeply to test Ian's assertion. He had often wondered if everyone breathed air that smelled this fresh. That's why *he* called it God's country.

Galley returned his attention to Ian. "What's

it like over there—where you're from?"

Ian plucked a small flat-topped blade of grass, placed it into his mouth and sat back, looking into the shading branches above. He shut his eyes and began to relate vivid tales of his English countryside and family in Chipping Norton, Britain's beauties and its large radio telescopes at the Neffield Radio Astronomy Laboratories in Jodrell Bank.

Hearing this, Galley finally lowered his book and began to ask questions about the telescopes and the people of science that used them. Ian, once an inquisitive kid himself, but now a senior cosmologist, was happy to point another eager youngster into a pastoral life of stargazing.

Ian spent an hour describing his cosmic career and the excitement that it had provided him. He told of his meeting the late Carl Sagan at the International Astronomy Conference. He excitedly told Galley how he was delivering a paper to the conference on his new theory of black hole jets and Carl came up to him after the presentation and praised his work.

He continued, describing his work at the Jodrell Bank radio telescope and the thrill of finding a new asteroid while working at the Kitt Peak Observatory in Arizona. Finally, in a stern but informative manner he explained to Galley the requirements to be an astronomer and that he *must* attend college and preferably get a doctorate to be a successful astronomer. Galley smiled as the admonition began to soak in.

After graduating high school *cum laude,* Galley investigated colleges offering degrees in astronomy, based on Ian's recommendations, and found that his first choice *was* the University of Texas in Austin. This was the same university that ran and operated the McDonald Observatory. Galley remembered that Ian had told him if he studied there, he would have access to the observatory on his home visits to Fort Davis. That sold Galley on UT Austin.

Shortly after applying to the University of Texas at Austin, Galley was accepted. He graduated with a B.S. in astronomy with honors four years later. During that period he had three chances to use the new Hobby-Eberly telescope at Mt. Locke, and jumped at each opportunity offered him.

During each of his uses, he searched in the near space just outside our Solar System for comets. His studies had shown that more comets, some still undetected, were sure to exist and eventually orbit into Earth's view. They would all have to have names and he wanted his name on one. Pruitt's Comet, or maybe, Galley's Comet, he couldn't decide.

Galley began to write in technical journals of his findings of interstellar debris like stardust orbiting just outside our Solar System. In his research he investigated a near-interstellar region, the theorized Kuiper belt, named after a Dutch astronomer, Gerard Kuiper. The region was so tagged because it was Kuiper who first postulated that swarms of minor planets in the orbital belt must be the source of many orbiting short-period comets. Another theorized belt, the Oort cloud, was thought to be home to the other, longer period comets, such as Halley's. In either belt, the floating debris is subject to gravitational pull from passing asteroids or planetary alignments, and could at any minute start a possible orbital trajectory toward the Sun.

Cosmic perturbations and orbital mechanics fascinated Galley so much that he continued on to graduate school in Austin and finally graduated with a Ph. D. in Astronomy in 2000. While performing his graduate explorations at the McDonald Observatory, Galley had the opportunity to use the Millimeter Wave Dish, a non-optical telescope that used millimeter-long radio waves rather than light to view stars and other cosmic disturbances. He was fascinated with this novel device for observing astronomical phenomena. Because of his new found interest he took a job there after graduation and stayed on the staff of the MWD. A year later, Galley received an unsolicited job offer from what was considered to be the grandfather of all radio telescopes, the Very Large Array in Socorro, New Mexico. He accepted the offer immediately and began packing.

During the two weeks before his move to New Mexico, he met the woman of his dreams while taking an overdue vacation in Albuquerque. He wasn't planning to start a relationship that early in his life. It just happened.

On a short excursion to Madrid, a quaint artists' colony on the Turquoise Trail near Santa Fe, Galley stopped for lunch at a busy little sidewalk bistro. The outside menu caught his eye and drew him into the crowded romantic courtyard. Once inside he realized the tables were all occupied. He started to leave but noticed a beautiful slender blonde by herself, eating a small salad and examining the cover of a CD. She glanced up from the jewel case and smiled at Galley. Shyly he glanced down to his hand and saw he had just purchased the same CD she held in her hand. Then he did something he had never done before. Driven by a mysterious force he didn't understand he walked slowly to her table and put his CD on the table beside hers. The titles, "Kindred Spirits" matched.

"Is this good Indian flute music?" he asked, hoping for a positive response.

"No," she answered with a roll of her eyes.

"Oh, I'm sorry." Galley blushed and picked up his CD.

"Wait!" she said, "It's not *Indian* flute music—that's for snake charmers. This is Native American flute music . . . and yes, it's very good music." She smiled and motioned to the empty chair by her, "That seat's not taken, if you'd like to have lunch. Of course, you'll have to buy mine, too."

Galley grinned. "Are...Are you sure?" He was mesmerized by her beauty but tried not to show it. His heart was pounding.

"Well, I hate to eat alone . . . yes, please join me and let's discuss kindred spirits. I'm Jalisa Foxlow." She held out her hand.

Taking it gently, Galley sat and started a conversation that lasted for over four hours. During that time they discovered very strange common tastes besides ethnic flute music. Both of them had small art collections by a particularly unusual and rather esoteric artist, Salvadore Dali. They both had competed in high school science fairs, which keyed Galley that this was no dumb blonde, and finally they seemed to know what each other was thinking, like soul mates or identical twins. He had never had such a spiritual —almost magical— experience before.

Galley was totally enthralled with Jalisa's beauty and knowledge, and she was quickly becoming interested in him. After all, she favored intelligence over brawn, but Galley wasn't lacking in either. As they left the bistro together at the end of the day, a little elderly lady stopped them. "I just have to tell you that you two make such a handsome tall couple," she said. "You should have beautiful children." Blushing all the way to her car, Jalisa interrupted the awkward silence, "Galley, if you're still in town tomorrow night, I'd like to cook you dinner and repay you for the wonderful lunch. I really enjoyed it."

"Well, I was planning on heading back tomorrow, but . . . . ."

The entire encounter came as a surrealistic shock to him. They had fallen in love at first sight, and he didn't really believe that could happen. After dinner the next night, he went back to Fort Davis, got his household goods and then rushed back to Socorro, where he would be only about sixty miles from Albuquerque—and Jalisa. A month later he asked her to marry him.

The next year they married. During the first year of his marriage he made great inroads into occultation and shadow analysis of passive objects, using radio waves. This notable work earned the facility much publicity and, best of all, Federal grant money. It also brought a visiting fellow astronomer from Sweden, Neemu Hatlem, to be assigned to work with Galley. They became best friends. So close, so in fact, that Neemu decided to stay on at the VLA, and applied for American citizenship.

Over the next years, their friendship grew even closer. Neemu married his fiancée, Rutha, who finally followed him over from Sweden. They had four children, two boys and two girls, in rapid succession. In time the two couples, Galley and Jalisa, and Neemu and Rutha, became best friends.

Then, a handful of years later came Galley's discovery. Nothing was the same after that.

CHAPTER 1
TWILIGHT APPROACHING
DARKNESS

"The Earth will soon go into total darkness as an opaque cloud of cosmic matter moves over our Sun from interstellar space. We as a species must brace ourselves for this impending darkness in our lives. In 2012 we will experience an Extinction Level Event. May God save us all."

GALILEO M. PRUITT, Ph.D., 2011

Outside, evening temperatures were dipping into the minus seventies. Galley looked up from his notebook as he heard Gus's familiar voice.

The small transistor radio lodged snugly between the salt and pepper shakers crackled out the gruff monotone of oldtimer Gus Freeman, Socorro's KTEK radio weatherman, ". . . is 7:05 p.m. and the outside summer—uh, Twilight—temperature is seventy-two degrees Fahrenheit—below zero, that is. And that's not wind chill either, folks. The low tonight will be minus seventy-five, high tomorrow only sixty-five below zero. Oh . . . and tomorrow's solar efficiency should continue to decrease to around 14 percent. The Endlight Event, those rocket scientists say, is only twenty-eight days away. Bundle up cowboys, it's only gonna get colder . . . Brrrr. Where's that global warming when we need it? Now for today's silent prayer . . ."

Old Gus had gotten pretty good at predicting these temperatures, Galley thought. He should have, they had been dropping about two-and-a-half degrees a day since Twilight began sixty-three days ago. At least *we* weren't experiencing the minus nineties they had up North. It was Cold for New Mexico . . . especially for July. *Brrrr.* A shiver rushed up Galley's spine.

Galley switched off the radio and stood, staring blankly through the frost-covered kitchen window into the freezing darkness. How strange to have been so thrilled at having finally accomplished his parents' dream of being a famous astronomer and then to be so devastated by the results of that same achievement.

Earth's Twilight had started over two months ago just as he had predicted. It began with a hardly noticeable cooling of the Sun's rays, weak rays like he remembered on his visits to Southern California and New York where the Sun barely filtered through the choking smog. That early phase of Twilight created an almost jubilant atmosphere across the world because of the eerie strangeness of the cool daylight. Worries of global warming were fading quickly.

Then as the Cloud slowly continued to move between the Earth and the Sun, the growing absence of radiant heat took him back to those very wintry overcast days of his youth. Yet now he could still clearly see the Sun as a pinkishgray disk with no blurring of the outline at all. It was as if a giant welder's mask had been placed between the Earth and its lifegiving solar furnace.

Even nighttime was strangely dark. The stars were just as bright as before, the only reminder of the Moon was a very faint black disk that occasionally eclipsed a visible star.

He knew that very soon the dwindling daylight would be no brighter—or warmer—than a full moon's moonlight, before Twilight. Now, even moonlight would be welcomed, but since the Cloud blocked the moon's sunlight, too, Earth was very quickly falling into the deepest darkness ever witnessed by life on Earth. An extinction level event, or ELE, was imminent.

The beginning weeks of Twilight were easier because the warmth had not yet faded. Dark and warm were fine—well, fine as they could be, considering—but dark and cold were just simply depressing. He thought of late May when rainbows of fragrant wildflowers were in bloom and temperatures in the mid-eighties blew warm bouquets of nature all around. He never realized how much he could miss the warm Sun on his face—or the smell of fresh cut grass. But then everybody was in this together. Everybody missed the warm Sun, but —.

Suddenly, he heard Jalisa scream from the front room. Rushing to her, he saw her tall slender figure wrenching in pain by the front door, trying to escape from it. Her blond hair was being thrown around her head in frenzied motion. Shadows from the roaring fireplace danced madly on the far wall.

Instinctively he ran toward her across the Saltillo tile floor and onto the Navaho rug. As he tried to stop, the rug continued with him under his feet. Like a ballistic missile, he slid across the room and crashed headfirst into the wall just inches from where she was being held captive.

"God! I'm sorry, honey," he mumbled, still dazed from the impact. Brushing the thinning salt-

and-pepper hair from his eyes, he felt for his missing glasses. Quickly he bent over, reached down and groped for them. After one accurate sweep he found the gold-rimmed spectacles nestled in the folds of the crumpled rug beneath him and put them on. He rose upright and looked at his wife, still shrieking in obvious trouble. Only then did her problem sink in, clearing his mind immediately: she was trying to break loose from the doorknob that had frozen to her hand!

"Help me, Galley! Dammit!" she said, childishly stomping her feet. "I'm sorry—I forgot. I was just trying to shut the door tighter to keep out this stupid cold—and my hands were wet."

"Damn!" Galley turned, ran into the kitchen and grabbed the warming teakettle from the stove. She could hear him muttering something about Lucy. He had always related her, lovingly of course, to Lucy and all her shenanigans. He even called himself Ricky sometimes just to rattle her. This time he knew Lucy was in trouble.

He returned a moment later to pour the warm water over her hand. As he began to tip the steaming kettle, she noticed the tendrils of white vapor rising from the spout and screamed, "Galley that's too hot! Don't burn me!"

"I won't!" he yelled back, now shaking at the tension of the situation. "It's only lukewarm, I promise!" His reassurances weren't helping her. She began to dance frantically in small steps, almost making Galley laugh. Her glaring eyes stopped him cold. Lucy was *really* in trouble.

As she watched Galley inspecting her predicament she began to sob. "Galley, how much longer do we have? I hate this!"

Galley ignored her question and methodically began to pour the steaming water, first over the knob, then on her hand.

"Ow! Galley, you liar! That *is too* hot!" she screamed, frenetically trying to pull her hand away. Finally, the icy grasp of the doorknob released with a tug, freeing her hand only to strike Galley square in the face, knocking his glasses to the floor again.

"Ow! That works," he said chuckling, as he bent down for his glasses once again. Strange how I'd know where they'd land, he thought. "How does it feel? Did it take any flesh?"

She was calmed somewhat by her hand's freedom. "No. I'm okay, I guess. Sorry, I didn't mean to hit you Galley, how much more time do we have?"

Galley hesitated as he started back into the kitchen. "I think we'll be okay for another month. Nobody has ever witnessed a total Earth cool down before, but at the rate we're dropping we'll be okay until lateAugust. By that time, at the current rate of cooling, daytime temperatures should be around minus 180 Fahrenheit or colder. Then we'll..." His voice faded.

"What happens then?"

Galley mumbled something from the kitchen and returned, carrying a dry towel. "Here, let me dry your hand and clean up this mess before you slip and break your head, too."

"What happens then?" she repeated persistently. "And I'm in no mood for joking, dammit!"

He carefully wiped her hand, frowning at the redness he found there. "Nobody really knows, but some experts are guessing that

19

eventually all bodies of water across the Earth will freeze. First the fresh water bodies, then the oceans and seas. If temperatures keep dropping the atmosphere might even freeze."

"But how would we breathe, Galley?" She was beginning to lose concern for her aching hand and tried to pull it away.

"Don't! We've got to get some blood flowing." Galley yanked at her hand and persisted in his vigorous massage. Without looking up he began to relate the plans of a group that called itself the Deep Earth Survival Colony.

"There's a group that has been studying projections of dropping temperatures and predicts that the atmosphere *will* freeze before life comes to an end on Earth as we know it. So they're preparing to try to continue living past that time and prevent everything from dying. They're trying to outlive the Endlight Event."

Jalisa finally freed her hand from his grasp, but became less interested in it word by word. "How can they do that without air?"

"They plan to go underground where it's much warmer, and then somehow mine frozen air from the surface. The expansion of the air during underground thawing will serve to provide energy for the process and the colony. The remainder of the group's energy will be supplied by geothermal generators from what I read."

"How many people are in this Deep Earth whateveryoucalledthem?"

"The Deep Earth survival colony. According to the newspapers, at last count, they had over a thousand people in their movement, and they're growing by several hundred each week"

Jalisa thought for a moment, staring blankly at her hand. "If these geniuses are so bright and really know what they're doing, why are there only 1000 members?"

Galley smiled at her comment and began to wipe the steaming water from the floor. "Ah, there's a catch. The group has some very elaborate and expensive plans. And since there's no government funding for such a private group, they collect a fee as each new member joins."

"How much?"

"They've successfully collected a million dollars from each entering member."

She dropped her hand from her gaze, now forgetting it completely, and paused. "That's over a billion dollars so far!"

"That's right. And they'll need *all* of it—or more—to reach their goals," Galley punctuated his statement with a final broad sweep of the damp dishtowel across the tile. He stood stiffly and grimaced, grabbing his back in response as he kicked the Navaho rug back into place. He turned, still bent slightly, and returned to the kitchen muttering something about getting old, as Jalisa, exhausted and still shaking, sat on the couch. She began to slowly reexamine her hand.

Her hand was still red and small pieces of skin had been torn from her palm when she freed it from the icy doorknob. "Galley, why are we even trying? There's no point to this is there?"

Silence.

"Oh well. At least we have each other."

Silence.

As Galley emerged once again from the kitchen he noticed Jalisa's sly smile. "Good! You're

21

smiling. What did I do now?"

"Galley, you're not getting old. You just worry about it too much."

Galley sat beside Jalisa, put his arm around her and said, "Thanks, honey. I guess I do. But it's probably justified by the way I feel . . . anyway, the group is trying to entice a few scientists to join the Colony Staff for future planning. They'll help the Colony members develop scientific strategies and tactics as they move to this new way of living. They especially need physicists, cryogenics experts and radio astronomers. I think they're probably going to ask me to join as one of their astronomers —"

Jalisa stiffened, somewhat astounded. "Galley, you know we don't have two million dollars floating around to join a crazy group like that! And if we did, why in the world would we want to?"

"Wait. Let me finish . . . scientists work their way in. Of course it means I'll have to quit my position at the VLA. But what good will the VLA be when everyone else is freezing or already frozen?" His voice quieted with seriousness, "Yesterday, Neemu and I detected a possible clearing moving into the Solar System that may produce a dawn by late October. It would be the Earth's savior—at least for the time being. Otherwise, we'll have to wait for the Earth to orbit back into sunlight sometime in late December around Christmas. Things will be getting pretty cold by then. If we join this Deep Earth thing, we might just make it through to the dawn."

Galley wished that he wasn't so logical. He knew the clearing was moving too slowly to save most of the planet, and the time from midAugust to late December was just too long for the Earth to stay in total darkness. The Earth would just freeze and become a cold lifeless place like Venus, with the exception of having about five or six billion dead bodies lying around frozen to death. Whenever the Endlight Event ends with its dawn, he knew, a gradual reheating is predicted to occur. The atmosphere would return to a gaseous state and lakes, rivers and seas would flow again. And then, out of the ground would come this paranoid group of one or two thousand survivors and have to clean the whole damn stinking, thawing thing up. And if the Cloud was still in the Solar System, Earth might orbit back into the God-awful Twilight all over again next May.

Great that I found this, he thought, I wanted to be a famous astronomer, and now I'm world renowned, at least for a few months until we all die. "*Mole People!*"

"What did you say, Galley?"

"Oh, I was just thinking out loud . . . thinking of that old corny Superman movie about the Mole People. We're all going to become just like that, living underground in tunnels like moles and scampering up to the surface to gather frozen air.'

"Galley, you're a scientist. Don't be so damn melodramatic. Leave the histrionics to all those doomsday nuts out there."

Galley stood and walked over to switch on the TV. "Why are you doing that when we we're talking?" Jalisa snapped.

"I need to clear my head and just not think about anything. Is that okay?" He returned to her side as the screen flickered to life.

"If you start watching the special reports on

23

the Endlight countdown you'll just start thinking all over again . . . you know that's all that's on."

"I guess you're right," he muttered as he returned to switch the TV off. "Oh, How's your hand, now?"

"It kinda stings," she said. "But I think it'll be all right."

He pushed the button on the TV and walked over to the fireplace to stoke the roaring fire. Poking aimlessly at the cedar logs with the heavy blackened rod, he said, "Honey, remember that all surfaces that touch the outside weather are extremely cold and can freeze to your skin. Please stay away from the windows and outside doorknobs—especially with wet hands. Now come over here and warm your hands."

Jalisa knew that sermon was coming, eventually. Galley had always tried to baby her. "I won't touch anything again. I just forgot, Galley . . . I'm really okay," she said with a repenting and childish pout. Good acting, she thought. She patted the cushion beside her, motioning for Galley to sit.

He paused, replaced the stoker on the hearth and returned to her side. "Honey, I know, I have trouble remembering sometimes myself. It's becoming a strange world out there . . . but I love you more than ever." He put his arms around her and embraced her lovingly.

Unresponsive to his gesture, Jalisa dropped her head and began rubbing her hand again. "I hate it Galley."

"I know. We have to adapt so quickly. Every day it's becoming more dangerous if we let our guard down. That's what I hate about this, too—

no more relaxing, only tension and worrying about what's going to happen next—but we can do it."

She finally responded and put her arms around him. "I love you too. We'll make it. With your knowledge and my beauty, we can't lose."

A subtle squeeze from Jalisa made Galley grin. "Yeah, we'll make it," he said, returning the squeeze, "and if we don't, we'll still be with each other—somewhere."

For moments, they just sat, snuggled warmly in each other's arms, silently contemplating what lay in front of each of them. She knew that he was under more stress than ever before since he had discovered this horrendous upcoming event. He knew and hated that she was ultimately destined to do whatever he did, because of his scientific interest and activity in predicting, detecting and then documenting Endlight. He had to consider each decision about changes in their lives very carefully.

A piercing electronic beeping jolted Galley from his sleep. Confused at first, he looked around to see that Jalisa was still next to him but the fire was out, the glowing red embers were now white and cold. Then his attention went to the window. He saw the pinkishgray glow of the Twilight daylight.

"Oh, crap!" Galley looked at his beeping watch. It was ninefifteen in the morning and he was late for work. He remembered setting the alarm to remind him of the meeting with the press. Galley jumped up and shook Jalisa. "Honey, I'm late. We slept all night and I've got to get to work."

She groaned as she stretched her arms and began a slow yawn. "What time is it?"

"Ninefifteen. I'm supposed to be in a press conference right now,"

"I'll call your office," she said, now realizing the urgency of the situation. "You just get ready."

"Would you go warm up the car for me, too?"

"Okay, I'll go warm up the car for you, too," Jalisa said in a mocking tone, still groggy from her waking sleep. She hated the cold, especially in the morning.

"Tell them I'll be there about tenthirty. Say I couldn't get my car started or something. That's getting to be a good excuse these days. Thanks." Galley smiled, kissed her on the head and whizzed past her into the bedroom to change clothes.

"Good morning, how may I direct your call?" the observatory operator asked.

"Extension 241, please." Jalisa requested. Four rings. Five rings. Jalisa began to tap her finger on the receiver. The sixth phone ring changed, signaling a rollover to a forwarded phone.

"Neemu here, can I help you?" a voice said.

"Hi Neemu, this is Jalisa Pruitt. Galley's gonna be a little late because his car froze overnight. He forgot to plug in the engine heater."

Neemu laughed. "Likely story . . . oh, and by the way, there are some hopping mad reporters around here. They've been waiting for him for twenty minutes already. They're not going to take kindly to another hour wait."

"Sorry, Neemu, just try to appease them with something. He should be there around tenthirty. Can't you talk to them until then? Maybe show them the control room."

"They want to talk straight to the horse's

mouth. Galley's become pretty famous you know, Jalisa. The press won't talk to just anybody about Endlight."

"Just tell them he's on his way and he's sorry to keep them waiting. If he's that important, then they can just wait. Thanks Neemu. Hope to see you and Rutha and the kids soon —," Jalisa paused as Galley brushed by, grabbed his briefcase and started toward the door.

She lowered the phone momentarily. "Didn't you forget something, Galley?"

"Oh, I'm sorry, honey," he said. "I'm really in a rush."

He spun around, gave her a gentle kiss on the cheek and said, "Love you, bye."

"Love you, bye," Jalisa said as her gaze followed him out the door into the cold dimness of Twilight.

His speedometer was holding at 95 miles per hour and the engine was humming like a precision machine as he flashed past the Socorro city limit sign. Times like these made Galley pleased that he bought the Porsche. He had to travel almost an hour each way along U.S. Highway 60 to go back and forth to his isolated work on the Plains of St. Agustin. He decided last year to get something he would enjoy driving—and it did make each trip easier.

Never had he been late for a press conference this important, and the pumping adrenaline made him press his foot closer to the floorboard. The tachometer raced over 5000 rpm. His Porsche's speedometer climbed to 100 mph.

The roadside signs flashed by in rapid succession; MAGDELENA CITY LIMITS, then VERY LARGE ARRAY RADIO TELESCOPE VISITOR CENTER — 20 MILES. He was making pretty good time. He looked at his watch. Ten-oh-five, I'll be there with time to spare, he thought. Just keep it on 100.

How eerie the scenery these days, he thought. Months ago, looking out of his window during the same trip, he would have seen stark mesas and the Magdalena Mountains, tumbleweed and cacti across the plains shimmering with the heat of the bright morning Sun. Now the pink dimness of Twilight created a very surrealistic effect on the landscape. And the skyline was even more remarkable. The Cloud covered the lower third of the morning sky, like a carbon fog rolling in from the east, so there was a very black, dark band toward the horizon with an ethereal pink disk peering through. Otherwise the stars were blazing brightly across the rest of the sky. Galley noticed Polaris off to his right. At least if I ever get lost, I can still find my way back, he mused. The dimness of the daylight and the lack of oncoming cars on the desolate road were causing his mind to wander.

Suddenly, out of the corner of his eye he saw a flash of motion off the side of the road in the pinkish glow. Then it was in front of him in the glare of his headlights.

"A deer!" he screamed at the top of his lungs as he pounded his hand onto the horn button and jammed his foot through the brake pedal. It had stopped right in front of him and there was no way for him to avoid it without swerving out of control.

He began to see everything in slow motion just as he would have expected to see the scene in a movie. I know I'm either going to die from the impact or freeze to death before help comes, he reasoned. If I swerve, I'll surely lose control and die. On the other hand, if I continue heading straight, I'll hit the deer and possibly be killed by flying glass or even one of those damn antlers coming through the windshield.

As quickly as it happened a moment ago, a second deer came bounding onto the roadway from Galley's right, sped across the road and continued on. The stag quickly turned his attention to the doe and raced across the road after his newest interest.

Not more than two seconds had passed since the event started, yet Galley had traveled almost 300 feet with tires screeching and his car wildly careening all over the highway. Finally, after completing a 540-degree spin, the car ended up in the sand off the side of the road. His heart was pounding and his gasping was beginning to fog the windows. While he sat there dazed with the engine still running he looked up through the settling dust outside his window to Polaris to get his bearing. It was over his left shoulder this time.

Well, right now I certainly don't want to go back where I came from. I'm late; I'm late for a very important date. He was amused at that thought. It must have been the dizzying spin that made him think that. "Galley, get a grip on yourself," he murmured under his breath. As he stared at Polaris he noticed a brief flicker of bright light in the sky slightly to the south of the nearby constellation Cepheus.

What was that? he thought. His heart was racing again. It appeared to him that a bright star had exploded or possibly a meteor had flared at one point of its trajectory across the sky. He watched for a trace of light on either side of the flare but there was nothing but the pink glow. The sector of sky that had flashed was now dim again.

Could it have been a supernova? I'll have to remember to ask the crew on scope duty about that when I get to the observatory.

He looked back over his shoulder searching for more deer. Wouldn't that have been a strange way to end this all, he thought. Then he muttered "Thanks, God," and slowly pulled the Porsche back onto the highway, his hands and knees still shaking, accelerating only to 60 mph.

At 10:20 a.m., Galley reached the mountain overlooking the twenty-seven dish antennas of the VLA Radio Observatory. Normally the white dishes, always organized in a Y shape of varying size, stood out from the surrounding desert in a starkly bizarre manner. He thought it was so strange that this ultra-hightech listening machinery now stands on the New Mexico frontier where Indians once placed their ears to the ground to hear approaching friends or adversaries. Here now are these giant white monuments to science, all standing at attention and facing the same direction like some mutant albino meerkat colony. He always thought of those silly little meerkats standing and turning together above their den to watch for intruders when he saw the antennas reaim themselves toward another galaxy.

Since Twilight, the antennas had taken on

a different look. The pinkishred reflection and very dark shadows gave them a heightened contrast from the desert floor. They reminded him of the little red lights on museum maps that indicate points of interest. But then, he thought, how appropriate. That's exactly what they are. Each of these dishes *is* a point of interest at the VLA visitor center. I wonder if they have a map like that in the visitor center? The thought of the visitor center jarred him back to reality and the crowd of reporters he was getting ready to face. He looked at his watch. He'd still make it by tenthirty.

As he turned off U.S. 60 onto the access road to the visitor center he could see the parking lot was full. Let's see that means there are about sixty to eighty reporters here today he thought, his nervous stomach churning to an audible growl.

As his car approached the main entrance to the visitor center, Galley watched the impatient crowd melt into the blinding brilliance of TV floods. Shielding his eyes from the glare, he heard shouting but could not yet understand what was being said. Soon the voices became clearer as he neared. Reporters jammed microphones up to his windows from both sides.

"Dr. Pruitt?" a window-muffled voice screamed over others, "when are you predicting total Endlight?"

"Dr. Pruitt," another interjected, "is it true the Endlight Event is the result of a disintegrated comet or planet?"

"Galley, John Ruster with CBS News," another announced loudly, his well-known face only inches from Galley's window. "Do you think there is any connection between the Endlight Event and the bright flash of light from the Northern sky this morning?"

Galley paused to open his window and then decided against it. He had already planned his speech and the answers to these questions would be pure conjecture.

He nodded to John, waved and smiled as he slowly released the clutch, moving forward. He continued on through the parking lot, moving slowly to avoid hitting reporters that surrounded him. After finally seeing an opening in the crowded lot, he crept his Porsche into the empty handicapped space in front of the Visitor Center and shut off the engine. He sat motionless for fifteen or twenty seconds, thinking of Ruster's comment. Well, at least I didn't imagine the flash, he thought.

A frigid blast of air hit his face as Galley opened the door. The crowd of reporters silenced to let him speak. Rushing through them toward the warmth inside, Galley pointed and mumbled, "I'll talk in there."

Inside the Visitor Center a speaker's podium had been placed next to a large whiteboard and immense plasma TV screen. The screen showed a computer-generated image of the Sun, Moon and Earth, the Moon encircling the Earth about every six seconds. The image also showed the Earth moving into a graying darkness; rotating about onequarter turn around the Sun and then moving gradually back into sunlight. This process occurred about twice a minute in a perfectly recurring pattern, like the repetition once seen on the daily satellite weather reports showing cloud cover. Back when there were clouds to see.

As Galley walked toward the podium through the buzzing crowd of reporters he felt a silent antagonism that he had never sensed before. It's probably just because they've been standing here over an hour, nothing to do but watch the world turn into darkness, over and over, he thought. He passed in front of the screen and paused to watch the repetitive high-definition computer graphic.

He was rather proud of his computer graphic illustration of the Endlight Event that he had spent the last few weeks programming. During the month following his discovery of an impending solar occlusion, he had insisted to NRAO Headquarters that he needed a Silicon Reality Xtreme Graphics computer to compose illustrative sequences for an Endlight feasibility demonstration. The execs back at headquarters simply explained that their money from the National Science Foundation was currently earmarked for other members of the NRAO group: a fivehundredthousand dollar supercomputer was just too much for one astronomer to need for himself. Besides, not many people believed his crazy prediction that the Earth would really go into darkness, much less stay there for three months. His frantic plea for assistance didn't help his credibility much either. Then exactly three weeks after Galley's discovery and announcement, an astronomer named Janet Lew, at Mauna Kea, an optical observatory in Hawaii, started noticing a very gradual, but persistent, decrease in solar efficiency and reported it through a bulletin from the International Astronomical Union bureau in Cambridge, Mass. Members of the Hubble Space Telescope team in the same bulletin confirmed

33

it. Galley remembered how he laughed the next day when the large white NRAO semi, complete with computer technicians, drove up to the Control Building to install his SRX Computer. No words of apology or humility or anything, just the five-hundred-thousand-dollar supercomputing titanium box he had been asking for.

"Galley, are you all right?" A hand gently tapped his shoulder. He turned away from the screen and saw Neemu standing by the podium holding several sheets of paper and what looked like a bulky red, blue and white cardboard envelope.

"Oh, hi Neemu," Galley responded. "I guess the drive got to me. What's going on?"

"The reporters have been asking about some secret society and your involvement with it," Neemu said. "What do you plan to tell them?"

"It's pretty hard to say something when I don't even know for sure, myself. I'll come up with something."

"Oh, here," Neemu interrupted. "These are the latest reports on Endlight. You might want to look them over before you start answering questions. And by the way here's a really curious news story fax from UPI. It says some eccentric multi-billionaire wants to buy or lease Carlsbad Caverns National Park before he dies. Seems he's always wanted to own it for himself. The press has been asking about that story, too. I guess New Mexico's just hot in the news right now. Too bad our weather's not."

Galley glanced up and smiled in response but his mind was still on Neemu's last comment.

He wondered why anybody would want to buy a National Park when the whole world was going to die by freezing.

"What's the eccentric's name?" Galley asked.

"The story says it's some guy named Jackson Morrow," Neemu related. "He was a wealthy real estate developer in California during the eighties. He rode the up trend and got out before it crashed. Now he wants to own more land, but this time with a campground on it and a cavern beneath it. He's offered over a billion dollars for the place."

"Hmmm, crazy people these days." Galley nodded and stared back at the papers in his hand. The top sheet was the Endlight projection sheet, now known by scientists across the world as the most accurate compilation of scientific opinions and conjecture about the impending doom of the Earth. The top lines read:

LATEST SOLAR PREDICTION:
ENDLIGHT ZENITH:
(Point @ solar efficiency < 1%) 26 days (August 18) @70% prob.
ENDLIGHT EVENT DURATION:
+135 days @75% probability.

"And one other thing, Galley," Neemu added, "You've got a FedEx package in that stack from that Carlsbad guy, Jackson Morrow. Just thought you might be interested in looking at it before the media wolves get you."

"Hmmm." Galley hesitated, then turned to the noisy audience and held out his hands, palms down, "Ladies and gentlemen of the Press, may I please have your attention?"

35

The crowd of reporters scrambled for notepads and pencils as a hush settled over the Visitor Center. Within moments the din had decreased to barely audible mumbles and the sound of small pages turning, as all awaited his first words.

"I have an urgent incoming phone call from Washington, D.C. I know you've been waiting over an hour for this conference, but I must beg your patience for a few more minutes while I take this call."

Galley stepped down from the podium and rushed toward the Visitor Center's main office, dragging Neemu with him. "Come in and close the door behind you," Galley whispered. "I want to see this thing from Morrow."

CHAPTER 2
RSVP

"When I heard the learn'd astronomer,
When the proofs, the figures, were ranged in columns
before me,
When I was shown the charts and diagrams, to add,
divide, and measure them,
When I sitting heard the astronomer where he
lectured with much applause in the lecture-room,
How soon unaccountable I became tired and sick,
Till rising and gliding out I wander'd off by myself,
In the mystical moist night-air, and from time to time,
Look'd up in perfect silence at the stars."

WALT WHITMAN, from *When I*
heard the learn'd astronomer

Galley ripped the tear strip from the top of the FedEx parcel and reached in to retrieve the contents. As the first page emerged from the envelope he noticed the stamped warning in large red letters:

DESC
*** TOP SECRET ***
(For Dr. Pruitt's Eyes Only)

"Uh, Neemu?" Galley said somewhat apologetically, "I need to read this in private . . . but don't leave right now. Just give me a few minutes." Pulling the envelope's contents out with intentional deliberation, Galley slowly sat on the office couch.

Neemu walked over to the desk, sat down and picked up a recent copy of "Time" magazine on one neatly arranged stack of papers. Flipping through the first few pages, he stopped and abruptly closed the magazine. Galley's picture was on the cover! The sideline under his picture read: "Dr. Galley Pruitt, Endlight Astronomer." Confused with a sense of joy—and some envy—Neemu quickly thumbed through to the cover story and began reading.

Galley threw the stiff envelope to the floor and began reading its message. The letterhead "Deep Earth Survival Colony," brought everything together for him. The return address was to Jackson Morrow, Founder. 10000 Los Altos Parkway, Beverly Hills, California. Now he began to realize the facts behind the mysterious newspaper story. He glanced over at Neemu who was still engrossed in his magazine and continued reading the letter.

"Dear Dr. Pruitt:

"As Founder and selfappointed President of the Deep Earth Survival Colony (from now on referred to as DESC), I extend an invitation for you to join us as our Colony Astronomer. Of course your wife Jalisa is also invited.

"As you will be a working part of our society, we require no initiation fee for your or your wife's entrance. However since you and the other Colony Scientists will be a vital part of our continuation through this Endlight Event, you must follow all rules

38

and requests from DESC implicitly.

    "If you decide to accept this invitation please contact me immediately thereafter at the above location. We are finalizing the core group of personnel to guide us through the upcoming cataclysm and we urgently need your answer. Please guard the identity of our group and its members. We must not let ourselves be known to the public for fear of reprisals and panic during our final Endlight descent into Deep Earth.

Respectfully,
Jackson Morrow"

    Galley looked to the left-hand margin of the letter where a sidebar listed the Colony Executives and Scientists. He recognized none of the names but did notice that their nationalities were from all over the world. Another item that caught his interest was the prior affiliation of the Colony Chief Scientist Geoff Chadwick, former Chief Scientist at Biosphere II. Not a bad choice, he thought. I guess this group will be the next Biosphere since the original project in the Arizona desert shut down many years ago. He read down the list of scientists looking for an astronomer. Then he noticed at the bottom a small note: Positions not yet filled: Colony Astronomer, Colony Botanist, Colony Veterinarian, Colony Geologist, and Colony Speleologist.

    Colony Veterinarian? Botanist? "Well Neemu, I think I'm ready to face the crowd." He replaced the contents into the envelope and laid it beside him.

    "Galley," Neemu puzzled, "did you know you

were on the cover of Time this week?"

"Yeah. I tried to get them to put you on there, too. Last month they asked me for some photographs and comments but I didn't know for sure what they'd do. I guess that's one of the reasons for this press conference."

As Galley started for the door, Neemu rose from the desk. The phone rang, startling Neemu. He grabbed the receiver, almost dropping it as he put it to his ear, "VLA Visitor Center, Neemu here."

"Hello. Is Dr. Galley Pruitt there?" the voice asked.

"Ya, he's right here beside me."

"Please put him on the line."

"Galley, someone wants to talk to you," Neemu said as he held out the receiver.

Galley took the phone. "Hello, this is Galley Pruitt."

"Dr. Pruitt, I'm sorry to bother you. We had to track you down through your secretary. This is Ed Micolo at the Naval Observatory in Washington. We here observed a bright visible flare in the Northern sky near Cepheus about an hour ago, well . . . twelvesixteen exactly, and wonder if you have corroborating radio telescope data from that event?"

"Is it *Dr.* Micolo?" Galley asked as he realized this was truly a call from Washington, D.C. What irony he thought, to use an excuse falsely and then have it come true. He whispered to Neemu, holding his hand over the receiver microphone, "Naval Observatory in D.C. calling, weird, huh?" Neemu nodded in agreement.

"Yes," Micolo said.

"Dr. Micolo, I'm sorry I don't have data immediately available on that event. I've been on the road during the past hour and a half and now I'm in a press conference about Endlight. As soon as I get through here, I'll be more than happy to find out about that event for you and myself. I saw it from my car window . . . What do the people up there think it was?"

"It appeared to have a very sharp intensity transition in going from dark to light and back. We don't think it was a nova or supernova. Some people here don't even think it was a natural phenomenon."

"Let me check our receiver activities when I get through here and I'll get back with you," Galley said. "It shouldn't take more than a few hours. Can I get your number?"

After trading phone numbers and Internet addresses, Galley placed the phone back into its cradle. Galley was glad that they were both on the new fiber optic Internet so that they could correspond by e-mail and VOIP — the phone system was beginning to act flaky from the cold. He thought for a few moments, looked up at Neemu and said, "Would you mind going over to the Control Building and asking the duty crew if they had any unexplainable observations in the northern sky around Cepheus about tensixteen, our time, this morning? I'll face the crowd by myself."

"Sure," Neemu said. "What should I be looking for?"

"At 1616 hours GMT there was a bright pinpoint flash in the northern sky just south of Polaris. The astronomers at the Naval Observatory saw it and are wondering if it had radio emissions during the flash as well as the visible ones. A Dr. Ed Micolo called wanting information. I said we'd help."

Neemu started for the door, opened it and looked back at Galley, still standing by the phone. "Good luck, Galley. See you after the conference."

Galley left the office and walked slowly toward the podium. As he looked around the room at all the visitor displays he noticed on the wall to his right a large floortoceiling map of the Plains of St. Augustin showing the Magdalena Mountains and the VLA complex. Then he saw the little red dots showing where the antennas were positioned in the Y today. "Well I'll be damned," he said to himself. On the visitor display map, he noticed the lights for antennas three, six and twenty-seven were not glowing red as all others were. They were dark. He'd have to tell the maintenance people about those burned out lights after the conference. He stepped back onto the podium and said, "Pardon me for the delay, but the Naval Observatory called to confirm a bright flash in the northern sky this morning. I don't think it's related to Endlight but we're checking on it."

Galley removed a small piece of folded paper from his coat pocket, unfolded it and began, "Ladies and gentlemen, before I begin I'd like to thank Time Magazine for choosing me for their cover story on Endlight last week. I really did no more than my normal professional duties during the discovery. I owe much of this honor to the hard workers here at the VLA including my old—uh should I say longtime—friend and co-worker Neemu Hatlem, those astronomers at the thousandfoot radio telescope in Arecibo, Puerto Rico and the optical astronomers at Mauna Kea, Hawaii, the McDonald Observatory in Texas and those at the Jet Propulsion Laboratory in California using the space-borne Hubble Space Telescope. Now at this time I'd like to present a short overview of the history of the Endlight Event discovery."

Galley paused momentarily, switched on an overhead projector and asked for the visitor center lights to be turned down. As the lights dimmed the large screen flashed the logo of the NRAO, a large outline of the state of New Mexico and a small Yshaped icon near Socorro. He began speaking as he carefully refolded the paper and placed it into his coat pocket. "Neemu Hatlem, my assistant, and I were investigating some unusual discrepancies between optical and radio telescope measurements of an object near a newly discovered comet when we first realized there was a visible blockage entering our Solar System. It began back in January of last year."

Galley placed a second viewgraph on the projector. The image on the screen showed the Solar System with a darkened band beyond the orbits of Neptune and Pluto. He continued, "Some astronomers at Mauna Kea were searching for comets and planets beyond Pluto in what we call the Kuiper belt. The Kuiper belt is a theorized vast ring, shown here, beyond our Solar System suspected to hold comets and comet debris in orbit before they enter our Solar System." Galley pointed his laser pencil to highlight the darkened ring. "Mauna Kea was tracking a small object, probably a comet or asteroid, no bigger than a few hundred

43

kilometers in diameter when they noticed it begin to fade, then disappear over a period of a few months. To verify their observation they called the Hubble Space Telescope scientists at JPL. They all agreed with the object's fading and ultimate disappearance."

He placed a photograph of the Hubble Space Telescope on the projector and resumed the presentation. "This telescope, since its upgrade, is one of the highest resolution optical telescopes in the world. If it sees something, it's there. If it doesn't, it's not. Finally they called on the radio astronomers at the 1000-foot diameter dish antenna at the Arecibo observatory to confirm the disappearance using radio waves rather than light." He placed a bird'seye shot viewgraph of the antenna at Arecibo onto the projector. The crowd of reporters responded with a gasp of awe as they recognized the immense size of the object they were viewing.

"The astronomers at Arecibo, using the same megawatt radar system they used to map the surface of Venus, saw the object just as it had been two months before, but their telescope's resolution was really too poor for them to be positive of the results." Galley's next viewgraph illustrated the silhouette of the Arecibo dish with focused rays ending at the outskirts of the Solar System. At the focus of the rays was a small round blurry object.

"There appeared to be no disappearance," Galley said, pointing to the blurry object with the laser pen, "but according to the blurry sky data from Arecibo, they couldn't be sure. The radio astronomers at Arecibo suggested to Mauna Kea that Arecibo transmit the radar signal and let us, here at the VLA, receive the signal since we had such a large baseline interferometer with our twenty-seven dishes. Positive results would refute the Arecibo data. Negative results would require further investigation by even more observatories. Additionally, since Arecibo and the VLA were both members of our National Radio Astronomy Observatory group, and our array can have an effective diameter of nine miles rather than Arecibo's 1000-foot dish, we agreed to cooperate in the largebaseline activeradar search." He placed a slide showing the silhouette of Arecibo's dish and the Yshaped silhouette from the VLA across the lower U.S. from each other. Rays emanated from the Arecibo dish to a focus in the Kuiper belt. Then the rays were shown to reflect back to the twentyseven VLA antennas. The ray's focal point in the Kuiper belt had a small bright sharplyfocused object shown.

"In April we began the experiment, cooperating with Arecibo, shown here, transmitting very powerful radar signals toward the object in the Kuiper belt. We, over here at the VLA, began receiving the signals about twelve hours later. In addition to the reflections from known objects there, we were searching for something we rarely searched for -void— where there was matter before, or an object's disappearance. Over a period of several days we began to assemble a fairly highresolution map of the objects in the vicinity we were scanning with our telescopes. I should add we missed very few because Arecibo was illuminating with 2.5 centimeter radio waves at over one-million watts of focused power—power so strong we had to warn air traffic to evacuate the airspace over the Arecibo dish for fear of cooking the people in the planes. It took three days of cleaning up after the experiment to remove the dead birds, small animals and insects from the Arecibo dish. Don't worry, though—they didn't feel a thing."

Galley placed another viewgraph on the projector. It obviously was a computergenerated stellar map showing a group of objects clustered within a few degrees of each other and another separated by some distance from the group. A red permanent marker line circled the isolated object. He continued, "The map that we created of this part of the Universe nearest our target looked exactly as we had expected, considering orbital mechanics. And it still included the optically invisible object shown over here circled in red!"

He pointed his laser pen so that the green point of light illuminated the circled object and paused momentarily to reorganize his thoughts. Then he resumed, "So Neemu and I started considering every plausible explanation for the disappearance paradox."

He placed a new viewgraph on the projector filled with lines of text preceded by bullet points, its title reading "Proposed Explanations."

"These are the postulates for disappearance we chose during our research," he continued. "The most obvious one was that the object had melted, exploded or evaporated for some mysterious reason. That would leave no radar echo. Out. Next we considered the possibility of an alien craft that sped off into the Galaxy. Nope, that wouldn't have left an echo either. Besides we ridiculed ourselves the whole time we were considering that idea. Finally we concluded that the object must still really be there but we just couldn't see it. It had become invisible like a black hole. But a black hole couldn't exist this close to the Solar System without sucking every planet and the Sun into it. This third postulate began to make more sense than any others. As a last ditch effort to solve the mystery, we contacted Arecibo to redo the experiment. When we went through the same radar tests again we found that the originally missing object had reappeared and a close neighboring object had vanished. It was as if something were moving across the sky blocking the objects' light reflections from us but not their radio reflections. It was if an extremely light absorptive black cloud were moving into the Solar System. Our discovery of this Cloud, over a year ago was then made known to the astronomical society through the standard messenger, the International Astronomical Union bureau. Most astronomers thought it a curious phenomenon but of little importance to them. Neemu and I began to track and study the Cloud over a period of months. We observed it pass in front of known stars with complete spectrographic histories. In other words, we knew exactly what these stars emitted in terms of light, infrared, X-rays and radio waves without the Cloud in front of them. As the Cloud covered and obscured them we again took complete spectrographic data on the stars to try to detect what was in the Cloud."

Galley placed another overhead slide on the projector. It showed what appeared to be a disorganized pattern of dark elongated small objects over a clear background, like looking through a handful of black rice that had been dropped onto a clear glass table.

47

"What you see here is our hypothesis of the Cloud's composition. We found that energy waves longer than ten microns passed through these objects almost unaffected while shorter waves, like light waves, having a wavelength from .8 to .3 microns, were reflected or absorbed by the shape of these opaque dipole objects. Additionally, light and other energy passing through the Cloud were not uniformly attenuated, suggesting the presence of an element like carbon in the dipole crystals. The presence of the element carbon explained why we could still receive longerwave radio astronomy signals through the Cloud from the object, yet not be able to see shorterwavelength light through it. It's like carbon black -- very opaque but not very conductive electrically."

He placed another viewgraph on the projector that simply contained the words ENDLIGHT EVENT DISCOVERY, and continued, "After determining the Cloud's composition we began to track its orbital movement over the next few months. Finally we realized that it was on an orbital course for our Sun, much like the one Halley's Comet travels every seventy-six years. However we estimated the size of the Cloud to be huge, some thirty-million miles long and nine-million miles wide. It would, we theorized, totally block our sunlight when it passed between Earth and the Sun at perihelion. That's when we put out the warning to all of mankind that Earth was coming toward the end of its light. We were possibly going to experience an Extinction Level Event. Skeptics and many scientists ignored us until we were supported by optical telescope confirmation of our darkening Sun sometime later from observatories in Hawaii and West Texas."

He placed the first, originally shown slide, with the NRAO logo and New Mexico outline, back on the projector. "Now we have been in what we refer to as Twilight for over two months with the sun gradually growing dimmer each day. We expect to experience the Endlight Event in less than four weeks. At that time our daylight will be no brighter than last winter's moonlight from a quarter moon. Our temperatures will drop drastically as that happens, with lows expected to approach those on the dark side of the Moon. All life on the surface of the Earth will freeze unless protected from the extreme cold. Even protection may not help if we lose our food and power supplies. The atmosphere may begin to freeze and separate into its primary component parts, nitrogen and oxygen. Carbon dioxide and nitrogen will freeze first, creating a super-rich oxygen atmosphere until that possibly liquefies and freezes, too. There are many unknown variables. We can only conjecture as to the disposition of the Earth as we orbit into Endlight. Then perihelion, the point in its orbit where the Cloud comes closest to the sun, should occur in December 2012, a few days before Christmas. The Cloud will then recede back to the Kuiper belt, we'll begin to regain our light and the Earth will once again warm to its current temperatures. Unfortunately most of life on Earth as we know it now will have frozen to death."

Galley hesitated and wiped his forehead with a handkerchief, "Incidentally, for those of you who track more esoteric interests, this exact date was predicted as the End of Days on the Mayan calendar—created by astronomers during ancient times. Let's hope and pray they were wrong."

Galley turned off the projector and asked for the visitor center lights to be turned back up. "It's not a rosy picture I paint, sorry . . . Are there any questions?"

As the reporters squinted at Galley through the brightened illumination, a few held up their arms at full length. Galley pointed to the reporter over by the wall map and said, "Yes?"

"Dr. Pruitt, I'm Jim Whitson with the New York Times. What are you scientists doing to save us from this catastrophe?"

"There's not much we can do to stop Endlight, Jim, it's a natural catastrophe," Galley answered. "Suggestions have been made by some scientists to try to fan or dispel the Cloud using multiple nuclear explosions in space. That's like trying to extinguish a thousand roaring bonfires with an eyedropper full of water. There have even been some plans talked about to launch a large spacecraft ark to save some of the humanity, but there's not nearly enough time to build it. NASA is conducting the most promising effort. They are frantically attempting to build the Advanced Mars Colony Habitat on Earth to withstand the elements of Endlight." He paused, then continued, "Two problems exist with this endeavor. The first is the size of the habitat, It only holds three hundred people. That won't save much of the humanity. The second problem is that the habitat is made to absorb heat during the hot Martian days and redistribute it during the frigid nights. And, since there will be no more days on Earth for three to four months, they are having to modify the design to use alternate sources of thermal energy."

"Why," the reporter asked, "can't they just plug in some big heaters in the city auditoriums all over the world to keep us warm? That wouldn't be nearly as expensive as building some Mars habitat. Plus, then we could *all* be saved from the cold."

Galley, somewhat irritated by the simple-mindedness of the question, replied in a staccato series of questions and statements, "Jim, what makes you think we'll still have power? Where does your power come from? Don't you think our generating plants will freeze, too? And besides, who would run them? Then, there will be no power for heaters. Anyone else have a question?"

From the center of the room a tall, well-groomed correspondent rose and spoke, "Scott Crocker, Fox News. Dr. Pruitt, does anyone really believe all that Mayan calendar mumbo-jumbo? You alluded to it, but nobody seems to put much faith in it."

Smiling, Galley responded, "Well, Mr. Crocker, you're with the news service. Why don't you tell me. I just know something big's going to happen at that predicted time. Correlation? I frankly couldn't hazard a guess. Next question?"

A reporter from CNN, Bob Cristman, was the first to speak at the new invitation for questions. "Dr. Pruitt, Bob Cristman—CNN News, there are rumors circulating in the press about a secret elitist society that is trying to outlive Endlight. It's said that people are paying one million dollars apiece to join. Have you heard of them or know who they are?"

"I've heard the rumors. I know nothing more than you about the nature of this group, if it does

51

in fact exist. However, I can imagine that some private factions will form in an effort to keep themselves alive through this," Galley replied in a cooperative and agreeable manner. "Any more questions?"

A familiar reporter at the rear of the room who had been patiently waiting for his turn stood up and interjected, "Dr. Pruitt, my name is John Ruster with CBS New. You mentioned that the Cloud is taking a path like Halley's Comet into the Solar System. Do you think it has ever been here before, and, now that it is here, will it ever come back?"

"That's a very good question, John," Galley acknowledged. "It's one we've been grappling with ourselves for the past year or so . . . the best guess we can make is that it has come before, maybe tens of thousands of years ago. And if that period is correct, then the periodicity of the orbit may explain, or at least reinforce, historical information about our periodic Ice Ages. If our guess is right that it is a periodic cosmic event, then it will come back in another ten- or twenty-thousand years from now."

Galley glanced down at his watch and noticed that it was nearing noon. He interrupted himself, "I'm afraid that's all the time I have for questions," as he started packing up his presentation materials. "Thank you for coming out today. I hope I've clarified the situation a little for your subscribers. I wish there were good news to report, sorry. Good morning."

As Galley arrived at the VLA Control Building where he kept a small, very untidy office he checked his mailbox for messages. Three pink "While You Were Out" slips and an advertisement for "Popular Astronomy" magazine met his hand as he reached in to get his mail. "Hmm," he mumbled as he looked over the phone message slips. "One from Neemu, one from Dr. Micolo at the Naval Observatory and a third from a Mr. Morrow in California."

"Hi, Neemu, what's up? Did you find anything out about that flash this morning?" Galley asked as his first return phone call was answered.

"Galley, I've got some bad news."

"Well, what else can go wrong besides Endlight?" Galley chided.

"The cold is starting to affect the waveguide-feed amplifiers at the dishes. They were not designed to take this kind of cold and keep on operating. Antennas three, six and twenty-seven have ceased to operate and —."

"Neemu, which antennas?" Galley interrupted.

"Three, six and twenty seven. Why?"

"When I was in the Visitor Center this morning I noticed that on the configuration wall map those same three antenna location lights were extinguished while all the others glowed."

"That's because those indicator lights are tied to the incoming signal feed at the control room. They were done like that to show visitors which of the twenty-seven antennas are really active and receiving."

"Oh, I didn't know that. You mean somebody around here was really thinking?"

"Anyway," Neemu chuckled and continued, "the lack of those three antennas means we must completely rewrite the baseline configuration software for only twenty-four antennas, and we

53

don't even know how long those will keep operating."

"I thought those masers were cooled with liquid nitrogen to keep the noise down. Why should the cold affect *them*? It's still much warmer outside than liquid nitrogen temperatures."

"I talked to one of the antenna technicians because I had that same concern," Neemu related. "He said the masers were working fine. It's the TWT feed amplifiers in the waveguides that are frozen solid. And, also he said the antenna rotation and tilt motors are freezing. We've probably got only a week or two of operation here before we have to shut the whole operation down."

"Damn it!" Galley was suddenly furious. The hopelessness of the situation was starting to hit home after the depressing press conference this morning. He had never thought that the radio telescope dishes would fail this quickly in the cold. "All right, Neemu. Thanks anyway. Did we hear any information at all on that flash, even from another observatory?"

"Well, we did have our antennas pointing that direction when it happened, according to the time you gave me, but we saw no unusual radio signals," Neemu said assuredly, "Oh, and I talked to your dear friend Childs, the jerk, at the McDonald Millimeter Wave Dish. He saw nothing, also . . . except he did say that they caught the optical flash through one of their spotter scopes. They just thought it was a meteor burnout. Probably was, too."

"I'm not so sure, Neemu," Galley responded. "I saw it and it didn't seem like any meteor flash I'd seen before. Oh well, I've got to make a few other return phone calls. I'll talk to you later."

"Oh, Galley, how did your press conference go?"

"I almost put *myself* to sleep I was so boring," he said with a chuckle.

"Well, I guess when you've seen one end of our civilization, you've seen them all," Neemu cajoled in return.

Galley chuckled again, said, "Neemu you're so weird," and hung up the phone.

Galley looked back at the pink slips. As he examined the slip for Micolo's call, he noticed the message "You were in the Visitor Center so I transferred his call there." Then he remembered he told Micolo he would call back to report their findings.

"Good afternoon, Naval Observatory," the switchboard operator answered.

"Dr. Ed Micolo, please."

"Dr. Micolo's office," the secretary responded.

"Hello, this is Dr. Galley Pruitt at the Very Large Array in New Mexico. I'm returning a call from Dr. Micolo this morning. Is he there?"

"He's in the Observatory Control Room right now, Dr. Pruitt. Would you like for me to page him?"

"Please."

As he was put on hold he heard the tinny strains of Muzak on the line. Listening and waiting for Micolo to answer, he began to recognize the song "Don't Let the Stars Get in Your Eyes, Don't Let the Moon Steal Your Heart." *Surely they didn't—*.

"Hello, Galley this is Ed," a voice interrupted his musing.

"Ed, I checked into our reception of that flash

this morning and found out we have a problem here."

"Oh?"

"Our waveguide feed amplifiers are slowly freezing. We've lost three antennas already, and we'll probably lose more," Galley explained.

"Well, don't be too upset. I talked to Arecibo right after I called you this morning and they're having the same problem—except, as you know, they have only one antenna and when it goes they're out of business."

"How's the cold affecting your telescope?"

"We try to keep it warm with the dome cover. That's working pretty well. The only problem we have is when we open the dome we have to wait a few hours for the optics temperature to stabilize."

"But at least you're still operational?"

"Yes."

"Good, please let me know of any new results, if you can get though. With *our* electronics freezing, I'm not sure how much longer the phone system will be working. Their satellite dishes will probably have the same problem."

"We've discussed that here," Micolo agreed, "and we expect to lose the entire worldwide telephone system in a week or so. We've been contacting some local ham radio operators to keep links open to the U.S. at least."

Galley replied, "We've got a number of hams at the facility. I'd better do that same thing then."

"I think it'll keep us in touch a little bit longer, anyway," Micolo conceded.

"What bands are you planning on using?" Galley probed, trying to get a calling card frequency for the VLA Hams.

"Eighty or 160 meters is what they're recommending."

"OK, I'll talk to our guys and try to contact you this week, if your people are on the air that soon."

"They have already started making contacts. You should hear us. Listen for W1AW."

"We'll do it. Thanks for the information, Ed. Sorry I can't be of more help. I guess I'll be out of a job soon if we can't warm up those amplifiers somehow."

"Good luck, Galley."

"Thanks, I think we're gonna need it. Bye," Galley acknowledged as he hung up the phone.
He paged to the last pink slip. It read, "Jackson Morrow called . . . He needs to talk to you. He says you've got his number." Galley reached over to the stack of presentation slides he brought back from the Visitor Center looking for the FedEx envelope to get Morrow's number. The envelope wasn't there!

"Crap! I must have left it in the office," he said to himself. Suddenly realizing the urgency of getting the letter before anyone else found it, he bolted for the door, grabbing his parka on the way out of the Control Building.

The walk back to the Control Building was only a few hundred yards but at sixtyseven below zero, it chilled Galley to the bone. The pinkblack sky, the lack of nature's sounds except for a gentile breathtaking breeze and the eerie shadow cast by the nearest towering antenna dish were depressing reminders of the Earth's plight. He walked faster to keep warm. Upon reaching the Visitor Center he entered the frosted glass doors to see it empty. He looked over to the office. That room was empty also. "Thank God," he muttered as he entered the office and saw the envelope lying exactly where he had left it earlier. Something in the back of his mind made him look again into the main room. Suddenly, the wall map caught his attention. It was changed! Now *more* indicator lights were out. He walked out to the board to see that antennas eight, nine and fifteen had gone dark since he was here just over an hour ago! "Holy hell!" he exclaimed. "My world is crumbling as I watch!"

Then a decisive calmness came over him. He looked down at the envelope in his hand and walked back into the office, shutting the door behind him.

"Hello," the voice answered through a noisy longdistance connection. It reminded him of the greeting for calls he had made to the nation's most secret agencies.

"This is Galley Pruitt calling for Mr. Morrow."

"One moment, please," the voice responded.

"Dr. Pruitt?"

"Yes."

"This is Jackson Morrow. Thank you for returning my call," Morrow said in a very businesslike tone. "Did you get my letter?"

"Yes, I have it right here."

"Good. If you have an interest in following up the matter with me, I'd like to meet with you."

"I'm very interested," Galley said as he looked over the invitation again.

"Can you meet me in Phoenix tomorrow afternoon? I'll be there on business and it's not too far from you."

"It's a little short notice, but things are rather slow here right now, anyway. Can I call you this evening with a confirmation after I talk with my wife?"

"That will be fine. What time?"

"About seven o'clock your time?"

"Exactly seven o'clock my time. I'll expect your call. Goodbye, Dr. Pruitt," Morrow said in a straightforward tone. The line went dead.

Galley hung up the phone and looked back at the letter. He never imagined he would face a decision like this. His mind was screaming for him to do something to save the world, his heart was whispering, *save yourself and your family*.

After walking back to the Control Building, he went onto his office, still shivering from the cold, and shut the door. He sat at his desk and logged into his computer as he had methodically done a thousand times before. The daily logon message, which normally explained the day's activity on the radio telescope, read "The VLA facility will close at 4:00 p.m. this afternoon for maintenance because of continuing antenna malfunctions."

"That's just great!" he said in a sarcastic manner to himself. Galley looked at his watch. It was 3:45 p.m. He hadn't had time to eat his lunch and he was getting very irritable. He picked up the phone and dialed Neemu.

"Neemu, did you get the early closure message?"

"Ya, I'm going home now," Neemu responded.

"Me, too. Hope they get those damn things thawed pretty soon or we'll all be out of a job."

"Don't count on it."

"I think I'm going to take a day of vacation tomorrow to seal up some cold leaks in the house."

"Have fun, I did that last weekend. We're a little bit cozier now."

"Well, Jalisa's been bitching at me for a month to do it, and I just haven't had time."

"See you next week, if we're still in business."

"Have a good weekend, Neemu."

"You too."

As Galley left the Control Building, he passed the receptionist and said, "Oh, Susan. I'm taking a day of vacation tomorrow. I'll be in next week."

"See you then," she acknowledged.

His drive back into Socorro seemed much more pleasant this time. He was making a decision that would change his life and he was accepting it. As he entered town and drove down California Street he looked at the businesses with their ice frosted windows and lights still aglow. Some had closed for business during the last month. He knew with each new uncontrollable change in his life he was making the right decision.

As he passed the closed Dairy Queen with the ice-coated lighted sign reading "Take a break from the heat—Get your Blizzards here" he noticed a small animal cowering against the door, trying to stay warm. He pulled into the parking lot and got out of his car, with the motor left running.

"Here puppy," he called. The little dog looked at him and cowered even closer to the door. He walked up to the little animal and saw its tail begin to wag slowly back and forth. The little beige dog looked up at Galley with its whiskers coated with icicles, its big warm brown eyes begging for help.

"Come here, little guy," Galley said as he picked up the frightened shivering stray in his hand and held it up to his face to see better. "Why, you can't weigh over ten pounds. How did you make it out here in the cold all this time?" he asked the pup with a baby-talk sound to his voice. "Come on boy, let's go home." The little dog licked his face with its cold tongue.

"Hi honey, we're home," Galley said as he walked in the back door.

From the living room he heard, "Hi dear . . . what do you mean *we're* home?" She ran though the living room and appeared at the door to the kitchen expecting to find, as usual, a dinner guest from work. Instead she saw Galley standing there holding a briefcase in one hand and a small puppy with a wagging tail in the other.

"How cute," she said. "Where'd you get him?"

"He was trying to buy a DQ Dude at the Dairy Queen but they were closed," Galley kidded. "No, really, he was just sitting by the door there shivering and trying to keep warm. I saw him look at me with those icicle-covered whiskers and couldn't leave him to freeze to death."

"Good, I love you for that," Jalisa said as she came over to hug Galley and pet the new addition to the family.

"Oh, incidentally Galley, it's not a he, it's a she," she said as she rubbed the puppy's tummy.

"Well, whatever it is I didn't want it to freeze. What do you want to name *her*?" Galley asked.

"What say we name her Frosty," Jalisa asked putting her nose up to the puppy's nose. The puppy sneezed.

Galley laughed as Jalisa grabbed a paper

61

towel and wiped off her face exclaiming, "Yuk!"

They spent the next thirty minutes looking through the kitchen gathering bowls and plates for water and food for Frosty. Each was trying to find a better one that the other could find. Funny how a new little dog could make them forget the world crisis that they, and everyone else, were facing and make them act like little kids.

Later, after they all finished dinner, Galley said, "Honey, come sit by me in the living room. I need to talk to you."

Jalisa knew by the tone of his voice that this was not a casual conversation they were going to have. She followed him in and sat down.

"Today, I received an invitation to join the Deep Earth Survival Colony. Well really, *we* received the invitation, it was for you too."

"What do you plan to do about work?" she asked.

"There's a really big problem with the antennas right now due to the cold. If they can't fix them, then there will be no more work. And nobody there really thinks they can get them working again." Galley explained.

"So if there's no more work, what's stopping us from saying yes?"

"Nothing, really, I just wanted to ask you before I committed us to this group. I think they really think they will make it through Endlight, alive."

"Well then, let's do it! Call him and tell him yes," she said and held up her hand for a high five.

He slapped her hand with his and said, "All right! But it's not quite that simple. I have to call him tonight to tell him I'll accept the invitation in a meeting with him in Phoenix tomorrow afternoon. What time is it now?"

She looked at her watch, "Seven forty-five. Why Phoenix?"

"I don't know, probably just a middle meeting spot for both of us. I'm supposed to call to confirm the meeting at seven o'clock California time tonight."

"Better start calling now," she said, "I've had some real trouble getting through on long distance lately."

After fifteen minutes of redialing and listening to that three-toned dee-dee-deeee sound and the operator saying, "I'm sorry, your call cannot go through right now," Galley slammed the phone back in its cradle. He looked over at Jalisa and said, "One of the things I found out today, too, is the worldwide phone system should quit operating during the next week because of the cold. Better call our families before that happens."

"Let me try it," she said. "What's his number?"

"Area 213-555-3444," he read from the letterhead.

"Shhhh, I think it's ringing."

"Lucky!" he whispered with a smile as she handed him the phone.

"Hello," the gruff voice answered.

"Mr. Morrow?"

"Yes."

"This is Galley Pruitt calling from New Mexico. Do you have time to talk now?"

"I've got a few minutes before my next meeting with the Colony Forum," Morrow responded.

63

"Okay, I'll be quick. As you requested, I'd like to meet you in Phoenix tomorrow to discuss the invitation."

"Have you decided your response to it?"

"Yes sir, I have."

"Good, then meet me at three-oh-seven tomorrow at The Phoenician Resort right off Camelback Road. We'll discuss your decision there. I'm six-feet, three-inches tall, 198 pounds, with gray-white hair. I'll be wearing a tee shirt, shorts and tennis shoes and drinking a Tequila Sunrise in the Lobby Lounge. Have me paged by JM if you don't see me there. Goodbye Dr. Pruitt," Morrow said as he hung up his phone.

CHAPTER 3
THE PHOENIX MEETING

The long drive to Phoenix on I-25 and I-10 was quite unnerving for Galley. The past two months of Twilight and cold had caused the amount of traffic along the US interstate highways to gradually dwindle and finally almost vanish. Even the open desert highways in New Mexico and Southern Arizona, where the traffic was normally sparse, seemed almost eerily void of motion and life. Nobody wanted to be stuck even *ten* miles from nowhere in these temperatures. "Is this strange feeling of empty depression due to the constant darkness or the lack of passing traffic on the highway?" he asked himself as he drove over the dark and empty superhighways. He had planned to travel the nearly 500 miles from Socorro to Phoenix in just under six hours, based on an average speed, he computed, of 85 miles an hour. To play it safe, he left Socorro at 8:00 a.m. that morning, giving him a good seven hours to get there and find 6000 Camelback Road, the Phoenician and JM.

Out on the open New Mexico road, his car raced for hours through the icy, frigid wind of Twilight. A tiny stream of outside air whistled in through a small crevice in the rubber seal near the front window vent. It kept the inside car temperature below freezing. As he drove, shivering and not really understanding why, he turned up the heater. He also increased the radio's volume to hear over the Porsche's engine roar—and the continuing, almost sub-audible, whistle. Singing and humming along with the music should get his mind off the cold outside and make the trip seem shorter, he thought.

Galley welcomed the sight of the sign reading WELCOME TO ARIZONA. Three miles past the border he saw an Arizona State Trooper's car on the side of the highway and slowed to sixty-five. As he passed it he realized it was empty. He immediately pushed back up to eighty. He was becoming nervous that he might not make the meeting on time.

Three hours and 250 miles later he finally began to realize that he was no warmer than before. Galley placed his hand around the front driver-side window trying to detect airflow and said, "Aha! That's why I'm so damn cold!" He felt the tiny frigid air jet coming from the vent seal and then, in the back of his mind, remembered opening his window at the VLA to talk to the reporters. Slowly he brought the car to a stop so that he could reseat the window in its seal. Everything was so damn cold! A voice in his head echoed Morrow's last statement before hanging up the night before, "I'll be wearing a tee shirt, shorts and tennis shoes."

"How can anybody do that in this weather when I'm out here freezing my butt off in wool pants and a fur-lined, sub-zero parka?" Galley grunted out loud as he struggled to lower the window, put it back in its track and then reclose it. He was becoming very irritated with this trip. "I should have flown!" he growled to himself. As he pressed the glass, the window stubbornly settled back into its seal with an assuring pop. Then he thought, but what if they had stopped flying because of the extreme temperatures: he would have been stuck in Albuquerque, anyway. *No, this is the right thing to do, Galley,* he assured himself. He sighed in relief. Once again he glanced at the window to insure that it had sealed as he closed it. His gaze refocused on the dim mountain range silhouette in the distance. He could see the glow of the city lights from Phoenix in the sky. I'm close, he thought. Suddenly, Galley was surprised by another brief flash from the western sky. This one was almost identical to the one he saw yesterday, just in a different part of the sky. It was bright, too—like distant lightning, flaring in a dark stormy sky. But there were no clouds—there hadn't been any for the past forty days with the increasingly colder Twilight climate. He turned up the radio hoping to hear some special report on the flash and pressed the accelerator pedal. The Porsche's engine roared and heat flowed from the dashboard vent. Galley pulled back onto the highway and immediately felt the effect of his efforts. Warmth!

Morrow must be really weird, and to top it off, he's really cold natured, Galley mused as he turned his attention back to Morrow and the weatherman over the car radio saying, "The temperature at 2:00 p.m. in Phoenix right now is 69 degrees below zero."

He looked at the odometer. "Only 32 miles more to go," he muttered as he sat back in the seat and pushed the accelerator pedal to the floor. The Porsche screamed across the frozen Arizona desert.

At 2:20 p.m. Galley reached the outskirts of Scottsdale, just past Phoenix, turned off IH10 onto 44th Street and immediately encountered a massive traffic jam. What in the world are all these people doing here, he thought. I may not make it to the Phoenician on time. He crept along at a few miles per hour for almost ten minutes. Then he saw the cause of the gridlock. The cars were backed up for almost half a mile waiting to get in the parking lot of a church. The impact of this experience stunned him into the realization of the social isolation he was experiencing while living in Socorro. He hadn't traveled into a large city since the temperatures began dropping, and the imminence of the World's end suddenly became evident.

Galley stared at the crowd of people waiting to enter the church as he slowly passed the entrance driveway. There must have been thousands, all looking as if they were waiting to depart on some polar expedition. The mass of people had a strange characteristic to Galley. In the open space of the church lawn, they were huddled together in a tight formation resembling crowds leaving a sporting event. There was no need to rush or crowd here; they were just trying to keep warm. People at the periphery of the group were trying to work their way inward. Some were conversing; others were looking upward in solemn prayer. He looked away.

His watch read 2:40 p.m. He intended on getting to the resort by 3:00 p.m. so he could gather his thoughts before meeting Jackson. Another traffic jam. This time he noticed the large eight-story building ahead with the lighted blue caduceus at the top. The medical symbol for a *hospital*, he realized as he sighed, saddened. These sights were not the greeting he expected upon entering Phoenix. But, of course, he remembered reading news stories of the tremendous number of growing cases of frostbite and hypothermia across the world. Reading news stories and seeing the effects on the population were two different things. As he crept past the busy hospital parking lot a sudden feeling of despair gripped his concentration.

He looked back at his watch, trying to ignore these newfound horrors. 2:52p.m. If only there was some way he could help. But he knew there wasn't really any way to help the masses. He wanted to help himself and his family survive, and to assist in the effort to preserve humanity through the Colony.

At 3:10 p.m. Galley pulled past the lighted tennis courts of the Phoenician and into the front parking lot. What a place, he thought as he scanned the semicircular pyramid-shaped hotel; at least Morrow has taste in his surroundings.

Galley parked his car and looked up at the large double-humped bluff behind him. Camel-back, he thought, what a beautiful setting for a resort — before Endlight. He turned and walked toward the main entrance, noticing on his way the tennis courts with their newly installed infrared heaters around the perimeter of each court. Heaters were also projecting over the tops of the courts looking like large flyswatters poised to smash the players below. Even with these glowing heaters surrounding them, people on the courts were dressed in ski parkas and warm-up suits, obviously trying to stay warm as they played. He smirked, mumbled, "Crazy tennis players," and shook his head as he passed the doorman. The doorman smiled back, winked and said, "Yes sir."

Entering the resort, Galley welcomed the

warmth and immediately noticed the aroma of food from a nearby restaurant. It reminded him that he had not eaten all day.

As he crossed the marble floors of the lavish lobby, he looked around to find the lobby bar. Directly in front of him, under a huge chandelier appearing to be made of Italian crystal, he spotted such a contradiction to his sensibilities he stopped. Amid all the people in the lobby with their sweaters and fur-lined parkas was a man looking to be in his late fifties, wearing exactly what he was told to expect—shorts, high-topped tennis shoes and a tee-shirt reading "CALIFORNIA — It's The Place You Ought To Be."   On the table in front of him the stranger had a reddish-orange drink in a tall half-filled glass.

Galley looked back at his watch and saw it was now 3:12 p.m. He approached the table and said, "Jackson Morrow?"

Morrow looked at his watch. "Dr. Pruitt, you're five minutes late."

"I apologize, I didn't expect the traffic jams here," Galley responded.

"One thing I will not tolerate from the Colony staff is a lack of discipline in any endeavor," Morrow retorted.

"Mr. Morrow —."

"Call me Jackson."

"Yes sir," Galley continued. "Jackson, I strive on attention to detail, it's demanded in my profession. I just hit some heavy traffic, and in a 500-plus mile trip, I don't think a five-minute delay in the start of a mysterious meeting is relevant to this discussion."

"It is *very* relevant to me. Just don't do it

again!"

"Yes sir." Galley cleared his throat, "Now, I've come to accept your offer to join the Colony. Do you still want me?"

"You were chosen from a large selection of potential candidates for the position of Colony astronomer," Jackson related. "I govern the Colony with a group of eight other very brilliant representatives I selected from the Colonists. This group is called the Forum. It was not just I that chose you but the other members of the Forum, too. Yes, we want you and your wife Jalisa to join us."

"Thank you for your confidence. We graciously accept your invitation," Galley said as a waiter approached the table. The conversation stopped.

"Would you like anything to drink?" the waiter asked, looking at Galley.

"I'd like some coffee, please. I need to warm up."

"Yes sir, will that be all?"

Galley nodded and looked back at Jackson as the waiter walked away. "Can you tell me a few more details about you and your plans for your Colony?"

Morrow hesitated a few moments, and then began, "Dr. Pruitt, I consider myself a very unique individual. I've built up almost unlimited wealth and I'm still not happy. Just when I think things are getting better, everything goes wrong. For example, I was just beginning to enjoy my earnings at my new palatial beach home in Southern Florida a number of years ago when Andrew, that damn big hurricane, blew it away. Then I moved back to

71

what I thought was a safe haven from the elements, Southern California. Right! First that huge quake of '09 hit. I rebuilt for several years and began to settle in again. Then Endlight comes. Now I've got to move again to keep going." Morrow nervously folded the corner of the napkin under his glass, looked down at his shorts and continued, "I've even got physical evidence of my constant misfortune." Morrow held out his bare arms in front of him. "Did you notice that my apparel is slightly unusual for this climate?"

"Yes, I've been a little curious about that," Galley admitted.

"On January 13, a number of years ago," Morrow related, "I was golfing in Palm Springs when a sudden storm blew over the desert from the surrounding mountains. My partner and I had no time to leave the course before rain and lightning were all around us. We felt the wrath of God was upon us. Then suddenly a bolt of lightning hit me on the thirteenth tee at one-thirteen in the afternoon. That's thirteen-thirteen in military time. My partner was killed instantly by the ground potential gradient around the strike, but somehow I survived. The doctors who examined me afterward found almost no physical injury to me but diagnosed me with a strange disorder called cryanesthesia. That's why I'm dressed like this."

"What's cryanesthesia?" Galley asked, noticing the waiter returning with his coffee.

Morrow paused while the waiter placed the steaming coffee in front of Galley. "It's a condition caused by a sudden neurological trauma that blocks the sensation of cold to the brain . . . I feel no cold, even in this Twilight climate."

"My God," Galley said. "What a strange malady."

"Yes, but it's been a rather fortunate gift for me during the recent months of decreasing temperatures. The only precaution I must observe is not to let my extremities freeze. I'm very prone to frostbite because of this condition."

Galley acknowledged his concern. "I can understand."

Morrow continued, "I wear a device called a Cryosensor. I had it developed by a small electronics firm that my brother and I own in California to warn me of impending freeze-danger to my limbs. It's really quite ingenious."

"It's fortunate for you that you could do that."

"Yes. But I don't consider myself a lucky man, even though the company has sold thousands since the Earth's cool down started and we've grossed several million from the sales."

Galley shook his head, trying not to show his lack of sympathy for the billionaire. "But you seem to be otherwise normal."

"Not really, I also developed an unusual fascination with numbers after the incident on the golf course. Sometimes it bothers even me."

"Is that the reason for the unusual meeting time?" Galley asked as he warmed his hands and sipped the steaming coffee from his cup. "I'm sorry for asking, I'm just curious."

"That and a great amount of recently acquired superstition often cause me to behave in ways that are even strange to me. I can't always explain my actions, but I assure you I'm as sane as you or the next person."

"I believe you. Now, what have you planned

for the Colony?" Galley asked, wanting to get the conversation back on track.

Morrow motioned for the waiter as he sipped the last of his Tequila Sunrise from his glass. "I'll have another," he said.

"Yes sir. Would you like more coffee?" the waiter asked, looking toward Galley.

"Please warm it up, and I'd like to see a menu if you serve food here in the lounge."

"Yes sir, I'll be right back."

Morrow looked down at the small pager-sized Cryosensor attached to his belt as Galley unzipped his parka. "It's quite warm in here; 78.6 degrees to be exact. You should be quite comfortable without that."

Galley responded obediently by smiling and removing his parka. He placed it over the back of his chair.

"I have devised a grand plan," Morrow continued, "to save most of the Earth's species during Endlight."

Galley raised his eyebrows. "Really, how?"

"You may have heard the news stories about my attempted purchase or lease of Carlsbad Caverns."

Galley nodded affirmatively.

"I was interested in legally acquiring the Caverns to use as a modern Noah's ark," Morrow added. "The reasons I'm interested are fourfold. First, as you and I know, the Earth will most likely freeze in a few months and kill every living thing on its surface. Second, the Caverns are 800 feet or so below the Earth's surface and have a constant temperature of 56 degrees inside. Third, it has over fourteen acres of floor space in the Big Room alone, all underground. That room also has a ceiling over 200 feet high. There are many more rooms and undeveloped caves in the area to house the Colony. Fourth, it has easy ingress and egress for heavy equipment and large animals through the cave entrance."

Galley took the Carlsbad Caverns tourist brochure as Morrow offered it, and paused, studying the photographs on the pamphlet cover. "Looks like a very large place for only a few thousand people," Galley noted, now examining the interior photographs. "What did you say about large animals?"

"Galley, I'm not saving just the human race. I plan to save *every* species alive on Earth today."

"Well, I don't think there's *that* much room in here," Galley retorted with a chuckle.

"Aha! That's the most beautiful part of my plan!" Morrow exclaimed causing the threesome seated two tables away to look at him. He looked down at his empty glass. "Sorry, I just get so excited."

Galley coaxed, "Go on."

"I have arranged the transport of one of each species alive today to Carlsbad. The Caverns are being modified to handle them all with hydroponics gardens, aquariums, aviaries, and biome habitats ranging from desert plains to rain forests. Of course humans also have their space."

"But how are you going to save the species with only one of each?" Galley asked with a puzzled look.

"There's the beauty! Now you've found it!" Jackson Morrow said with the same excitement as before. The threesome looked back at Morrow. He continued in a lower voice, "I'm bringing only the female of each species into the cave. If the gestation period is over four months, I bring them in pregnant. That way they won't have the baby before Endlight's over and we're out of the cave into a thawed world. It just makes sense to save space that way."

Galley showed appreciation of the plan by smiling and tilting his head, "Hmm . . . that's pretty ingenious. But what of the shorter gestation species . . . and what happens if you have spontaneous abortions during the confinement? What if the offspring is another female?"

"I have that planned, too. I'm bringing on staff, specialists from the Cincinnati Zoo's Center for the Reproduction of Endangered Wildlife—CREW for short—and from the San Diego Zoo's Center for Reproduction of Endangered Species, or CRES. Together, the two groups currently have cryopreserved the eggs, sperm and embryos for over eight-hundred species of animals in what they call the Big Sleep."

Morrow looked around the room for their waiter and continued, "Under the direction of Dr. Janet Sherman, a reproductive physiologist from Cincinnati, a group of twenty scientists will maintain our Cryopreservation Lab and oversee eventual repopulation of the animals of the world after Endlight. She and her team have all been working for years in the science of cryogenically freezing sperm and embryos for saving endangered species. They didn't realize how important their jobs would be until you predicted Endlight. Then, suddenly they realized every species on Earth was immediately endangered. Because of that, I have built a thirty-million-dollar cryogenic chamber and storage system for the cave. It will store the frozen sperm and embryos from every species captured . . . and we hope to capture them all before they freeze to death during Endlight."

The conversation paused as the waiter returned with the cocktail for Morrow and refilled Galley's coffee cup. He then handed the menu to Galley and said, "I'll return for your order in a moment." Galley nodded approval and opened the menu.

"Well, Jackson," Galley added as he looked over the menu fare, "it sounds like you do have an organized plan. Where do I fit in?"

Morrow stirred the grenadine in his drink, making the visual sunrise effect in the glass disappear. The glass took on the pinkish hue of Twilight. "Most members of our colony are wealthy businesspeople, politicians, entertainers and their spouses. They were all personally invited in under the highest secrecy based on their wealth and integrity. They have all paid a substantial fee to join. The entrance fee supports the cave modifications and colony life-support system. We are now over twelve hundred people strong including spouses, and have collected almost 3.2 billion dollars in fees. Of course nobody needs their money if they don't live past Endlight, so they don't mind the charge. It's kind of a life tax—you pay it to live or you just don't live. It's that simple . . . and many members have given their entire fortunes over to me."

"You certainly don't mince words," Galley interjected. "Isn't that a rather cold attitude to have about this situation we're in?"

"Galley, I'm a businessman. I thrive on setting and accomplishing goals, no matter how I get there. I am not cold in my thoughts, just logical to a fault, as some of my friends will admit. You must also realize these people in the Colony are paying to keep all species of life on Earth from vanishing forever as the dinosaurs did. That gives each member a mission to continue, even if some don't want to live through the event. Why, we've even had a few close friends of some Colony members pay the entrance fee and not join."

"Why?" Galley asked, carefully sipping from his full cup.

"They believe in our mission to save all life on Earth for posterity, and they wanted to help financially, but they're ready to give up now. They don't want to start anew after Endlight. They're at peace with themselves. These are some of these most amazing people I've met. They and the other members have funded the recent development and construction of one of the most amazing high-tech facilities ever conceived of above or below the ground. We're moving in this week —"

Almost choking, Galley put his cup down and interrupted, "I thought I just read about your trying to buy the Caverns last week. How could it be complete this fast?"

"You *did* read of my offer to the National Parks and Wildlife Department to buy Carlsbad Caverns last week. It was merely a formality. They closed the cave to visitors and abandoned it about two months ago when you announced your Endlight discovery. It seems nobody is interested in recreational trips after that bombshell."

"So you just moved in and started modifying

it for your use?"

"Yes, for my use and yours, and to help us with the preservation of life on Earth."

"Jackson, it sounds like you've been very careful to ensure the preservation of the wildlife species. How are you handling the continued propagation of the human race?"

"I've specified that for each male and female adult couple entering the Colony with us, there must be at least two opposite-sex children. That will ensure rapid human repopulation of the Earth when we come out. Those that don't qualify just don't get in."

Galley frowned as he dropped the menu. "But my wife and I have no children."

"Then you must simply find two youngsters, one male and one female, to bring with you before we seal the Cavern doors to Endlight," Morrow responded showing no concern.

"Are you serious? That's ludicrous!"

"Galley, there are billions of people that will freeze to death during Endlight. Their children will freeze with them . . . just give them a chance to save their children and you'll have more children than you can handle."

Galley wanted to call Morrow a heartless bastard to his face, but suddenly realized he was only doing what he felt was necessary . . . and he was probably right. "If we can't find the children then we can't join the Colony?"

"That's right. I'm sorry but that *is* one of our rules. The rules of the Colony are not arbitrary ones, they are carefully thought out by our Forum to continue life on Earth."

The waiter returned to take Galley's order.

"Are you ready to order?"

Galley handed him the menu. "No, I think I've lost my appetite."

"Very well, sir. Would either of you like anything else?" Morrow nodded no. Galley concurred. "Fine, then. I'll bring your check."

Morrow confided as the waiter left, "Galley, this has not been easy for anybody. I have spent days with stomach-wrenching indecision, as you probably will. Just think of it as being on the roof of a burning ten-story building when the flames finally reach your feet and your shoes begin to burn. Would you jump?"

"Probably, if there were no other escape."

"Good," Morrow continued. "Then I'd like to see you, your wife and new family at the Caverns next Wednesday. That will give you four days to get your business in order in Socorro. We need you with us to oversee the final construction of our observatory. We'll have a small optical telescope and a fully heated ten-meter radio telescope at your disposal in the Cavern. Those should be adequate for observations during our brief confinement there."

"Yes sir. Thank you for your confidence, again, "Galley responded, still stunned by the new condition placed upon him.

"Are you staying the night?" Morrow asked.

"No, I think I'd better head back to Socorro tonight and discuss this with my wife."

"Well, why don't you just call her from here?"

Galley rose from his chair. "Okay, I think I'll try."

As Morrow paid the check, Galley returned

from the direction of the phones. "There's a problem with the phone lines, I couldn't get through. I'm just gonna head home."

"Then I look forward to seeing you next Wednesday, Dr. Pruitt. Welcome to the Colony and please remember to keep our identity and location of our underground habitat in your deepest confidence."

"I will. Oh, Jackson, the phone malfunction reminded me. Do you have any hams—amateur radio operators—in the Colony?"

"Hams? No, not that I know of. Why?"

"Then I suggest that you place one on your staff to keep us in touch with other parts of the world that might survive Endlight. The entire worldwide telephone system is quickly failing. It will be our only link with the surface in a week or so."

"Thank you for the suggestion, Dr. Pruitt, I think you'll be a fine addition to our staff."

Galley rose to. put on his coat and shook hands with Morrow. "See you Wednesday, Jackson."

"Drive safely, Galley. We need you."

"Thanks," Galley responded as he started for the door.

Morrow rose from his chair and addressed Galley as he walked away, "Oh, Galley!"

Galley spun around and returned to the table. "Yes sir?"

"I neglected to mention a few details you will need to know now in case the phones stay down through next Wednesday. Bring only one-hundred pounds per person of personal items. Leave your other things in your house; they should be there

81

when things thaw out after Endlight. You will need no food. We'll supply that. You *will* need money for personal items you may want to buy in our Cavern commissary. Most people are bringing around one-hundred-thousand dollars spending money for the four-month stay. I believe it will be hard to spend that much in the time we're down there."

Galley asked, "What about family pets? Are they allowed?"

"No! Absolutely not!" Morrow exclaimed, startling several people entering the lounge area.

Galley's heart rose to his throat as he thought of having to put Frosty back into the cold. He begged, "But what if it's only a small, under-ten-pound, dog, couldn't you please make an exception?"

"I said *no*, and that's that, Dr. Pruitt. The Forum will simply *not* allow it." Morrow commanded with a stern frown.

Galley mumbled, "Jerk!" under his breath and in final resignation said, "Well fine, I'll see you Wednesday, Morrow."

"Goodbye Galley, I'll be in the Operations Center Control Room most of the day Wednesday. If you don't find me there, have me paged through the PCC System, that's the Personal Cavern Communicator. We all have one."

"I will. Goodbye," Galley said as he walked away.

As Galley reached his car he noticed that the doorman had plugged his Porsche's oil pan heater into one of the recently installed power outlets in front of each parking space. Strange he hadn't noticed them when he parked. Galley looked back over his shoulder and yelled, "Thank You," before unplugging the cord and stowing it under the wheel well. He then kicked the tire in anger and screamed, "Damn you, Morrow!"

Having relieved some of his anger Galley unlocked the door, smashed himself into the driver's seat and started the car. He slammed the car door. Quietly, delicate ice crystals from the windshield broke loose and drifted gently in front of him reflecting the parking lot lights like shimmering stars. Tears welled up in his eyes as he began his miserable journey back to Socorro.

CHAPTER 4
TRANSMISSION RECEIVED

"The World is too much with us; late and soon,
Getting and spending, we lay waste our powers;
Little we see in Nature that is ours;
We have given our hearts away, a sordid boon!
This sea that bares her bosom to the moon;
The winds that will be howling at all hours,
And are up-gathered now like sleeping flowers;
For this, for everything, we are out of tune;
It moves us not. —Great God! I'd rather be
A Pagan suckled in a creed outworn,
So might I, standing on this pleasant lea,
Have glimpses that would make me less forlorn;
Have sight of Proteus rising from the sea,
Or hear old Triton blow his wreathed horn."

WILLIAM WORDSWORTH, *The World*
Is Too Much With Us

Galley drove through Socorro and pulled into his driveway shortly after midnight, feeling the immediate anxiety of having to relate his story to Jalisa. He knew she'd be waiting up.

Hearing the garage door open, Jalisa ran into the garage screaming, "Where have you been? Why didn't you call me? I've been so worried about you! I thought you were dead."

Opening his door, Galley stepped from the car shouting to be heard, "I'm sorry. I tried to call you from Phoenix before I left but the phones weren't working. I really did."

He closed the garage door, then walked over to her and put his arm around her. "Sorry I worried you."

She reacted coldly and said, almost sobbing, "I *was* so worried about you. I thought you might have had an accident or broken down on the highway. I'm sorry, I'll be all right, and I was just so scared."

Galley held Jalisa trying to reassure her of his presence. "I'm home, everything will be all right. Well, almost."

She stood there quietly in his arms for several seconds and then responded, "What do you mean, well almost?"

"Come on, let's go inside where it's warm— I'm freezing—and I'll tell you about the meeting."

They walked through the back door together to find Frosty jumping into the air and barking in happiness. Frosty ran up to Galley and stood up, putting her front paws on his leg and wagging her tail. Jalisa said, "Look how happy she is to see you home."

Looking down, Galley stood motionless without emotion.

"What's wrong, Galley?"

After several seconds of thought, he smiled and reached down to cuddle Frosty in his arms. She licked his face in appreciation. In between licks, he managed to say, "I've just got . . . a lot of things . . . on my mind, and . . . the welfare of this little pup . . . is one of them."

Jalisa laughed at the pair, not knowing the real concern in Galley's mind. "She's fine. She just ate a big dinner of leftover roast beef and carrots."

"She ate . . . carrots?" he questioned in astonishment.

"I think she would eat anything now that she's found a home," she confided, almost in a whisper.

Galley, suddenly feeling the weariness from his trip, took off his parka. "Honey, let's go to bed, I'm exhausted from the drive. I'll tell you about the meeting in the morning."

"Well, how did it go? Please don't keep me in suspense until morning," she pleaded.

As they walked into the bedroom Frosty jumped on the bed, still wagging her tail. Galley reached down and petted her on the head, trying not to show his sadness. "The best news is that we're in! They accepted us into the Colony. The Colony governors had a large number of astronomers to pick from and they chose me . . . I guess because I was the first to discover Endlight."

Jalisa called from the closet while putting on her nightgown, "That's great! I'm so happy and proud of you! That's the other thing I was worried about while you were gone. I thought surely you would call me and tell me if it was good news."

Now sitting on the bed, playing with Frosty he called back, "Jalisa, I told you the phone system was failing with the falling temperatures. I tried but couldn't get through to Socorro."

She emerged from the closet in a very sheer teddy and said, "Galley, get ready for bed."

He rushed into the closet past Jalisa to take

off his clothes and yelled back, "Just a minute." Three minutes later he was asleep as his head hit his pillow.

He awoke Saturday morning to the glow of Twilight coming through the mini-blinds in the bedroom. Glancing at the clock by his bedside, he noticed that it was eleven-thirty. He shook Jalisa gently on the shoulder. "Rise and shine, honey, you're the only sunshine I'll see all day."

Rolling over to face him, she opened one eye, then the other. "Very funny, I tried to get *you* to rise and shine last night, but you pooped out on me."

"I'm sorry, I promise. I *was* interested, but I guess I was just exhausted. I'll get up and make the coffee. You lay here in bed."

She rolled back over causing a high-pitched screech. "Oh, Frosty, I'm so sorry. Come here little girl," Jalisa whispered as Galley left the room.

Jalisa, still yawning, followed Galley into the kitchen after a few minutes and sat at the breakfast table. "Galley can we turn the heater up some more? It's really getting cold in here."

Galley finished putting the filter and coffee into the coffee maker, turned it on, and left the room. "Sure, I'll do it. I'm cold, too."

As she sat waiting for the coffee to finish perking Jalisa turned on the radio to get the weather report. Because temperatures had dropped below the lowest readings of most commercial thermometers, everyone in Socorro relied on the readings from the scientific thermometer that KTEK bought last month. After a short while Gus reported, "The local noon temperature in Socorro is—are you ready for this—minus seventy-four degrees."

Galley, hearing the report, yelled from the living room, "Damn!"

"What happened? Are you okay?"

"It's already four degrees colder than predicted for today. That means the temperature drop is speeding up. We've dropped over six degrees since yesterday."

Jalisa poured her coffee. "What does that matter? It's still cold."

"The Cloud must not be equally dense throughout. We suspected that but didn't think it highly likely. We couldn't measure it either."

"So?"

"It means we all have less time before things get *really* cold, to the point of requiring artificial environments to sustain life cold. It also means we go into the Endlight Event, and total darkness, sooner than expected. We need to get to the Cavern and the Colony pretty damn fast."

Disturbed by his answer, she continued, "Okay, then tell me all about yesterday's meeting."

He sat beside Jalisa and carefully described Morrow's entire plan and all of its details to her, except the no-pet condition. After he finished talking and had his second cup of coffee, Jalisa sat there stunned by all the information she had just been subjected to. She was even more amazed at the conditions they were to follow if they wanted to enter the Colony.

"Galley," she pleaded. "Where in the world are we going to get two kids from? Kidnap them? You don't just go up to someone and ask them if you can borrow their kids for four months and then leave them to freeze to death."

"I know, honey. I've been worried sick about that stipulation. I've also been doing a lot of thinking about it, and I think I may have a solution."

"Really?"

"Yes. You know Neemu and Rutha have the two girls and two boys?"

"Yeah?"

"Well, I'm going to ask them to lend us two of them for a few months."

"Are you going to tell them about the Colony, Galley?"

"I have to, but I'm not saying where it is or who its leader is. Otherwise, Neemu would suspect Carlsbad from the newspaper article he told me about last week."

"But Galley, I hate for you to do that. We're such close friends with them."

"Jalisa, they will all freeze anyway in a few weeks, so we might as well try to save some of the kids. It's the only choice I can think of for us."

Jalisa began to sob, at first quietly with her face in her hands, and then almost uncontrollably as the realization of it all began to sink in. Galley got up and walked around the kitchen table to her. He squatted by her chair and hugged her, trying to comfort her distress, "Jalisa, I'm sorry. Nobody can stop this horrible event. We just happen to be fortunate enough to have an escape. At least Morrow thinks it's an escape. I haven't seen this new place yet. It might be more hazardous than taking our chances on the outside here in Socorro."

She looked at him, tears still in her eyes. "Galley, I... I don't want us to die. We're too young. Make it go away."

89

"Don't worry, honey. I think we'll make it with the Colony. Everything sounds really well thought out. Now let's you and I make a plan; we've got only four days before we leave for Carlsbad."

Now controlling her crying to just an occasional slight sniff, she agreed, "Ok, I'll help, but first things first. Go call the Hatlems and ask them about the kids. If we can't get them, we can't go at all."

Galley stood abruptly. "I can't call. This is too important a question to ask over the phone, and besides, the phones may not be working reliably, anyway. I think I'll drop in and pay Neemu and Rutha a personal visit."

"That's a good idea, honey. Want me to go with you?"

"No, I want to ask Neemu in private, before I approach Rutha with the subject. I'll be back shortly," Galley said as he kissed her on the head and went into the garage.

"Bye, be careful," she whispered and began crying again.

Galley arrived at the Hatlem's house hoping he would see the lights on. Good, they're home, he thought as he walked up the front walk and noticed activity inside. He knocked twice.

"Oh, hi Galley," Rutha said as she opened the door. "How have you and Jalisa been lately? I haven't seen you in weeks."

"I know, Rutha, we've been busy getting ready for this," he said pointing his finger up to the dimming pink-grey sky.

"That's what Neemu's doing right now. He's out in the garage sealing cold air leaks. Why don't

90

you go out there and give him some moral support?"

"Ok, I'll do just that. I've gotten to be a pretty good leak sealer, too," he said as he walked toward the garage. "Oh, Rutha where are the kids?"

"Jan and Klas are in their rooms watching cartoons and the girls are asleep."

"I'll say hi on my way back in," he called as he opened the door and went into the garage. "Brrrr, Neemu . . . I thought you were out here trying to fix cold-air leaks. It must be zero in here. And why is your car engine running with the garage door closed, that's dangerous as hell!"

Frustrated, Neemu looked up from his contorted position in the corner. "I *am* trying to fix leaks. There are just a lot of them in this old garage, and the car is running to keep me warm. I've got a hose on the exhaust pipe that goes outside." He put down the caulking gun and stood up slowly. "Ow! That hurts." He groaned as he grabbed his back.

Galley laughed at Neemu's appearance. He had white goop all over his hands and face. His parka was dirty and torn, and his beard was covered with ice. Galley joked, "Well Neemu, who's winning, you or the leakers?"

"Very funny, Galley. I need to take a break anyway, I'm glad you dropped by. What's up?" Neemu asked. He took a handkerchief from his pocket and wiped his face.

"I wanted to talk to you about a small problem Jalisa and I have."

"Okay, let's go inside where it's warm. I'm freezing."

"No. I'd rather not right now. Can we talk out here privately?"

"Sure, but first let me go in and get some coffee to warm up. Want some?"

"I'll take a half-cup. I just finished a pot about an hour ago, and I'm already floating."

"Okay, I'll be right back, Galley. Make yourself comfortable," Neemu said, laughing at the thought of being comfortable in his messy garage in below-freezing temperatures.

Neemu returned with their coffees and handed one steaming cup to Galley. "This one's yours."

"Thanks, Neemu," Galley said.

They both leaned back against the car hood to keep warm, sipping their coffee for several seconds before Neemu spoke. "So what's this small problem you and Jalisa have?"

"We've been invited to join a survival group that plans to outlive Endlight. Remember those rumors about a secret society you heard about a few days ago? "

"Ya."

"Well, they were true. They asked me to join them as their astronomer and I accepted. They say they are going to protect us from dying in the cold during the Endlight period."

"Galley, that's great!" Neemu responded trying not to show his envy. "Do they have room for two astronomers?"

"No Neemu, I'm afraid not," Galley answered quietly. "There's only limited space in the survival habitat."

"Oh, the NASA Mars habitat? Good for you and Jalisa," Neemu said now showing resentment in his voice.

"Neemu, there's more," Galley carefully

continued. "I don't really know how to ask this since we've been friends for so long, but the Colony rules state that we must bring two opposite-sex children into the group to help preserve humanity."

Neemu felt uncomfortably pleased knowing that Galley and Jalisa never had children. He interrupted, "Ask me what?"

Galley paused momentarily. "They won't let us in without children so we need to borrow two of yours for about four months. We'll save two of your family, at least."

Neemu suddenly seething with anger yelled, "Which two do you want, you bastard? You're actually going to leave the rest of us out here to freeze to death?" He lunged at Galley, knocking him backward.

Galley spun around to break his fall with his hands.

"Neemu, I'm *sorry*." Galley pleaded. His head slammed against a tarp-covered workbench. Galley fell to the floor and pulled the tarp with him exposing some old electronics equipment covered with dust. He looked back up at Neemu and noticed the equipment. It wasn't fully recognizable to Galley, with the blood now flowing over his eyes, but on the bench appeared to be a radio transmitter, complete with microphone, and a short-wave receiver. On the face of the transmitter were the call letters SM3WAM.

Galley wiped his eyes with his hand and yelled, "*Neemu, stop!* What's all this radio equipment?"

Neemu attacked again, going for Galley's throat this time, as he screamed, "Why do you care, you cold-hearted son-of-a-bitch? Don't you

93

remember that I told you that I was an amateur radio operator in Sweden?"

Galley trying to talk, but gasping for oxygen, rasped, "Neemu, stop! I can get you in."

"What?" Neemu relaxed his grip on Galley's throat.

Still gasping for air, Galley responded, "They're looking for an amateur radio operator. I think I can get you and Rutha and *all* the kids in, if I'm not too late."

"Galley, you knew I was a Ham. That's what got me into electronics and radio astronomy. I've just never had time to get my license transferred over here. Don't you remember that?" Neemu asked, still kneeling over Galley, his legs straddling Galley's chest.

"No, I'm sorry! *Now let me up*! Neemu, I've got to get in touch with someone. I've got to get through to the leader before he selects someone else," Galley yelled frantically, looking at the equipment and still thinking of the kids.

"Okay, then. Hurry! Use our phone. I'm sorry I lost my temper but you really pissed me off," Neemu said rapidly as he helped Galley up from the floor.

Five-hundred miles away the switchboard operator at the Phoenician Resort took a call. "Good Afternoon . . . Phoenician Resort. May I help you?"

"Hello, this is amateur radio station KZ7V0X in Phoenix. I have a phone-patch request to speak to Jackson Morrow from amateur radio station SM3WAM/portable in Socorro, New Mexico," the voice on the phone responded.

"One moment sir, I'll connect you with his room," the operator replied.

"Hello?" Morrow answered, somewhat startled by the ringing phone. Nobody was supposed to know where he was except members of the Forum and they were all in California or New Mexico. He knew they couldn't be calling because the phone lines to California were out, as were the lines to New Mexico.

"Mr. Morrow?"

"Yes? Who in the hell is *this*"

"This is Vic Dolger, operator of amateur radio station K Zed 7 Victor Zero X-ray here in Phoenix. I have a long-distance radiotelephone patch for you from Socorro, New Mexico."

"Is this call from Dr. Galley Pruitt?" Morrow asked.

"Just a minute, let me see," the ham operator responded.

Morrow could hear muffled talking in the background between Vic and the other radio station in Socorro. "Sugar Mary 3 William Allen Mary, What is the name of your party? Over," Dolger asked.

The response crackled, then clearly said, "KZ7V0X this is SM3WAM/portable. It's Dr. Galley Pruitt. Over."

Vic came back on the phone line, "Yes, Mr. Morrow, the calling party *is* a Dr. Pruitt."

"Well, then I'll talk to him," Morrow agreed.

Dolger continued, "First let me explain something, Mr. Morrow. Because this is a half-duplex radio communication, it's a little different from your normal full-duplex phone conversations."

"Oh? How is that?"

"Well, you can't both talk at the same time. When one of you finishes speaking you must say 'over' to let us know to change from transmitting

95

to receiving at our ends in Socorro and here. Otherwise, you'll over talk each other."

"That seems simple enough. Put Galley on. Over."

There were several clicks and buzzes in Morrow's phone receiver as the two hams connected the phone patch lines into their transmitters and receivers. Then there was a momentary hissing after which Morrow clearly heard, "Mr. Morrow, this is Galley Pruitt calling from Socorro. Can you hear me all right? Over."

"Yes, I can Galley, loud and clear. Are you all right? Did you make it back to Socorro okay? Uh, over."

Hissing came from the phone, then a click. "I'm fine, Jackson. I've got a question for you that can't wait until next Wednesday. Did you find an amateur radio operator for us yet? Over."

"No, Galley, you know that the long-distance phone lines are out. Why, have you found us someone? Over."

Sssssss, click. "Yes, an International ham from Sweden who is also an astronomer and electronics expert. He has two male and two female children so he can help us with our two-child requirement, too. I think if you'll let him, his name is Neemu, incidentally and his wife, Rutha, join us, it will solve a lot of problems for all of us. What do you say Jackson? Over."

"Galley, did this Neemu person set up the radiophone link we're talking over right now?" Jackson waited several seconds for an answer and then remembered to sign off, "Oh, I forgot, Over."

The hiss returned, then the click of the received incoming signal on Morrow's phone. "Yes,

Jackson, he connected us through his equipment here at his house. When we tried to call you by long-distance telephone the lines were still down— and probably will stay that way—so Neemu decided to try a radiophone patch link into Phoenix. It only took us about ten minutes to complete the patch. Over."

"Okay, Galley, it's obvious that we need someone like him to retain contact with the rest of the world. You're authorized to invite him to join us. Tell him the details, since I don't want to discuss them over the phone, much less radio. Is he there now? Over."

Sssss, click. "Yes, he's right here beside me here in this damn leaky, freezing garage," Galley looked at Neemu and smiled. "He can hear everything you're saying. Over."

"Well, Neemu I'd like to have you, your wife and children join us at Antron next week. Galley will tell you the details. I'm sorry for the informality of this invitation, but considering the circumstances, it's the best I can do. Over"

Sssss, click. "Mr. Morrow, this in Neemu. I deeply appreciate the offer and *do* accept for my family and me. After we finish this call I'll get more details from Galley and just a minute, Galley wants to ask you a question,"

Morrow heard Neemu hand the microphone back to Galley, "Jackson, do I know Antron? Over."

"Yes, Galley, it's our code name for the place we talked about here yesterday. Over."

"Fine, here's Neemu back."

Neemu took the microphone. "Anyway, Mr. Morrow thanks again. We'll definitely be there. And Galley sends his thanks, too. Over and out."

Morrow hung up the phone and looked out onto the red-glowing tennis courts. After staring out into the dimness for a few minutes, he picked up the phone, dialed his driver's room and said, "Are you ready to take me to the meeting at Hydrolox?"

"Yes, sir," the driver replied.

Galley waited while Neemu shut down the radio station and turned off the car engine. They went inside to tell Rutha and the kids. Galley walked over to the phone and tried to call Jalisa. Neemu called for Rutha and the kids to come into the room. The phone began to ring. Thank God the local circuits are not dead yet, he thought.

Jalisa answered the phone. "Hello?"

"Hi hon, I'm over at the Hatlems' house. Sorry for the delay, but we had a complication develop."

"Have you asked them about the kids yet?"

"Yes, that's the complication. I asked Neemu and he split my head open," Galley said dabbing the cut with a damp cloth Neemu had brought him.

"My God, Galley, are you all right?"

"Yes, I think I'm fine. We just had a little scuffle. Then everything worked out."

"What do you mean, Galley? How can you say that if you're injured?"

"I'm not injured, I just have a little cut on my forehead."

"What happened?"

"I asked Neemu to borrow the kids."

"And he beat you up?"

"Well, sort of —"

"Galley, stop it with the riddles. Tell me what happened."

"Remember I told you we needed an amateur radio operator in the Colony?"

"Yes, why?"

"Well, I found out during our scuffle that Neemu has been a ham for many years in Sweden. He said he'd told me that long ago and I just forgot. He's got all the equipment we need for communication."

"Galley, what does that have to do with anything? Can they join us?" Jalisa asked impatiently.

"Well, Neemu just set it up so I could talk to Morrow —"

"You talked to Morrow in Phoenix? What did he say?"

"He asked them to join."

"How did you talk to him? I thought the phone system was out."

"Only long-distance calls using satellite links are out. Obviously, the local lines are still operational since I'm talking to you right now. Neemu linked Socorro to Phoenix by short-wave radio and then coupled the radios to the local phone lines in each city. Ingenious, huh? We ..."

"Just a minute, Galley, someone's at the front door," Jalisa interrupted.

Galley turned to Neemu and whispered, "I'll be off in a second. I just had to tell Jalisa the good news."

Neemu, still somewhat upset by the recent events, called out again, this time screaming, for Rutha and the kids to come into the living room. Three kids quickly filed into the room, followed by Rutha carrying the youngest. Each took a seat, waiting for the mysterious news. Neemu sat and quietly described the details of the phone conversation to them while waiting for Galley to hang up with Jalisa.

Jalisa came back on the phone with a very disturbed voice, "Galley, I think you'd better come home right now, there are two military men here waiting to transport you somewhere."

"What? What kind of military men? Are you sure?" Galley asked in disbelief.

"Yes, Galley, they came in a military Hummer and are in full uniform. There's one guy here named, let me see, Colonel McMurphy. And the other one's Major Stancey. Do you want to talk to them?"

"Put the Colonel on the phone. I want to ask him a few questions."

"Ok, Galley, just a minute." The line went silent as she handed off the phone.

"Dr. Pruitt, this is Colonel McMurphy. I've been sent up from Holloman Air Force Base in Alamogordo to escort you to a waiting plane in the desert near us"

"What do you mean a waiting plane in the desert?" Galley interjected.

"Dr. Pruitt this is a very classified mission. Sir, I can tell you no more over the telephone. Please try to get here as quickly as possible. We can't leave until you leave with us."

"Ok, put my wife back on the phone . . . please."

"Yes, sir."

"Galley, what's going on? Have you done something wrong?" Jalisa asked with despair in her voice.

"Jalisa," Galley explained in exasperation,

"I have no idea what's happening there but I'd better get there as soon as possible like they said. I'm walking out the door right now."

"Bye, Galley. See you in a minute. Please drive safely."

Galley hung up the phone and looked over at the Hatlem family sitting patiently around the living room in deep anticipation of more details on their new lifesaving adventure. "Guys, I'm sorry, I have to leave immediately."

"Why, what was that phone call about?" Neemu asked.

"I don't really know. There are some men at my house who want to take me somewhere right now. They won't tell me where. I can't imagine what this is about."

"Can't you tell us about Antron before you go? You just can't leave us up in the air like this, Galley. Our lives are all at stake," Neemu pleaded.

Galley looked down at the family sitting there eagerly waiting for an answer. He thought for several seconds as their eyes pleaded with him. "I just can't right now. Something very strange is happening at my house at this moment and I have to get back. I'll have Jalisa come over in a few minutes and tell you everything she knows. I've filled her in on everything I know."

"We understand," Neemu conceded. "We'll just talk to Jalisa when she comes over."

"I'm really sorry I have to leave like this." Galley said approaching the front door.

"Bye, and have a good trip. Call me when you get back, if the phones are still working," Neemu said. "I *am* rather curious about your mysterious trip."

Galley drove slowly by the front of his house to inspect the vehicle parked in the street. His headlights showed that it was an olive-drab military Hummer with USAF— HOLLOMAN AFB stenciled in large white letters across the passenger door. Below that was FOR OFFICIAL USE ONLY. The license plates read US AIR FORCE—FOR OFFICIAL USE ONLY. *Well, I guess they're real*, he thought as he drove into the garage and shut off the engine. Galley entered the house to find Jalisa sitting in the living room having coffee with the two uniformed soldiers. He walked to the middle of the room and looked at the two officers. "Hi, I'm Galley Pruitt. Now what's this all about?"

Colonel McMurphy rose to shake hands with Galley. He extended his hand outward but the gesture was ignored by Galley. "Dr. Pruitt," he said as he dropped his hand, "I've been ordered to see that you get safely to an Air Force runway not far from here and board a plane. That's all I know. You'll find out more after takeoff."

Galley looked at Jalisa. "Are you all right?"

She responded, "I'm okay. I'm just confused, and a little bit scared. How's your head?"

"It's okay," Galley said as he looked back at McMurphy. "Do you know where I'm being taken or when I'll be back?"

"Dr. Pruitt, all I've been told is that this is a matter of utmost priority for national security."

"How long will I be gone? I have to be back by Tuesday."

"Well, sir, I've also been ordered to pick you up from the airstrip on Sunday, tomorrow evening at five p.m. You should be home by six."

Galley looked back at Jalisa. "Can you

handle that? Honey, you know you've got to start packing while I'm gone. Oh, and I told Neemu and Rutha you'd come right over and explain the situation to them. You know what I'm talking about. They're dying to know more details."

Jalisa answered with resignation in her voice, "Ok, Galley. I'll do that, and have everything under control by the time you get back. You better go pack a few things for yourself."

Galley left the room and reentered several minutes later with a small carry-on bag. "Ok, let's go," he said as the officers rose from their chairs. He kissed Jalisa goodbye and left, leaving her wondering what had just happened. She grabbed her parka and headed into the garage on her way to the Hatlem's.

As they climbed into the Hummer in front of Galley's house, Galley asked, "What's this really all about guys?"

Major Stancey replied, "Dr. Pruitt, as the Colonel said we're under strict orders to take you to a classified Air Force runway for a very important top-secret mission."

Galley responded, "How can that be, I have no clearances? I've been around enough secret projects to know that clearances are required for this type of thing."

Colonel McMurphy looked over his shoulder briefly at Galley and said, "This project has been given a code name by the President of the United States: Darkstar. We have just done an intensive background search on you and your wife, and have verified your integrity."

Galley said sarcastically, "Thanks for the confidence."

103

McMurphy continued, "Everything you will see and hear from this point onward, until we return you to your house, is to be considered Top Secret, code name Darkstar. The President has granted you the clearance personally. Here, sign this acknowledgment."

Galley turned on the overhead light and read the security agreement. He felt a lump come into his throat as he noticed the President's signature under his. He regretted what he had just said.

McMurphy asked, "What was that conversation all about, back there, you had with your wife? You know, about the Hatlems and more details?"

Galley answered, trying to conceal the deception in his voice, "We just found out that my wife is pregnant and I wanted her to be the first to tell them . . . in person."

"Oh, well congratulations, Dr. Pruitt," both soldiers said, almost in unison.

After traveling for twelve minutes along Interstate 25 they turned left onto U.S. 380. The windows were beginning to fog from their breath. Galley used his parka sleeve to wipe a small hole in the condensation. Looking out over the familiar New Mexico lava beds he asked, "Where are we going?"

McMurphy pointed to the right far ahead and said, "Up there. We'll be there in a little while."

As he stared out o the nothingness for what seemed like hours, Galley finally noticed a road sign in the headlight beams that read TRINITY SITE with an arrow pointing to the right. The Hummer slowed and turned off of U.S. 380 onto a dirt road as the dim glow of Twilight was fading into sunset. Galley began to feel uneasy with the situation.

Forty minutes had passed when the Hummer eased onto another side road. The headlights illuminated a large sign reading: ENTRY PROHIBITED—EXTREMELY DANGEROUS RADIATION PAST THIS POINT.

Galley sat upright in his seat. "Wait a minute guys, can't you read?

The Major looked back at Galley and chuckled sarcastically. "You don't really think *we* would be here if we thought it was dangerous, do you?"

"No. I guess not," Galley said as he relaxed back into his seat. He started to drift off to sleep. As the Hummer squealed to a halt, Galley awakened to hear, "We're here with Dr. Pruitt."

"Yes sir," the heavily armed guard responded with a salute.

Galley, still groggy from the short nap asked, "Where are we now?"

Major Stancey looked back at Galley. "This is an extremely sensitive outpost for the Air Force. Do not *ever* reveal its location."

"We'll I don't think I could if I tried, I fell asleep back there," Galley admitted. Then he looked ahead, rubbing his eyes, to see a small well-lit concrete building and a immense runway with its blue lights aglow. He also noticed a deep rumbling like nothing he had ever heard before.

The Hummer stopped in front of a flat-roofed concrete-block building. A small lighted blue and white sign read USAF SITE 44. The Major and Colonel exited the Hummer and waited for Galley to climb from the back seat. "This is it," the Major said. "Please follow us."

Galley stood up, once again feeling the biting cold. "Let's go."

Galley entered the austere outpost noticing the whiteboards all around the walls with what looked like flight schedules. A uniformed man walked from a room at the rear of the building with a very large bundle over his arm. "Here Dr. Pruitt, put this on. It's a pressurized flight suit. All personnel flying over fifty-thousand feet are required to wear them for safety. You'll be way over that."

Galley thought *fifty-thousand feet* and then automatically responded, "Where do I change?"

Major Stancey said, "I'll show you. And besides, you'll probably need some help climbing into that suit." Galley followed Stancey into the back room, noticing the rumbling growing in intensity. It began to shake the concrete walls.

Five minutes later Galley walked from the dressing area resembling an astronaut. The suit was lined with pressure hoses and tubing. Over his head was a helmet that looked like a prop from a futuristic science-fiction movie. Then Colonel McMurphy reappeared saying, "I'll walk you to the plane. That's as far as I go."

Galley followed the Colonel out the door toward the brightly glowing lights of the runway and saw, as he gasped, the sleek black-gray body of an advanced airship with an almost un-recognizable shape. It was an airplane like he'd never seen before. Embedded in the center of each sleek wing were two engines that glowed red through their nacelles. The rumble was deafening. It vibrated his stomach. He hesitated.

"*Come on*, Dr. Pruitt," McMurphy yelled over the roar.

They ran up under the aircraft to an open hatch in the belly of the plane. A small ladder extended down to the tarmac. "Have a good trip, Dr. Pruitt," McMurphy screamed over the engines' roar. Galley nodded back, not hearing, but recognizing the phrase from his lips.

Galley climbed inside and saw two other astronaut-looking crew members reaching for his hand. One shut the hatch, slightly silencing the noise, as Galley rolled onto the floor of the darkened compartment. Galley mouthed, "Thanks," and looked around the space filled with electronics as he regained his night vision. He saw the pilot and co-pilot sitting in their seats several yards in front and above him. The roar from the engines was making his headache worsen.

The crewman who had reached out to help Galley looked down at him and yelled, "Welcome aboard the Aurora 2."

Galley sat quietly stunned for a few moments as the aircraft began its taxi. He screamed over the engines' roar, "Is this the same ship we've heard about that has been causing all the noise over California?"

"Yes, sir, it is. My name is Captain Chuck Garner. I'll be your flight officer during the trip."

"Where in the hell are we going? Nobody's told me yet," Galley yelled.

Captain Garner screamed back, "If you'll wait a few minutes I'll tell you." He pointed to a small black panel in front of Galley, "Take that coiled cord hanging from your helmet and plug it in there.

107

It's got your audio . . . and oxygen." Galley quickly obeyed.

The deafening roar muffled to a rumble once again as the aircraft approached the end of the runway. Unable to see out because of the lack of windows, Galley carefully observed the sway of each turn and reasoned that they must have just left the taxiway and now be on the runway. As the roar grew in intensity almost to the point of pain, they began their ascent from the runway. The tremendous acceleration of the takeoff was more than Galley had ever experienced. His body was pressed back into his seat uncontrollably.

Five minutes of pure horror had passed for Galley when there was a slight shudder in the ship's airframe and then everything went quiet, except for a throbbing rumble. Galley finally spoke into the microphone, "What happened? Are we okay?"

Garner responded through the headset, "Yes, we just outran our sound. We'll now be traveling faster than the speed of sound for the rest of the flight . . . until we land, that is."

Galley said sarcastically, "I can't wait. Now, where are we going?"

"We've been ordered to deliver you to Ramey Air Force Base. You should be there in about twenty-five minutes."

"Where's Ramey Air Force Base?" Galley questioned.

"It's an abandoned U.S. military base in the northwest corner of Puerto Rico."

Galley paused and then confirmed, "*Puerto Rico*?"

"Yes."

"That's almost three-thousand miles from

central New Mexico. How can we get there in twenty-five minutes?" he inquired with incredulity in his voice.

"Dr. Pruitt, you're aboard Aurora 2. Don't ask questions . . . and remember you never *saw* this plane, much less *flew* in it."

Galley sat quietly thinking for more than ten minutes trying to absorb the strange events of the past hour of his life. He looked over at Garner, now scanning what appeared to Galley to be the display of an advanced navigation system. A small label below the display read AURORA NAVSAT. Galley recognized the acronym used by the Global Positioning System, a satellite navigation system in widespread use for a number of years and asked, "Captain Garner, can you tell me what this trip is about?"

"All I know, sir, is that we have been ordered to take you to Puerto Rico under Project Darkstar."

"Great. I know that. Can you tell me how fast we're flying?" Galley asked, now letting his curiosity get to him.

"No, sir, that's classified information."

"More classified than Darkstar?"

"No, sir, you just don't have a need to know our exact air speed," Garner replied. "I can tell you that we're flying at several miles per second . . . you'll be able to compute that from our transit time. Scram jets don't waste any time"

Galley looked at his watch. It read 4:30 p.m.

At 4:40 p.m. Garner said, "Dr. Pruitt, I suggest you brace yourself. We're going subsonic again." Galley tightened his harness. He clumsily repositioned himself in his small jump seat and noticed Garner was smiling back at him. Five

109

minutes later he felt the thump of the tires hitting the runway as they landed.

"Welcome to Puerto Rico, sir," Garner said as he opened the hatch. "I think someone will be waiting for you outside the aircraft."

Galley stepped down the hatch ladder to see another Hummer waiting. This one had a decal across the top of its windshield. It read ARECIBO RADIO OBSERVATORY - VEHICLE. In the glow of the runway lights a tall, heavily dressed figure left the Hummer and moved across the tarmac toward the plane. The stranger approached with his gloves over his ears and motioned for Galley to follow. As they entered the Hummer, the stranger extended his glove to Galley and said, "Welcome to Project Darkstar, Dr. Pruitt, I'm Andrew Witherhouse, Project Manager."

CHAPTER 5
DARKSTAR

"When earth's last picture is painted, and the tubes are twisted and dried,
When the oldest colors have faded, and the youngest critic has died,
We shall rest, and faith, we shall need it—lie down for an aeon or two,
Till the Master of All Good Workmen shall set us to work anew!

And those that were good will be happy: they shall sit in a golden chair;
They shall splash at a ten-league canvas with brushes of comets' hair;
They shall find real saints to draw from — Magdelene, Peter, and Paul;
They shall work for an age at a sitting and never be tired at all!

And only the Master shall praise us, and only the Master shall blame;
And no one shall work for money, and no one shall work for fame;
But each for the joy of the working, and each for his separate star,
Shall draw the Thing as he sees It for the God of Things as They Are!"

RUDYARD KIPLING, *L'Envoi*

On the hour-and-forty-minute drive from Ramey to Arecibo, Galley began to learn more about

111

Witherhouse and his work. He was an Australian radio astronomer from Canberra who had come to Arecibo many years ago as part of NASA's newest SETI—Search for Extra-Terrestrial Intelligence—effort named HRMS for High Resolution Microwave Survey. He had been working for the past thirty years on some of the most intense investigations into intelligent radio emissions from the sky, without results.

Galley looked over the island's dark landscape and noticed in the dim light the tropical foliage still looking fresh and luscious. Then he realized the freezing temperatures had preserved it all. Everything was in suspended animation. He took his mind off the scenery and asked, "Where did you attend school?"

Witherhouse responded, "U of W., sorry, that's the University of Wollongong to non-Aussies."

"Oh? What then?" Galley probed.

"Well, after graduating from UW with a Ph.D. in Theoretical Physics I worked at the Deep Space Network at Tidbinbilla, Australia. Soon after that I left Australia for Puerto Rico to join Frank Drake in his search for extraterrestrial intelligence at the Arecibo dish, searching single radio channels, one-at-a-time."

"That must have been really exciting. Drake is a famous figure in radio astronomy."

"It was. Then I moved to the META—Mega-channel Extra-Terrestrial Assay—program for several years at the Harvard-Smithsonian radio telescope in Harvard, Massachusetts, searching 8.4 million channels simultaneously."

"Yes, I've collaborated with that facility on some of my observations," Galley agreed.

"Finally about ten years ago, I was asked by the BETA—*Billion*-channel Extra-Terrestrial—program to join them at the Goldstone Deep Space Communications Complex in the Mojave Desert. I obviously jumped at the chance"

"I don't blame you. I've heard that program is the most exciting SETI effort around."

"Well, it *was* . . . I remained there until the beginning of Twilight earlier in the year, just before Arecibo sent out its second signal into the universe, like the one previously sent by Drake and Sagan on November, 16, 1974."

Galley said, "I've read articles about that. It caused quite a bit of controversy—letting Earth's existence and location be known for the second time."

"It was the same transmission . . . except for one thing. This new message was an SOS to save all life on Earth from freezing during the Endlight Event. It was also to serve as a beacon of our previous existence if we were not saved."

Witherhouse excitedly related that only last week, just before the Arecibo radio telescope and its crucial receiving element, the maser, froze, they found the most promising transmission they had ever received. Yet the signal seemed to be juxtaposed to all their expectations. They tried to repeat the observation but couldn't because of the antenna's cold-temperature malfunction. Witherhouse continued to explain, "We first thought the signal to be terrestrial interference because it had no Doppler shift associated with the Earth's rotation."

The relative velocity between a receiving station and transmitter causes the Doppler shift phenomenon. It is the same effect as a train whistle, increasing in pitch as it approaches and decreasing as it departs.

The SETI program had used Doppler for many years to eliminate unwanted Earth-based signals. The assumption was that if a signal came from the Earth's surface then it would be traveling the same speed as the surface-based receiving antenna. However if it came from space, it would appear to have motion based on the Earth's rotation as the receiver revolves toward or away from the transmitter.

Witherhouse admitted, "What our reasoning failed to take into account was the possibility of a space-based signal with a zero velocity relative to the Earth's surface. This unexpected yet measured data meant the signal source would have to be in a geosynchronous orbit, and all sources in that orbital shell, out at 36,000 miles, were documented and known."

Galley agreed, "Of course."

Witherhouse continued, "Crikey, never in our wildest dreams did we think we would find a geosynchronous source at a distance of more than ten-million miles from Earth. That's exactly what was indicated by the triangulation measurements from this observatory and two others during the previous week."

Galley raised his eyebrows as he listened with increasing interest.

"Having had some apparent success, we then hit a snag. The antenna froze and that frustrated everyone at Arecibo on the SETI project. It frustrated everyone so much, in fact, that every available astronomer at Arecibo went immediately to the six-hundred-foot-high suspended amplifier room and antenna assembly to see what was wrong."

"Every astronomer?" Galley queried.

"Yes. Some rode the cable car up. Some took the catwalk. Sixteen astronomers worked constantly for a week hanging above the 1000-foot diameter aluminum dish until they warmed the maser and waveguides back into operation."

"Wow!" Galley shook his head in amazement.

"They just got it working yesterday, the official beginning of Project Darkstar. It's a project originated by the President of the United States to investigate the newly observed signal from interplanetary space."

Galley said, "Oh. I see. I feel honored to be involved in it."

As they drove up to the guardhouse an armed guard waved them through. Galley looked around at the razor-wire-topped chain-link fence. "Is this security for Darkstar?"

Witherhouse said, "Only partially. Some of the locals around here are suspicious of our research and think we're doing black magic or something. A few think we're doing secret government work and others are just super-stitiously scared of the antenna and towers. We had attempts at sabotage to our antennas and our control room before we put up the fencing. If you look closely at the base of that support tower over there, you'll notice an armed guard pacing around the tower."

Galley looked over at the sentry near the concrete tower. The huge white-tiered monolith behind the guard reminded Galley of a four-stage rocket quietly waiting on its launch pad. It was brightly illuminated at the bottom with a gradual darkening toward the top where it reached out of view. "My God, how tall is that thing?" He craned his neck to see the brilliant red lights at the top.

"There are three towers all alike," Witherhouse answered. "Each is slightly over 1000-feet tall and supports the antenna's focal structure and the bow, by four steel cables. Those cables are each larger than your arm."

"This is really some impressive antenna," Galley commented as the Hummer approached the control building, its overlook platform and the jagged aluminum rim of the enormous metallic dish nestled in the valley of the surrounding mountains.

"We, too, were all awed upon arriving at this facility, but it soon wears off. Then it becomes just another job . . . except when we have to go up to the antenna house. There's still something terrifying about climbing around in a thirty-ton metallic structure, bigger than a football field, when you're suspended sixty stories in the air by just twelve cables."

"I can imagine," Galley agreed.

The Hummer stopped in front of the antenna control building. Witherhouse got out and waited for Galley to get his bag from the back seat. Galley climbed from the Hummer and followed him through the bitter cold to the front door of the control building. Galley looked around at the gigantic antenna with its huge, suspended triangular focal assembly and felt as if he were in some "Close Encounter" movie and those were the starships. The smell of cold metal pierced the icy air.

As they entered the control room, Witherhouse called to the astronomers at the control console. They looked around. "I want you to meet Dr. Galley Pruitt. He discovered Endlight, as you probably know." The two astronomers rose and moved toward Galley and Witherhouse.

"Dr. Pruitt, I'm Joshua Samuels," said the first to extend his hand.

Galley shook hands and said, "I've heard your name, before. Aren't you from South Africa?"

Samuels smiled and in a distinctly South African accent answered, "Why yes, Johannesburg . . . I had no idea I was famous."

Galley continued, "I've been interested for quite some time in your work on radio wave gravitational lenses. I believe you presented a paper on your work several years ago at the International Radio Astronomy Conference in Austria. We used some of those techniques to discover Endlight."

"Ah yes, I remember," Samuels replied. "I'm glad someone found some use for that work. I finally ran out of steam and joined the SETI program. My work is really quite interesting and exciting now."

Galley reached his hand out to the second astronomer, "Hi, Galley Pruitt."

"Hello Dr. Pruitt, I'm Sondra Anderson. I've heard quite a bit about *you*."

"Hope not all bad," Galley joked.

"I'm the one who took the call from Dr. Micolo at NRL last week. He spoke quite highly of you and your work."

Galley's ears reddened as he began to blush.

She continued, "Of course, I've also been following your work since you discovered the Cloud

117

last year. I think that discovery would probably have won you the Nobel Prize in Science, if we hadn't happened onto this strange little signal from the cosmos. I think we've just found intelligent life out there."

Galley looked at all three astronomers with astonishment in his eyes, "*Really?*"

Witherhouse answered, "We only *think* we've found it. That's one reason we brought you here, to help us validate our discovery."

"Why me? I haven't been involved with SETI," Galley asked, now puzzled by his association with Darkstar.

"Galley, you're a radio astronomer," Samuels volunteered. "You found the Cloud and then predicted Endlight. At first nobody believed you. Now everybody believes you . . . unfortunately."

Galley nodded reluctantly in affirmation.

Samuels continued, "We're in the same situation now. We want you to help us verify our finding so we can get some non-astronomers to believe us. The President, for example, would like irrefutable proof that what we found is intelligent life, not from this Earth—non-human. You can help us with that."

"How?"

Smiling, Witherhouse patted Galley on the back and said, "Crikey, Galley, that's what *you're* supposed to tell *us*, according to the President."

Galley paused, staring intently through Witherhouse. He broke his trance seconds later, scooping the overnight bag from beside his feet. "Well then, let's go to work. I've only got a day before I have to return to Socorro."

As Samuels and Anderson returned to the

computer consoles and the large windows overlooking the dish, Witherhouse took Galley into the Computer Room. "Here, let me show you the Target Search Screen we recorded last week just before the maser froze." Witherhouse pulled up a colorful computer image on the screen showing a small radio telescope logo in the upper left corner. It was a stylistic drawing that reminded Galley of a Mexican sombrero tossed over one of those highway department orange marker cones. Under the drawing was TARGET SEARCH. Across the top of the screen in bright red letters were the words: Multi-channel Spectrum Analyzer – sub-band 8820. The lower part of the screen was a black background filled with white stationary dots.

Galley puzzled at the monitor's appearance as he rubbed his eyes, trying to focus. It appeared to be a fuzzy TV screen with no station tuned in except the blurry dots were stationary, not dancing around. "Exactly what am I looking at?" Galley asked, not being accustomed to SETI tools.

"This is a frequency-time frame-stack from our multi-channel search analyzer. Here, put on these glasses, they might help." Witherhouse smiled as he handed Galley a sleek pair of black-framed plastic spectacles. They reminded Galley of cheap sunglasses. As Witherhouse put his glasses on, so did Galley. The screen suddenly filled with depth receding into a black infinity behind the glass screen.

"Wow! What *are* these glasses?" Galley asked in amazement.

"They're cross-polarized lenses like the ones we wore in old 3-D movies," Witherhouse explained.

"We've just modified the computer monitor to act like the 3-D projector. That way we can see more detail in our data—we add a third dimension, so to speak."

"They're really neat but how do they help?" Galley asked.

"Look at this horizontal line of dots on the screen," Witherhouse pointed with his pencil to the top line, almost indistinguishable from the one below because of its closeness. "Each white dot on this line represents a received signal in which its strength exceeded our preset threshold for terrestrial noise. Across each horizontal line are almost one-thousand dots, representing one-thousand channels per line. There are also one thousand lines stacked vertically on the screen, to give a single time-slot scan of one-million channels."

"That's quite impressive," Galley said.

"The time slot we used here was one second in length. We call it a frame," Witherhouse continued. "If a signal is received that is not on the surface of the Earth, we get this effect." Witherhouse pointed to a bright line of white dots on the 3-D screen. The illuminated line started at the left front edge of the glass and appeared to recede into the right corner of the monitor to a depth of several feet.

"The depth you see on the screen, Galley, is due to the time that the signal remained on the air. This one went the complete frame stack of three-hundred frames so it was on the air for at least three-hundred seconds, or five minutes." Galley nodded his head, understanding.

Witherhouse continued, "The movement

across the screen is due to the Doppler shift caused by the Earth's rotation. I think I mentioned that effect to you earlier?"

"Yes, I'm familiar with the effect."

"As you see this signal *does* appear to have the expected Doppler shift to suggest it *is* extraterrestrial, and it's on the air for over five minutes."

Galley asked excitedly, "Is this the signal you spoke of from another intelligence?"

Witherhouse smiled and answered, "No, this signal is one we use for calibration of the system. We bounce our own signal off the Moon to verify proper operation of all systems. It just looks like an extraterrestrial signal because it's really being reflected back to us from our Moon."

"Oh," Galley said quietly, embarrassed for his apparent ignorance.

Witherhouse brought another screen up on the monitor. This one looked similar to the other differing in the message "Multi-channel Spectrum Analyzer – sub-band 9000." The million-channel display area below the legend also looked quite different. Galley immediately noticed that the Moon bounce calibration signal was gone. Now there was a new strong signal that appeared to extend into the screen in an intermittent fashion. It looked like a dashed line projecting out at him from the rear of the monitor.

"What's that?" Galley asked as he pointed to the mysterious signal.

"That's the Darkstar signal," Witherhouse confirmed. "Dr. Anderson found it last week almost simultaneously with the visible flash in the Northern sky last Thursday."

121

"Wait a minute, "Galley said as he looked back to the control room. "I thought Dr. Anderson just told me she's the one who talked to Micolo after the flash."

"She was. I was standing by her when she talked to him."

"Well, if I remember right Micolo said he called you for radio signal verification of the flash and you said your antenna was frozen, you heard nothing."

"That's right Galley, that's what we told him. According to a set of very strict rules we follow here, called *Post Detection Protocols* we are not allowed to tell anyone but authorized individuals of suspected discoveries. That particular signal looked like a discovery immediately. We had signal capture for almost two minutes during the time the flash occurred. Then it quit. Then our maser really did freeze. And *it* quit, too. Since then we've been trying to warm the system back into operation."

"And now it works?" Galley interjected.

"Yes, it appears to be fully operational."

"Have you found the Darkstar signal again?"

"No, but we found another similar signal that appeared just before the second flash, last Friday. Did you see that one?"

Galley said, "Yes, I did. It appeared to be brighter than the first. It almost appeared to me to sweep across the sky."

"We saw it too. We had received a pulsating signal from the Western sky just before it flashed, then nothing. It's almost as if both of those flashes were preceded by a beeping signal like the ticking before a time bomb explodes or a homing missile radar lock-on signal before the missile strikes," Witherhouse related.

"That's a ridiculous thought," Galley stated, "unless those are some kind of missile or bombs launched from Earth. Even if they were launched from here I don't think we have the technology to generate that amount of light from ten-million miles out"

"I don't think so either," Witherhouse admitted as he typed into the keyboard, pulling up the Target Search screen for the second flash. "There, see how the second signal matches the first."

"Yes, there's a strong similarity," Galley agreed. "How far away is this signal from Earth?"

"We didn't really have time to triangulate it with another telescope, but it appears to be the same distance as the first, about ten-million miles."

"Hmm," Galley puzzled as he moved his head across the 3-D screen to create motion parallax, thus emphasizing the second signal's depth. "And there's no Doppler shift at all?"

"No. Not that we can measure," Witherhouse said, rolling his chair back to get out of Galley's way.

"So, we know that both signals are stationary over the Earth, as if they were in geosynchronous orbit."

"Correct," Witherhouse said, rolling back up to the monitor.

Galley then put his hand on his chin and rubbed his short graying beard. "Andrew, would you leave me alone for a while. I'd like to scan some more search screens and try to absorb everything I'm seeing here."

"Sure, Galley, I'll be in the antenna control room if you need me. The extension there is 219. There's the local phone," Witherhouse said as he pointed to the dusty old black dial telephone sitting on the sleek ultramodern Cray XX1 supercomputer. "Our local lines are still working, barely."

Galley spent several hours scanning more search screens and looking over computer printouts. All the data seemed to be consistent with the premise that the two signals *were* extraterrestrial, but there was no definite evidence sufficient for proof. He put his head down on his arms to rest his neck momentarily. He was realizing what a hectic life he had been living the past few days. He thought back to Jalisa and Frosty and wondered what Neemu and Ruth had said when they found out about the Colony at Carlsbad.

The phone rang, waking Galley from a sound sleep. He raised his head, looking quickly at his watch. It read three-thirty. "Hello, Computer Room," he answered as he looked out the window seeing darkness. It must still be morning, he thought.

"Galley, a few of us are going over to the observatory cafeteria for a bite to eat, would you like to go with us?" Samuels asked. "It's the only place to eat within thirty miles or so."

"Yeah, I'd better get something to eat to clear my head. Thanks for asking," Galley said as he groggily walked into the antenna control room stretching his arms over his head.

"Find anything?" Anderson asked.

Galley yawned and looked at Sondra and answered, "I think I found exactly the same thing you found. It appears to be extraterrestrial, but it can't be proven." Galley yawned again. "Sorry, I also think it put me to sleep."

Anderson, Samuels and Pruitt drove to the observatory cafeteria by the staff swimming pool, leaving Witherhouse to man the radio telescope. As they left the car and walked up to the small frame building Galley commented on the luxury of having a pool—before it froze. His director would never agree to it at the VLA. Then Galley was reminded by his hosts that he was now out in the middle of God-forsaken nowhere, and to keep his opinions to himself, thank you.

During the meal of jerk chicken and black beans, the three revisited the strange events of the past few weeks. They knew there must be some common thread to the flashes and radio signals from space. It just couldn't be found. Then there was an even more remote possibility that this was all linked to the Endlight Event. That would be harder to prove. Finally, having come to the realization that they all needed more information, they finished their late dinners with a cognac and returned to the Control Building.

As they entered the Control Room they found Witherhouse sitting in front of the antenna console white-faced. He sat motionless for several seconds staring out the window.

Sondra said, "Andrew?"

He slowly turned and looked around at them.

"What's wrong? What happened? You look like you've seen a ghost." Samuels inquired, knowing this was not Witherhouse's normal character.

Witherhouse stared back and slowly began, his voice trembling with emotion, "The geologists were right in their predictions. The Earth's crust is freezing."

"So?" Galley asked, showing no concern.

"I was just in contact with Joo Chang, Director of the Beijing Radio Observatory. I was trying to verify the location of the Darkstar signal by triangulation of its pre-flash direction we received last Friday. We've had a terrible, terrible cataclysm."

"Witherhouse, you need to get hold of yourself, what happened?" Anderson asked as she walked over and grabbed his arm, trying to subdue his disturbed state.

"The Island of Japan just experienced an earthquake of estimated magnitude 10.2. That's greater than all of humanity has ever experienced. Tokyo was essentially leveled. According to initial reports, there's nothing left over two stories tall. There are fires burning all over the island and they can't put them out. Their water system is frozen. Tens of millions of people are dead. And now the coasts of Korea and China are expecting tidal waves of unprecedented magnitude. The people can't outrun the tsunamis."

Samuels ran into the bathroom to throw up. Galley stood looking at Witherhouse and Anderson in disbelief. The room went totally quiet, except for the hissing noise from the shortwave receivers, for several minutes as they bowed their heads in prayer.

Galley looked up and asked, trying to regain his composure, "Andrew, what did you mean about the geologists?"

Witherhouse explained that geologists around the world had been studying the effects of another possible ice age for many years. Several of them hypothesized that as the Earth's crust began to freeze and contract around its warmer core, faults would become extremely active. They predicted earthquakes of extreme magnitudes around the world as the crust continued to shrink.

Samuels, who had now returned to the Control Room still looking rather green, verified the details. He too, had followed the research with interest, and knew that other locations were to follow in the fate of Japan. He explained that Mt. Vesuvius would erupt followed by a quake that would destroy most of Eastern Italy.

Another fault would activate near Mt. Pele in Martinique, destroying that island with volcanic eruptions and much of the Caribbean around it with major quakes. Finally the San Andreas Fault in California would awaken, shearing off the coast from the rest of the state and taking Los Angeles and San Francisco with it. He had not really expected to see the geologists' prediction come true, but now he knew the terrible chain of events was starting.

In the flurry of conversation that followed the news of the disaster, the astronomers failed to notice the weak pulsing signal appearing on the Target Search screen.

Galley asked, "Did those geologists say anything about earthquakes in New Mexico?" thinking of the underground Antron.

"Possibly," Samuels answered. "They even predicted huge earthquakes would level the island of Manhattan in New York."

As the signal became stronger it set off a high-pitched alarm on the console. A red light next to the alarm flashed brilliantly, indicating signal interception.

Galley jumped at the noise and asked, "What's that?"

Witherhouse whirled around in the console chair to see the dashed line on the screen, "*It's the signal again!*"

Without a word, they all ran to the observation window to look at the sky. Moments later there was a flash! It came from the Southern sky. It swept from south to the north like cloud-to-cloud lightning—but there were no clouds. The event lasted less than a second.

Galley yelled, "What time is it?"

Witherhouse looked at his watch and said, "Exactly five-fifty-two."

Witherhouse ran back to the console as Galley and Anderson followed. The signal was gone from the Target Search screen.

"*Damn it!*" Witherhouse exclaimed. "We've lost it."

Galley pushed Witherhouse from the screen, "Look where the antenna's pointed, Ursa Major! Towards the Southern horizon, have you observed the signal from there before?"

"No, our only two interceptions of these signals have been from the Northern and Western skies," Anderson commented.

"Those are three points of the compass. What are we seeing here?" Galley asked as he reached for the 3-D glasses. "How long did the other signals last before the flash?" He scanned the display looking at the dashed line coming out of the screen toward him.

The others sat silently for a few seconds,

trying to recall the information. "Roughly one minute and fifty-seconds, why?" Anderson answered.

"This one was on the screen for . . . let me see . . . one minute and forty-eight seconds." Galley commented, now seeing a correlation in the events.

"Well, what does that tell us?" Samuels asked the group.

They all looked at the screen. Samuels and Witherhouse put on their 3-D glasses. Anderson walked to the observation window. She noticed a crescent of the pink Twilight sun beginning to peek over the morning horizon.

"I don't see a solution to this puzzle," she said, now staring up into the dark sky. "We don't know any more than we did before we got that signal, except it seems to be moving across the sky."

They looked closely at the signal. "No. It can't be," Witherhouse said. "Remember there's no Doppler shift."

He picked up the microphone for the short-wave transmitter and said, "NASA Watch Gold this is NASA Watch Air. Come in please."

Galley whispered to Samuels, "Who's he calling?"

"Goldstone, "Samuels answered.

"NASA Watch Gold here. Go ahead, Air. Over," the voice crackled over the console speaker.

"This is Witherhouse. Did you receive a pulsing signal at oh-five-five-two — no Doppler shift — from the Southern sky?"

The receiver hissed. "Before that bright flash?"

Witherhouse said, "Yes."

"We have it in the Southern sky at elevation

thirty degrees, twelve minutes and 42.916 seconds."

Witherhouse moved to the keyboard and began keying in data. A few seconds later the computer flashed on the screen: 9.8 MILLION MILES.

"Aha!" Witherhouse said. "This is the third match. We have three distances, all within a few percent of each other. That's too close to be coincidental."

"I agree," Anderson said, approaching the console. Then she noticed something no one else had observed. "Andrew, what frequency band line did we just receive the signal on?"

Witherhouse looked closely on the screen, "Seems to be . . . hmm . . . 9180 megahertz.

"Andrew, can you pull up the first Darkstar signal Search Screen from Thursday, please?" she asked, suddenly with a plan in mind.

"Sure. Just give me a few seconds . . . here it is."

"What's the frequency band line for that first signal we found in the Northern sky?"

"It appears to be 9000 megahertz."

Excited with the answer she asked once more, "Andrew, pull up the second signal from the Western sky."

"Okay, got it."

"Now Andrew, is the frequency band line of that signal exactly 9270 megahertz?" she asked, pacing rapidly between the window and console.

Galley and Samuels stood watching the ping-pong interaction between Witherhouse and Anderson in amazement. They felt they were watching an event that would change mankind forever.

Witherhouse hesitated as he looked back to the screen, "Now how would you know tha—." He stopped in mid-question.

"Come on Andrew, what is it?" Galley impatiently questioned.

"Tell me it's not 9270, Andrew," Samuels said in disbelief that they were on the verge of finding and proving extraterrestrial intelligence.

Witherhouse looked back at the two astronomers standing in front of the console. Sondra was still pacing and had begun to wring her hands, nervously.

Witherhouse calmly announced, "Yes, it's 9270 megahertz, the exact point on our compass where it came from. Just like the others, if you subtract nine thousand."

"That's it! We found it!" Samuels shouted.

Galley, still trying to rehash the details of the discovery, looked at the Search Screen for several seconds. Then he threw up his arms in excitement, "We've just found intelligent life out there only ten million miles away. Can you believe that?" He finally smiled and stepped over to hug Sondra. "That was brilliant! How did you know?" he asked.

"Galley, I think when you mentioned that the signals and flashes were coming from the three points of the compass, I subconsciously formed the connection. Then I saw that last frequency line at 9180 from the South and something snapped," Anderson answered as she began to shake from the realization of her discovery.

"Do we know any more about the signal than it can change its frequency to match its location?"

Galley asked.

"No," Witherhouse said, "but that's enough to prove intelligence. Someone or something out there is sending us a signal that is meant to be decoded. A very simple signal and it's locked to our Earth's rotation . . . and centered on Arecibo. Could it be trying to talk to us? Could it be from our own planet? Could it possibly be an answer to our distress signal?"

They all stood there quietly for several seconds looking at each other and then answered in unison, "Naaaaaah." Then they broke into laughter and high-fived each other all around.

After a few minutes of reliving the discovery with the others, Sondra Anderson said, "Andrew, as Project Manager, you'd better go call the President and tell him to expect another flash from the Eastern sky at 9090 megahertz."

Witherhouse looked across the room, "Galley, you do it. That's why he sent you here—"

Samuels interrupted, "I think Sondra should do it, she discovered the correlation."

"Yeah, Sondra, you call him," Galley and Witherhouse said almost simultaneously.

"You do it Sondra. I command you as Project Darkstar Manager," Witherhouse said with a smile across his face.

"I didn't really do anything. Andrew, please call him."

Witherhouse picked up the transmitter microphone and began calling, "Darkstar One this is Darkstar Two, come in."

After several minutes of calling, Witherhouse heard the response he was searching for, "Darkstar Two this is Darkstar One. Go ahead. Over."

Suddenly Witherhouse handed the microphone to Anderson. She nervously took it from him and responded into the little black sponge ball, "This is Anderson at Darkstar Two. I have a short message for the Boss. Tell him a star is born. Did you copy? Over."

The receiver hiss stopped immediately, indicating that the transmitter at Darkstar One had been turned on. There was just no sound. Then came the familiar Presidential voice that everyone knew from the White House, "Darkstar Two this is Darkstar Center. Boss speaking. Let me speak to Pruitt, over."

"This is Galley, sir," he said after taking the mike from Sondra.

"Pruitt, do you confirm a star is born? Over."

"Just a minute sir," Galley said as he clicked off the microphone. He looked at Witherhouse. "What in the hell does that mean—a star is born?"

"It's a code phrase. It simply means we've had detection of extraterrestrial intelligence with obvious but not rigorous proof," Witherhouse confided.

Galley paused momentarily to organize his response then clicked on the microphone, "Yes sir, I confirm a star is born. Over"

"Hello, Darkstar Two this is One. The Boss just handed me the mike and asked me to sign off. Congratulations, you guys."

Galley said, "Thank you Darkstar One, over and out."

"Over and out, Darkstar Two."

Witherhouse looked at Galley as he gently placed the microphone on the desk, "Well that should keep the guys in D.C. happy for while."

"Yeah, for what it's worth at this point in time," Galley replied. "I guess they at least got their money's worth. Will we hear back from them?"

"Probably not," Witherhouse conceded, "Now it will go to NSA, the CIA and all the other space spooks, wherever they are."

Anderson interjected, "And who really cares now that the Earth is slowly dying?"

For the next few hours the group sat around the Control Room discussing the exhilaration of the discovery and how to follow the *Post Detection Protocols* as strictly as possible. Finally, realizing that there was much work to do for final verification of the signal's unearthliness, they broke for a short lunch—with champagne—at the cafeteria.

After a well-deserved, two-hour nap in their rooms, the team of four astronomers returned to the Control Room for a final review of their work. A few hours later, still in active conversation about the discovery and its implications, Witherhouse looked at his watch and saw it was five in the afternoon.

"I'd better get you back to your magic carpet Galley if you want to get home on time. Would you like to stay with us a few more days?"

"No thanks, Andrew, I've got some pressing business to complete when I get back."

"Okay, do you need to get your bag and things?" Samuels asked.

"Yes, they're in the entry hall."

Samuels reached out his hand to Galley, "It was a pleasure, Dr. Pruitt."

"My pleasure," Galley responded.

"Goodbye Galley. It has been fascinating

working with the discoverer of the Endlight Event," Anderson said as she held out her hand.

"Goodbye to you, Sondra. It is *my* thrill to have worked with the discoverer of extraterrestrial intelligence," Galley said. He shook her hand and bowed his head to her. "Good luck in your future analyses of these signals. They may say more than we think."

"I hope so," she acknowledged.

"Are you ready, Galley?" Witherhouse asked.

"Yes, I'm dead tired. Can I sleep on the trip back to Ramey?"

"Sure, if you can sleep through all those bumps and hairpin turns."

As Witherhouse and Galley donned their parkas, there suddenly came a tremendous boom that shook the entire Control Building. One of the observation windows cracked, then shattered. A coffee mug flew from the console desktop onto the floor. The suspended antenna assembly building swayed gently above the expansive dish below. Large ice crystals drifted softly down onto the giant aluminum dish below.

Witherhouse smiled at Galley, standing terror stricken next to him. "I think your ride's here."

"Is that all? God, I thought we were having an earthquake." Galley said, breathing a relieving sigh.

"We went through that just before you landed yesterday," Samuels said, "but it wasn't nearly as bad. It didn't sway the antenna structure or break that window over there."

"Or my damn coffee mug," Anderson grunted as she bent over to retrieve the shards of her mug.

"Okay guys," Witherhouse said, "while I'm taking Galley would you please call the maintenance shop and see if you can rouse someone for help. We need a sheet of plywood or something to plug that gaping cold air vent before you and the equipment freeze."

"Yes, sir," Samuels responded reaching for the phone.

"Goodbye again," Galley said as he walked out into the cold dimness.

The return trip to Ramey had been extremely short for Galley. He had fallen asleep just past the observatory guard gate and was awakened by the thundering roar of his plane as they approached the runway.

Witherhouse looked at Galley and motioned toward the back seat of the Hummer, "Better climb into your pressure suit. Jump into the back seat, you'll have more room."

"Thanks, I'll only take a few minutes, "Galley shouted over the rumble of the awaiting aircraft. He could see the engines glowing through their skin. The belly door was open and the ladder extended.

Witherhouse and Galley walked up to the airship together. Galley smiled and extended his hand. Witherhouse shook it, returned the smile and mouthed, "Goodbye." Galley mouthed, "Goodbye," then climbed the ladder.

As he lifted himself into the familiar darkened navigation compartment he saw Captain Garner. He gave a thumbs up to Garner as he shut the belly hatch and sat back into his seat. Reflexively, Galley plugged his helmet's cord into the helmet jack in front of him.

Quickly the plane began to taxi and Galley felt a rumble with the roar that he hadn't remembered feeling in New Mexico. The plane's engines roared louder as they moved to the end of the runway. Then painful rumble-roar again, much worse than before, as the plane hurled down the runway swaying up and down and from side to side.

As they lifted off from the runway everything seemed okay. Then after only a few minutes Captain Garner was signaled by the co-pilot to look down. Garner leaned forward and stared in disbelief.

Galley, looking around at all the equipment in the darkened navigation compartment, finally noticed Garner frantically motioning for him to come forward into the cockpit. He got up and began moving forward so that he could see where Garner was pointing. The airship was in a sharp bank so he had to almost crawl over the equipment.

"*Oh, my God!*" Galley screamed over the engines roar. Out the cockpit side window he could see the radio telescope that he had just left below them, its antenna assembly building swaying twenty to thirty feet from side to side like a kite in the wind. Then the tower nearest the Control Building began to slowly topple toward the aluminum dish below. As it did the antenna bow structure fell into the dish, shooting sparks and throwing dust and debris high into the darkened air.

Slowly, the other two towers began to lean and then gently crumble into the dish, being pulled by cables and the vibration of the strong earthquake. Tears were appearing in the surface of the Earth below him, leaving deep chasms. Within seconds it was all over. Galley could see almost nothing left of the Control Building. A large part of the dish had been catapulted, like tiddlywinks, onto the building. Amidst the dust and debris below, Galley knew there could be no life remaining.

Galley went back to his jump seat and waited for the plane's rumble to subside. Shortly the welcome quietness came.

"I'm sorry," Garner said.

Galley nodded in acknowledgment and closed his eyes awaiting the end of the trip.

CHAPTER 6
INTO THE ARK

"All the animals in my poems go into the ark
The human beings walk in the great dark
The bad dark and the good dark. They walk
Shivering under the small lamp light
And the road has two ways to go and the humans
none.

JON SILKIN - from *Prologue*

Jalisa dropped the perfume bottle she was packing upon feeling and hearing the thunderous sonic shock wave of Aurora 2. *"Oh, my God, was that an earthquake?"* she asked herself taking a deep breath. Then all was calm.

Moments later on the secret runway near the Trinity Site, Galley dropped out of the belly hatch onto the tarmac. Holding his hands over his ears, he ran toward the blockhouse. He looked frantically around for his ride.

As suddenly as it arrived, Aurora 2 reentered the runway and rumbled away leaving Galley alone on the dark taxiway. The Hummer wasn't in sight. Only the blue runway lights and the deep pinkish-black Twilight sky filled his view. He walked quickly to the concrete bunker to find warmth . . . and quiet.

Galley closed the door and entered the warm room. "Boy, Garner was in a big hurry."

"Yep, sure was. Hello, Dr. Pruitt. Have a good trip? I'm Sergeant Duncan . . . U.S. Air Force," said the middle-aged Master Sergeant behind the duty desk. His feet were crossed and resting on its surface as he reclined lazily in the chair.

"Good and bad," Galley answered as he walked into the room and removed his parka.

"Sorry about that. Want me to help you out of that pressure suit?" the Sergeant asked as he lowered his feet to the floor and sat upright. He laid his crossword puzzle on the desk where his feet had been.

"No, I think I can handle it myself," Galley said, heading for the dressing area. "Oh, Sergeant, what's our outside temperature now?"

"Thermometer says ninety-five below . . . but I don't believe it. Must be at least 105 below, according to my predictions," the soldier responded.

"Oh? How's that? Your predictions, I mean." Galley questioned as he removed his tube-lined leggings.

"Well, you see, I've been plotting our daily temperatures out here in the desert and I think I've found a pattern that predicts the Cloud's uneven density. It says we should enter Endlight much sooner than expected."

Galley finished removing the pressure suit and reentered the room handing the bundle to Duncan. "Do you have the plots here?" Galley asked, curious to see the new prediction.

"Sure, right here," the Sergeant said, pulling a stack of ruled yellow paper from the desk drawer.

"What's the new date?" Galley asked.

"You mean for solar efficiency to drop below 1 percent — what you considered Endlight conditions?"

"Yes."

"My numbers say August 5. That's three

weeks earlier than your original prediction."

"What makes you think it will happen three weeks early, Sergeant?"

"Dr. Pruitt, see this constant temperature drop over the past few months?"

"Yes, I'm aware of our daily 2.5 degree drop."

"Well, over the past few days we're dropping at about ten degrees per day—almost four times faster than before. And if you measure the current sunlight intensity with a photometer and correlate the increased temperature drop to an increasing loss of light, then you get August 5. It's that simple."

Galley knew Duncan was probably right since he had mentioned the same theory to Jalisa only yesterday. He just hadn't had time to sit down with the numbers and do the projections. "Sergeant, what are you planning to do the next four months during Endlight?"

"Far's I know, I'll be ridin' out on A-2 assigned to Shy Mountain. They're closing down this radioactive hellhole out here . . . too hard to maintain in the cold."

Galley thought momentarily and realized there wasn't much in that sentence he understood. "What's 'on a two'?" he asked.

The Sergeant laughed and responded, "Oh, I'll be on Aurora 2 — A2 — that's our nickname for that damn fast noisemaker you just rode."

Galley laughed, realizing the simplicity of his confusion, "Oh okay. Well, where's Shy Mountain? Is that an Air Force base?"

"Yeah, it's the old North American Air Defense Command Post—NORAD for short. It's buried under Cheyenne Mountain in Colorado.

They dug a hole deep enough under the mountain to survive a direct nuclear blast and then put four acres of military base in there."

"In a cave, huh?" Galley asked.

"Yep. It's supposed to be easier to maintain livable temperatures down there in a cave. I think there'll be three or four hundred people lucky enough to be assigned there during Endlight, living quarters and everything there underground."

"When are you going—brrr!" Galley was interrupted by a blast of freezing air as the front door flew open.

"Hi, Dr. Pruitt, sorry I'm late," McMurphy said, rushing into the room. He slammed the door behind him and rubbed his gloves together. "Brrrr, it's cold out there."

"Damn straight, Colonel," Galley answered. "And don't worry about the little delay. Sergeant Duncan and I have been keeping each other company for a while. Are we ready to go?"

"We'd better. I told your wife yesterday that I'd have you back by six p.m. and we've still got a distance to go to get back to Socorro."

"Okay, then let's go," Galley said, pulling on his parka.

On the road back to Socorro, Galley asked about Major Stancey and discovered that he had taken ill with a strange form of asphyxia aggravated by the thinning air.

"Will he be all right?" Galley asked with concern in his voice.

"We think so. He's under heated oxygen treatment now and it seems to be helping. We took him down into the valley to get him to a lower altitude. That helped, too."

Galley thought for a few moments and asked, "I've heard about the theory of the air thinning as we get colder. Does Major Stancey's illness mean it's happening already?"

"Well, the atmosphere's not freezing yet, if that's what you mean. It's just getting thinner as it gets colder because of several other reasons."

"The lack of vegetation to replenish the oxygen?" Galley interposed.

"Yes, that's the main reason. The other is simply due to the lack of moisture in the air and cold-temperature chemistry and physics interactions."

"Oh, I see," Galley said in amazement at the breadth of the Colonel's knowledge.

"What do you do in the Air Force, Colonel?" Galley asked out of curiosity.

"Intelligence. I worked three years in Thule, Greenland before I came here. That place was almost as cold as it is here, now. That's how I know about the atmospheric thinning problems."

Galley sat quietly thinking of the bitterly cold landscape he was observing as the scenery passed by outside the Hummer. A shiver ran up his spine. "Oh, no wonder," he said.

The Hummer pulled up to the front of Galley's house at 5:46 p.m. Galley bid farewell to McMurphy and noticed how much darker it was now than when he left. Jalisa had forgotten to leave the porch light on and he had to find the lock by feel. It wasn't easy through gloves.

Galley entered the house to a blast of sweet-smelling something filling his nostrils. "I'm home, honey," he said sniffing around in the air for a directional clue to Jalisa. She walked into the room

143

and hugged Galley, "I'm glad you're back. I was so worried about you."

"I'm fine and I'm glad to be home," he responded as he returned the hug.

"Where in the world did you go, Galley? What was so important that you had to leave so quickly?"

"Jalisa, if I told you, you'd never believe me anyway, so let's just say I had to investigate a suspicious signal from space from a local radio telescope."

"Local? I thought you were going to be taken to board a plane in the desert."

Galley bluffed, "Oh, I meant local, relatively, in terms of radio telescope sites. By the way honey, did you hear about that big earthquake?"

"Which one, you mean that terrible one in Japan?" she questioned with a grimace on her face.

"Yes, but how many have there been? What do you mean which one? I haven't had much time to listen to news." Galley said, walking to the hall closet.

Jalisa answered factually, "Well, there was the 10.2 in Japan. Then another bad one in Martinique, I don't remember its size. Then there was a 9.9 in Puerto Rico. I think that's all."

"What was said about the ones in the Caribbean? How many died?" Galley probed, trying to learn of his friends' fate at Arecibo.

"I don't really know for sure, but I just heard a special news report on TV a few minutes before you walked in. They said it's too early to tell much about widespread damage but that the quake in Puerto Rico destroyed the town of San Juan and its airport. No one can enter or leave the island anymore. That includes the Red Cross or any other humanitarian aid groups with ground maintenance and planes still working in this cold, sad."

Galley looked blankly into the floor beneath him and then took off his parka. For seconds he was frozen, mentally transported back to the nightmare just hours ago. Abruptly he shook it off and squatted to play with Frosty, who had been jumping up to his knees since he entered the room. "Hi little frisky thing," he said to the puppy. "I guess you're warm and happy now."

Jalisa said, "She's been fine. Just a little sad and missing you while you were gone, I think. She slept on the cold floor by the front door last night."

Galley picked Frosty up and looked her in the eyes, "Frosty, you're going to be fine now. I'm back to stay." The little beige puppy licked his nose with its lightning-fast tongue. "Oooh! Skunk breath!" he said as he wiped his arm over his face.

Jalisa laughed. "It's good to have you home, Daddy. I just want a little kiss."

Galley gently kissed the pup on the head and placed her on the sofa. "Jalisa how's the packing going, and what's that smell?" he inquired, now turning his attention back to his nose—and reality.

"Oh, Galley, I heard this loud boom that shook the house about an hour ago. It scared me so much I dropped a bottle of perfume I was packing. After all the news about earthquakes, I thought *we* were having one here in New Mexico."

Galley stood and walked into the bedroom to drop his overnight bag. "I assume you dropped that perfume in here," he said, now scrunching his face at the strong pungency of jasmine.

"Yes, sorry, I was putting it on for your return," she said quietly. "I tried to clean it up. It just needs to dry a little while longer."

"Well, we only have a few days longer to be here, anyway. Just imagine we're living in a jasmine garden," he said in a kidding style. "Got a clothespin for my nose?"

Jalisa laughed and went into the kitchen calling back, "Galley, are you hungry?"

"I think so. I haven't really eaten much in the past day. What have we got to eat?"

"I'm fixing your favorite meal, chicken-fried steak and gravy, just like your mom used to make. And mashed potatoes from scratch," she called, still in the kitchen. "Plus, I made you some fresh coffee. Want some?"

"I'd love a cup, thanks," he said as he walked into the kitchen, kissed Jalisa on the back of her neck and sat at the breakfast table.

"You get up and get it, lazy. I'm making dinner," Jalisa said, jamming the masher into the potatoes another time. She looked sternly over at Galley, then cracked a smile and winked.

Galley poured a cup of coffee for himself and one for Jalisa and then sat back at the table. "Tell me what happened yesterday at the Hatlems' house after you went over there."

Jalisa stopped mashing momentarily. "Neemu said he had worshiped the ground you walked on since he came to the VLA, but that trick yesterday about borrowing the kids nearly made him kill you. I think it was really fortunate you found that ham gear or you might be in the hospital – or morgue – right now."

Galley gulped as he swallowed the coffee he had just sipped. "Weren't they happy at all?"

"Of course they were happy about the results, honey. It's just that initially they saw you leaving them in the cold, so to speak," Jalisa admitted. "They knew about the society all along and expected you to find some way to get them in since we were best friends."

"Oh, now it makes more sense. But I don't know how I could have gotten them in. Morrow's a real stickler for rules and regulations. He won't even let Frosty—." He paused in mid-sentence, realizing what he almost said.

"He won't let Frosty *what*?" Jalisa asked curtly.

Galley paused for several seconds looking down into his cup, then spoke slowly, "Jackson Morrow says that the Forum, the group that rules the colony, has prohibited any animals but those selected for preservation from entering the cave. He won't let us bring Frosty with us."

"Screw him! We're bringing Frosty with us anyway," Jalisa quipped loudly back at Galley.

"They may not let us in if we do," Galley responded, "but I'm willing to take the risk, too. I say we sneak her in. I've been thinking about that all week. It's almost made me sick."

"Do you mean to tell me, Galley Pruitt, that you've known about this stupid no-Frosty rule for a whole week and haven't told me?"

"Well I've known almost a week, and only because I didn't want to worry you. That's why I didn't say anything. I was just going to sneak her in," Galley replied.

"Oh," her voice shook, "you'd *better* do that.

That poor little dog just can't be put back into the cold again."

"I know."

"If you put her back out, I'll never speak to you again."

"Don't *worry!*" Galley assured Jalisa in a louder voice.

Sweating, she finally put the potatoes down. "Boy! I've never mashed potatoes that smoothly in my life."

Galley laughed so hard that Jalisa started laughing, too. He handed her a cup of coffee and they sipped noisily a few seconds with both in quiet concentration. Then Galley asked, "Ready to eat?"

"Yes, come dish it up," Jalisa said as she handed him his plate.

He took it and headed toward the stove, spooning himself big heaps of smashed potatoes and lumpy cream gravy. During their dinner they talked about their excitement over Antron and on the Hatlem's being able to join them there. Galley told Jalisa that Neemu had even reworked and polished his ham equipment just so he would be sure to be indispensable in the Colony. He was thrilled with his family's selection but still not completely happy with Galley. Neemu had told Jalisa they would be packed to leave for Antron on Wednesday morning. That afternoon, they would follow Galley and Jalisa down to Whites City and enter Antron together. Finishing the meal, Galley said, "That reminds me, Jalisa, I don't remember your answer about how the packing is going."

"The Blazer's loaded and set to go, at least with everything Frosty and I need. I weighed the whole thing on the bathroom scale and it was only ninety-three pounds. You may want to look over this list and see what other things you want in terms of personal items."

Galley took the list, "Thanks. I'll look it over tomorrow after work."

"You're going to work tomorrow? Isn't that a waste of time? "

"I thought I would at least go in and tell them it's my last day."

"Okay, now that I think of it, Neemu wanted to talk to you anyway. You might as well meet him at work as at home."

"Good, then I think I'll turn in. It's been a very strange and tiring two days for me," Galley said as he placed his dishes in the sink. "Thanks for dinner, it was scrumptious. Just like mom used to make."

Jalisa smiled and kissed Galley as he walked by. "Good night honey," he said.

Galley awoke to a darkened Twilight sky. His watch read 7:15 a.m. He looked at the mini-blinds in the window and realized he was having trouble seeing them. The Endlight Event *was* approaching much sooner than expected. He reached over, turned on the light and then touched Jalisa's shoulder. "Morning honey," he said, gently rocking her awake.

Frosty ran up to lick her face. "Morning," she groggily answered between licks.

Galley headed off to the bathroom to get ready.

Ten minutes later Galley reentered the bedroom. Jalisa and Frosty were now snuggling together, asleep. Frosty had her head on the pillow beside Jalisa's and was under the covers on her back just like her master.

Galley smiled and whispered, "Bye, honey."

Jalisa opened one eye and whispered back, "Bye. Be careful . . . I love you."

Galley kissed Jalisa gently on her forehead and said, "I love you more. I shouldn't be very long. I'll see you when I get home."

Galley drove into the Control Building parking lot shortly after 8:40 a.m. He was still thinking how much darker and colder it was now than last Thursday when he last made the trip to the VLA. This trip he could barely see the antennas as he came over the ridge onto the Magdalena Plains. Their shadows were gone. The pink Twilight Sun disk had dimmed to a glowing ember, reddish and ominous.

Galley noticed, as he rushed by the flagpole in front of the Control Building, that the flag was at half-mast.

"Good morning, Galley," the receptionist greeted him as he entered the lobby.

"Good morning, Susan. Did you miss me Friday?"

"No, we were too busy trying to put out fires, if you know what I mean."

"How many antennas are working now?"

"I think there are only four still operational. We lost a few on Friday, quite a few on Saturday, and then a bunch yesterday."

"Damn this cold! Why is our flag at half mast?"

"For the astronomers at the Arecibo and Beijing radio observatories, they all died. Wasn't that horrible?"

Galley mumbled to Susan as he continued past her toward his office, "Yeah, I felt like I was there."

She turned to look at Galley but he was gone from the lobby.

Galley walked to his office door then stopped. He walked on toward Neemu's door. "Good morning, what's up?" Galley asked, seeing Neemu packing the box on his desk.

"Hi Galley," Neemu responded in a cold tone. He kept packing, not looking up.

"Look Neemu, I'm sorry. I've been under a lot of pressure with this damn discovery and I don't always do or say the right thing lately."

Neemu glared at Galley, "Galley, I helped you with that discovery. You couldn't have done without me. Do you think I feel great? You're getting all the recognition and all the perks that go with it. I'm getting nothing, unless you hand it to me."

"Yes, you're right. I really apologize, Neemu. You and your family have been our best friends for so long. Can't we just forget that anything happened?"

"It may take awhile," Neemu responded as he returned to his packing. "Where did you have to go so damn fast Saturday with all that secrecy and crap?"

"Okay, since you want to be a part of everything, I'll tell you. You can't repeat this to anyone. I went to the Arecibo radio observatory and—."

"Sure, and if you think I believe that, I've got some icy swampland in Stockholm to rent you," Neemu snidely interjected.

151

"Neemu, you've got to believe me."

"Galley, I know how long it takes to go to Puerto Rico and return. If you did go there you wouldn't have had time to do anything. You weren't going to be gone more than a day, according to what Jalisa told us. Besides, everybody at Arecibo was killed in the earthquake, according to our communications with NRAO Headquarters."

Galley paused, trying to control his frustration, continued, "We detected intelligent life beyond Earth before the earthquake, Neemu. Doesn't that interest you?"

Neemu put a notebook into the box and hesitated, "Do you have proof? Who can verify your story?"

"Sure I have proof." Galley started, paused. He suddenly realized that all the people and records from the discovery at Arecibo were gone. He also realized that the knowledge of each portion of his trip had been carefully kept from the next portion. McMurphy delivered him to the plane but didn't know where he was going. Garner took him to Ramey but didn't know why. "The President!" Galley realized. He was the only other living person that knew!

"The President of the United States," Galley uttered. "He knows."

Neemu looked at Galley for a second and said, "Galley, I think this Endlight thing is really getting to you. You need to lighten up."

Galley stared back in disbelief.

"When are we meeting to go to Antron? Are you and Jalisa packed?" Neemu said, trying to ease the tension.

Galley restrained his anger and tried to

regain his composure. "Never mind."

"Well, when should we go? Have you talked to Morrow since Saturday?" Neemu prodded.

"You *will* believe me, Neemu," Galley stated, then resigned himself to the situation at hand. "We were going to meet day-after-tomorrow, Wednesday, but with the advancing rate of cool down I think we should go this afternoon. Endlight's coming much faster than we thought."

"I know. The predicted high tomorrow is minus 145. That's a 40-degree drop from today. At that rate it will be minus 220 by Wednesday. I don't even think our cars will work in that temperature."

"Let me clear out my things and get home. We'll be at your house about three this afternoon to meet up and leave. Okay?"

"Sure. We'll see you then," Neemu said as he struggled to close the box by interleaving the flaps.

"Got a spare box, Neemu?"

"Sure, take this one."

Galley returned to his office and gathered the few Endlight documents he would need for Antron.

On his way out of the building he stopped by the VLA Control Room. He entered the room with the box under his arm and noticed the hissing and beeping of the receivers was absent. So were the people. He walked over to the Antenna Control Console to read a small handwritten sign. On it was written GONE ICE FISHIN'. He smiled and turned to exit. A figure entered the room.

"Galley, I heard you were in the building ...

I've closed the observatory for obvious reasons," said Karl Chaffee, director at the VLA. "Sorry. Stop by Susan's desk and pick up your last weeks and severance pay. It's cash this time for obvious reasons."

Galley tried to look disappointed. "Oh, okay."

Chaffee continued, "It's been a pleasure working with you. You really are a brilliant astronomer . . . one of our best."

Galley looked down at the sign and said quietly, "I owe a lot to Neemu. He worked beside me for the past several years without many thanks. Could you tell him I said that?"

"Sure Galley, I'll stop by and tell him. I haven't told him about the closing yet."

"Thanks, Karl. I hope it doesn't hit him too hard. He's got those kids to support, you know."

"Galley, I think you'll both find your severance pay to be quite generous. If he can stay warm he shouldn't have any trouble with finances until this God-awful thing is over."

Galley shook hands and left the Control Building for the last time. He looked back and wiped his eyes with his glove.

"Hi honey, I'm home," Galley said quietly as he walked in from the garage. The effect of opening any outside door had begun to resemble the opening of a walk-in freezer; a dense fog filled the air around him as he entered.

"Hi, Frosty! How's my favorite girl?" he said as he placed the box on the kitchen table. She was jumping on him and cheering him up, as usual.

154

"What do you mean your favorite girl?" Jalisa asked, entering the room with a large scrapbook in her hand.

"I'm just kidding . . . what's that?" Galley asked with a grin..

"A photo album of our stay here at Socorro, I thought it would remind me of home while we're in the cave."

"Good idea," he said. "You know how cold it's getting outside?"

"No, Gus said earlier today that his thermometer broke. How cold is it?"

"It's cold enough for us to be leaving. I told Neemu that we'd meet them at three this afternoon and head toward Antron."

Jalisa went into the garage with the scrapbook causing another frozen fog storm in the kitchen.

Galley thought, I hate when that happens! He laughed at himself and went into the bedroom to pack, with Frosty following at his heels.

At 2:45 p.m. Galley and Jalisa put the final suitcase in the Blazer and slammed the rear door. Galley asked, "Did you put the antifreeze in like I asked you?"

"Yes, I poured the maximum amount recommended for sub-zero cold."

"Well, let's hope it never gets below Zerex out there."

Jalisa laughed and said, "Galley, that's bad."

He unplugged the oil heater and helped Jalisa into the front seat. "Are you ready?" he asked.

"Yeah, let's go." She buckled her seatbelt as he opened the garage door.

Galley returned, rubbing his hands together.

He entered the car and started the engine. "Well, old house, we'll see you in a few months, if all goes well," he said as he backed out of the garage. Moments later, Jalisa quietly began to cry as Galley returned to close the garage door.

Galley ran back, now shivering, to the car after closing and locking the garage. "Didn't you forget something, Galley?" Jalisa asked as he opened his door.

"Brrrr," he said, frustrated with the cold. He fell clumsily into the driver's seat and looked around the inside of the car. There were the suitcases, the duffel bag, the—.

"Damn! We forgot Frosty!" he yelled. Galley sprang from the car, opened the garage and ran back into the house. Jalisa laughed until he returned.

They arrived at the Hatlems' at 3:07 p.m. A thought of Phoenix flashed through his mind. Strange, the same time as the meeting, except he was late for that.

"Hi Galley, we're ready," Rutha said as she answered the door. "We'll let Krista and Jan ride with you, if that's okay."

"Sure, we'd love to have them with us. I think we'll get to know them better over this experience," Galley responded appreciatively.

"Hi Galley, you ready to go?" Neemu asked as he walked into the room. He was wearing a Nordic fur-lined parka that would have kept a desert native warm.

Galley laughed and said, "Yes, follow us. We know where we're going, on to Whites City and Antron!"

Galley had planned the trip to Carlsbad on I-25 then onto U.S. 380 into Roswell, then south on U.S. 285 to 396, which would take them to Whites City and the cavern entrance. The total trip, about two hundred and fifty miles, was to take a little over four hours. That would put them into the parking lot at Antron about seven o'clock in the evening.

As they turned off I-25 onto U.S. 380, Galley looked back in the rear-view mirror to ensure the Hatlems were still behind them. *Good, headlights*, he thought. Moments later he passed the right exit with the sign reading TRINITY SITE. He looked back to the road quickly, trying not to remember the incident. The headlights were still behind him.

At six forty-five they passed through the town of Carlsbad. Galley stopped the car in an abandoned gas station and went back to Neemu's car.

"About fifteen more miles and we'll see a sign to the caverns. Follow us in to the visitor center at the top of Walnut Canyon. It's about seven miles past the park entrance," Galley said, shivering from the cold.

"Okey Dokey, Galley," Neemu shouted over the kids playing in the back seat.

Galley continued on 396 through what had been the Chihuahuan desert. The yuccas and prickly pear cacti were frozen in a perfect state of preservation. Century plants stood majestically over the desert in a gossamer white covering. Then he saw the park entrance. A small concrete guardhouse stood where nothing had been before.

157

As Galley slowed to approach, a heavily armed guard exited the building and walked to the car.

"Who are you?" the guard asked rudely with what appeared to be a drawn firearm.

"We are Dr. Galley Pruitt and family. Behind me are Dr. Neemu Hatlem and family. We're here to meet Jackson Morrow."

The guard grabbed a clipboard hanging from his belt and scanned several pages. "Do you have any identification?"

By this time, Neemu had left his car and began walking up to the guard. "Hold it there, mister!" the guard commanded, now pointing the gun at Neemu.

Galley handed his drivers license through the window and yelled, "Neemu, watch out he's got a gun!"

The gun fired, knocking Neemu to the ground. He grabbed his leg and yelled, "Galley I'm hit. Help me!"

Galley jumped from the Blazer, and ran to Neemu's side. He glared at the guard and screamed, "*Why did you do that? You bastard! We're here for Antron!*"

The guard moved swiftly to Neemu's side, squatted and said, "I'm sorry, Dr. Pruitt, the gun went off accidentally. I didn't mean to shoot."

"Get me some help. I've got to get him into the car and up the hill," Galley screamed as he looked back to Rutha, now watching in horror through the front windshield. He ran back to her window and said, "Rutha, get into the driver's seat and follow me. I'm taking Neemu in our car. He's okay, just a leg wound. The guard fired accidentally."

Galley and the guard helped Neemu into the car. As he got his balance the guard grabbed the radio microphone from his shoulder, "Antron Control, this is Antron Gate. I've got an emergency coming up the hill. Get the medics to the entrance, *now!*"

Galley sped up the entrance to the visitor center with Neemu moaning in pain. He hardly noticed the two dimly lit immense white spherical tanks looming over the building. On their sides were the giant letters "HYDROLOX." A small ornate golden sign over the entrance to the visitor center read, "WELCOME TO ANTRON."

CHAPTER 7
ANTRON

"In the naked bed, in Plato's cave,
Reflected headlights slowly slid the wall,
Carpenters hammered under the shaded
windows,
Wind troubled the window curtains all night long.
A fleet of trucks strained uphill, grinding,
Their freights covered, as usual.
The ceiling lightened again, the slanting diagram
Slid slowly forth."

DELMORE SCHWARTZ, from *In the*
Naked Bed, in Plato's Cave

A team of medics dressed in white met Galley's Blazer as it pulled up to the Visitor Center's entrance. One of them yelled through his window, "Which one of you is hurt?"

Galley opened his door and ran to the rear of the Blazer to help Neemu from the car, "Okay, Neemu, the medics are here. You'll be fine."

"This is Dr. Neemu Hatlem. He's the Colony Radio Operator. The guard shot him in the leg," Galley yelled in anger to the medics as they loaded him onto the gurney.

"Yes sir, Dr. Pruitt. I'm Dr. Jim Mason, one of the Colony Physicians. We'll take him down the elevator to the infirmary for immediate attention. He'll be okay."

Rutha approached Neemu as the medics moved his gurney toward the entrance of the Visitor Center. "Neemu, I'm going with you." She looked at Galley and pleaded, "Galley, can you and Jalisa please take care of the kids for a while?"

"Of course, Rutha."

The Visitor Center door opened as Rutha and the medics approached. Galley saw a tall figure holding the door for them. In the dim glow of the building lights he recognized Jackson Morrow.

Morrow approached Galley. "Hello, Dr. Pruitt. Welcome to Antron. Sorry for this inconvenience."

"Hello Jackson. I hope this isn't a sign of things to come."

"I assure you, Galley, everything's under control. Now park your cars and I'll have some of our staff help you with your belongings."

Galley walked to the Hatlem's car and got the kids. They ran to the Blazer and jumped in the back seat, glad to be reunited with their siblings. There was a high-pitched squeak.

Galley got into the driver's seat and told Jalisa, "Put Frosty in the duffle bag, quick."

In she went.

He continued, "Now kids, don't say a word about the little dog. Let's all keep it a secret. Okay?"

They nodded in agreement as they all giggled with their hands over their mouths. Jalisa laughed and said, "Okay, guys, we're going to take care of you for a while until we see your mom and dad again. That shouldn't be long."

They quietly stared back giving Jalisa their full attention, now. "Mrs. Pruitt, what happened to daddy?" Jan asked.

"He had a little accident. Daddy got an owie on his leg but he'll be fine," she responded with tenderness in her voice.

They eased back into the seat comforted by her response.

Galley drove the Blazer into a parking slot near a Rolls Royce and got out to move the Hatlems' car. He parked it in a slot by a Mercedes. As he walked back to the Blazer he looked over the parking lot and saw what looked to be a luxury car used car lot: Mercedes, Jaguars, Rolls Royces, Ferraris, Lexuses and even a few Cadillacs. Then his attention was drawn to the deep growling of diesel engines from the road down to the cavern's entrance. He squinted to see the cause of the roar and saw ten, maybe twelve, large earthmoving trucks, their loads covered with tarps. From the covers he spotted a few protruding irregularly shaped cylinders. The trucks were slowly leaving the entrance, one by one. Then he noticed the waiting empty earthmovers in the opposite lane. *What could they be moving that's that heavy?* he thought. *Those trucks sound like they're really straining to get up the hill.* Galley walked back to the Blazer to find Jalisa peering through binoculars out the front window. "Are you looking at those trucks?"

"Yes. They're ruining the cave," Jalisa answered.

"What do you mean?"

"Those trucks are filled with huge stalagmites and stalactites."

Galley sat quietly for several seconds as the trucks droned on and then said, "Well, I guess they're ruining it for its original natural beauty but now it will have another beauty. Let's just call it Morrow's Ark."

162

Jalisa put down the binoculars and thought. "I guess you're right. It just won't ever be the same. I'm glad I got to see its timeless beauty before he destroyed–changed—it."

Galley was startled by the knock on his window. It was Morrow. Four men dressed in dark-blue uniforms accompanied him. Galley opened the door to Morrow's request, "Ready to go? We'll take your bags."

Galley stepped from the car and said, "I'll take the duffle bag. I've got some important stuff in there."

Morrow paused at the high-pitched yip as Galley lifted the bag over his shoulder. One of the kids in the back seat immediately made the same noise in response. Morrow hesitated and then smiled, "Our kids' area is quite noisy. We have all gotten used that."

Galley glanced at Jalisa as they both breathed a sigh of relief.

Morrow and his entourage entered the elevator together for their seven-hundred-and-fifty-foot decent into the Earth. The kids were squealing with delight. Galley could still hear the slight whimper coming from the bag over his shoulder.

"I hope you'll be pleased with your new home in Antron for the next few months. Everyone here seems to be already enjoying it," Morrow said sounding like a tour guide.

Galley asked, "How many are here, so far?"

"Because of the accelerated onset of Endlight we've had many people come in early. I think about fifteen hundred so far. In fact, I expected you, Neemu and your families early. I'm just sorry about the guard incident. He'll be replaced."

"Neemu will be well taken care of, I assume?" Galley inquired.

"Yes, we have an expert staff of physicians on call. Many are from the best hospitals in the U.S. You don't have much trouble filling an ark with an oncoming flood."

Ninety seconds after they entered the elevator it slowed to a halt. The doors opened to what had previously been the Underground Lunchroom. Jalisa and Galley stood in amazement at what they saw. In what had been a dimly lit cavernous room with a few lunch tables and a cafeteria line, they viewed with awe a room resembling the lobby of a five-star luxurious hotel. Bright lights gleamed from the chrome furnishings. Glistening tubular chandeliers hung from the expansive ceilings. People were gathered in small groups with cocktails discussing the day's activities.

"I think you'll be pleased," Morrow said as he observed their expressions.

"Wow! Mr. Morrow."

"Jalisa, call me Jackson."

"Yes sir. Jackson I never expected this. I thought this would be like a survival camp."

"It is a survival camp, Jalisa. It's just that all our survivors are very wealthy and expect to be treated in certain ways."

As they walked from the elevator Galley noticed an elderly couple across the room from them with a small dog on a leash. He nudged Jalisa with his elbow and motioned for her to look in that direction. She saw them too.

"Jackson, I see a couple with a small dog over there. I thought the Forum forbid pets."

"Well Galley they did . . . but the Colonists put up such a fight over their pets they changed the rules."

"Do you mean pets *are* allowed?" Galley excitedly asked.

"Yes, do you have one at home you'd like to go back and get?"

Galley quickly pulled the duffle bag from his shoulder and unzipped it. A little fuzzy white face poked out. The other end of the bag moved rapidly from side to side with the accompanying whishing noise of tail against canvas.

Morrow laughed. "I see you've already taken care of that. That's why we changed the rules. After the first thirty Colonists sneaked their pets in, we felt we were just outnumbered in our opinion."

Jalisa hugged Morrow and said, "Thank you, Jackson. We just couldn't leave her."

"I know," he said smiling and returning the hug. "Now let me show you to your quarters."

As they wound through the Hall of the Giants and Temple of the Sun, Galley and Jalisa traveled most of the way with their mouths agape. They saw large stainless steel rooms built where limestone pillars had stood. The rocky walking path was now a ten-foot wide concrete road. They had been passed several times by small-unmanned motorized carts carrying some kind of food trays. The atmosphere of Antron reminded them of a busy metropolis.

Galley and the group rounded a bend in the road and viewed what appeared to him to be a giant concrete wall extending from the floor to the ceiling of a gigantic room. It had rows of balcony walkways all the way up.

"Here is the Big Room," Morrow said. "This will be your home. You're in cubicle 874 up there. The Hatlems are next door in 875." Morrow pointed to a door at the end of a balcony row, eight stories above the ground on the side of the wall. "They're not large but they're comfortable and I think you'll like the views. You'll spend very little time in them anyway. We've insured that."

They scanned the cavernous chamber trying to understand what they were looking at. It was a small apartment complex built into a single one-hundred-foot-tall manmade wall in the cavern. The top of the wall seemed to be secured to the cave ceiling along its entire length. And, the wall was so long it almost disappeared from view at the other end.

In the distance, the rear of the wall could not be seen nor could the cavern behind it. Abutting concrete walls made the wall structure into a large closed half-dome taking up the entire left side of the cavern's Big Room. Elevators and stairs went all the way up the wall to each walkway balcony. The doors to all rooms on any floor were accessible by the same walkway.

Opposite the wall, the remainder of the huge chamber was brightly lighted with sodium vapor lights. Radiant heaters were glowing from the ceilings and walls. Here and there a remaining stalagmite or stalactite could be seen as a translucent red tower in front of a glowing heater. Huge convection heaters blew through the right side of the cavernous room keeping the air temperature at exactly seventy degrees.

Galley looked around in amazement and asked, "How did you do this? This is an amazing structure."

"Not everyone has the advantage of being able to bolt their skyscrapers to the sky. We brought in the prefabricated rooms one by one and stacked them on top of and beside each other until we reached the ceiling. Then we bolted them all together. They all have windows and balconies facing the rear. This gives each and every one of our one-thousand-plus cubicles a view that we carefully planned for. There's more than eight acres of scenery behind that wall. When you get to your room, you'll see."

"But where are the animals? I thought you would have a cave full of animals."

Morrow laughed and replied, "We *do* have a cave full of animals, Galley. They're just separated from our everyday life for safety and sanitary reasons. I'll show most of them to you tomorrow when we visit your telescope."

"Hey, kids, would you like to go up to our rooms?" Galley asked the little ones. They were obviously getting weary from the trip and the walk through the cave.

In a very mannerly style the three oldest nodded yes in unison. The youngest had already fallen asleep on Jalisa's shoulder.

Galley and Jalisa bid Morrow good evening and took the four kids and Frosty up the elevator to their room.

The room was small but cozy. It reminded Jalisa of her cabin on the cruise through the Panama Canal. There were two large comfortable sleeping bunks below and two pull-down bunks

167

above. A small stainless steel bathroom seemed also to serve as the shower by pulling the curtain-door.

What ingenuity, Galley thought. The entire walking space in the cabin couldn't have been more than twelve feet by five feet but it was cozier and warmer than their house had been in months. At the opposite end of the room from the door was a floor-to-ceiling curtain, drawn shut.

"Well, honey, what do you think?" Galley asked. Jalisa was putting Krista into the lower bunk nearest her.

He walked over by the large window to find the cord to open the drapes.

"I think it'll do just fine. As long as we're warm and alive I'll be happy," she answered with a smile.

"Me, too," Galley said quietly. He quickly pulled the drawstring and opened the drapes their full extent.

They both drew a deep breath at the beauty they saw out the balcony door window.

"Oh, Galley, have you ever seen anything so beautiful?" Jalisa asked, wiping a small tear from her eye.

"No. I don't think so," he said as he put his arm around her waist.

They were looking over a tropical rain forest with magnificent trees and greenery. Brilliantly colored birds flew through the air from tree to tree. Lights were placed around the high ceiling behind existing stalactite structures to hide them from view. It almost appeared that a hole had been cut in the top of the cave and the previous warm daylight was still beaming brightly in. In the far distance they could see a tall slender waterfall, its water tumbling into a small blue lagoon below.

Galley opened the door to the balcony. A rush of warm, moist air met his face as he stepped onto the balcony. He could hear the waterfall over the call of tropical birds. Then he heard an elephant trumpet. He looked for the source of the noise off to the left and saw an African elephant rubbing its trunk against a tall Banyan tree. Several hundred yards away a hippopotamus was wallowing in the small river flowing from the lagoon. A small monkey swung between trees on a thick hanging vine.

"Jalisa, come out here and look at this," he said, poking his head back through the sliding glass door.

She stepped over to the balcony door and carefully looked out. The eight-story-drop below made her feel a little uneasy. She had always feared heights a little bit. "Wow," she said, "this is unbelievable. Where'd he get all the animals from?"

"He said he's been collecting them for almost a year, now. I guess the zoos had no problem giving them up since they would probably die anyway."

"Yeah, I guess so," she agreed.

Galley looked back out, "Jalisa, notice that you only see one of each species. That's Jackson's grand plan to save space. They're all females, too."

"Well, Galley, I don't care what they are or how many there are, I just think this is like vacationing in a tropical paradise. I never thought it would be like this."

"Neither did I," Galley admitted.

He stepped to the edge of the balcony to look down. "Galley, be careful," Jalisa said. He looked straight down to see what separated the animals from the cubicles. He saw what appeared to be a large deep moat filled with rapidly flowing water. The water flowed from left to right in front of the lower cubicles then was diverted back into a large whirlpool far in the distance, away from the living complex.

"He's ingenious," Galley said.

"Why, Galley?" Jalisa responded. She was still worried about his proximity to the edge of the balcony.

"If an animal tries to get to the living quarters, it falls in the moat and is swept rapidly into that pit back there where the water drains through that grate. See it?"

"Yeah, I see the water going into the pit."

"Well, then the animal gets up and just walks back were he came from, a little wetter than before."

"Galley, come in here. You're worrying me," Jalisa said, forgetting about the ingenious system.

Galley stepped back inside and picked up Jan. He held him up to the window so he could see over the balcony safety rail. "Wow!" Jan said scanning the terrain below with wide eyes. After a few minutes of looking over the landscape, he put his head down on Galley's shoulder and closed his eyes.

Jalisa said, "Galley, he's getting sleepy like the rest of them.

Galley put Jan into the bunk over Krista's and pulled the covers over him.

A few minutes later all the kids were sound asleep, taking all the beds in the Pruitt's cubicle. Frosty had jumped into the lower bed with Krista and was now sleeping, curled up by her side.

Galley looked around the tiny room and spotted four small cell-phone-looking devices lying on the dresser between the lower bunks.

"What are those?" Jalisa whispered as Galley picked one up to inspect it.

"It says PCC on the side. Under that, this one has Jalisa P. engraved into the metal. This one has Galley P. under the PCC."

"Well, what are they?" Jalisa asked again.

Galley thought momentarily as he examined the devices. There was a small white plastic clip on the back and a black plastic grille over the front. The top had a little red push-button protruding from it. Suddenly the PCC he was holding emitted a shrill "Beeeeeep." He jumped, accidentally throwing the PCC into the air. The beep was followed by, "Dinner is now being served in the dining room, first seating—*squawk*," as the PCC landed on the floor and bounced. A second voice continued after the first announcement, "Doctor and Mrs. Pruitt, you and your children are in first seating."

"*Now* I remember," Galley said. "Jackson said something about a Personal Cavern Communicator when I talked to him in Phoenix. I'll bet that's a PCC, and these are our communicators. Here, put yours on." He took the PCC on the dresser and handed it to her looking to ensure it was the one with Jalisa P. on the side.

He reached down and picked his up from the floor, clipped it on his collar and said, "We'd better get the kids to the dining room, wherever that is."

Jalisa said, "But Galley, we just got them to sleep."

"Okay then. Why don't you stay here with them and I'll go down and see if I can bring some food back. That way they can eat when they wake up from their nap. We've got a microwave over there."

"Good idea, I'll just wait here. I can see what's on our TV. It'll give me something to do. If all else fails, I can just start unpacking," Jalisa said with a quick wink.

"Good, and if you have any trouble or need anything, my best guess would to push that little red button on top of your PCC. I assure you something will happen when you do. Just don't ever drop these things, it sounds like you're killing them when you do," Galley said with a chuckle as he grabbed for the PCC on his collar. It was still there.

"Yeah, thanks Galley," she answered back with a pantomimed kick to his rear end. "You'd better get to the dining room, Galley. They may have a time limit for serving."

"Okay, bye. Oh, I may try to stop by and find Neemu on the way," he said, racing out the door. It slammed behind him, rousing Frosty from a deep, twitching sleep. She cuddled more into Krista and nodded back off.

At the base of the wall Galley looked around trying to find some directions. He saw a group of blue directional arrows on the wall with large white writing. Walking up to them he noticed one pointing to the dining room. It appeared to be back near the Underground Lunchroom, according to the direction and distance given. Above the dining room arrow were two more arrows. One pointed straight ahead. It read MEDAID. A second arrow pointed right and had written on it AQUARIUM. He assumed the first arrow was the direction of the infirmary and started off in that direction.

A few more buildings down the Big Room's path toward the Bottomless Pit, Galley saw a white concrete-block-walled structure built into the side of the cave. It appeared to be the size of a small two-story house. Over the door was a sign that read EMERGENCY MEDICAL AID. He stopped and entered through the shiny metal doors.

Inside, a woman dressed in a tidy light blue uniform looked down at the computer terminal on the counter in front of her and then up at Galley. She said, "Hello, Dr. Pruitt. I'm Nurse Glenda Carson, R.N."

Galley looked strangely at the nurse, not knowing how she knew his name, and said, "Hi, I'm here to see how Neemu Hatlem's doing. Is he here?"

"Yes, he is. I'll get his wife for you."

As Nurse Carson left, Galley looked around the room noting that the surroundings had all the appearances of an ultramodern hospital. On the nurses' station in front of him were cardiac monitors awaiting patients and television monitors sequencing, showing empty beds. He looked carefully for Neemu in the changing TV images but saw only meticulously made beds. The sheets were light blue with dark blue comforters bearing the large gold embroidered letters ANTRON. Beside each bed were electronic IV stands with inactive lights and dials covering their fronts. Galley shook his head in amazement.

173

"Hi Galley," Rutha said, emerging out of the swinging doors from the rear rooms.

"Hi, Rutha. How's Neemu?"

"Dr. Mason said it was only a grazing wound. Neemu was really lucky."

"That's great Rutha! When will they release him?"

"He was supposed to be out five minutes ago, but they had to rewrap the wound because of some continued bleeding."

"Oh, well then I'll just wait here for him with you," Galley said as he sat on the modern chrome and black fabric chair.

Ten minutes later Neemu entered the room with Nurse Carson walking behind. He preceded her in a black motorized wheelchair that looked somewhat like a futuristic automobile, shiny and sleek. A joystick protruded from the control panel over Neemu's lap. LEDs flashed and changed colors with each movement of Neemu's hand on the joystick.

Neemu, with a somber face, wheeled over to Galley's chair. He hesitated several seconds then looked directly into Galley's eyes and asked, "Wanna race?"

Galley laughed a single loud, "Ha!" Then he started laughing with joy at Neemu's attitude and appearance. "You look fine and you're even acting normal," Galley said with relief.

Neemu looked at Rutha and winked, then turned to Galley and replied with a big grin, "That's funny, Dr. Pruitt, I never acted normal before . . . I think I need a second opinion."

Galley continued laughing then countered, "Okay, Dr. Hatlem, you're also ugly."

After Rutha and Neemu had signed out and were waiting to leave, Galley walked over to Nurse Carson's station. She looked up once more at him. "How did you know my name when I walked in?" he asked. "My curiosity's gotten the best of me."

Glenda smiled and pointed to the computer readout in front of her. "Dr. Pruitt, the Antron Control Computer continuously monitors the location and status of each PCC. I simply looked on the screen to see who was in the room with me and it said: Dr. Galley Pruitt, thirty-six years old, six-feet tall, 185 pounds, born in Ft. Davis, Texas, married to—."

"Never mind. Never mind. I understand," Galley interrupted. He turned to leave with Neemu and said, "It's nice to know someone up there cares."

Neemu looked up smiling from the chair and pushed the joystick forward as Galley opened the door. "Speaking of that," Neemu said, "Morrow came to visit me while ago. He apologized deeply and said he dismissed the guard that shot me. Because of me that guard will probably freeze to death."

Galley frowned and replied, "Just be glad the guard was caught before he made a really serious mistake."

"Like what?" Neemu inquired.

"I don't know yet, but I'll bet you that with a closed, confined colony like Antron, there could be some doozies."

"I guess you're right," Neemu conceded.

On the way back to the room Galley described the accommodations, but left the scenery to be discovered. Finishing his description he said, "The

175

kids are all asleep in our room. I'm on my way to the Dining Room to see if I can get some take-out food for them and us. Want me to get you some, too?"

"Sure. I'm starved," Neemu replied. Rutha shook her head in agreement.

"Okay, then take the elevator up to your room. I think it's number 873 . . . or 875. Ours is 874 and it's next door to yours. Just knock on our door and ask Jalisa which is yours. She'll remember."

"Okay, Galley, see you in a while," Neemu said, rolling toward the elevator and leaving a little cloud of sparkly dust behind him.

Galley was walking toward the direction of the dining room when a small, motorized cart putted up beside him and stopped. Jackson Morrow asked, "Need a lift? I'm going to eat."

"Sure, why not? Thanks," Galley said, hopping into the front passenger seat.

"I wanted to talk to you tonight anyway, Galley. I'm glad I caught you."

"Oh?"

"Yes. I'd like to meet you tomorrow morning at oh-seven-thirty-two in Antron Control. From there I can give you a tour of the cave and show you your telescopes. I'm quite proud of them"

"I'd like that."

"I also want to introduce you and Neemu to the Colony Staff. There should be a few of them there in the morning, but I'm having a staff meeting tomorrow afternoon at thirteen-oh-six hours. You'll both get to meet everyone then, at least all of the Colony Staff that are here so far."

"I'll be there. I'll also tell Neemu." Galley

said, scanning the immense room as they drove through.

"Don't worry. You'll both be reminded over your PCCs with ample time for response. Our MIPS computer schedules all events and reminds every Colonist involved well in advance of the scheduled times."

Galley nodded in acknowledgment and then, still looking up, asked, "What are all those pipes on the ceiling?"

Morrow looked up at the large color-coded pipes overhead, "Oh, those? They're part of the ecosystem here, Gas and water lines to the surface. I'll show you more tomorrow . . . here we are."

"Thanks for the lift, Jackson" Galley said climbing from the cart.

"No problem. Where are your kids . . . and Jalisa? Where are Neemu and *his* wife? I just saw them and I thought they were coming to dinner."

"No, we're all so tired I volunteered to come down and pick up some food to take back for us. Do you know where I go for take-out orders?"

Morrow laughed, "I think you need to read the AGB, er, the Antron Guide Book. There *is* no take-out service. However, you'll find that if you push the little red button on your PCC, you'll be connected to room service by just asking. We guarantee room delivery in fifteen minutes."

"Can you use this thing to speak with anyone?" Galley asked in apparent confusion.

"Yes, just push the red button and call the party you want by first name and last name. If there are ambiguous names then you must use their nickname or middle name, too."

"Then what?" Galley asked.

"Then just talk in a normal conversational voice. The computer listens to each of you talk and decides when to end the conversation and shut off the link . . . usually when one of you pauses or says goodbye."

"Ingenious, Jackson," Galley said as he reached to pull the PCC from his collar.

He pushed the button and heard a monotonic voice ask, "PCC. Command?"

"Call Jalisa Pruitt."

The metal device answered, "In the Hatlem's room, 875. Connecting." A quiet pulsating tone followed.

Galley looked in amazement at Morrow, "How'd you do this?"

"I think I mentioned to you about my electronics company in California?"

"Oh, Yes. I remember. They invented that cryo-something you wear."

"Cryosensor. Yes, they invented that device as well as the PCC technology. We had very little use for the PCC until you discovered Endlight and I decided to move into the cave."

At that moment in the Hatlems' room, Jalisa's PCC beeped loudly and announced, "Incoming call from Galley Pruitt. To answer, push the red button."

Jalisa reached down to her belt and pressed the button. "Hello, Galley?"

"Hi hon, aren't these neat? I'm with Jackson down here at the Dining Room. He says to just call in our dinner like room service . . . they don't have carry-out here."

Jalisa looked at Rutha, Neemu and the kids with her eyes wide open. She laughingly said to them, "Oh, poor babies. We have to use room service."

Galley's voice came over the PCC, "I heard that. Now, when we finish talking, push the red button again and say 'Call Room Service'. Then just order normally like you would in a hotel . . . but be sure to order something for me, too."

"What do you want me to order for you?"

Galley playfully answered, "A chicken fried steak with lumpy gravy and smashed potatoes."

Jalisa said, "Galley, that's not funny!" and pushed the red button. A voice from the device said, "PCC. Command?"

Galley looked blankly at Morrow as the PCC went dead. "She hung up on you," he said. "She pushed the red button just like you said. That aborts the old session and starts a new one."

Galley said, "Oh," slightly embarrassed by the incident. Then he continued, "I'd better get back to the cubicles before they eat my food."

As Galley turned to leave, Morrow asked, "Galley, what do you think about your living area?"

"Jackson, it's wonderful. We were so surprised at the beauty *and* functionality."

"I was really proud of our architect. He fit over four-thousand people comfortably into a little over twenty-two thousand square feet of land—a mere half acre. That's only about six square feet of cave floor space per person . . . a floor area of just two by three feet apiece."

"I hadn't stopped to realize that. It has a very efficient plan. How did you develop it?" Galley asked.

"It happened through a series of logical steps. I was thinking metaphorically of Antron as

179

an ark. Then I realized an ark is a boat, and a luxury boat has extremely comfortable and efficient quarters. So, I called in a cruise ship architect to complete the design. I think he did a wonderful job."

"So do we, Jackson. Now, I'd better get back to the room. I'm starving."

"See you in the morning, Galley. Oh, why don't you take the Hoxcart back? There are plenty available in the cave. Just leave it when you get off. It homes back to Antron Control, AC, automatically for refueling. When you need one again and don't feel like walking, just push the red button on your PCC and say, 'Send Cart'."

Galley hopped aboard the cart, said, "Thanks, Jackson," and motored back toward the Big Room.

A few minutes later Galley left the Hoxcart in front of the cubicles and walked up to the elevator. As he stepped on the elevator and pushed the eighth-floor button, the cart pulled slowly away on its way back to Antron Control.

Galley entered room 874 to find Jalisa, Jan and Krista sitting around the small pullout dining table waiting for dinner to arrive. He walked over to the window to see the rain forest scenery was now darkened, bathed in a dim blue light like moonlight during a full moon. All was quiet except for the waterfall roaring in the distance. He looked at his watch, of course, nighttime. It's 10:00 p.m., he thought. He hadn't seen the stark day-night contrast in so long he had almost forgotten it existed.

"I guess the animals are sleeping," he said quietly.

Jan said, "Galley, when can we go see the animals?"

"Jan, we'll have plenty of time to see them . . . maybe tomorrow."

A knock at the door signaled the arrival of dinner. Jalisa opened it to a tuxedoed waiter pushing a chrome cart carrying four glass-dome-covered plates and four crystal goblets. He brought the plates to the table two at a time. The children had hamburgers with French fries and chocolate malts served in crystal stemware. Jalisa's steamy glass dome was removed to reveal a broiled white fish filet crusted with braised almonds, broccoli with hollandaise sauce and new potatoes in a light butter cream sauce. She bent over the plate, inhaling the aroma and said, "Ahhhhh."

Galley's plate was uncovered at last to show a thin pancake-shaped piece of meat covered in browned cracker crumbs. On the side was a large helping of silky smooth mashed potatoes covered with a light gravy sauce full of knotty lumps. The waiter looked back and winked at Jalisa as he began to leave the room with the cart. Jalisa jumped up, ran to the door and gave him a sizable tip, saying, "Thank you, very much. It looks wonderful, just like home." She smiled and winked back.

After dinner, Jalisa and Galley put Jan and Krista to bed. It was already 11:45 p.m. and everyone was exhausted, especially the kids. Jalisa pushed the red button and said, "Call Rutha Hatlem." The PCC answered, "In the Hatlem's room, 875. Connecting." A hushed pulsing tone followed.

181

"Jalisa?" Rutha answered.

"Rutha, I just thought I'd tell you the kids are asleep and everything's fine here."

"Same here, Jalisa. Neemu's painkillers knocked him out right after dinner and the kids went soon after that. I'm just sitting out here on the balcony pretending I'm visiting Africa."

"Isn't it beautiful out there?" Jalisa asked.

"Yes, I would never have thought it would be like this. I wonder what's happening topside."

"On the surface?"

"Yes," Rutha clarified.

"I turned on the TV set in the room today and got terribly depressed. You know you can get most major city telecasts in here?"

"No. I didn't. I haven't had time to turn the set on yet. Neemu, you know."

"Well you may not want to," Jalisa added, "the news is all bad everywhere."

"How bad?"

"Several hundred thousand people died today across the U. S. alone due to hypothermia, asphyxia and suicides."

"Oh, dear God," Rutha exclaimed in a soft voice.

"I'm sorry, Rutha, I didn't mean to upset you. Get some sleep. You must be worn out too."

"I am Jalisa. I'll see you in the morning. I guess Neemu and Galley are supposed to be somewhere early. I'll call you on this little beeper after they leave."

"Okay, goodnight Rutha."

"Night, Jalisa." The PCC fell silent.

Jalisa looked over to talk to Galley but found him laying half-on and half-off the bottom bunk sound asleep. As he exhaled, his lips separated and made a soft "pooh" with each breath. Jalisa smiled and lifted his legs into bed. After pulling up the covers for the kids and Galley, she lay on her bunk silently for several minutes thinking about the unbelievable events of the day. Her eyes closed and she was asleep.

At 7:02 a.m. the PCC by Galley's pillow began beeping loudly. After five seconds the beeping stopped and a computerized female voice said, "Dr. Pruitt. You have a meeting at Antron Control in thirty minutes. Please wake up."

Galley rolled over and said, "Okay, okay. I'm up."

The PCC voice said, "Thank you," and went silent.

Galley jumped up, bumping his head on the bunk above him. "Damn, that hurts!" he mumbled to himself trying not to wake everyone up.

"Are you okay, Galley?" Jan asked after being jolted awake by the big bump under his bed.

"Yep, I'm fine, Jan. Go back to sleep."

Jan put his head back on the pillow and said "Okay, Galley." He closed his eyes and dropped back into a deep sleep as Galley finished dressing.

Galley arrived at Antron Central at 7:29 a.m., three minutes early for his meeting. He had walked almost one-and-a-half miles to get there and was winded beyond his expectations. Nearing Antron Control, he thought about his condition and attributed it to the thinner air and uphill climb to the Center. He also was thinking about the amazing sights he had seen traveling to the Center as he approached the white

183

concrete-block windowless building. A plaque by the entrance read;

ANTRON CONTROL CENTER—AUTHORIZED PERSONNEL ONLY.

Galley noticed a small clear darkened window by the door. A sign over it read;

PLACE RIGHT HAND ON WINDOW

Galley raised his right hand and put it carefully on the window. There was a bright flash of light from the window followed by a computer-generated female voice that said, "State your name, first, then last."

Galley kept his hand over the window and said, "Galley Pruitt."

"Thank you, Dr. Pruitt. You may now remove your hand from the scan window. Your clearance is approved. Please enter at the buzz," the soft voice continued.

A loud buzz from the door lock signaled Galley to push. The vault door swung open then closed behind him automatically as he entered.

"Good morning, Dr. Pruitt. I'm Geoff Chadwick, Chief Scientist for the Colony," said the grey-haired and bearded man approaching Galley in the anteroom. Galley thought he would be taller from his reputation. He was only slightly over five-feet tall but his British accent made him seem quite stately.

Galley bowed his head slightly and responded, "Good morning, Dr. Chadwick. It's really a pleasure to meet you. I've read many of your papers on artificial environments as they were used in the Biosphere 2 biomes."

"Thank you, Galley. I, likewise, have read all of your Endlight Event papers from prediction to discovery with avarice. I, as well as many others, understood the consequences on the Earth of such a catastrophe. In fact, I began planning for Antron, a virtual Biosphere 3, almost a year ago, right after your discovery of the Cloud, and approached Jackson with the idea."

"Thank you, but it's not an accomplishment I really want to be remembered by. I want to help us live through Endlight. Now what can I do to help?" Galley asked with eagerness in his voice.

Almost as on cue, Morrow entered the anteroom through swinging double doors and said, "Well, Galley, I see you've met Geoff. Have you had time to discuss our facility yet? And where's Neemu?"

Galley stood silent, realizing that in his rush he had forgotten to wait for Neemu.

Chadwick answered, interrupting the silence, "I haven't seen Neemu yet but Galley just arrive..." A banging on the outside wall interrupted him.

"Who in the hell is out there banging?" Morrow asked walking over to the TV monitor screen by the front desk. "It's Neemu. Why didn't he...? Oh, I see! He couldn't reach the hand scanner window from his wheel chair." He laughed and felt embarrassed at the oversight. "I guess I should have planned better for the disabled . . . sorry, just an accident."

Chadwick and Galley smiled at each other for a moment just before Morrow exploded, "Well, don't just stand there like dummies, someone let him in!"

Chadwick stepped quickly to the wall by the door and pushed the button labeled 'OPEN VAULT'. The door swung inward revealing Neemu sitting impatiently at the entrance. "Galley, why didn't you wait for me?" he asked, glaring at Pruitt.

"I'm sorry, Neemu. With the anticipation of this meeting I simply forgot."

Neemu put his hand on the joystick and wheeled into the anteroom. "Okay, just don't let it happen again," he said with a straight face. Then he cracked a brief smile at the waiting group.

"Now, let me show you the Control Center," Morrow said, "but first, Neemu this is Geoff Chadwick, Colony Chief Scientist. He developed most of our Antron biomes as well as those in Biosphere 2."

Neemu questioned, "Biosphere 2 in the Arizona desert?"

"Yes," Morrow answered, "he successfully led eight people in a closed environment there for two years. I felt he would have no problem with four months here. It's a few more people but the principle's the same."

"I'm pleased to meet you," Neemu said extending his hand.

Geoff exchanged formalities and excused himself to the aquarium biome.

At Chadwick's departure Morrow turned to Galley and Neemu and said, "Now, if you'll both follow me, I'll give you a short tour and then show you to your new offices."

They passed through the swinging doors into

a technological wonderland.

As they approached the closed cypher-locked door labeled ANTRON CONTROL CENTRAL, Morrow placed his hand over the cypher lock and punched in a code indiscernible to Neemu and Galley. The door opened to a large gleaming black cube sitting on the floor in the middle of the room. Six-foot-tall equipment racks filled with electronics lined the far wall. Illuminated numbers and rows of multicolored blinking lights covered the equipment panels. At one end of the room was a sleek black sloping-front console filled with color plasma panels. A woman sat in one of five massive black chairs at the console, scanning the monitors.

Five computer keyboards covered the surface of the console desk. The room was warm and smelled of freshly operated electronic equipment. The soft whine of cooling fans blended with the silence.

"This is the MIPS Medusa Computer room. From here we control and monitor all of Antron's activities," Morrow said, sweeping his hand across the room. He continued, "That black box in the center of the room has one-thousand-and-twenty-four separate processors in it, each running at 9.8 gigahertz, to ensure that every environmental, power and scientific system in Antron is at peak efficiency."

They moved to the console and Morrow introduced the operator, "This is Molly O'Quinn, our Chief Computer Scientist. She comes to us from Epcot Center."

Galley and Neemu looked at each other and asked almost in unison, "Epcot Center in Florida?"

Morrow laughed and explained, "That's the

187

reaction I get from almost everyone. Epcot Center has hundreds of artificial environments operating simultaneously under complete computer control. Thousands of processes have to happen in perfect sequence. She's accustomed to the constant pressure of exact synchronization. That's why she's ideal for this job."

Molly stood and said, "Dr. Pruitt, Dr. Hatlem, Pleased to meet you."

Neemu said, "Sorry I can't stand Ms. O'Quinn."

Galley shook hands, saying, "Molly, pleased to meet you. Are your computers tied into the radio telescope, also?"

"Yes, Dr. Pruitt, you have the full power of Medusa at your disposal from your Control Room. Have you seen your facility yet?"

"No, we're on our way there now."

O'Quinn continued, "We'll, I'm sure that you will be quite impressed with your capabilities. Jackson insisted that I give you every computational advantage here since you'll be our watchdog for the return of the Sun, so to speak."

"Good, I'll try to use your processors wisely. Is there any chance of my affecting the Antron control system's operation by taking too much computational power for my telescope?"

O'Quinn walked up to the cube and opened a black side panel. Inside were hundreds of tiny flashing red and green LEDs. There was also one larger pair of blue and white LEDs on a separate inner panel. She pointed to the larger pair and said, "No, A sequencer in Medusa insures that critical cave control computations always have priority over non critical computations. When this blue light is lit, the cave is being managed for survival. When it goes out and the white one comes on, other computations are being made. Antron control is effectively asleep then . . . but since we wake it back up over one-hundred-thousand times a second everything is perfectly managed, and synchronized. In other words, don't worry about taking too much computer time from Medusa, here." She closed the panel and patted her hand on the top of the cube as if petting an animal.

"Okay, thanks for the info," Galley said.

"Dr. Hatlem, you also have the use of Medusa in your Communications Center . . . same rules apply."

"Thanks, Molly," Neemu said.

Molly turned her back to the monitors and her keyboard and Neemu begun to scan the small color monitors at the console. There must have been forty nine-inch plasma panels, each with a different image showing. Some screens showed motionless panoramas. Some showed adults, some showed children, moving through hallways and rooms. Others showed animals in the Rain Forest near the moat. Still, others showed rows of metallic devices and white objects rotating in harmony.

A single larger screen to the right of the smaller ones had a continuous sequence of closed-circuit camera views switching from one view to the next at a rate of one per second. It appeared to be showing external dimly lit views of the parking area and cave entrance area seven-hundred feet over their heads. Galley and Neemu both noticed almost simultaneously the dim image of two very large spheres near what seemed to be the Visitor Center, above.

Galley pointed to the large screen and said quickly before the image changed, "What're those spheres. I noticed them as we drove up Walnut Canyon last night. They've never been there before when we've visited Carlsbad."

Molly looked at Morrow and said, "I'll let him explain them." She pushed a button on the keyboard under the monitor that froze the picture of the immense white spheres on the screen. Seconds later they were brightly illuminated from their base so that the large red letters HYDROLOX could be read on the side of each sphere.

Morrow stated, "Our energy source in Antron is quite unique. That's what you're looking at. It's a binary gas power system developed for me by Hydrolox in Phoenix. One tank holds enough liquid hydrogen to power this cave for six months, when mixed with oxygen. The other holds liquid oxygen, or lox, for us to breathe in the cave and also mix with the hydrogen for power. Both gases, combined and called hox, are mixed in the gas-turbine power plant near the cave's surface entrance in the old Bat Cave. Control of the power system occurs from this console and this keyboard." He pointed to the monitor and keyboard at the left of the console. "But the hox turbines are located safely away from the living biomes. The water resulting from the hydrogen-oxygen reaction in the power plant is piped into the lower caves and used wherever water is needed."

Neemu looked at Galley, then back at Morrow and said, "Quite impressive . . . and you don't have to worry about your fuel freezing, do you?"

"No, it has to get pretty damn cold for oxygen

or hydrogen to freeze solid. I don't think that will happen in the next four months. Isn't that beautiful? The colder it gets outside, the more efficient our gaseous liquefiers become. We had some trouble keeping the tanks at capacity before the temperature started dropping but that's not when we needed it. In fact, as we brought Antron online, our hox liquefier plant used so much power from the New Mexico power plants they finally rationed our use. We're at full capacity now and the system is percolating perfectly, pure oxygen and hydrogen gases to energy and pure water then dirty air and water back to pure oxygen, nitrogen and hydrogen."

"Kind of like a perpetual motion machine, isn't it?" Neemu inquired.

"Not really. The efficiency *is* high enough though that we can be self sustaining in a closed loop system for over six months after we close the doors and seal ourselves in."

"Isn't there some danger in having those tanks so close together outside? If they develop the slightest leak then the gas from both tanks could mix and go *blooey* and we'd all be dust?" Galley questioned.

"Don't worry. We're so deep below the surface we'd hardly feel a thump from the explosion. Then we would just walk out of the cave from its natural entrance."

"And freeze to death outside?" Neemu asked.

Morrow laughed. "You scientists worry too much! We'll cross that bridge when we come to it, if we ever do. The Hydrolox power system is designed to be highly reliable and safe. Now, let's continue our tour."

191

Five steps and one door down the hallway from Control Central they stopped at a door marked ANTRON COM CENTER. Morrow reached his right hand to the cypher lock and said, "One, nine, six." He pushed the lock buttons with his fingers as he spoke the numbers. "That's your code for entry, guys. Push them one at a time, in that order."

The door swung open to a large futuristically styled room. Neemu quickly wheeled in. On the left side of the room was a short-wave radio station that he had dreamed of all his life. Against the wall was a long desk covered with electronic gadgets, only some of which he recognized from across the room. On the wall over the desk were twelve IBM-style clocks set with different time zones from across the world. He wheeled up to the desk and pulled the chair out of his way. The chair legs made an irritating screeching noise as they slid across the concrete floor.

As Neemu was exploring his new equipment like a child on Christmas morning, Galley had looked to the right end of the room and found the radio telescope control console. It was newer equipment than that at the VLA. He sat at the console and began studying the equipment panels.

"Hey Galley, look at this!" Neemu said excitedly as he turned to look behind him. He saw Morrow standing in the middle of the room smiling as he glanced between Neemu and Galley in their chairs. "Thanks, Jackson," Neemu continued, "this equipment is wonderful . . . and very expensive. I've only seen this Icom 1508 HF transceiver in pictures. It costs over twelve-thousand dollars. And this IC-9KL amplifier! They're almost ten thousand! What a dream! I can talk to anyone in the world with this rig!"

"That's the idea, Neemu. I'm glad you like it. I though we needed the best for our Colony," Morrow answered with a self-pleased grin.

"How did you know to buy equipment this good?" Neemu asked. "You said you didn't know any hams."

"I *don't* know any hams. I just picked up a ham radio magazine, think it was something like *QUEST*."

"*QST?*" Neemu suggested.

"Yes that's it. Anyway, I just picked it up from the newsstand and ordered the most expensive equipment in it," Jackson answered. "It came in yesterday."

"Well, you did fine by me," Neemu said, still pushing buttons and turning knobs on the radio transceiver.

Galley turned to look back at Neemu and said, "Neemu, come look at this antenna feed and receiver system . . . don't forget you're a radio astronomer, too."

Neemu backed from the radio desk almost knocking Morrow down. "I'm so sorry, Jackson," Neemu said. "I still haven't gotten the hang of driving this thing in reverse with a joystick."

Morrow caught his balance and laughed. "Boy, what a way to treat someone that just spent a fortune on your equipment."

Neemu carefully drove by Morrow, trying not to hit him again, on his way over to the radio telescope control console. He slid in beside Galley's chair and said, "Wow! And this is a *private* enterprise radio telescope?"

Galley said quietly to Neemu, "Neemu, this

cost some megabucks, I'll guarantee that." He turned back to Morrow. "Thanks, Jackson. This is a beauty."

Morrow walked over to the console and said, "How would I expect Picasso to paint without a brush? Besides, Galley, you are our eyes while we are here. Neemu is our ears. You both deserve the best equipment to keep the Colony informed of external world activities."

Galley asked, "Where's the antenna for the system?"

Morrow replied, "It's topside under a protective radome with the spotter scope. You have to take the elevator to get to it. It's behind one of the Hydrolox tanks, that's why you didn't notice it on the way up."

"I'd like to see it later," Galley said.

Neemu agreed, "Me, too."

"Good, then let's start moving," Morrow said. "Let me show you the rest of Antron. You can both come back in here and acquaint yourself with the equipment this afternoon. Remember you've got over four months with not much to do. There's no hurry to do anything, just wait for sunlight to return."

Morrow walked Galley and Neemu by the PCC Computer Room on the way out of the Control Building. They were using their PCCs to call each other and test the system like two kids with Christmas-fresh walkie-talkies. "Can you hear me now?"

Leaving the Control Center, Morrow pointed to the pathway to the left and said, "Let's visit the Aquarium Biome first."

Galley and Neemu moved to the left and were

almost hit by a driverless hoxcart autonomously returning to the Control Center. The cart stopped only inches from Neemu's wheelchair.

"Whew! That was a close call!" Neemu exclaimed.

Morrow said, "These hoxcarts are designed to avoid hitting obstacles at all costs, even if it means jumping into reverse to do it. They often turn themselves over trying to avoid collisions. They're very clumsy but reliable and safe."

Galley asked, "Morrow why do you call them *oxcarts*? I can't imagine how they got that name. Is it because they're so clumsy?"

Morrow put his hand on the stopped cart and pointed to a small sign under the steering wheel. It read: DANGER - Hydrogen/Oxygen Powered Cart. KEEP AWAY FROM HEAT OR FLAMES.

Galley read the small label and said, "Oh! *Hox*carts! Now I see."

Neemu laughed and said, "Galley, sometimes I wonder about you. Didn't you hear Morrow say that everything in the cave is powered by hydrogen and oxygen? That way there's no pollution and the only byproduct of the process is water. Look! There's the Hoxcart's water collection tank." Neemu pointed to a small stainless steel cylinder labeled H_2O under the passenger seat.

Galley blushed and responded, "Guess that was just too obvious for me. By the way, Neemu, I am *not* a rocket scientist, you know, just a radio astronomer."

Morrow laughed at their bickering and motioned for them to follow him. "We're heading

195

for the Aquarium biome. It's located in the old Lower Cave. The Lower Cave is now a ten-million gallon warm ocean aquarium, complete with a coral reef and over one-hundred thousand species of marine life. Follow me."

CHAPTER 8
BIODIVERSITY

"What is man without the beasts? If all beasts were gone, men would die from a great loneliness of the spirit. For whatever happens to the beasts soon happens to man."

CHIEF SEATTLE, 1854

Morrow led Neemu and Galley out of the Big Room. They followed the blue arrow on the cave wall that read AQUARIUM and started down a tunnel that obviously had been recently widened. Ninety or so feet into the lighted tunnel they approached a very large set of stainless steel double doors set into a thick concrete wall, blocking the tunnel. The shiny metallic doors were at least forty feet wide and thirty feet tall. Morrow approached a small human-sized door off to the side of the big doors, turned the doorknob and opened it.

Neemu looked briefly at Morrow's invitation to enter and said, "Sorry, Jackson. I can't go through there. There's a ledge under it. If you'll just lift my chair up…"

Morrow glanced down to see a small two-inch high ridge of stainless steel under the pathway that he had stepped over a thousand times. He interrupted, "Neemu, I'm sorry. More bad design."

Morrow walked to a small box on the side wall and pressed a green button. A sign by the door had the instructions: CHILDREN UNDER 13 NOT ALLOWED WITHOUT PARENTS. The giant doors opened slowly from the center as the steel panels retracted into the wall. A low rumble echoed through the tunnel shaking the ground beneath them.

Galley watched as glistening snowflakes of crystallized calcium drifted down from the ceiling reminding him of his Phoenix trip. He was suddenly taken a thousand miles and a nightmare away from Arizona and New Mexico. He was breathing warm fresh sea air.

Warmth and humidity rose past them in wafts. Neemu's glasses fogged to the point that he took them off and wiped the lenses on his shirt. The smell of fresh salt air reminded Galley of his youthful college spring breaks on the Gulf of Mexico, near South Padre Island. The doors closed behind them with groaning thud.

After walking for several minutes past the doors, Morrow mentioned that the room they were approaching was one of the lowest caves in the caverns. That's why it had been chosen as the Aquarium biome. "We began filling the room with sea water four months ago and just finished last week. I think we have done a respectable job of simulating a natural ocean environment. You'll see in a minute. It's part of the biodiversity program here."

Galley asked, "Are those waves I hear?" as he cupped his right hand to his ear. The faint sounds of surf washing against a shore echoed up the tunnel from the Lower Cave.

"Yes. Isn't that pleasant? Chadwick installed wave machines to simulate ocean currents as closely as possible," Morrow explained. "We've even created artificial tides by carefully filtering and pumping some of the sea water into a million-gallon reservoir on twelve hour cycles. Every other half-day, the water is returned to our ocean. It creates tides of several feet — tides large enough to fool our marine life into believing they're in a real ocean."

They continued the trip down into the lower cave. As the descent drew steeper Neemu noticed that his wheelchair was beginning to smell of burning rubber. Neemu asked, "Galley, I think my brakes are giving out on this machine. Could you grab the handles and help me down the road gently? I'm afraid if these brakes fail, I'll end up flying down this road like some cartoon character screaming and waving his hands just before he hits a bump and sails through the air into the ocean."

Galley chuckled and said, "Sure, Neemu. I'd hate to see you lose your dignity like that."

Neemu said, "It's not funny. And don't you dare let go."

"Okay, Neemu. I've got you."

At the bottom of the tunnel the steep incline leveled to a gradual slope. They rounded the last corner and noticed that the wave sounds had become quite loud. The light from the end of the tunnel was intense, resembling daylight on a sunny day at the beach.

As they neared the mouth of the tunnel the ocean came into view. Neemu and Galley stopped and gazed into the blinding brightness of artificial sunlight. A gentle breeze smelling of marine life wafted across the surface of the water.

They left the tunnel and moved slowly out into the glaring light. Galley squinted as he looked up into the hundreds of infrared and UV lights.

They were evenly spaced across the cave ceiling, painted a light blue to resemble the sky. Then he looked across the water. The opposite shore around the ocean must have been several hundred yards away from where they were standing.

Morrow walked across the sand beach to the ocean's shore. "Gentlemen, the Antron Ocean." He held out his hand to present the view to them as its proud creator.

Neemu said, "Jackson, this is truly beautiful. I feel like I'm in the South Pacific."

Morrow replied, "Thank you, Neemu. I thought, since I had to make an ocean to save the marine life, I might as well make it pleasurable for humans, too. The only thing allowed here is wading, no swimming."

"Why not swimming?" Neemu asked.

"The ocean's over two-hundred feet deep in some places," Morrow explained. "The waves and tide create a severe undertow at times. We lost several divers during the construction and testing of the tide generator system to undertow. They were killed instantly as the waves smashed them into the coral reef over there."

Neemu said, "I don't think I wanted to swim anyway," and laid his head back in his chair to feel the radiant heat from above. "I love the warmth," he sighed.

"You'll find that the visible radiation from the illuminators on the ceiling is almost exactly the composition of sunlight on a summer day in Southern Florida. You can get burned very quickly," Morrow explained. "Also, the inside cave temperature here often reaches ninety degrees to simulate temperate climates. Watch out for heat stroke."

Galley rolled up his sleeves and asked, "What about the colder climate oceans? Are they in here, too?"

Morrow smiled and replied, "No, I've left most of them to take care of themselves, just like the bottom dweller species. We don't expect the freeze to be bad enough to kill anything deep under the sea. We're just trying to protect the tropical marine species here."

"Man, this must have been some undertaking, getting all the water and fish in here," Neemu said.

"It wasn't too bad. But, I do remember we had some trouble with the humpback and killer whales, they barely fit through the tunnels getting down here. We can't let them gain any weight while they're in here or they won't be able to get back out."

Neemu frowned and said, "That would be terrible, but you could put them on an Atkins diet just in time to leave." A wry smile replaced his frown.

Morrow chuckled and shook his head in agreement. "We've already thought of that as a contingency plan. It'll work."

For several minutes they stood looking over the seascape from the edge of the water. The foamy surf roared closer to their feet with each new wave. The tide was coming in. A voice behind them suddenly bellowed, "I see our guests found our jolly warm ocean."

Morrow said without turning around, "Hi Geoff."

Neemu and Galley turned to Chadwick and returned the smile. Galley said, "You've got quite

201

some artificial ocean here. Is it as big as the one you had in Biosphere 2?"

"Oh yes, much larger. The Aquarium biome in Biosphere 2 was only about nine-hundred-thousand gallons. This ocean would hold over ten of that one. Incidentally, we call it a *biome* after the Biosphere terminology. It just means an artificial biological habitat. We also have a rain forest biome behind the living quarters. Other parts of the cave have the savannah and aviary biomes. You'll get to see them later in your tour of Antron's biodiversity."

"Yes, we must be moving on," Morrow stated, looking at his watch. "I'll see you in the staff meeting this afternoon, Geoff?"

"I'll most assuredly be there, Jackson," Chadwick said as he stepped into the shallow water and reached a long-handled sampling net into the ocean surf. "Now, if you'll excuse me again, I must check the plankton level."

"Thank you, Geoff," Morrow said. "See you later."

"Cheerio," Chadwick answered and continued to drag his sampling net through the surf.

Galley and Neemu returned the pleasantry, and then followed Morrow back into the tunnel. Thirty feet into the passageway Neemu's chair motor stalled from the steepening incline. Grumbling about his current inability to walk, Neemu asked Galley to help him up the path by pushing the chair. Galley agreed and they continued toward the next stop on their tour.

As they neared the giant doors leaving the Aquarium biome, Morrow said, "We expect to open the Aquarium biome to the Colony Public in a week or two. By that time all of the marine ecosystems should be stabilized and ready for our Colony to encroach."

Morrow opened the large double doors again to let Neemu through and said, "I've got to get someone down here to fix that damn ledge under that little door. There's no reason for that inconvenience. Someone's going to trip on it and break their neck."

Galley, pushing Neemu through the doorway, asked, "Do you still have workmen here in the cave for repairs and construction?"

"Oh yes, Galley," Morrow replied. "We have a contingent of about three hundred workers and their families here. In addition to our brilliant scientific staff we have talented carpenters, masons, metalworkers, food service staff, custodians, security guards, animal keepers and feeders—."

Galley interrupted, "Yes, I guess you do have a full staff here. I just haven't had time to see many of them yet."

"You probably won't either, Galley. They've all been instructed to work invisibly in their chores. Many of the guests here in Antron are not used to seeing their help work, so we try to continue the facade."

As they entered the Big Room again, they veered right, away from the living quarters and toward the Bottomless Pit and the MEDAID Center. Galley asked, "Is the Bottomless Pit still up there? I remember it from my vacations here as a kid. I loved that thought . . . a bottomless pit."

Morrow answered, "Yes, it's there, but that's what we now use for our ocean tide reservoir.

There's nothing to see anymore."

"Oh," he answered with some disappointment in his voice.

Several hundred feet after they entered the Big Room they approached the MEDAID building and saw more buildings built into the rock beyond it.

"Where are we going now?" Neemu asked fearing that his fuel was running low. "Do I have enough power left to finish the tour?"

Morrow walked to the wheelchair's control panel and looked at it. He tilted his head back to read through his bifocals and said, "Neemu, you've still got 60 percent left. That should run you another hour or so. If you do run out during the tour, there are refueling stations throughout Antron."

"Good," Neemu answered, breathing a sigh of relief.

Morrow pointed past the MEDAID building to a connecting white concrete building, "In that building, gentlemen, is one of my pet projects here."

Galley said, "Okay, I'll bite. What's in there?"

Morrow said, "Our cave CAVE."

"What?" Neemu questioned thinking he had misunderstood the statement.

"I said 'Our cave CAVE'. It's an acronym for a Cave Automatic Virtual Environment room."

"Jackson, what in the world are you talking about? You're not making any sense," Neemu added.

Morrow started to explain more slowly what he was trying to say, "I am using a new technology first developed at the University of Illinois in Chicago. There's a laboratory there called the

Electronic Visualization Laboratory, or EVL, that created a walk-in virtual environment with a frosted glass floor and walls. Television projectors throw a three-by-three-meter image in full three-dimensional fidelity onto the floor and each wall of the room. Then people inside wear 3-D glasses and feel as if they're in another reality."

"Oh, it's a virtual reality room?" Galley asked.

"Basically, yes. Dr. Hertzberg, our Colony Psychologist warned me that even with our attractive biomes and artificial environments, some Colonists might become violently claustrophobic after a few months. It's a little like cabin fever and there are few remedies for the malaise except for the sufferer to leave the place of discomfort."

"I've experienced that feeling in Sweden during some of our long winters," Neemu agreed. "You don't care what you have to do to leave, you just want out."

"That's right. That's why Hertzberg recommended I try the CAVE room for release of cabin, or cavern, fever tension in our case. If people try to leave Antron after we're closed in, there will be no way back in. We have to do that for our safety from possible interlopers and trespassers."

"So people can come in here to get away from Antron?" Neemu questioned.

"Yes, virtually get away, so to speak. When they begin to feel closed-in they simply enter the CAVE and place these 3-D glasses over their eyes," Morrow held up a pair of darkened spectacles that looked like cheap sunglasses. "Then using a hand-held tracking wand, the participant may, by waving his or her hand, direct a journey to almost any place on the Earth. The feeling is like you're really there. We've even added smell and temperature feedback to the experience to make it more realistic."

"Can I try it?" Neemu asked in a manner resembling a shy kid.

"Sure, Neemu. Here." Morrow handed the glasses to Neemu and grabbed two more pairs from the desk outside the CAVE room. "Put these on Galley. We can ride with him on his journey." Morrow shoved Galley into the white-walled CAVE room and followed him in.

"Are you sure it's okay, Morrow?" Galley asked. "I mean, to tag along on his trip?"

Neemu looked up at Galley through the gray-lens glasses and said, "Don't worry, Galley. *I* won't leave *you* behind."

Galley was preparing to respond when the room flashed to life!

They were flying several hundred feet over a craggy valley covered with green vegetation. The smell of lush greenery enveloped the room as the humidity and temperature rose. Galley estimated their speed to be eighty miles per hour or so. Off in the distance snow-capped mountains rose above the tundra.

Neemu pointed the wand toward the mountain peak and the room began to climb upward. Twenty seconds later they were circling the peak. The temperature in the room had dropped so much that Galley began to shiver. Suddenly, out of nowhere, a large yellow paper airplane almost four feet long sailed directly toward them from the front. Neemu pointed the wand downward. The room appeared to dive under the oncoming paper aircraft. They all ducked their heads as it passed overhead.

Galley asked, "Wow! Did you see that?"

Morrow smiled and nodded affirmatively in response.

They continued dropping until the room was rushing through the crevasse of a narrow valley, bumping between walls. The blue sky, high above, had a thin layer of clouds that looked like sparsely scattered cotton.

Neemu asked, "How do you stop this thing, Morrow? I think I'm getting sick."

Morrow reached over and took the wand from his hand. He pointed to a small red octagon off in the distance over the mountain peak they had just left. The paper airplane was still circling near the peak. Rapidly, the room rose from the valley toward the sky and headed straight for the object. A small red shape, at first barely visible, grew larger and larger until it eclipsed most of one wall. It was a gigantic stop sign floating in the sky.

Neemu yelled, "Oh no! We're gonna crash!"

Galley raised his arms over his face as if to protect himself. Then the room went dark

As the background lights came on, there was complete silence in the CAVE room except for Galley's and Neemu's heavy breathing.

Morrow looked down at Neemu removing his glasses and said, "Okay, Stopped! Well, Neemu, what did you think of that?"

"Jackson, I'm just glad I skipped breakfast this morning. And this machine is supposed to relieve claustrophobia?"

"Yes. The panic associated with the fast-paced reactions needed for flying takes people's minds off their immediate problem. It's a very compelling experience, almost like really being there."

"I noticed," Galley said. He was still swaying on his feet.

Morrow continued, "Over each mountain is a small colored portal like the red one we just entered. All of them are ports to different worlds you can fly into. Depending on the color of the portal, the CAVE room can take you to Africa, Egypt, Antarctica, Paris, Rome, Brazil and even the Moon. If people have specific destination requests we can usually accommodate those, too. Of course the red stop-sign shaped port always ends the trip no matter where you are."

"I'll have to remember this if I get bored with this cave life," Neemu commented as he rolled his chair out of the CAVE room.

Morrow added, "You don't really have to come here if you don't want to. Each living cubicle has four head-mounted-display helmets—some people call them virtual reality goggles—complete with 3-D sound that plug into the jacks by your TV set in your room. You and your family may want to use them to travel from your living room by virtual travel methods like those used here."

Galley said, "That's really something, Jackson. I'll have to show Jalisa and the kids when I get back to the room."

Morrow said, "I've got a feeling they've already found them Galley. Most kids that arrived here went straight for them when they entered their rooms for the first time."

Neemu said, "Well our kids grew up in New Mexico. I think maybe they've been a little technically sheltered. They probably won't know what to do with them."

Galley nodded in agreement.

"But thanks anyway, Jackson. We'll all enjoy having some diversion like that once in a while."

"I thought mentally-well people might enjoy the therapy, too. Dr. Hertzberg's afraid we'll all be a little skittish by the time we get to leave Antron."

"I hope not," Neemu said. "That guard was skittish enough for me, and he hasn't even been closed up in here yet."

Morrow said, "Yes, he has Neemu. He lived here for the past two months. Maybe that's what got to him."

"Well, I just hope the other security guards in here are more stable than he was."

"I'll see to it that the Colony Psychiatrist stays busy keeping them in line," Morrow stated. They left the CAVE room building and Morrow said, "Next stop, the Egg Lab."

Passing back through the Big Room, Galley noticed for the first time the number of people wandering through the complex. He had been so intently focusing on the technology of the cave he had overlooked the people. They were everywhere, young and old, walking and strolling in pairs as if in a Seurat pointillism painting on a sultry Sunday afternoon. "Where are all the kids right now?" Neemu asked looking over the landscape of the huge room and seeing few children.

Morrow pointed to a large round concrete building off to the left nestled snugly in a side cave of The Temple of the Sun and said, "In there. It's our school and daycare center. For those kids over five that don't want to stay home, we have a highly trained staff of volunteer teachers. We have grades K through twelve in there."

"What about kids who were in college before they came here?" Galley asked.

Morrow answered, "Yes, we have a few of them. Our college-age kids can study by our DVD library of correspondence courses. Of course, they can't get the degrees since the schools have all closed. At least they can still learn. We also have a number of our scientific staff that have agreed to teach courses during the Endlight Event and afterward, too. Would either of you like to volunteer to lead a course or two in our middle school or college level classes?"

"I'll be glad to teach science or physics," Neemu quickly volunteered, still thankful to be part of the Colony Staff.

Galley thought momentarily and offered, "Astronomy, that's what I would like to teach, if anyone wants to enroll in that subject, of course."

"Okay, I'll make a note of that for both of you," Morrow replied.

They continued past the school into the Hall of Giants and encountered a crowded hallway where people seemed to be standing in line. "What are all these people waiting for?" Galley asked.

"Oh, that's the line for the commissary. It appears that quite a few Colonists forgot to bring something or other. If so, they can probably buy it in there. We tried to stock the store with a good number of necessities."

A familiar voice from the crowd said, "Hey, Galley!"

Surprised that someone would know him, Galley turned to look into the crowd. He scanned the unfamiliar faces for several seconds before he saw Jalisa standing in line midway across the hallway. He excused himself from Jackson and Neemu and walked over to her, "Hi, hon, what are you doing here? Did we forget something?"

"Yes. Dog food, dummy."

Galley closed his eyes in apology and said, "I'm sorry. I didn't even think about that, I was just so worried about just getting Frosty in the cave."

Jalisa smiled, "It's all right. I found out from our neighbors that the commissary staff made a special trip to Roswell this week just to stock up on dog food for the Colonists. They brought in three tons of it."

"Wow!" Galley shook his head in amazement. "I'd better get back to Jackson and Neemu. We're still on the tour. This place is fantastic, I'll show it to you later," Galley said excitedly looking back toward the Aquarium biome and the CAVE.

"Okay, honey. I'll see you later this afternoon," she said, taking a small step forward in line.

Galley walked back to his position between Morrow and Neemu. "Sorry. I thought she needed something. She's just waiting to look in and investigate the shop."

Morrow looked over and motioned emphatically for Jalisa to join them. She looked away from Jackson to the line she had been standing in for the last thirty minutes. There were still twenty people in front of her and at least forty behind her. She knew if she left the line she would have to start all over. She hesitated for several seconds then finally stepped

211

out of line and walked toward Morrow.

As she approached, he whispered, "Our Colony Staff members don't have to stand in line with the Colonists. We need to get them rapidly in and out so they can get back to work. There is a back entrance for employees and spouses. Use it."

She smiled and blushed, "Jackson, thank you, but I don't want special."

He held his hand up to stop her in mid-sentence. "Antron rules, you must use that door. Just show the guard your PCC. It says you're an employee and don't forget to wash your hands before returning to work." He stared at Jalisa sternly for a brief second before the edges of his mouth slowly turned up into a friendly smile.

"Thanks, Jackson," Jalisa answered as she headed toward the rear of the commissary.

Shortly after passing the Underground Lunchroom and elevators to the surface they encountered another large concrete wall with sliding stainless steel doors just like they found at the entrance to the ocean. A small door off to the side of the large one had a cypher lock on the knob. Writing on the door read;

COLONISTS PROHIBITED BEYOND THIS POINT

Jackson walked to the small door, reached for the cypher lock and punched in three numbers. "Nine, two, then nine," he said to Neemu and Galley. "That's the number you must use to start the entry security procedures for the upper cave rooms. You'll see those—?"

Morrow was interrupted as a small aluminum plate on the wall near the doorknob slid back making a swishing noise. Behind it was a glass window with small instructions printed below the glass. Morrow placed his hand over the glass and waited for the flash. The computer announced, "Handprint recognized, please verify identity, speak first name, then last."

He responded, "Jackson Morrow," to the soft female voice's request.

A quiet click came from the door lock as the door began to swing open.

As they passed through the door Neemu said, "Hey, look! They forgot the ledge here. I can roll through without help."

The door closed behind them as he wheeled through. Several seconds passed before the long dim uphill cavern hallway began echoing with a high-pitched beeping. Then in unison from their PCCs came the shrill announcement, "You are entering a secured area. Please observe all instructions and warnings during your presence."

Then all went quiet except for the remaining echoes returning from the hallway ahead. Morrow said, "It's kind of irritating, but you get used to it after a few times."

"Uh-huh," Galley and Neemu responded together, relaxing their painful grimaces.

An eerie quietness filled the cave as they continued on, with an almost sub-audible hum coming from the far distance. Each of their footsteps echoed for several seconds after each step. Neemu's wheelchair rolled over tiny fallen stalactites making a steady crunching noise as it blended their footsteps in the calcite dust. They

213

veered to the left and began descending into a large round cavern. A strange view appeared as they continued to descend. The rough cave walls surrounded a large building that looked like an elongated marshmallow. Its exterior walls were iridescent white and had the texture of a puffy cumulus cloud on a summer day.

Galley stopped to look at the strange structure, "What's that?"

Morrow pointed to the room and answered, "That's the Egg Lab. What you see is thermal foam insulation around the building to keep it warm inside."

Neemu added, "Look's like that insulation is several yards thick, must work real well."

"Neemu, it's over ten feet thick all around and on top. Also, the lab floor is ten feet above the cave floor, suspended by support beams over more insulation," Morrow explained. "Come on, let's go in."

They moved up a small concrete ramp from the cave floor to the Egg Lab entrance. It reminded Galley of a Halloween spook house entrance with all the spider-webbed white insulation around the door. A black pull handle stuck out of the insulation just far enough to be easily seen. Morrow grabbed it and pulled on the heavy door. As it opened, they moved into a small anteroom and saw a brightly lit massive stainless steel door. Shimmers of moist heat flowed past them into the cavern as the door opened fully.

"Come quickly. Let's not let too much heat out," Morrow quipped.

Neemu shot into the door in front of Galley almost tripping him. "Watch out, Neemu you almost ran over me," Galley said irritably as he stepped out of the way of the wheelchair.

"I'm Sorry, Galley. My glasses are all fogged up and I still don't have full control of this thing. I just barely moved the joy stick and it shot forward, it's so powerful I think it could do wheelies if I gunned it."

"Just try to control it better. I don't want to have to take you back to MEDAID with another injury," Galley crabbed as he entered the room behind Neemu. Both were squinting into the room's white glare.

Morrow entered the airlock room and closed the door behind him. Galley looked toward the end of the room and saw two stark silver metal benches in front of a wall with large picture windows over them. On the side walls hung bright yellow plastic and paper suits ready to be worn.

"Do you two want to go in?" Morrow asked. "If you do, we have to put on those clean-room suits." He looked down at Neemu sitting in the wheelchair. "No, I think that would be a little difficult for you, Neemu. Let's just look through these windows."

They all moved up to the large picture windows. On the other side was a long expansive white room filled with gleaming stainless steel machines. Each machine had several rotating carousels that looked somewhat like Ferris wheels filled with multicolored eggs. Some were white; some were gray; still others were almost black. The sizes of the carousels and eggs ranged from the smallest at the left of the room, which appeared to be tiny blue ones, almost hummingbird-egg size, to large white ostrich eggs in the machine on the extreme right. As they scanned the maze of churning machines, each turning its eggs in a perfectly synchronized rhythm, a cartoonish puffy figure dressed in a yellow and white clean-room suit appeared and waved from the tenth tier back. It looked like a two-tone Pillsbury Doughboy.

"Ah, it's Dr. Sherman," Morrow said as he motioned for her to approach.

She waddled to the center window and pushed the intercom button below the glass. The quiet airlock room was instantly filled with sounds of humming motors and whirring gears.

"Hello, Jackson. What can I do for you?"

"Janet, I'd like for you to meet Drs. Pruitt and Hatlem. They're new on the staff, our astronomer and our radio man."

"You mean *The* Dr. Pruitt that discovered the Endlight Event?" Janet asked, suddenly realizing the connection of name and avocation.

Morrow nodded affirmatively, "Yes, one and the same." He turned to Galley and Neemu and continued, "Gentlemen, this is Dr. Janet Sherman, our head Noah here in Antron. She studied under Dr. Ginnie Wilson in the Frozen Zoo and Garden at the Cincinnati Zoo. Accordingly, she's come to us with excellent recommendations."

Janet nodded through the window and said, "I'll be out in a jiffy. I've only got to check on the reptilian section, that shouldn't take more than two or three minutes."

Morrow responded, "We'll wait. I'd like you to talk with them briefly."

Janet disappeared back into the machines with their revolving cages of precious treasures.

Six minutes later Janet appeared from the

egg rotators and walked into a small room to the right of the large windows. She then exited the side room into the airlock, in which they were waiting, through a small sliding metal door that had previously gone unnoticed. She stepped over to the dressing benches as the door hissed closed and unzipped her clean-room suit.

As she removed her head cover and jacket, Galley noticed her T-shirt that read "CREW - The Frozen Zoo" across the back. Then she removed the bulky yellow paper trousers revealing a petite figure in snug blue jeans.

"Jackson is this the same person we were talking to in there earlier? I mean Dr. Sherman?" Galley asked, pointing toward the center window.

Morrow, understanding the confusion, smiled and answered, "Yes, it's Dr. Sherman."

"I thought she was this huge woman, oh, I'm Sorry," Galley whispered as his face reddened with a blush.

She had heard him and looked over with a smile

Morrow noticed the uneasiness in the atmosphere and said, "Well, Janet would you like to explain your project to the gentlemen?"

"Sure. We have three major plans here in the cave to save as many of Earth's species as we can during Endlight."

Neemu nodded with interest and noticed Morrow looking rather impatiently at his watch.

Sherman continued, "We've had over thirty years experience at the Cincinnati zoo in our Frozen Zoo and Garden. There we were trying to preserve endangered species for futurity..." A high-pitched beeping interrupted her.

A tinny voice from Morrow's PCC crackled, "Mr. Morrow, we need you in the Control Center. Could you please come as soon as possible?"

Morrow looked at the three scientists standing around him waiting for his response, "Yes, I'll be there shortly . . . I'm in the Egg Lab now. What's wrong and who is this?"

"Sorry, Jackson. This is Geoff. We have a small problem with the hydrogen liquefier. Someone from Hydrolox wants to talk to you."

"Okay, Geoff. I'll be there in a minute." He walked over to Janet and asked, "Would you mind completing the tour, Janet? I've shown them their labs, the Aquarium and Control Center. I think they might enjoy seeing the Cryolab and Power plant. Oh, and you can walk them by the carnivore zoo, too, if you don't mind."

"No problem, Jackson. I need to check out the freezer anyway."

Morrow left the room quickly and headed back up toward the Big Room.

Janet paused briefly, trying to remember her stopping point, then continued, "In Cincinnati one of our major objectives was to preserve and propagate those plant and animal species that were then at risk of extinction. We also succeeded in setting worldwide research standards into wildlife reproduction, including interspecies surrogate mothering through embryo transplantation."

Neemu tilted his head to the side and asked, "Exactly what does that mean?"

"Oh, well for example, in one case we used a domestic housecat named Desi and implanted in her an embryo from an Indian desert cat. As a result of the surrogate motherhood, Desi gave birth to a beautiful spotted desert cat. We named him Noah."

"Oh, I see. Like surrogate motherhood in humans but with different species."

"Yes, exactly. We've also had luck with antelopes in saving the endangered African bongo." She paused to take a breath and Neemu asked, "But those don't have eggs, like these?" He motioned to the windows.

She laughed and answered, "No, Neemu, but we extract eggs or ova from their wombs, freeze them and later fertilize them with frozen sperm. The fertilized ova are then implanted in the wombs of surrogate mothers by several techniques, including laparoscopic surgery. In fact, that's our second method of preserving species here in Antron."

"You said there were three. What's the third?" Neemu inquired further.

"Simply maintaining the natural settings you see in the biomes, like the one behind your living cubicle. We can artificially inseminate any of the females in the biomes if we later find the frozen embryos or ova are defective for implantation."

"Wow, I didn't realize wildlife reproduction was so advanced," Neemu responded.

Janet continued to explain, "People began to realize many years ago that life is a tremendously intricate web of biological dependencies and balances. The loss of one species could possibly wipe out hundreds of others . . . I'm not just talking about animals but plants, too. If we were to lose a few hundred species the web would continue to grow but in a different direction. It's not inconceivable that the web could grow to

219

exterminate the human species."

"Really?" Galley asked with raised eyebrows.

"Considering the current situation, we shouldn't worry about that. But not too long ago, ecologically speaking, groups started to actively prevent the decimation of endangered species by scientific means, rather than just protesting on the Capitol steps. Our current technologies here in Antron are based on those insightful activities. They were considered somewhat pointless back then. People said, 'So what if we lose a few rare species, there are not enough of them around to make a difference saving them.' Now we're going to make a *big* difference."

"Yes, I guess you are," Galley agreed. "Are you pretty sure it's all going to work?"

"We have high confidence based on our experience, but then, what alternatives do we have?"

"Good point," Galley admitted.

Janet looked down at the floor and said, "Sorry. I've digressed. Let's get back to the tour." She turned back toward the windows and pointed toward the left of the room, "What you see are the eggs of most species of reptiles over there. We have acquired fertilized eggs from zoos across the world. Each species has at least four eggs each for redundancy."

"Redundancy?" Galley asked.

"Not all eggs are expected to hatch so we make sure that we still have a viable crop of hatchlings." She hesitated and swept her hand from the center to the left of the room, "Those eggs are all the avian species from the smallest hummingbird to the ratites."

Galley asked, "Like ostriches and emus?"

"Yes, those are the big white ones and the smaller gray ones over there." She pointed to the largest rotator to the right of the room. Its gleaming chrome egg racks holding large white and gray eggs were slowly rolling in a silent and relentless vigil over species preservation.

Galley and Neemu stared into the room and watched the rotating machinery almost hypnotically. Then Neemu, breaking from the trance, asked, "Aren't some of these going to hatch before we leave the cave?"

"Of course, we have a hatchery and nursery behind this room. It has living space for up to several hundred hatchlings. When they get large enough, we move them to the appropriate biome. The process has taken quite a bit of cooperation between Geoff and me, but we think it's a pretty airtight plan."

Neemu yawned and said, "Sounds impressive."

Janet looked at her watch. "We'd better get moving. I know you both want to get back to your labs."

Galley nodded negatively and said, "No, Janet, this is really interesting. Continue."

Janet moved toward the airlock's outer vault door and opened it slowly, "We'll move on to the Cryolab."

As they left the strange puffy building, Galley looked back at the surreal scene behind him. He never thought this would happen in his lifetime, or forever, for that matter.

After traveling for fifteen minutes uphill toward the Devil's Den the group began passing large concrete block rooms lining one side of the cavern hall. Janet began, "These rooms are where we keep the female carnivores. Separately, of course, so they don't devour each other. They're not really interesting to visit. Kinda like going to a zoo."

Galley and Neemu looked at each other.

Neemu said, "We'll pass, if that's all right?"

"Sure, the Cryolab is just ahead."

They could feel the hall chamber getting colder as they neared the cavern's outer surface opening. Even the infrared wall heaters were losing their effectiveness as they continued.

The constant hum also grew in intensity as they walked. After a few minutes of steep uphill walking and pushing, there appeared several hundred feet in front of them a large glistening metal building without windows. From the top of the building came plumes of billowing white gas illuminated by bright light.

Janet said, "That's the lab. The gas you see is escaping nitrogen fog from the cryopreservation Dewars."

"You just let it escape into the cave?" Galley asked, worrying about his heavy breathing from the long uphill climb pushing Neemu.

"Don't worry. We mix enough oxygen with it to make it perfectly breathable air. You know Earth's air is only 20 percent oxygen; the rest is mostly nitrogen and a few other gases."

"Yes, of course." Galley remembered and breathed easier as they neared the building.

On the outside wall of the Cryolab hung eight fur-lined parkas. "Put these on," Janet said as she handed them two parkas. "It's really cold in there because we don't like to waste the liquid nitrogen we use for cryo-preservation." She removed a parka from the wall that had J. SHERMAN embroidered into the lapel and pulled it on.

"Why nitrogen? I didn't see a third tank on top when I drove in here." Galley asked.

"We extract the nitrogen from the outside atmosphere and freeze it using liquid oxygen from one of the large tanks you saw. There's such an abundance of cold nitrogen in the air outside the cave it's really a pretty simple process to cool it a little more. Plus there's no explosive hazard with nitrogen and it's cold enough for our purposes. That's what we used in the Frozen Zoo for cryo-preservation and we're familiar with its effects."

"That makes sense," Galley said as he zipped the parka to his neck. "Mmm, this is *warm*."

Janet approached what looked to Galley and Neemu like a walk-in freezer door and pulled the handle. A loud *ker-chink* echoed through the cavern hallway. Then suddenly they were in darkness. Total darkness like they had never seen before. Even the dull red glow from the radiant heaters on the walls faded away.

The constant rumbling hum that they had grown accustomed to hearing and feeling slowly lowered in pitch until it became inaudible. Gradually, the generator shuddered to a halt causing various resonances throughout the cave. The metal Cryolab they were about to enter rattled and trembled as the resonances periodically matched the building's. Then all was silent except for the occasional hiss of the escaping nitrogen gas and the sounds of their breathing. In the

223

distance they heard the roar of a lion or tiger. The echoes produced an eerie moaning sound that chilled Galley to the bone. Finally, there was nothing but hissing-breathing-hissing-breathing.

CHAPTER 9
LOCKDOWN

"What the hell just happened?" Galley asked in confusion while feeling aimlessly in the air for something substantial to hold on to. His hand bumped Janet on the shoulder.

Obviously upset, Janet said, "Stay where you are. I think we just lost our power plant. Maybe that's why Jackson was called to Antron Control." Suddenly she thought of the consequences. "My God! We'll lose the animals."

Off in the distance from deep in the cave they could hear a steady droning motor growing in amplitude. Janet began to fumble through the pockets of her parka, "I know I've got a flashlight in here somewhere."

Momentarily, a small pencil beam of blue light illuminated the floor in front of her. "I hate the dark," she said staring at the small illuminated area. Calcite crystals glistened their icy-blue reflections back into her light.

"What about the Colony down below?" Neemu asked from the darkness, worrying about his kids and Rutha.

"They have emergency fuel-cell lighting down there. At least they won't be in total darkness," Janet answered.

The droning noise now became recognizable as a Hoxcart coming their way. They could see a dim headlight in the far distance approaching, its rays reflecting randomly from the crystalline walls.

Janet pointed the light into the dark hallway, "Looks like someone's coming . . . fast. They're probably heading to the power plant at the head of the cave. I just hope to God that they can fix this problem quickly."

In the increasingly colder cavern hallway a speeding Hoxcart approached the scientists, "Get that damn light out of my face," a voice bellowed from the cart as it stopped abruptly beside them.

Janet turned off the flashlight as Morrow activated a large Cyalume light stick and handed it to her, "What happened, Jackson?" The light stick gradually brightened its illumination until the cavern walls returned the strange green glow.

"Hydrolox says they just found a hydrogen leak on the surface so they had to shut down the pipes into the cavern to fix it. It shouldn't take more than an hour or so. All life support systems will be okay for that long."

"Are you sure, Jackson?" Janet asked, shivering from the growing coldness.

"Absolutely, we have enough thermal insulation and inertia in the biomes to keep them perking for at least an hour or two. The rotators are running on emergency fuel-cell power from Hox gas stored in tanks nearby. I just checked them. The living area is under emergency power lighting. Everything's fine. Believe me, Janet." As he finished speaking, a quiet warbling whine began that sounded like an electronic siren in the distance. It quickly grew in loudness until the wailing echoed up and back down the hallway. The discordant echoes made Galley and Neemu cover their ears.

"Now, what's that?" Janet screamed over the wailing tone.

"My damn Cryosensor!" Morrow yelled as he pushed a small button on the unit. The deafening tones stopped. He looked down, holding his light stick over the thermometer on his belt, "Damn! It's ten degrees in here and dropping quickly. My body core temperature has dropped to ninety-five. Janet, throw me one of those parkas."

She pulled a fourth parka from the wall and tossed it to him.

He slid his arms into the parka, "Thanks, I'll see you back at Control." He gunned the Hoxcart and sped up the cave toward the main entrance and the power plant.

Left only with her light stick and guests in the darkness, Janet decided to resist the temptation to panic, and finish the tour. She said, "Gentlemen, follow me. I'll now try to show you the Cryolab." They followed her through the sleek metallic door into a room in which the green glow seemed to hang motionless. She fanned her hand through the nitrogen boil-off trying to clear the green fog. It swirled around creating green and black patterns in the air like a living malachite wall.

Janet said, "This will never do. We can't see a thing." She retrieved her pencil flashlight and shined it across the expansive room. There were at least several hundred stainless steel vacuum Dewars, looking like giant thermos bottles, standing upright on tables all over the room and the floors under them.

Janet slipped a metallic-foil-covered glove over her right hand and reached for the nearest Dewar. After removing the thermos-like cover with her left hand, she pulled a small round tray from the bubbling liquid nitrogen. It appeared to hold hundreds of small half-inch long white straws dangling from a perforated metal retainer plate. A dense blue and green fog was falling to the floor from the lower tips of the straws. "Gentlemen," she said, "this is the future of continued life on Earth. Our Noah plan."

A short distance further toward the mouth of the cave Morrow began to feel the only effect of Twilight he had ever noticed, a shortness of breath in the cold air. He had been told to expect this and that it was normal, yet it now bothered him. The cart pulled up past the cave entrance area that still had the old sign reading TWILIGHT ZONE. Morrow always thought this was such an ironic name. It had been given to the entrance many decades before, yet it was now the Twilight barrier between Antron and the forthcoming Endlight Event.

Morrow drove the cart wildly out of the cave and up the hill toward the Hydrolox tanks. As he neared the top of the hill he targeted a bright orange street light over the pathway several hundred feet away. He continued racing toward the light and noticed a small bright obstacle in the path under the light. He was going to run over it, he decided, since there was no room to go around it.

Only twenty feet from the obstacle, as the Hoxcart headlights finally caught the object, he realized it was a reflective yellow warning sign on a striped sawhorse. The sign read;

WARNING?
HYDROGEN GAS
EXTREMELY EXPLOSIVE
NO SPARKS OR OPEN FLAMES

In the dimming Twilight, a strangely dressed figure frantically waving his arms over his head ran toward him from under the towering spherical white tank. Upon seeing the barely visible figure running in the distance and hearing shouting, Morrow stopped the cart and reached down to turn off the ignition. The engine quieted as it reached idle.

"Hey! Don't turn it off! You'll blow us all up!" the approaching voice screamed.

Morrow slowly lifted his hand from the ignition key and looked at the technician rapidly nearing his cart. He was running clumsily in a loose-fitting black rubber suit with a black head cover. The narrow eye slits barely showed the consuming panic in the technician's eyes. Having fallen several times as he ran to catch Morrow, his hands were scratched and bleeding profusely.

As the figure neared the cart, Morrow could see that he was gasping for air and tearing at his rubber hood. His futile efforts left streaks of a frozen dark red liquid smeared across the black fabric. "What in the hell is wrong?" Morrow shouted.

"Get that cart out of here! Are you crazy?" the voice screamed back. *"There's hydrogen gas all over this area. We'll to be blown to bits!"*

Morrow yelled, "Jump on," and wheeled the cart around for the technician to climb on. As they sped off, away from the hazardous hydrogen, the technician pointed toward the cave entrance and yelled, *"Go in there!"*

The cart was quickly inside the safety of the cave entrance pit. Morrow jumped off the cart and ran to a side wall toward a lighted console. He yanked the PCC from his shirt collar and spoke rapidly but clearly into it, "Antron Control, this is Jackson Morrow. We have an emergency at the entrance! I'm closing the cave and taking us into Lockdown, *now!*"

The technician overheard Morrow's communication and sprang from the cart running toward him. *"Wait! You can't do that now! We've got four other men out there working on the leak!"*

"Well then . . . how much longer are they going to take?" Morrow asked hurriedly.

The technician calmed slightly at Morrow's hesitation. "We were out there doing a final checkout and there's a big problem. It appears that there's been some recent sabotage to the hydrogen pipeline to cause a leak. We just found it. At first we thought we could have it fixed in forty-five minutes to an hour, but now we're estimating four hours. They won't even finish in *that* time if I don't get back there to help them." He looked back toward the large spherical tank. "Working around hydrogen is really touchy. Any spark or static discharge and *boom*, we're all gone."

Morrow's eyebrows narrowed as he stared at the technician, "Well, four hours is too long for the cave to stay open in the cold without power, and I don't like the danger of hydrogen loose out there . . . I've got to close the entrance."

He reached to a large panel on the wall and flipped up the yellow safety cover over a red pull switch. Above the switch was a large label reading PULL - LOCKDOWN START. Morrow grabbed the red T-bar handle and pulled. With a loud click, it popped out of the panel into Morrow's hand leaving a red light glowing in its place. Morrow dropped the handle to the floor.

The technician, now in an unbelieving state, looked rapidly between Morrow, the switch and the cave entrance waiting for something to happen. Then quietly, in an almost surrealistic atmosphere, a thin curtain of steaming water began to fall over the cave entrance. It was as if a warm rainstorm had formed above the gaping cavern entrance.

The technician laughed defiantly. "That's Lockdown?"

Morrow looked down at the entrance floor to the fine wall of falling water. A small ridge of icy stalagmites had begun to form as the warm water landed. "You see those tiny ice formations there?" Morrow asked the technician as he pointed to the floor.

"Yeah, so what?"

"In eight hours or so, those little icicles will grow into an impenetrable icy wall more than ten feet thick over the cave entrance. That means you and your crew have several hours to fix the problem and get into the cave while you can still break through the forming ice gate. Depending on the outside temperature, it may freeze even faster. As long as the power's out the elevator can't be used, either."

The technician, now obviously agitated by the finality of the new threat, screamed loudly at Morrow, "*You crazy bastard!*" and ran through the falling water to the outside. He looked back to the icy ridge that had now grown to several inches in height. The water that had fallen on his conductive black-rubber suit shoulders and hood quickly crystallized into sparkling green diamonds reflecting back the Cyalume light from Morrow's hands. He turned, looked toward the large hydrogen storage tank and began a full speed run back to his team, yelling, *"Hurry! The bastard's going to lock us out! We've got to hurry!"*

Morrow climbed on the Hoxcart and headed back down into the cave. Moments later he neared the Cryolab and saw the green glow of Janet's light stick bobbing rhythmically down the cavern pathway as she returned her team to civilization and the Colony. "Hop in the back," he said as he approached.

Janet and Galley obeyed as Neemu challenged, "Bet I can beat you down this hill, even without power."

Morrow frowned. "Neemu, this is no time for joking. Follow me."

Several hundred feet later as they neared the carnivore pens, Janet said, "Jackson, please stop here. I've got to check on the animals in there. I'm worried about the cold." He stopped the cart and she stepped to the pathway. Slowly she walked toward the building, holding her light stick at waist level in front of her.   Ahead, the white stucco carnivore chamber began to reflect the greenish glow.

While he waited for Janet to return, Jackson explained the hydrogen leak problem, raising his voice to be heard over the idling Hoxcart. "It seems we have a hydrogen leak in the lines above the cave. The technicians think it will take several hours to repair it, we'll be without power for that long—."

"What was that?" Neemu interrupted, looking into the darkness of the far cave wall.

"What was what?" Jackson asked.

"I heard something over there when you paused, sounded like footsteps."

"It's probably Janet tending the animals."

"No. It came from over there," Neemu said, pointing away from the carnivore building.

"Well then, it's probably just a stalactite falling or even a rat from outside. We have quite a few interlopers up here trying to stay warm in this part of the cave."

As Morrow finished speaking, Janet returned to the Hoxcart. "Okay, let's go. They're doing fine. It's still pretty warm in there," she said as she hopped into the cart.

Jackson gunned the Hoxcart heading back toward the Colony. With the cart picking up speed, he looked back to Janet and said, "We've begun Lockdown."

"Why? I thought that wasn't scheduled until Endlight—."

"What's Lockdown?" Galley interrupted.

"We block the cave entrance with a gate of frozen water for the duration of the event," Morrow replied. He looked back to Janet. "We have a potentially catastrophic hydrogen leak on the surface that's going to take three or four hours to fix. The technician thought it might have been caused by sabotage. We just can't take a chance on surviving the minus 145-degree outside temperature with an open entrance in a cave without our warming power. There's also a chance

233

that, with the entrance open, a hydrogen explosion could send shock waves tearing through the cavern, it could destroy everything. *Everything*." Morrow, with an uncontrollable fear in his eyes, looked back toward the cavern entrance.

"*Watch out!*" Janet screamed. "There's someone..."

Morrow turned forward just in time to see the Hoxcart hit the left leg of a figure walking near the wall. The impact knocked him to the ground. Morrow slammed on the brakes causing a gritty crunching sound as the tires dug into the pathway's calcite crystals. The sudden deceleration threw Galley off the side of the cart. He tumbled alongside for several feet. Milliseconds later, Neemu ran his motorized chair into the rear of the Hoxcart, causing his front fender to slide under the cart's bumper. Janet tumbled forward into the front seat upon impact.

As the dust settled, Morrow looked into the darkness at the victim lying on the ground. "Are you all right? I'm sorry. I didn't see you." In the reflection of the headlights, Morrow saw a face he recognized.

"Well, Jackson. That's a fine way to treat your only brother, just run over him."

Morrow jumped from the cart and offered his hand to the prone figure. "I'm so sorry, Jon. Oh, this is my twin brother, Jon Morrow," he said loud enough for the group to hear. "Are you hurt?"

Galley stood, brushed himself off and walked over to help. "Hi Jon, I'm Galley Pruitt. Do you need any help?"

"No. I don't think anything's broken, but *ow*, my leg hurts where I fell on it."

Galley noticed in the reflecting headlights the sparkle of shimmering ice diamonds on Jon's fur-lined parka hood. He reached his hand out to help Jon up, but found himself, instead, brushing Jon's shoulder. *His parka was covered with fine droplets of frozen water!* "Jackson, I didn't know you had a brother."

Jackson laughed. "He's kind of the black sheep of the family, but he's still my brother. You were going to meet him in the staff meeting this afternoon." Jackson looked back at Jon. "What in the world are you doing up here in this part of the cave?"

Jon stood and brushed himself off. "I just needed to walk in the cold. The warmth down there started getting to me. Sorry I got in your way. But now, I don't think I can walk back."

Jackson walked to the cart and looked at Janet, "Are you okay? You're bleeding."

"I think so, just a cut. I'll be all right."

Jackson sat in the front beside Janet and looked to the back of the cart. "I think we have room for one more back there now that Janet's up here. Get in."

Jon and Galley squeezed into the back of the cart and sat side-by-side, almost on top of each other. "Everybody secure?" Jackson asked.

"Too secure," Jon said. He tried to find more space for his rather large frame.

Jackson pushed on the accelerator but nothing happened. The engine strained but there was no movement . . . the tires spun in place.

"Uh, Jackson . . . I think we're stuck," Nccmu said from the darkness at the rear of the Hoxcart.

"Oh, Neemu, I'm sorry I forgot about you.

235

Are you okay," Jackson asked.

"I'm all right but I think my vehicle has a problem. I can't move either."

Jackson stepped from the cart and walked to the back carrying his light stick. "I see the problem. You're stuck under our bumper." Jackson stepped on the front of Neemu's motorized chair and shoved it back with his foot. The two vehicles separated with a clunk. Neemu's chair rolled back several inches then crashed back into the cart. "Neemu, take your hand off the joystick," Jackson demanded.

"Sorry, Jackson. I just bumped it when you broke us loose."

"See if you can back up now," Jackson asked. Neemu obeyed and the chair slowly backed away from the cart. "Okay, now we're free."

"Th-Th-Thanks, J-J-Jackson. L-L-Let's g-g-go. I'm getting c-c-cold," Neemu said through chattering teeth.

Jackson moved to the driver's seat and started back toward the Colony. "Are you with us, Neemu?"

"Ya. I-I-I'm c-c-coming."

After delivering Janet back to the Egg Lab, Galley and Neemu to the area in front of the living cubicles, and his brother to the MEDAID facility, Jackson Morrow rushed back to the emergency-powered Antron Control Center. He jumped from the Hoxcart and began banging on the door. *"Someone open this damn door and let me in!"*

Twelve seconds later, Molly O'Quinn manually opened the massive door. "Sorry, Jackson, the door is not on emergency power.

What's wrong?"

Morrow pushed her aside and rushed to the control panel. He pushed a large switch labeled EMERGENCY SECURITY POWER. Morrow then switched the black-and-white TV monitor to the surface surveillance cameras to view the large liquid gas storage tanks. The darkness flashed into brilliance as he touched another push-button on the control panel labeled EMERGENCY SURFACE LIGHTS. In the monitor he saw five men working busily around a section of large-diameter pipe at the base of the hydrogen sphere. One held up his hand and waved as a gesture to welcome the helpful light.

Jackson flicked the monitor to the VCR position causing the screen to go blank. He reached to the one of the many VCRs above the monitor and pushed the rewind button. The rewinding VCR was labeled SURFACE ACTIVITY TAPE. Two minutes later, Jackson hit the play button. The monitor showed the two large spherical storage tanks towering over the Visitor Center in the dim Twilight. The five technicians were gone from the picture and the area where they had been standing in the "live" shot could now be barely seen in the recorded ambient Twilight lighting.

Good, he thought. Maybe he could see something happen. He touched the fast-forward button on the VCR to speed up the viewing speed. After four minutes of viewing the tape at fast speed, Jackson noticed in the darkness a shape move from the cave entrance toward the hydrogen tank and pause at a lighted sign several hundred feet from the hydrogen tank. "Who's that?" Jackson shouted as he grabbed the sides of the TV panel with his

237

hands.

Molly walked over to stand behind Morrow. "What's going on, Jackson?"

"Shhh," he said. As Jackson, and now Molly, quietly watched, another figure came running from the direction of the hydrogen tank waving its arms. He could be seen to fall several times during the trip to join the first figure. The figures then joined and both returned to the cave. Some thirty seconds later a single figure ran out of the cave heading rapidly back to the large sphere. Jackson quickly pushed the rewind button, watching for the restart of the sequence he had just observed. As the video tape reached the point that the first shape just exited the cave, Jackson pushed play, stopping the fast viewing speed and slowing the picture to normal speed. There! He saw it! The Hoxcart left the cave entrance and headed up toward the large white storage tanks. It could barely be seen, but it was a Hoxcart for sure, he could see the headlights.

The cart moved slowly up the hill to a sign illuminated by the Hoxcart headlights. Morrow moved his face within a few inches of the monitor, trying to see more detail. The second darkly dressed figure came running from under the hydrogen tank tripping and falling to the ground several times on the way to the cart. Then the figure climbed on the cart as it spun around and headed back to the cave. Morrow said, "Aha! There are two of them! See them?" His nose was almost touching the monitor screen.

"Actually no, Jackson, I don't. Your head is in the way."

"Oh. I'm sorry. I didn't realize I was in your view. Now do you see them?" He stepped several feet from the monitor, letting Molly approach the screen.

"Why yes, Jackson, I do see two people," she replied, "and one of the, the cart driver, looks very much like you."

He jumped back to his position in front of the screen peering at the dark shape of the Hoxcart driver. "Damn! It *is* me. That must be when the technician told me of the leak. Just before he runs back out, I start Lockdown — watch." Thirty seconds after the Hoxcart was seen to enter the cave, the entrance began to glimmer in the Twilight. "See, that's the waterfall starting. Now the technician runs back to his buddies." A figure leaves the entrance running back toward the tanks. Jackson looked back toward Molly and said, "That *is* how it happened. I thought I might have captured something on tape, if there really was sabotage to the pipeline."

"Why would anyone want to sabotage our fuel supply, Jackson?" Molly asked.

"A few members of the Forum thought it was inevitable that someone would find us and want to stop our efforts. There are just some crazy people out there that—."

"*Jackson! Look!*" Molly interrupted, pointing toward the monitor.

He looked back just in time to see another figure run toward the entrance from the under the oxygen storage sphere. "Who is *that?* There's not supposed to be anyone out there but the technicians," Jackson said.

"I can't make out any details. The parka's covering the person's face," Molly replied. They watched as the figure ran to the cave entrance,

239

stopped just before entering to examine the embryonic ice gate at its feet and then bolted through the Lockdown waterfall into the darkness of Antron. Jackson reached out once more to touch the rewind button on the VCR. Suddenly the Control Center was plunged into total darkness. The bright monitor screen gradually dimmed into invisibility and left darkness in its place. Emergency power had failed!

CHAPTER 10
ENDLIGHT

The large chamber was filled with a cold eerie green glow. Males and females moved slowly through the room with light sticks hanging from their necks, casting strange shadows on the craggy crystalline rock ceiling. "May I have your attention?" Jackson asked. "I'd like to get this staff meeting into some kind of order . . . ."

Jackson Morrow fumbled with his light stick to illuminate his arm, and looked down at his watch. It read 1:06 p.m. He raised his eyes and gazed around the darkened Antron Meeting Room. There in front of him was *his* select scientific staff—some of the greatest minds on Earth—at *his* command. At his side was *his* Forum—seven of the richest and wealthiest businessmen in the United States . . . and his brother, Jon. Jackson was proud of his choices and his decision. "Please. Come to order!" he repeated in a slightly louder voice. The room of scientists continued mingling and talking about the recent loss of emergency power. *"Shut up! Can't any of you scientists hear?"*

The room dropped into a deep silence surpassed in intensity only by the emerald darkness in the corners of the room. Everyone eased quietly into his or her chairs. Jackson held up his green light stick in front of him so he could be seen. "Thank you for your attention. Now, I'd like to start our first official Antron Staff meeting."

After several minutes of introductory information and a quick introduction of his Forum,

241

Jackson asked that all the staff in the room introduce themselves and their duties. They started at the front left of the room and moved systematically toward the right rear. All in all, there were some 118 scientists on staff. Many were husband and wife. Others, like Galley and Neemu, had brought their spouses into Antron. Each told about themselves, their spouses and children and their previous employment and achievements. A few had won Nobel prizes in Science or Peace. Other had won Presidential Scientific Awards. The Colony Speleologist, Dr. Claro Gonzalves, had even attained a Pulitzer prize for his recent autobiography *Inside the Cave Man*. Accordingly, after sorting through almost two hours of self-introductions, the Forum unanimously appointed him to the unofficial post of Colony Scribe — to document all future staff meeting activities in writing for posterity. Graciously, CG, as he was affectionately known throughout the Colony, accepted the sole nomination. After an unofficial inauguration, Jackson walked to CG's table and handed him a small notebook computer. CG examined it curiously at first, then smiled. "Gracias. This is just like the one I use," he said.

Jackson walked back to the front of the meeting room and said, "As your first piece of recorded Antron history, CG, please enter into the record that Antron went into the ice-wall Lockdown at 11:34 a.m. this morning."

"Bueno. ¿Porque? Oh, sorry. Why?"

"Let it be recorded that we have a hydrogen leak on the surface that has been attributed to a saboteur. It appears that the same person is now

242

a member of our Colony." There was an audible gasp from the staff as Jackson Morrow paused to look around the room. "Right now, technicians are working above the cave entrance, racing against time and the growing ice gate, to fix the leak. If they fix it in time they get to come back into the cave and warm themselves with power. If not, then they freeze . . . and we *all* begin to die a slow freezing death without our emergency power." His last statement hushed his audience so that only the dripping of a few stalactites could be heard throughout the cavernous meeting room. Slowly a subaudible rumble began to quietly vibrate the room. The vibration increased in pitch until it could be heard, almost as a distant rumbling thunder. The assembled staff sat quietly waiting for something to happen. Gradually the rumble transitioned to a whine and then on to the high-pitched whistle of a jet engine. Suddenly the meeting room was bathed in the brilliance of incandescent and fluorescent light. A waft of warm air began to circulate through the room. Jackson raised his hands upward. "They fixed it! We're saved!" The room of scientists squinting through the abrupt illumination cheered with nervous relief.

Several minutes passed before the room returned to normalcy. As the room quieted, Jackson called for Geoff Chadwick to summarize the Colony emergency in detail. "I'd like our Chief Scientist, Geoff Chadwick, to describe the recent events of this unfortunate incident so that we may all understand it better. Geoff?"

Silence filled the atmosphere. Everyone waited for Chadwick to stand and address the group. Nothing happened. He wasn't present.

Seconds later the rear doors burst open, shattering the expecting quiet in the room. ". . . didn't fix the bloody emergency generator, sir. Those Hydrolox blokes fixed our main power," Geoff yelled over his shoulder to an appreciative Colonist as he rushed into the meeting room. He slowed his pace, seeing the room of waiting staff, and quietly said, "Sorry I'm late."

Jackson waited for Chadwick to take a seat at the rear of the room. "That's quite all right, Geoff. Can you bring us up to date on the emergency?"

Geoff, still breathing heavily from his hurried trip to the meeting, looked around at the audience, stood and stepped quickly to the front of the room. He paused briefly to catch his breath. "Obviously you all see that we have regained our power. This is not emergency power, but main power. I just came from the emergency power station and it appears that the standby generator overloaded during the power outage. That's why we lost emergency power. It also appears that it's no longer usable for emergency power."

"What happens if we lose power again?" a member of the Staff in the audience asked.

Geoff looked down at the floor. "Let's not think about that now . . . the Hydrolox repair team did a jolly good job of fixing the hydrogen leak, considering the circumstances up there. They're back safely in the cave, now. It seems like they had only a few inches of ice gate to break through to get in. They're some happy, but very cold and tired workers. Right now the repair team is heading to the MEDAID Center to be checked for frostbite."

Chadwick rubbed his hands together trying to bring warmth into them. "Now about the emergency . . . slightly less than two hours have passed since the main power was shut down, yet some members of the Colony have not taken the failure well. A few went into screaming panic attacks at the initial darkness . . . they were quickly calmed as the emergency power generators chugged into operation. A large number of Colonists showed a fear of a recurring darkness coupled with a mild claustrophobic reaction. It's all expected and understandable, according to Aaron Hertzberg, our Colony Psychiatrist. Isn't that right, Aaron?"

Aaron stood at the rear of the room. "Yes, Geoff. We have, in Antron, a delicately balanced artificial environment disguised to fool all the inhabitants into thinking they're in their natural environment. However, humans are not so easily fooled when they remember what's happening on the outside of this cave. Every day enormous numbers of people out there are dying. Life on the surface has become extremely tenuous, and our people know that we could follow in the same path if we have the slightest perturbation in our system. Consequently, some of our Colonists here in Antron may experience very unusual forms of psychoses. We'll just have to wait and see."

"Well said," Chadwick responded. He thanked Aaron for the information and continued, "Now that power has been returned to us, our environment should begin to stabilize. Temperatures dropped rapidly during the power outage because the cave entrance was open with no heating power. Those problems have both been solved—the cave entrance is proceeding into closure through Lockdown and our warming power is back. Activities within Antron should quickly return to normal. If any of you—and I mean any one of you—has a problem with your equipment or your specialization area here, please let me know and I'll work with you to solve the problem as quickly as possible. That's one of the reasons I'm here. My door is always open and my PCC always on." He nodded his head in appreciation, quietly walked back to his chair and sat.

Jackson Morrow moved back to the front of the room. "Thank you, Geoff. Now, since the emergency, and this meeting, have disrupted our activities for the past four hours, I'm sure that you all have projects you'd like to get back to work on . . . I know that I do."

Galley looked over to Neemu sitting beside him and whispered, "Finally! This is the most boring meeting I've ever attended."

"At least we all got to meet each other. Looks like a pretty sharp group," Neemu whispered in response. "I want to talk to that guy—I believe his name is Joe Shoole—that runs the cave communications."

Galley asked, "Why? Do you know him?"

"No. I'm just interested in how these PCCs work . . . just curiosity," Neemu whispered over Jackson's droning monologue.

" . . . So now go back into Antron and continue with your duties. I expect that we will be approaching Endlight Event conditions very soon. I'll check with the Colony Astronomer, Galley Pruitt, and let everyone know the status outside. Thank you for your attention and patience. Let's all try to get back together next week . . . I'll schedule a meeting and notify everyone a day before by PCC. Goodbye. Now, get back to work." Morrow walked from the front of the room toward Galley.

"Galley, as I said in the meeting, I'd like for you and Neemu to go back to our observatory and get a status on the Cloud. I'd want to know exactly when the Endlight Event officially starts . . . for the records. I'm going back to the Control Center to investigate this sabotage incident so just page me on the PCC when you find out something."

"Okay, Jackson . . . but before we do that can I talk with you in confidence? I really think we need to talk about—"

Jon had walked from the Forum table to stand by Jackson and interrupted, "What's the verdict on Endlight?"

Galley continued, ". . . something in private."

"Sure, Galley. Er . . . Jon could you excuse us for a minute, please?" Jackson asked.

Jon looked at the three beside him. "What you have to say to Jackson you can say to me, too. Isn't that right brother?" He stared at Jackson waiting for the answer.

Galley said, "Jon, I'd rather talk to Jackson in private."

Jackson looked at Galley then back to Jon. He paused momentarily in thought. "No, Jon. I have to respect his privacy. I'll report anything important to the Forum at a later time . . . if I deem it necessary."

Jon stared indignantly at Jackson. "No, brother, *I'll* report this incident to the Forum." He turned and stormed away.

As soon as Jon was out of hearing distance Jackson turned back to Galley. "You we're saying?"

"Jackson, can you tell me a little about your brother?"

"Why?"

"I have a suspicion that Jon is the one who sabotaged the hydrogen pipeline outside the cave."

"Don't be ridiculous, Pruitt. Why would you suspect my brother?"

"Jackson, that's why I wanted to know more about him . . . I want to clear or confirm my suspicions."

"You're being absurd, Pruitt. How dare you accuse one of the Forum, especially my brother, of a malicious act to our environment?"

"Look Jackson, please just humor me. Tell me about Jon's past . . . you said he's the black sheep of the family . . . I just want that statement clarified in my mind. Why *is* he the black sheep?"

"Okay . . . many years ago when I was making a killing in real estate, Jon asked me to fund a startup electronics company in Silicon Valley with him. He wanted do it as a partnership with both of us putting up equal funding. His vision was to create exotic and extremely high-tech electronics. I trusted him and bought in."

"Go on," Galley said.

"Jon is an engineer, and a very damn good one. That doesn't necessarily mean he's a good business man . . . I put over three million dollars into a small corporation he named TwoMorrows Electronic Systems . . . he lost it all on some stupid dream he was chasing to get rich. I found out later he didn't have a cent to match my money. I trusted him as a brother and he cheated me like a crooked used car salesman."

"Really? What happened then?" Neemu

asked.

"He prepared to file for Chapter 13 bankruptcy while still begging me for more money to keep operating. I refused. Then a few weeks later I was struck by lightning as I told you before, Galley. I thought it an omen."

"Yes, I remember."

"I took my problem of cryanesthesia to my brother and asked him to help. I gave him another five million dollars to create something . . . anything, and he invented the Cryosensor I wear." Morrow looked down at the instrument on his belt. It read sixty-four degrees. He pointed to a small logo on the side. Embossed in the metal casing were the letters TMES.

"So, Jon took advantage of you at first, then later almost saved your life," Galley reasoned.

"Yes, but he's cost me a pretty penny. I haven't regained my original investment in him, yet. His last effort was to develop and manufacture these PCCs we all wear . . . I made no money on that, either. Now, that Jon's in here with us, and our company's closed, I guess that I never will."

Galley put his hand on Jackson's shoulder. "Well, Jackson, that's not so bad. If that's all your brother did, it appears he made a few honest mistakes. At least he didn't do anything malicious or destructive to you."

"Galley, Jon has always been jealous of my success and wealth. In some ways I think he started that foolish company just to try to run me broke. Also, I did find that several of my potentially large Beverly Hills property deals worth millions were screwed up by him—he submitted false offers for unbelievable amounts on the properties, knocking real prospective buyers out of contention. I found that out through a friend at a private detective agency. Jon doesn't know, to this day, that I know it was him."

"Are you sure? Why would he do that?" Galley asked.

"Envy. Even as a kid Jon coveted my friends and accomplishments. We'd start a lemonade stand together and I'd outsell him, hands down. He made plain lemonade exactly by the recipe . . . I used half lemons and half limes. When we counted our money at the end of each day, I had twice as much as Jon did. Each time that happened, he beat me up. It got to the point I was trying to get people to buy his lemonade instead of mine so I wouldn't get beat up at night."

Galley glanced over to Neemu who was sitting quietly enthralled in the story. "Neemu, did you have lemonade stands in Sweden?"

Neemu rubbed his chin in thought, then answered, "No. But I understand the concept. I think our equivalent moneymaking pastime back then was shoveling snow. The faster kids always made more money . . . sometimes they got beat up, too."

Jackson smiled and continued, "Since we've grown up it's been the same. He's been jealous of my fortune in real estate for a long time, saying it was just my being in the right place at the right time . . . and it probably was. But I also made it happen by making sure I *was* there. I sometimes worry that Jon might do anything to damage my reputation or status."

Galley looked over his shoulder to Jon across the room then back to Jackson, "Jackson, that confirms my suspicions. I have to tell you something I now believe to be true."

"Yes. Go on."

"Do you remember when you ran into Jon with our Hoxcart this morning?"

"Yes. Why?"

"Didn't you think it a little strange for him to be walking in that part of the cave in the cold and darkness?"

"Why, yes, I do remember thinking it was an odd occurrence, at the time."

Galley lowered his voice. "There was an even stranger incident, Jackson."

"What happened?"

"When I came over to help Jon up from his fall, I felt the shoulders of his jacket . . . they were covered with frozen water drops. So was the fur and fabric on his parka hood . . . ice pellets."

"So what?"

"Jackson, don't you see? To get wet, Jon had to pass under the cave entrance after you started Lockdown. That water on him was from the warm waterfall overhead. It froze as it hit his parka because he had been outside in the extreme cold. If he had been in the cave and walked under the waterfall, the water wouldn't have frozen so quickly—it would have still been wet."

Jackson thought back to the video tape of the stranger entering the cavern. In his mind, he couldn't see a face but the build was similar to that of his brother. "Thank you for your concern, Galley," Jackson said coldly. "I'll look into this. You may be right. I hope not." He turned to walk away and hesitated. Then he stepped back to face Galley and reached out his hand. "Thank you

251

again, Galley. I really do appreciate your honesty and integrity."

"I just wanted you to know what I saw, Jackson. I'm not forming any judgments about your brother but I have some doubts about his activities."

Jackson turned away and walked from the meeting chamber into the open hall, heading toward the Control Center. Neemu looked back to Galley. "Did you really see all that, Galley?" Neemu asked.

"Yes. Did you see anything?"

"Galley you know I was looking at the smashed rear end of the Hoxcart the whole time. All I could see was darkness and shadows from your movements in front of the cart."

"Yes, of course. Sorry, Neemu I forgot about your accident . . . oh, by the way, how's your leg?"

"Doing better, thank you. I'm going to try to use a crutch this evening. My success depends on the strength of the painkillers Dr. Mason gave me. Strong . . . I walk. Weak . . . I fall down. Ya. Simple as that."

Galley chuckled. "Come on Neemu, let's get back to work."

They arrived at the Com Center after stopping to chat with several other staff members on the way. Colony scribe, CG, asked them if he could be the first to know when they discovered the Endlight Event condition. Galley agreed. He also found that Claro could be reached on the PCC by simply calling "CG." That made his life seem simpler.

Upon entering the Com Center room, Neemu rolled his chair to the short-wave radio console and switched the power control to ON. Galley went to the opposite side of the room and switched on the radio telescope computer and optical monitor scope. Slowly, the room began to sizzle and crackle with radio noise. The Com Center's hard floor and ceiling created an irritating reverberation from the crescendo of static. Galley frowned at Neemu. "Hey Neemu!" he screamed, "turn that damn thing down and see if you can raise anybody up at the Naval Observatory in D.C. . . . I want to ask about their Endlight prognosis."

Neemu complied and lowered the volume. "Okay, Galley, but what call signal and frequency are they using?"

"If I remember right, the guy I talked to there was named . . . something Micolo . . . let me see, now . . . Ed? Yes! That's it. But the radio station call he gave me for NRL was—I've got it here in my pocket—where in the hell is that note I wrote to myself?" Neemu waited patiently while Galley rummaged through his pockets. Seconds later he removed a small pocket organizer from his inside coat pocket and scanned through the screens. "*Here* it is!" Galley exclaimed, jamming his finger onto the organizer's screen. "W1AW—on 80 and 160 meters."

"Got it. Thanks, Galley." Neemu acknowledged as he began turning knobs on the receiver. The static quieted to a few lightning crashes per second, those occurring mostly over the cooling oceans and seas far from Antron. "Calling W1AW . . . CQ W1AW. This is—." Neemu looked at Galley and whispered, "What call should *I* use?"

"Use Darkstar. I think it'll get their attention faster."

"Wha—? Oh, okay. Whatever you say."

Neemu turned back to the microphone. "This is Darkstar calling. Over."

Galley noticed the computer monitor begin its power-up tests, but saw nothing on the optical telescope monitor. It remained blank and dark. He patiently waited several more minutes. Finally, he moved his hands to the telescope keyboard and typed in SCAN WESTERN SKY DENSITY, hoping to wake the system up and measure the amount of solar attenuation from the Cloud. The computer screen glowed without response for seconds. Then came the messages:

RADIOTELESCOPE MALFUNCTION:
RADIOTELESCOPE AZIMUTHAL FINAL
ALIGNMENT - INCOMPLETE

SIDEREAL CLOCK DRIVE MOTOR -
    OFF
MASER LN COOLER -
    OFF
WAVEGUIDE FEED AMPLIFIER -
    OFF

OPTICAL TELESCOPE MALFUNCTION:
CCD CAMERA IMAGE SENSOR ARRAY -
    DESTROYED

MISSING ARGUMENT:
SKY SCAN FREQUENCY RANGE -
    UNSPECIFIED

Galley sat motionlessly staring at the screen as the messages appeared. After several seconds of sustained disbelief, he muttered, "Dammit! I thought Morrow said this thing was working." He stood and began pacing across the front of the confusing screen looking up at it each time he passed by.

Unaware of the problem, Neemu continued his radio search for NRL. "Calling W1AW . . . Calling W1AW . . . this is Darkstar. Come in." He put down the microphone and glanced to the other side of the room to see Galley pacing in front of the radio telescope screen. "What's up Galley?"

"Let's just say our telescope has some problems."

"What kind of problems? Are they serious?"

"Neemu, come look for yourself. I just asked it to do a simple sky density scan and it gave me a book of error messages back." Neemu rolled his chair over to Galley's console and read the computer's output.

Neemu scanned the error readout. "Well, let's see . . . the alignment calibration isn't finished, the drive motor needs to be connected, the liquid nitrogen valve needs to be opened and the TWT amplifier has to be turned on." He scanned down to the second malfunction indication and touched the screen, pointing to the CCD camera error. "Those other things all look fixable but this blown image sensor doesn't make much sense. Something or someone blinded the telescope."

"Let me look at that again," Galley said as he moved to examine the monitor screen. "You're right Neemu. Those other things are just oversights in setting up the telescope. The CCD problem is something else. I think I'll take the elevator to the surface observatory dome and check the telescope to see if these messages are right. I'll also fix the problems, if I can, and try to finish the telescope alignment."

"Does the elevator still work?" Neemu asked as he rolled his chair back to the radio console.

"I think Jackson said it would be available throughout Endlight since it can only carry a few people at a time. It shouldn't pose much of a threat for invasion from the outside."

Neemu laughed. "Ya. If they do try to get in we'll just get them two-by-two like you people got the British."

Galley turned to leave the Com Center laughing. "Shhh . . . don't let Geoff hear you say that, Neemu. Bye, I'm going topside. It's pretty cold up there—even inside the dome. Send someone out for me if I don't come back in an hour." He pulled on his heavy fur-lined parka and started for the door.

Neemu called out to Galley, "Be careful. You may want to stop by the Control Center and check the security monitor on your way out just to make sure everything is all right up there."

"I'll do that. Thanks." Galley left the room and headed toward the Control Center.

"W1AW . . . this is Darkstar calling. Do you read?" Neemu continued. As he listened and turned the radio dial, trying to find a signal, he began to feel the emptiness of the airwaves. Signals had previously been piled on top of each other on this band trying to work stations across the world. Now it was just silence . . . and static. Humanity had disappeared from the face of the Earth—at least from a radio signal standpoint. He keyed the microphone once more. "CQ W1AW . . . CQ W1AW . . . This is Darkstar calling. Is anybody there?"

"Darkstar . . . this is A-F-Zero-C-M . . . do you read?"

Neemu jumped to attention in his chair at the unexpected interruption in silence. "Yes. Loud and clear. Could you repeat your call? I'm sorry I didn't get all the letters."

"It's Adam-Frank-Zero-Charlie-Mary—AF0CM—and what is this Darkstar stuff? This isn't citizens' band, you know. Over."

Neemu quickly grabbed a pencil to record the call in his logbook. He finished the entry and picked up the microphone. "AF0CM, this is SM3WAM from New Mexico. I was asked to use Darkstar as a code to call the Naval Observatory. I don't know what it means. Where are you located and what's your handle? I'm Neemu. Over."

"Okay, SM3 . . . uh, Darkstar. This is the U.S. Air Force Command Center at Cheyenne Mountain. My name is Captain Bill Zyda, Com Officer. There are about 500 people in here trying to stay warm. Yours is the first signal I've heard all day. What's your situation? Are you in trouble? Over."

"No, but thanks for the concern, Captain." Neemu knew the existence of Antron had to be carefully guarded. He suddenly realized he would have to be evasive in his conversation. "There are several of us here roughing it in a small cave in Southern New Mexico but we're okay and warm for now . . . have you heard the Naval Observatory on the air lately? I'm an astronomer and would like to find the status of Endlight. I don't even know the outside temperature. Over."

"Darkstar . . . this is AF0CM. No, Neemu, I haven't heard their signal in a few days but I

257

understand they have a few hundred people in the underground War Center there, holed up against the cold. Just keep trying; I think you'll get through. Oh, and as far as Endlight goes—it's officially here, as of ten-hundred hours this morning. We've got about a month to go, now. Then it's over for us. Over"

"AFOCM . . . Darkstar. Thanks for the info . . . but what do you mean you've got a month to go? Endlight is supposed to last three to four months. Over."

"Sorry for the confusion, Neemu. At our current rate of consumption we'll be out of supplies in about thirty days. That's our own problem. This facility deep in the mountain was designed to protect us from nuclear war and keep us safe from three weeks of fallout. Nobody ever planned for a four-month stay. I just don't know what we'll do about that. Over."

Neemu paused for a moment of prayer before keying the microphone. "I'm sorry to hear that, Captain. We're not sure how long we'll last either . . . we just have to keep the faith." Neemu hesitated, wondering if even Antron could really last through the four-month Endlight Event, then continued, "Stay in touch. I'll be on this frequency several times a day to check the outside status. We have a small telescope here and I'll be tracking the Cloud, looking for its end. I'll report our prognosis daily. Over."

"Thanks. It's been good hearing from the outside world. Stay warm. AFOCM over and out."

"Darkstar over and out." Neemu turned the volume down on the receiver and moved to the radio telescope control console. He flipped the switch on the console marked SURFACE INTERCOM and called, "Galley, are you up there?"

Inaudible to Neemu over the cooling fans, a radio signal slowly began its call from the quietened receiver. "Darkstar, this is W1AW. Darkstar this is W1AW. Come in please . . . This is Andrew Witherhouse here . . . please come in . . . ."

"Yes, Neemu, I'm up here and it's cold as shit, even in this plastic dome. Must be zero in here," Galley responded over the intercom. "Check the scope status."

Neemu typed   SCAN WESTERN SKY DENSITY   into the radio telescope computer console. The screen paused then displayed:

RADIOTELESCOPE MALFUNCTION:
MASER LN COOLER -
    OFF

OPTICAL TELESCOPE MALFUNCTION:
CCD CAMERA IMAGE SENSOR ARRAY -
    MISSING

MISSING ARGUMENT:
SKY SCAN FREQUENCY RANGE -
    UNSPECIFIED

Neemu scanned the error messages and smiled. "Looks like you've been busy up there. What have you found about the CCD array?"

"It appears to be melted. I can't understand that. It's like we pointed it directly at the Sun . . . but there is no Sun up there. There's nothing out there bright enough to do this . . . and it doesn't look like sabotage–it's well protected by lenses."

259

Neemu reread the error messages. "Hmm. That's very strange. Why haven't you turned on the liquid nitrogen to the maser?"

"I can't find the stupid N_2 valve."

Neemu grabbed the manual sitting by the console and flipped to the page describing the maser cooling system. "Hold on just a minute. I've got the manual here."

"What does it say?"

"Wait a minute! I haven't taken Emily Woods Reading Dynamics yet."

"Evelyn."

"Who's Evelyn?"

"Evelyn Woods, not Emily."

"Well, Evelyn or Emily, they both sound the same to me—American."

"Neemu, I'm up here freezing my butt off and you're making jokes. Hurry up."

"Okay, okay . . . here it is. It says the valve is at the focus of the antenna, just under the feed line."

"Great! That's ten feet over my head—way up there."

"Got a ladder?"

"I don't see one . . . wait . . . there is one over there by the optical telescope. Let me get it."

"Okay, I'll wait. While you're doing that you might be interested to hear that I made contact with the outside."

"With NRL?"

"No, the Air Force installation at Cheyenne Mountain."

"What's happening there?"

"Same thing as here. Staying warm underground."

"Who did you talk to? Was it a Sergeant?"

"No, a Captain Zyda. He said they only have enough supplies for a month."

"Oh, God help them . . . uh . . . just a minute Neemu while I get up here to this feed line . . . I see it! There's that stupid valve. Now, just a turn . . . umph . . . damn! It won't move, Neemu . . . frozen shut."

"Do you have anything to beat on it with, Galley?"

"Just this wrench in my hand."

"Try tapping gently, but not so hard as to bust the valve. We don't need liquid nitrogen all over the dome—the cold vapor would disable all the telescopes."

"Yeah. It would probably disable me, too. Okay here goes . . . umph . . . now twist you damn bastard . . . umph. . . it moved! Neemu, I turned it but I'm not sure if I turned it all the way on. Can you try the scan again?"

Neemu re-keyed the sky scan command. The screen now displayed:

OPTICAL TELESCOPE MALFUNCTION:
CCD CAMERA IMAGE SENSOR ARRAY -
    MISSING

MISSING ARGUMENT:
SKY SCAN FREQUENCY RANGE -
    UNSPECIFIED

"Looks like you did it buddy. We're back in the radio telescope business!"

"Okay, now I'm going to replace the CCD with the spare I found up here . . . that Jackson thought

261

of everything."

"Give me a call when you want to try the sky scan again. Oh, you might to be interested to know we're officially into the Endlight Event . . . Captain Zyda told me we entered it at around 10:00 a.m. this morning."

"I think I could have told you that. It's really dark out there. The pinkness is gone. I can't even see the Cloud, now . . . just a pitch black band of starless sky."

"That's just great. Now we just wait for four more months. Galley, I'm going back to the radio and see if there are any more souls out there. Call me when you're ready to retest."

"Okay. It'll be a few minutes. I've got to disassemble the optical eyepiece."

Neemu returned to the radio console and turned up the receiver volume. The speaker boomed, ". . . calling. Are you there Darkstar? This is W1AW."

Neemu excitedly grabbed the microphone. "W1AW . . . W1AW . . . this is Darkstar. Do you read?"

"Yes, Darkstar . . . loud and clear. Who is this? Galley, is that you?"

Neemu thought *how did he know that?* "No, this is Neemu Hatlem. Who is this?"

"Andrew Witherhouse in the War Center."

"How do you know Galley?"

"Project Darkstar in Arecibo. Over."

"You mean what he told me really is true . . . about your discovery there?" Neemu asked anxiously.

"Yes, Neemu I was there. I lived through the quake and was picked up by that bloody Aurora right after it dropped him off in New Mexico. It brought me straight to Bolling Air Force Base here in Washington."

The air went quiet as Neemu recounted Galley's story. He had never believed the whole story. He thought it just a cover to explain Galley's predicament with the kids. "Just a minute, Andrew. Galley *is* here with me—he's just unavailable to talk right now. Can you call back in an hour or so . . . or we can call you."

"Sure. I'll be around the Star Wars observatory all evening watching for more flash events."

"*More flash events*?" Neemu asked almost trembling with anxiety.

"Yes. Those events we found in Arecibo have been coming more frequently and are getting brighter with each flash . . . the one we had this afternoon, about 1:00 p.m. here, was almost as bright as the sun. So bright, in fact, that we saw a fraction of a degree warming in the atmosphere shortly thereafter—and it melted our telescope CCD image array."

"Wow! Where did the flash come from?"

"The Eastern sky, sweeping from north to south . . . like a giant spotlight from the sky."

Now realizing that the flash must have destroyed their CCD camera too, Neemu crushed the microphone button with his thumb. "Andrew, I've got to go tell Galley. We'll get back to you within the hour. W1AW this is Darkstar. Over and out."

Neemu turned rapidly to move to the surface intercom, almost toppling his wheelchair. "Galley, are you there? You're not going to believe what just happened. I finally believe you. There *is* someone out there."

Silence. "Galley are you there?" Neemu shouted into the intercom.

Several more seconds of silence followed his call to topside. Then Galley replied, "Yes, I'm here. I was in the middle of an intricate process with my hands full. Now what's so damn important that you had to interrupt me? And what do you mean you believe me?"

"Galley, do you know someone named Andrew Witherhouse?"

Silence, again. Then a somber voice from the intercom speaker said, "Yes, Neemu. I knew him . . . he died in the quake at Arecibo. Remember I told you about that trip and you didn't believe me?"

"Galley, I believe you now. I just talked to Andrew."

"*Neemu, what did you say?*"

"Andrew is alive in Washington, D.C. I just talked to him over the radio. He left Arecibo right after you got back on something called Aurora. You're supposed to talk to him over the radio within the hour."

"That's wonderful! I'll be right down. Give me a few minutes to replace this image array. I'm almost done . . . I still can't figure out what happened to it."

"Er, Galley, I think I've got the answer to our mystery. It's a long story so I'll tell you when you get here."

"See you in a minute." Galley left the intercom station and resumed the telescope repair.

Neemu pulled his PCC from his collar and said, "Call CG."

The PCC responded, "In living quarter . . . calling."

"Hello, this is CG."

"CG, Neemu here. You wanted you to be among the first to know. We're officially in the Endlight Event as of 10:00 a.m. this morning. I just received word from the Air Force Command Center in Colorado.

With sadness in his voice he answered, "Thanks, Neemu. How many souls are *there*?"

"Where?"

"At the Command Center."

"I think there are about 500 there . . . but they only have a month's worth of power and supplies."

"O Dios mio . . . sorry, Neemu, I'll note that information for our records."

"There's more noteworthy information, but I'd rather tell you in person."

"Okay. Come by the room tonight about 9:00 p.m. . . . room 217."

"See you then." Neemu clipped his PCC back on his collar and left the Com Center for the Control Room.

Jackson Morrow, pacing the floor in the Control Room, screamed, "What do you mean you were out there following someone?"

Jon pointed to the security monitor's freeze-frame image of the figure entering the cave entrance. "See that person entering the Lockdown gate?"

"Yes!" Jackson answered angrily.

"That's *not* me! See that hood on the parka? It's not fur lined!" Jon shouted.

265

"Well it *looks* like you . . . and your jacket *was* covered with ice when I ran into you . . . remember?"

"Wait a minute, Jackson. Watch. You'll see another person enter the cavern behind him."

Jackson thought back to when he originally viewed the taped replay of the figure running into the cave. He played the scene over in his mind. Then he realized that the power failed immediately after he watched the first figure enter. "Okay, Jon, I'm game. Let's watch," Jackson conceded.

Seconds later another figure, this one with a fur-lined parka, entered the cavern entrance with a Pink-Panther-like sneaking movement. Jackson laughed. "Well brother, that does look like your dorky style . . . but it just shows that there were two people out there. Who's the other person? If you really were following him you should have seen his or her face."

"Jackson, you know how dark it is up there. In the shadows we were in, there was no light for identification."

"Why didn't you get —?" Jackson's shouting was halted by Neemu's entrance into the Control Room.

"Jackson, we fixed the telescope and discovered we're in Endlight. Oh, sorry. Did I interrupt?"

Jackson, half-frowning from the argument and half-smiling from the news, looked around at Neemu entering the room. "You and Galley measured Endlight with our telescopes? That's wonderful! Uh . . . well, not that we're in Endlight. I mean our telescopes measured Endlight? "

"No, not exactly. We just fixed the optical

telescope . . . it had a burned-out CCD. The radio telescope only needed some operational tweaking to make it run."

Jackson walked from the security console to stand by Neemu. "Well, Neemu, I told Galley a long time ago he needed to be here to finish putting the thing into operation. He knew that. How *did* you determine that we're in Endlight, then?"

"I talked to another underground facility in Colorado. *They* told me we're in Endlight," Neemu said.

"Another underground facility? Where? Who's in charge? How many animals?"

Neemu could immediately sense Jackson's jealousy but found it hard to understand. Other lives were being saved, elsewhere. Why would that make him angry. "The Cheyenne Mountain U.S. Air Force Command Center, that's where. And I don't know who's in charge. . . maybe the President. There's also another underground colony in the War Center under Washington, D.C. All combined, there are probably another eight or nine hundred people hibernating elsewhere in caves. Don't know if they have animals, though. Probably not."

Jackson smiled again. "No. No animals. I'm the only one to think of them. I knew I would be."

As Jackson finished his sentence Galley rushed by the door. He glanced through the window to see Neemu and the small gathering, and entered. "Hi, folks. What's up—besides the Cloud? We're in Endlight, you know . . . and all the telescopes are working."

Jackson walked back to the console and glanced again at the still-frame frozen image of the fur-lined hooded figure. "We just found that out. Now, according to your earlier predictions, we only have to keep going another four months."

Galley walked across the room to stand by Jackson and view the monitor. He nodded politely as he passed Jon who looked through his gesture, ignoring him.

"Yes, I believe that to be true," Galley answered. However, now that our telescopes *are* working we can analyze the Cloud in more detail and possibly update our prognosis."

Jackson moved his head closer to the security screen and tilted his chin upward to see the figure through his reading glasses. "Good. Why don't you and Neemu go do that for us?"

Galley peered at the figure on the monitor and asked, "Who is that?"

Jackson turned to look at Galley. "Don't know, but I'm going to find out. Now, go study Endlight. I want more reliable data."

Galley looked down at Neemu and said, "Yes sir. Let's go, Neemu." Galley followed Neemu from the Control Room and noticed that Jackson and Jon restarted their argument as they left.

Reentering the Com Center, Galley moved to the telescope console and looked back at Neemu. "What were you saying about the CCD burnout? You said something about solving the mystery."

"Ya, when I talked to Witherhouse—"

"I still can't believe you talked to Andrew. And he's okay?"

Neemu continued, ". . . ya, and he said something about flashes becoming more frequent and brighter. One this morning was so bright it burned out the image array at the Naval

Observatory. That's what made me realize what happened to ours."

"It makes sense, Neemu. I think you're right."

"Galley, what are the flashes? Where are they coming from?"

"All we found out is that they are connected to some form of intelligence not of this Earth. Why they are out there, nobody knows . . . possibly some elaborate signaling system that we don't have time to decode because we're all freezing to death down here. What irony to finally find the signals we've all been searching for when nobody cares. Maybe—"

Suddenly the short-wave receiver's speaker boomed, "Darkstar this is W1AW. Darkstar, come in. Andrew Witherhouse here. Galley are you there?"

Galley rushed to the radio console, grabbing the microphone and pushing the talk button simultaneously. "W1AW, this is Darkstar. Galley Pruitt here. Andrew, I thought you died down there in Arecibo. I can't believe you're alive! What's going on up there?"

Neemu looked at Galley and mouthed, "I'm supposed to be keying the transmitter, not you, Galley . . . you're not a ham."

Galley covered the microphone with his hand and said to Neemu, "I don't think the radio police are out in force today, Neemu. You don't have to play ham operator any more . . . you and your family are already in. Remember?"

Galley quickly uncovered the microphone and continued, "What happened to the other people there at Arecibo . . . and what's with these flashes?

Are these the same ones we saw there?"

"Galley, I think so. Our radio telescope here has found the preceding radio signal now possesses the Doppler shift it never had before. That can only mean that the signals or beacons, or whatever they are, have lost synchronous lock on Arecibo. It's like they suddenly stopped tracking the Earth's rotation and just stopped in space, letting us revolve below."

"What do you make of that, Andrew?"

"We have several theories but none of them are provable. We're just watching and waiting. I wish we could go back to Arecibo and try to communicate with the bloody things."

"Me, too, Andrew. However unless these things just go away with the end of this event, I think we'll have plenty of time to study them later."

"Righto, Galley. We're hoping."

"Andrew, what happened to Sondra and Samuels after the quake?"

"I never found out, Galley. I was still at the runway when the earthquake hit. I left on Aurora about fifty-five minutes after it dropped you off. It came back for me. The runway was beginning to develop some cracks from the large aftershocks so we barely made it out ourselves. I asked the pilot to fly over the dish as we left the island. The towers and the bow assembly had basically decimated the dish. The antenna control building was crushed to the ground. I just don't see how anyone could have lived through it, I'm sorry to say."

"Well, at least you made it. I'm happy for that. Have you found any more about the Cloud? We just got our telescope working here and haven't had time to study it yet."

"Where are you, Galley?" Galley looked at Neemu, waiting for a suggestion.

"Tell him a small cave in Southern New Mexico. I used that earlier," Neemu said.

Galley shook his head no. "We're in the Luray Caverns in West Texas. It's rustic and crude, but somewhat warmer in here than outside. We don't know how long we can hold out, but we think we can make it four months."

"You had better be able to make it longer than that, Galley."

"What do you mean? Why?"

"I was just going to tell you when you asked me about the Cloud . . . we found a large center of mass about three months away. The internal gravitational attraction of the Cloud has changed its shape. It's getting longer and thinner. But it's still in our light for the duration."

"Well, Andrew, if you found the center of mass at three months away—that means Endlight will last *six months instead of four*?"

"I'm afraid that's true, Galley. Can you make it that long?"

"How cold will it get by then?"

"We have predictions all over the temperature scale, but the consensus is about minus 350 Fahrenheit."

"Oh, God, Andrew . . . we're all going to die. We can't stand those temperatures for that long."

"Neither can we Galley. We've got enough supplies for just over four months. Then power goes and we freeze in a week or two. Shortly thereafter our civilization dies. All trace of life is gone from the Earth."

271

Galley slowly placed the microphone on his lap and sat silently looking down. "Galley are you there? Galley are you there? Can you hear me? I'm losing you . . .."

CHAPTER 11
THE KANGAROO DECISION

Neemu reached out to grab the cord and pulled the microphone from Galley's lap. Neemu slowly pushed the button. "He's all right, Andrew. Just a little saddened by your news. We'll talk later . . . same frequency. W1AW—Darkstar. Over and out." Neemu put his hand on Galley's shoulder. "Galley, we can still probably make it. If we tell Jackson right now, we can ration supplies to add another two months to our stay—that's only 50% more time here."

Galley looked up, wiping his eyes. "Sorry for the emotion, Neemu. I never dreamed my *thrilling* discovery would really wipe out all life on Earth . . . but now, you know Neemu, I think you may be right. Our power *is* coming from liquid oxygen and hydrogen. That should last a long time . . . and as it gets colder, it will be easier to liquefy the gases from our atmosphere. We had better start liquefying right now to keep our tanks full. It just might work. We've got to tell Jackson."

"He's not going to like this news, Galley. Will you tell him?" Neemu asked.

"Yes, chicken, I will," Galley answered with a smirk. "Let's go back to the Control Center."

As they neared the Control Room, the shouting could still be heard. Jackson Morrow was accusing Jon Morrow of attempted sabotage and conspiracy. Jon was trying again to explain his reason for leaving the cave, while Jackson screamed

273

insults and indignities in return. The fight was hopelessly deadlocked.

Galley took a running start and burst through the Control Room door, startling both Jackson and Jon. They stared at him in silence for several moments. "Well, it sounds like we need a jury here. This argument is only going to be solved by evidence and testimony. Do we have legal due process in Antron?"

Neemu wheeled silently into the room and backed up Galley. "Ya. *Do* we have that here?"

Jackson Morrow looked between Neemu and Galley and stood silent for seconds. Then he put his hand to his chin and began pacing slowly around the room. "No. I never actually thought we'd need anything besides the Forum . . . another oversight. But that's all right. We can improvise. Neemu, go outside and find thirteen Colonists walking by. Bring them in here. We're going to have court and they'll be the jurors."

Galley raised his eyebrows as Neemu left the Control Center. "A kangaroo court? Jackson, I'm surprised at you."

Jackson Morrow looked directly at Jon. "We can't have a potential saboteur running around here threatening the existence of our Colonists and biomes. *I want a decision, now!* I'll get it through due process, just like on the outside. Do you have a problem with that, Jon? I promise —."

Galley interrupted, "Let's wait for your jurors, Jackson."

Several minutes later Neemu reentered the Control Room alone. "Where are the thirteen jurors?" Jackson Morrow screamed. "You came back without them. Why?"

Neemu rolled back to his previous position by Galley. "Jackson, do you have any idea what time it is?" Neemu asked.

Jackson looked at his watch. "Yes, of course, it's 10:32 p.m."

Neemu continued his explanation, "I didn't bring people back in with me because there is nobody out there. Everyone's asleep, or in their cubicle for the night."

"Okay then you and Galley are the jury. Let me see if Molly is still here." Jackson walked out of the Control Room toward the rear of the building.

"I think my brother's gone nuts," Jon said quietly. "Can you believe he's doing this to me?"

Neemu looked at Galley pleading for help. "Neemu, I think our news can wait . . . I don't know about the rest of you, but I'm exhausted," Galley said, yawning.

"Me, too. It's been a really long day . . . I'm also starving," Neemu added, then yawned in response.

"I'll buy you dinner, Neemu. If Rutha has eaten, do you want to eat with us?" Galley asked.

"Sure. I'll do it even if she hasn't eaten. Let's go." Neemu said as he started for the Control Room door. "See you in the morning, Jon."

"Night, Neemu."

Galley followed Neemu from the Control Room out of the Center, leaving Jon alone. Jon looked briefly around the empty room and also left for his cubicle, leaving Jackson alone to close up the Control Center.

The next morning Galley awakened to find Jan sitting in the center of the living room with one of the virtual reality helmet displays on his head. His hands were jabbing wildly into the air in front of him. With each stab Jan yelled, "Yah!" and Frosty nipped playfully in the air at his fingertips. Galley smiled, rolled over and kissed Jalisa on the cheek.

"Good morning. What time did you get home last night? How did you sleep?" Jalisa asked.

"When I finally hit the bed, about eleven-thirty, I was out like a light. Didn't you hear me come in?"

"No. I crashed about nine-forty-five right after the kids. I think the tension of being here makes you really tired, both mentally and physically."

"Yeah, I agree," Galley said, yawning and stretching his arms over his head.

Jalisa yawned back. "What happened yesterday? I was worried about you being out all day."

"It's a really long story. How did y'all fare in the blackout? Were the kids scared?"

"Of course they were scared, Galley . . . but not nearly as scared as they might have been had we not brought the flashlights. Those were a Godsend, believe me."

"Good. I glad you brought them . . . we had those chemical light sticks in the upper part of the cave. They worked fine . . . this place is really amazing, you know. I wish you could see everything," Galley said.

"I'm sure I'll have time. Right now I think I'll call for breakfast. I'm hungry." Jalisa picked her PCC from the charger and called room service.

In Neemu and Rutha's cubicle a PCC was beeping to be answered. Neemu picked it up and said, "Good Morning. Neemu here." Rutha looked to Neemu and rolled her eyes after glancing at her watch—it read 5:15 a.m.

"Help, Neemu! Y-Y-You've got to help me! P—P-Please help!" the voice pleaded.

Neemu sat straight up from his bed and looked back at Rutha. Her eyes were as large as his. "Who is this? How can I help you?" Neemu responded.

"Neemu, this is J—J-Jon Morrow . . . Jackson l-l-locked me up. He s-s-sent some s-s-security guards to my c-c-cubicle late last night to arrest me. They've l-l-locked me up in an animal cage in the carnivore p-p-pens and I'm soooo c-c-cold."

Neemu could hear Jon's voice trembling and teeth chattering from his shivering. "I can't believe he did that to you, Jon. Is there a carnivore in the pen with you?" Neemu asked cautiously.

"No. Th-Th-They said it was s-s-sick in the animal infirmary so they c-c-could use the cage for me—except I don't h-h-have the hairy coat that animal d-d-did. I don't even h-h-have a c-c-coat at all."

"Who is *they*, Jon?" Neemu asked.

"J-J-Jackson and Geoff Ch-Ch-Chadwick . . . They l-l-locked me up. They g-g-got some security guards and t-t-took me at g-g-gunpoint and p-p-put me in here."

"What's all this about, Neemu?" Rutha abruptly interjected as she, too, now sat upright. She couldn't listen to the obvious discomfort any longer. It reminded her of her childhood when she was accidentally locked out of her house in Stockholm. There, she almost froze to death that cold winter morning in waist-deep snow before her father opened the door to leave for work. "Neemu, we've got to help him! Where is he?" Rutha was extremely agitated and irate at the situation.

"Jon, are you up by the Cryolab in one of *those* pens?" Neemu inquired.

"Yes, I th-th-think s-s-so."

"I'll get Galley and we'll come free you."

"N-N-No! D-D-Don't, Neemu. D-D-Don't bring Galley. He th-th-thinks I did it, too. R-R-Remember?"

"Oh, ya. I'll come get you by myself. Don't worry. I'll be there within fifteen minutes."

"P-P-Please hurry . . . it's s-s-so cold."

Neemu signed off with Jon and grabbed his crutch and a sack from the closet. As he left the cubicle he blew a kiss to Rutha and whispered, "I'll see you in a little while," taking care not to wake the kids.

"Bye, be careful." she whispered back.

Five minutes after Neemu's Hoxcart had arrived for him, he sped past the Egg Lab cave entrance heading for the carnivore pens. Driving the Hoxcart was quite a bit different from his motorized chair, more like a snowmobile. This machine, he thought, would even be good to drive on the New Mexico highways. In the distance, but growing quickly closer, he saw the outer carnivore pens glowing cherry red in the light from the warming infrared illuminators. As he neared, he pulled the Hoxcart to a gradual halt in front of them. With the crutch snugly under his arm, Neemu stepped carefully away from the Hoxcart. He had adapted quite easily to his crutch since it gave him back some of the freedom that he lost after the accident. Neemu called out, "Jon Morrow . . . are you in there?"

A small voice answered, "I-I-I'm over h-h-here, Neemu. Hurry, p-p-please!"

Neemu moved toward the voice and saw Jon in the inner pen. It was shadowed from the warming heat. In cages on either side of him were pacing, snarling tigers. The left cage held a Siberian; the other, on the right, an unrecognizable species. Neemu walked closer to Jon's cage looking for a door. The tiger on Jon's left suddenly reared up on its hind legs and swatted at Neemu through its cage. Neemu jumped back. Standing erect, it must have been over eight feet tall!

"W-Watch out, Neemu!" Jon screamed.

"I'm okay, Jon. How are you?" Neemu looked back at the cage enclosing Jon and realized it had no doors other than those into the adjoining cages. "Jon! How did they put you in there? There are no doors out."

"I-I-I know, N-N-Neemu. Th-Th-They brought in that t-t-tiger after they l-l-locked me in. C-C-Can you h-h-help me g-g-get out?"

"I don't see an easy way right now, Jon . . . I did bring you a heavy parka to keep you warm. I also brought some down-filled overpants, boots and gloves. They kept me warm on the coldest days in Sweden . . . they should work for you up here."

"Oh, th-th-thank you, N-N-Neemu. Do you m-m-mind?"

"Of course not." Neemu limped back to the Hoxcart and picked up a large plastic sack. He returned to Jon's cage and handed the garments through the bars, being careful not to disturb the neighboring tigers.

279

"Th-Thanks," Jon said as he took the clothes. He hurriedly donned the still-warm suit. Minutes passed as Jon stood frozen like a newly sculpted statue, absorbing the warmth from the suit. Then, quietly, Jon moved toward Neemu and stuck his gloved right hand through the front bars. "God bless you, Neemu. I can make it a little while longer this way. But you must get me out before Jackson comes back . . . he'll know someone was here. I'll freeze to death if he takes *these* clothes from me, too."

Neemu took Jon's hand and tightly grasped it. "Don't worry, Jon. I'll get you out, somehow. Just stay in touch with your PCC."

"Neemu, I don't have a charger so I've only got about five more hours of use before the batteries run down."

"I'll be back before then, Jon. Stay calm . . . and stay away from those tigers!"

"Don't worry, Neemu. I've found out exactly how long their arms are when they reach into my cage. I'm staying in the safe region, now."

"See you in a little bit, Jon. Hold tight." Neemu turned toward the Hoxcart and hobbled slowly away, trying to avoid placing his crutch on the small straw stalactites that had fallen to the floor.

The breakfast ordered by Jalisa had just arrived. Galley looked at his watch. It was only 5:50 a.m. and he was still waking up. As Jalisa set up the children's plates with cereal and juice, Galley poured them both a steaming cup of hot coffee from the silver decanter. The smell of fresh-cooked bacon and blueberry pancakes filled the room. He sat at the dining table and slowly sipped from his mug, looking over the simulated dawn in their backyard biome. He wondered if the animals out there could make it six more months. Interrupting his thoughts, Jalisa sat beside him and removed the serving covers from their plates. "Yum," Galley said, "I'm so hungry I could eat a horse."

"Galley, shhh. Don't let the kids hear you say that. They'll take it wrong." Jalisa whispered.

"Oh, sorry. I forgot that's not a universal saying, is it?"

"No. Not in the Swedish culture, I don't believe."

"Okay, then please pass the sea salt. How's that?"

"Fine," Jalisa answered with a smile and reached for the shaker.

Galley placed a fork loaded with syrup-and-butter-soggy pancakes into his mouth just as a banging came from the front door.

Jalisa said, "Who can that be at this hour? I'll get it."

Neemu hobbled quickly into the room on one crutch as Jalisa opened the door for him. "Galley, we have to do something, *now!*" he said frantically.

"Wait a minute, Neemu. What exactly is going on?" Galley asked still savoring his first bite of pancakes.

Neemu paused to catch his breath and organize his thoughts. "Remember last night when Jackson tried to convict Jon Morrow of sabotage in that marsupial court?"

"Kangaroo court," Galley corrected with a smile.

"Okay, kangaroo court then," Neemu said, not appreciating the humor. "Well, Jackson did it by himself . . . He, Geoff and security arrested Jon and locked him in the carnivore pens, between two tigers. There's no way for him to get out except through one of their cages."

"What? Did you see this, Neemu?" Galley asked with sudden concern in his voice.

"Ya, I went to his pen this morning. Jon called me on his PCC . . . Galley, we've got to get him out."

"Okay, Neemu, calm down. Jon *may* be guilty but I can't see doing that without proof . . . call Janet Sherman and ask her to meet us up at the pens in twenty minutes. And tell her to bring her tranquilizer gun. I'll change clothes and meet you in front of the habitat in five minutes. Oh . . . and call a Hoxcart for us."

Neemu walked to the door barely using his crutch.

Galley watched him move quickly across the room and said, "Congratulations, Neemu. Glad to see you're up and about again . . . how's your leg?"

"It's fine. I think I've forgotten about the pain with all this going on. Hurry!" Neemu shut the door behind him.

Three minutes later Galley exited the habitat elevator to see Neemu waiting in the idling Hoxcart's driver's seat. He jumped aboard and asked, "Are you able to drive this thing, Neemu?"

"Ya. I drove it earlier. Shouldn't be much different from a snowmobile, should it? I've driven hundreds of them." Neemu said as he pressed the accelerator to the floor. The Hoxcart jerked into motion toward the carnivore pens.

During the trip Galley almost fell from the cart as Neemu rounded the first corner. A brief heated verbal interchange followed until Galley buckled his seatbelt. The wild ride continued uninterrupted, thereafter. Seven minutes later they arrived outside the carnivore pens.

As the Hoxcart crunched to a stop at the top of the caverns Galley said, "Neemu, you could have killed us. I'm driving back."

"Galley, I'm trying to save someone . . . besides, that's how I drive a snowmobile. I didn't fall off, did I?"

Their bantering was interrupted as footsteps approached the cart. "It's too late." Janet Sherman said remorsefully.

Neemu stared at her as she neared. "What do you mean, it's too late?"

She looked back to the pens and said, "He's dead. The Siberian tiger got him."

Unbelieving, Neemu jammed his crutch under his arm and started for the pens. "I've got to save him. I promised him I would."

Janet grabbed his arm and pleaded, "Neemu, don't go. It's terrible. He's torn apart . . . not much left of him. I've seen it before with animal handlers."

Neemu stopped and looked between Janet and Galley, then dropped his head in sadness. "I should have helped him . . . when I was here earlier. I don't understand . . . how he could have gotten that near to the tiger's cage . . . he said he knew their reach limits."

Janet placed her arm around Neemu trying to console him. "Neemu, I think it was quick. It got the upper part of his body first. He's unrecognizable. I'll call Dr. Mason to do some forensics on the accident and see if we can find a little more out about what really happened here."

She grabbed her PCC and said, "Call Jim Mason."

"Is there anything we can do Janet?" Galley asked solemnly.

She looked down. "I'd like for one of you to tell his brother, if you wouldn't mind terribly. I've had enough trauma for this morning."

Fifteen minutes later Galley appeared alone at the doorstep to Suite 1000 and rang the doorbell. Neemu had asked Galley to be the one to relate the incident because he wanted to stay at the cages and wait for Mason to arrive.

"Good morning Galley. What are you doing up at this hour? Is something wrong?" Jackson Morrow asked, opening the door wide as an invitation for entry.

Galley walked into Morrow's cubicle and immediately noticed the opulence of this suite. It was not like theirs, but instead larger and more like a Presidential Suite, plush and ornate.

"Well, Galley?" Jackson Morrow asked, shutting the door.

"Yes, something's wrong. Jackson, did you have your brother locked up in the carnivore cages last night?"

"Well, yes. I want him to be confined until I can further investigate the sabotage incident. . . I plan on convening a court at 9:13 a.m. to return a verdict immediately."

"No point, Jackson. Your brother Jon is dead . . . the Siberian tiger in the next cage got him. He was severely mutilated, according to Janet Sherman."

Jackson looked directly into Galley's eyes and gasped. "Wh-What? Are you sure, Pruitt?" Galley's answer was unheard by Jackson Morrow as the lightning-bolt induced amnesia began to lift from his mind. He was plunged back to those lemonade-stand days of his youth again. This time his recollection was different than before. Why had he put salt in Jon's lemonade every time he asked Jon to go for more ice? Young Jackson Morrow knew that he would be beaten each time, but was so ambitious he took the punishment, again and again. He *had* to outsell his brother Jon at any cost.

Jackson's newly unclouded mind jumped forward in time to the real estate deals in Beverly Hills. He remembered now that he had *asked* Jon to overbid the spoiled-rich buyers. That way he could make more money on each deal. A few clients had refused to counter offer and caused Jackson headaches. However, the majority of clients that did overbid Jon's offers brought Jackson a great fortune. Jon had complied with Jackson's requests and made him extremely successful, risking Jon's own reputation. Jackson repaid him by starting Jon's dream, TwoMorrows Electronics . . . now there was only one Morrow. *What have I done? My baby brother is dead!*

"Jackson . . . Jackson! Are you all right?" Galley asked.

"I-I need to be alone, Galley. Maybe Jon . . . Jon was right. Maybe . . . there *was* another person he was chasing into the cave."

"What do you mean, Jackson? Galley asked with growing concern about Jackson's immediate state of mind.

"H-He told me he was out there following another person who sabotaged the tank . . . I didn't believe him. I saw the tape . . . so did Molly."

Jackson paused, looking down at the delicate pattern in the oriental carpet on his floor. The swirls were so intricate, like his life with his brother, Jon—so interwoven. He put his hands to his face and began to sob uncontrollably.

Galley waited several minutes for Jackson to regain his composure. "Jackson, would you like for me to leave or stay?"

"Stay for a minute . . . I'm sorry, Galley. I loved my brother . . . I've just realized what I told you about him earlier was wrong."

"What did you tell me about him, Jackson?"

"That he was the black sheep of the family."

"He wasn't?"

"No. It was I. I deliberately lied to him and stole him blind in my futile attempts at grandeur . . . but I didn't lie to *you* intentionally. I've just realized that since the lightning strike, I've even been lying to myself. The shock of your news has brought some very dark memories back to me— ones I'd rather not remember."

"Jackson, tell me. I'd like to know."

"Galley, I'm going to tell you something I've never told anyone before . . . *anyone.*"

Galley sat upright in his chair and listened attentively. "Go on."

"I was the one who doctored Jon's lemonade so it wouldn't sell. Remember? I was the one who asked him to overbid my real estate clients, at risk of his own reputation, so I would make larger commissions. It worked. He made me wealthy beyond my dreams. And Galley, this is the worst thing."

Galley, beginning to feel uneasy about the sudden confession, interrupted, "Jackson, are you sure you want to continue?"

"I *have* to Galley . . .." Jackson looked back to the floor. "When Jon and I were in college, he was a freshman and I was a senior, our parents died in a terrible car accident on Arrowhead Mountain. It was January 13, 1970 at one-thirteen in the afternoon—the exact same day and time I was struck by lightning years later. Their brakes failed as they left the mountain. Their car plummeted over three-hundred feet into a canyon . . . both died instantly."

"Jackson, I'm so sorry," Galley said sympathetically.

"Don't be, Galley. I was the one who fixed their brakes so they would fail. I killed our mother and father for their money so Jon and I could be assured of a successful future. Nobody ever found out. The investigators thought it was a true accident . . . Jon loved them so . . . and now he's gone too."

"Well, I better go, now." Galley stood to leave and started for the door.

Jackson waived his hand and said, "Wait, Galley. I need to tell you more. I think that the subconscious knowledge of my dark past made me found the Colony. I did it to try to repent for all my greedy wrongdoings. Now that I'm remembering clearly again, I know that's why I did it. I just had to tell someone. I'm no hero . . . I'm sorry."

Galley frowned. "Jackson, you've done some bad things and some good things in your life but now I think you should go tell the Colony about your past."

Jackson lifted his pajama shirttail and looked at his Cryosensor. "I have to —."

287

Galley interrupted, "Before that, while we're still confessing, I need to tell you something. Yesterday Neemu and I talked to the Naval Observatory. They've been tracking the Cloud while we were setting up, here in Antron. They now say that Endlight will last six instead of four months."

"Oh, my God! I'm getting sick," Jackson said as he stood from his seat. "Just a minute, I have to the restroom before we go. Will you excuse me for a moment?" Jackson quickly left the living room. Five minutes had passed as Galley patiently sat and waited for Jackson to return from his bedroom. Finally, his patience wearing thin, Galley called, "Jackson, are you coming . . . we need to go."

No answer.

Galley called out again, louder, "Jackson. Are you ready?"

No answer.

Galley rose from his chair and slowly entered Jackson's bedroom. Jackson wasn't there! Galley scanned the room to find a possible exit. Then his eyes focused on the only escape . . . the open balcony door! At the sill of the door he saw Jackson's Cryosensor smashed into small pieces.

As he ran to the balcony and looked over the railing, he screamed, "*No! Jackson, no*! The horror he saw ten stories below was a crumpled figure lying in the drain at the end of the safety moat. Jackson had jumped to his death and been carried into the Rainforest biome by the same system he designed to prevent animal escapes. Animals were beginning to wander curiously up to the lifeless shape in the drain. Galley pulled the PCC from his collar and slowly said, "Call Neemu."

"Neemu, here." the PCC responded after several seconds.

"Neemu, I'm in Jackson's room. I told him about his brother and he broke down—."

Neemu interrupted, "Is he okay?"

"No, Neemu. Right after I told him, he jumped over the balcony to his death. He's caught in the Rainforest biome safety moat drain." Over the PCC's audio Galley could hear gasps and screams in the background.

Neemu's voice returned after moments of loud confusion. "Galley, I'm sorry you had to be there alone. I would never have expected that."

"Neither would I, Neemu, but it appears that Jackson had some dark secrets nobody knew about . . . until now, that is. His brother dying and the two-month Endlight extension were just too much for him to take . . . he just went nuts and jumped. Before he jumped he smashed his Cryosensor. Strange, isn't it?"

"Ya, very. We've had some rather startling developments here, too, Galley . . . Jon wasn't killed by the tiger . . . he was first shot with a gun and then fell toward the cage as he died. Then the tiger got him. The tiger didn't kill Jon—a bullet did."

Galley walked to the apartment door and opened it, then slowly continued, "Who would want to . . . Neemu, where you?"

"I'm in the Medaid Center."

"I'm on my way . . . we've got to talk about this. Jon *did not* commit the sabotage. Someone else damaged the hydrogen tank pipeline . . . and he's still here in Antron with us."

Galley pushed the little red button on his PCC. "Call 911."

Seconds later a soft voice answered, "Antron Security. What's your emergency?"

"This is Galley Pruitt. Send a team of paramedics to the Rainforest moat drain quickly. Jackson Morrow jumped from his balcony. He's down there."

Galley looked back into Jackson's empty apartment, closed the door and left for the Medaid Center.

CHAPTER 12
TWO MORROWS' FATE

O Raven Days, dark Raven Days of sorrow,
Will ever any warm light come again?
Will ever the lit mountains of To-morrow
Begin to gleam across the mournful plain?"

SIDNEY LANIER, from *The Raven Days*

Moments later, Galley crossed the main cavern hallway and entered the Medaid Center. Dr. Mason was passing through the lobby, heading toward a closed room on the left. "Excuse me, Doctor. Is Neemu Hatlem in here?" Galley asked quickly before the doctor exited.

Dr. Jim Mason stopped and looked at the visitor to his clinic. "Why yes, Dr. Pruitt, he is. Follow me, please."

Galley followed Mason past an operating room to a rear conference room where Neemu, Janet Sherman and Geoff Chadwick sat around a large oval mahogany table. The tension in the air could be cut with a scalpel as they waited for Dr. Mason's analysis.

Mason motioned with his hand for Galley to sit. Galley pulled his chair out from the table and sat with his legs and arms feeling awkwardly stiff. He was still in shock over the past few minutes of his life. Dr. Mason placed an X-ray negative over the large illuminated viewer and began to address the group, "Here we have an X-ray of the Siberian tiger's stomach taken *in vivo*, obviously. We don't

291

want to kill any species here—they're too valuable. You may notice this small dark spot here next to the ingested human spinal vertebrae. I believe Jon was shot in the neck and died almost instantly. His spinal cord was pierced by this projectile." He pointed with a pencil to the small black dot in the shadows of the large rib cage.

"I am convinced this is the bullet that matches the spent shell casing outside of cage C-113, where Jon was being detained. Unfortunately, we will have to wait a day or two until the tiger eliminates the object to determine its true identity."

Galley looked directly at Geoff. "Jon told us you and Jackson locked him up last night. Did you have anything to do with the shooting, too?"

Geoff stood and walked to the front of the room. He paused before speaking while examining the X-ray. He mumbled, "Hmmm . . . does look like a bloody bullet," then continued aloud, "I was ordered by Jackson Morrow to assist him in incarcerating his brother last night. All I did was tranquilize the animal while the guards placed Jon in the cage. The two guards then held him at gunpoint until the cages were closed and locked. It was the only place we could think of to keep him locked up without supervision. I was not in favor of the imprisonment nor did I believe Jon was guilty of sabotage—I was simply following Jackson's orders just like the security guards. And no, I had nothing to do with the shooting."

Galley looked back to Neemu who had now begun scribbling on a small notepad. "What do you think about this, Neemu? You found him first this morning."

Neemu faced Jim Mason now standing at

the side of the meeting room and asked, "Do you know what kind of bullet it was? From the casing, I mean?"

"Yes, Neemu," Mason said. "The spent shell is a .38 caliber magnum."

Neemu, looking down at his scribbles, continued, "Are colonists allowed to possess guns in Antron, Geoff?" As Neemu directed his question, his gaze moved to Chadwick's eyes.

"No, they're not supposed to need them or have them, for that matter . . . that's why we have security here. In addition to myself, only Jackson, Janet Sherman and our security force have any type of guns—and mine's a .45 caliber."

Neemu looked to Janet, questioningly. "I have a .22 caliber pistol and .50 caliber rifle for emergency animal control—that's all," she admitted.

"Does anyone know what guns Jackson has?" Galley asked, probing for additional clues.

"I think he has the same weapon that our security force uses—a .38 caliber revolver," Geoff recalled.

Neemu scribbled more notes on his pad and stared silently at the information. He was observing that only two entities in Antron owned guns like the one alleged to be the murder weapon: Jackson and the entire Antron security force. That left out Geoff and Janet. Jackson knew that Jon was in the cage last night—but so did security. Jackson had a reason to get rid of Jon and make it look like he was accidentally shot by security, or anybody for that matter. Jackson hated his brother and was convinced that it was he who sabotaged the hydrogen line . . . that's the motive. It wasn't

293

security—they had no motive to kill Jon. "Well in my logical and analytical opinion, we've just had a murder-suicide here in Antron," Neemu said, breaking the uneasy silence in the room. "Two rather off-kilter brothers didn't like each other, so one of them fixed the problem—permanently. Jackson simply shot his brother, then killed himself in grief afterward."

Galley rubbed his chin, thinking, for several seconds. "No, Neemu, I don't think so. If you could have seen Jackson's reactions and emotions after I told him about Jon's death, you wouldn't think he could have done it."

Neemu looked at his pad. "Galley, did you tell Jackson that his brother had been shot?"

"No. I believe I told him that the tiger mutilated and killed his brother. Why?"

Neemu looked up from his pad to the X-ray negative at the front of the room. "Galley, don't you think that if Jackson thought he had just shot his brother to death, he might still react totally differently when told his brother was, in fact, mauled and eaten after being shot?"

"Well, I guess so, Neemu. But to the point of killing himself?" Galley questioned. "I think if Jackson knew Jon was already dead, the knowledge that he was later mauled would not have affected him so severely."

"Okay, Galley. Then who did it, and why? We still don't even know who really sabotaged the hydrogen tank."

"Jackson told me before he died that his brother was chasing someone into the cave," Galley related. "At first Jackson didn't believe him, but then he said he did. That was just before he jumped.

He also said something about a tape that he and Molly watched."

"Maybe the two incidents aren't even connected," Janet offered. "Just possibly, this could be some terribly bizarre coincidence."

Mason stepped to the X-ray viewer and peered again into the image. "Possibly—but I don't really think so. There's just something that doesn't make sense here—and I can't identify it."

Galley grabbed his PCC and said, "Call Molly O'Quinn."

The computer responded, "Calling—in Antron Control."

"Hello. This is Molly O'Quinn," a voice answered.

"Molly, this is Galley. Could you please come over to the Medaid Center? We're in the back conference room. Oh, and Jackson said you and he were watching some tape together, recently. Do you know what I'm talking about?"

"Sure, Galley, the security surveillance tape showing the saboteur entering the cave? It's right over here in the stack of archive tapes."

"Well, could please bring it with you when you come over?

"Just give me a minute and I'll be there," Molly said as she placed her PCC in her pocket and began searching through the video tape stack. Fifteen minutes had passed in the Medaid Center and Molly had not shown up. Captain Steven Kane, recently retired Police Chief of Los Angeles and now head of Antron Security, *had* arrived at the Medaid Center following his initial investigations at Jackson's suite and the Rainforest safety moat drain.

Entering the conference room where the group still awaited Molly's arrival, Captain Kane looked across the room to Galley and asked, "Dr. Pruitt, did you see him jump?"

Galley sat up in his chair. "No, sir. Sorry. I last saw him when he went into his bedroom headed for the bathroom. He said he was sick. When I later went in to find him, he was gone. He had jumped and his body had already been swept into the drain."

"What were you doing in Mr. Morrow's suite, Dr. Pruitt, at that time of morning?" Kane continued.

"I went to tell him that his brother Jon had been killed," Galley answered innocently.

"*What? His brother is dead, too?* Why wasn't I told about that?" Kane asked angrily.

Jim Mason stood and attracted Kane's attention. He spoke slowly and distinctly, "I chose not to tell you until I performed some forensic tests and analysis. It was only a few hours ago when this whole nightmare started . . . at least when everything that we know happened started."

"Well, doctor, would you mind filling me in on a few of your inside details?" Kane asked indignantly.

Jim Mason began to relate the events of that morning with occasional assistance from Neemu and Chadwick. Kane was not pleased with the involvement of his security force, especially since he had not been previously told about Jon's arrest and confinement. He was also upset that he had not been made aware of Jon's suspected participation in the sabotage. As Mason finished relating the morning's strange activities, Kane stood motionless, staring out the conference room door into the hallway. Then he turned back to Mason. "Why in the hell am I always the last person to find everything out?" Kane yelled. "Christ sakes! You'd think in a small elite society like this we could keep some kind of goddamn order . . . now we've got one murder and one possible suicide. Mason, can I see Jon's bod —?"

Kane was interrupted in mid-sentence as Molly O'Quinn flew into the room. Her patience was obviously at the edge of its limits. "I've torn the entire Control Center apart looking for that surveillance tape without success. What's Jackson going to say?" Molly blurted as she rushed to the conference table and fell nervously into an empty chair. "I've lost that damn tape. I can't find it anywhere . . . it has to be in there. Jackson and I just looked at it yesterday . . . it has to be there."

Molly looked around the room at the somber faces waiting for her tirade to finish. "I'm sorry. I'm just very keyed up right now," she said, "and a very important tape is missing. Jackson's going to have my hide." Molly looked again at the frowning faces around the table and quickly realized something else was wrong. Why would Mason, Chadwick, Galley and Neemu be sitting in a room with the Chief of Security this time of morning, she thought . . . and where's Jackson?

"Good morning, Molly," Geoff said, rising from his chair. "We've had some strange and bizarre occurrences in Antron this morning. Jon Morrow was shot to death near the carnivore pens."

"Jon? Dead?" Molly stared back in disbelief.

Galley waited for a further response then spoke, "I asked you over, Molly, because before

Jackson jumped to his death, he said something about another intruder during the sabotage. He said you and he had seen it on tape."

"Jackson? Dead?" Molly shifted her disbelieving stare to Galley.

"Ya, Molly, we need to clear Jon's name from this accusation, if we can. Somebody shot him and left him in the cage. Poor man . . . eaten by that tiger."

"Eaten? Tiger?" Molly's eyes opened even further in disbelief as she snapped her gaze to Neemu. Her stare was gradually broken as she began to tremble in her chair, mildly at first, then quite violently. Her hands gripped the armrests so tightly her knuckles began to whiten.

Jim Mason jumped from his chair. "I got to get something to calm her down."

He disappeared into a nearby treatment room and returned holding a small syringe in his hand. "This should do it," he said as he moved swiftly toward Molly.

Her trembling was increasing in intensity as she, now terrified, watched the doctor approach. Her eyes, almost to point of exploding, widened as she saw the needle enter her right arm. Then came peace for Molly O'Quinn. She slumped forward into the chair hitting her head slightly on the table as she relaxed.

"There. That should keep her quiet for a while," Dr. Mason said returning to the treatment room with the empty syringe.

Kane excused himself and left the conference room. He planned on joining Mason to examine Jon's corpse.

As they sat there quietly thinking, Galley

looked at Neemu and said, "I wonder what happened to that video tape? Think Jackson took it back to his room?"

"Possibly," Neemu answered. "Does he have a video player there?"

"Neemu, we all have one, remember?" Galley said tapping his finger to his temple.

"Okay, then, when Chief Kane comes back let's get him to search Jackson's suite for the tape," Neemu suggested.

"Good idea, Neemu," Galley said with a smile and a wink. "You're becoming a regular Sherlock Holmes."

Five minutes later Kane and Mason returned to the conference room together, laughing. Kane was completing the end of a story, ". . . from Disney World and did you see the look on her face when he said eaten by that tiger?" Kane and Mason muffled their laughter as they took their seats at the table.

Kane looked at the five seated around the table with him. Molly was still out cold. He began, "I believe, having seen all the evidence available, that this was probably a murder-suicide . . . Jackson locked his brother up to keep him from further sabotage activities. Then he probably worked himself up and got so mad at Jon that he shot him, not expecting him to be eaten by the tiger. When Jackson found out the strange fate of his brother, his remorse made him jump off his balcony."

"I don't believe it happened like that, Chief Kane," Galley challenged.

"Oh, Galley, do you mean that you pushed Jackson from his window? Would you like to explain that? You *would* have had a reason if you were really distraught about Jon's shooting."

"No, of course not. I mean . . . I don't believe Jackson shot Jon . . . someone else did."

"Care to offer a suspect, Galley?" Kane smirked.

"I don't know, but I think it's someone that wanted to silence Jon—keep him from talking about something he knew or found out. The way it was done in secrecy would certainly point the finger at Jackson, too—not the real suspect. Probably the real saboteur, too."

"Galley, I think you've been watching too many television movies," Kane said as he turned to leave. "I'm going to have a Colony meeting to announce the loss of two great leaders of Antron. If you all don't mind, I'd rather tell everyone they met with an accident . . . together."

The group shook their heads in affirmation as he left the room.

"Oh, Chief Kane?" Galley yelled as he ran to the door.

Kane stopped and turned back. "Yes, Galley?"

"Would you please check Jackson's suite for any surveillance video tapes? We have reason to believe he might have taken one to his room for private review."

"I'll do that right now, Galley. I was on my way back up there for one more look, anyway."

"Thanks, Chief," Galley said as he returned to the table.

Neemu looked from the empty doorway back to Galley. "I think the whole incident this morning is beginning to sink in, guys. All at once, I'm very tired and need to get some rest."

Janet and Galley yawned almost in unison.

"Me, too," Janet said.

Geoff Chadwick looked at Molly still resting her head on the table and said, "Well, we can't leave her like that, can we? Can you chaps help me get her onto the floor? We can lay her there to sleep it off."

After Galley, Neemu and Geoff carefully placed Molly onto a blanket on the floor, they left the Medaid center. As the group separated and headed for their individual cubicles, Janet looked back and commented, "What a morning! I certainly hope nothing else goes wrong."

CHAPTER 13
THE INTERLOPER

Two weeks passed uneventfully in Antron just as Janet had wished. The Morrow brothers had been buried in an elaborate ceremony three days after their deaths. They were laid to rest in a large chamber next to the Egg Lab room because of its solitude and beauty. The entire ceremony looked as if it were taking place in heaven, on a giant puffy cloud. Everyone in Antron wept as the Morrows entered their final resting places. It was a very sad time.

Geoff Chadwick, Chief Scientist of the Colony, assumed the role of Colony leader. Although several of the Forum thought they themselves were better suited, Geoff reminded them that he was Jackson's first choice and right-hand man in running Antron smoothly. They agreed and quickly announced the election of Dr. Chadwick to Colony Governor.

The video tape was never found, so the theory of a second intruder and saboteur slowly faded away. Jackson *had* taken some surveillance tapes to his room for review, but that particular one was mysteriously missing. The consensus of thought was Jackson had put it in a hiding place known only to him.

Analysis of the tiger-ingested bullet had proved little since the barrel rifling-marks had been half chewed away and half stomach-acid eaten away. It was assumed that Jackson's gun was the murder weapon so Chief Steven Kane had closed the case.

People were getting on with living in the cave, although most families had begun to conserve and save food and supplies, since they were told of Endlight's expected two-month extension. Some had panicked when the news came. Several people locked themselves in the Jackson's Cave CAVE and had to be forcibly removed from their virtual world escapades. They were immediately placed directly under Aaron Hertzberg's care and supervision. Most families began to grow closer together as they spent more time with each other. Others grew apart with the extreme smothering closeness and constant familiarity of the confining cavern. All in all, Jackson's plan was working. He had created an ark that was surviving beautifully. Then the inevitable happened—his dream began to crumble.

It was on Janet Sherman's evening tour of the carnivore pens when she first noticed the sickness. She immediately thought unforeseen environmental elements were affecting the animals: humidity mixed with continual cold and night. The jaguar had developed a hoarse cough that seemed to come from deep in its lungs.

As Janet paused near cage C-114 to listen to the rale in the jaguar's breathing, she seemed to remember hearing the same sound before. Where had she heard that rale before? Then she remembered! It was from the sick snow leopard that had been in cage C-113 across the aisle, before it was taken to the infirmary. The thought brought a deep gloom as she realized that was the cage Jon had been killed in. But that animal had the same symptom of the raspish cough. Could there be a connection? She retrieved her tranquilizer dart gun from her Hoxcart and gave the jaguar a small

303

injection, just enough to put it out for five minutes. Then she took out an empty syringe and drew a vial of blood from the drugged animal. She relocked the cage and went to the bio-analysis laboratory near the Cryolab to analyze the sample.

Not knowing what to look for, she decided to first search for viruses. She began with cold weather strains and slowly moved to warm weather strains. She found nothing in her lengthy search. Then she remembered something Jackson had said about the interlopers in the upper parts of the cavern. Field and deer mice, and rats had been trying to escape the cold and take comfort in the cave for many weeks before the giant Lockdown gate was built. She went back to the testing bench and slowly performed another analysis.

This time she found what she was looking for, but it did not make her happy . . . she had found a rare strain of the hantaan virus. She was aware even at the Cincinnati Zoo of the hantavirus cases that been discovered in the Southwestern United States, particular in the Four Corners plains of New Mexico. *That disease had entered the cave! It could reach epidemic proportions in weeks. Everything and everyone could die!* Janet frantically took the ailing snow leopard's blood sample from the refrigerator and subjected it to the same test. Positive again! Janet pushed the button on her PCC and called Geoff. "Geoff. This is Janet," she said as he answered the call. "I've got some rather bad news for us."

"Oh? What's up, Janet?" he responded.

"I've found two cases of the hantavirus, specific strain hantaan, up here in the carnivore pens. I'm afraid that we could have a possible epidemic on our hands unless we get these animals separated."

"And Janet, where would you like to suggest we separate them to?" Geoff asked sarcastically.

"I don't care, we have to stop the spread of the virus or we'll all die . . . the cages with the sick animals are C-113 and C-114."

"Oh, dear God, Janet.   I was in C-113 when I put Jon in there and you and I were in there when we got him out. Are we infected?"

"Possibly. I need to perform some blood tests on us to know for sure. I'll notify Dr. Mason. He's seen the hantavirus in L.A., I'm sure."

"Janet, I'll meet you there in ten minutes. Call Mason and get the tests ready. We can't wait any longer." Chadwick said as he walked through the large vault door leaving the Antron Control Center.

Down the hall Galley and Neemu were in the Com Center performing their nightly duties. Time of day and night had begun to fuse in the cavern. With the exception of the Rainforest biome's synthetic light behind the living habitats, there was nothing to delineate night or day . . . only the clock. Everyone had begun to set their own work patterns, and Galley and Neemu chose to work from late afternoon until after midnight. That way they had more time to stay at home and visit with their wives and kids.

At 9:00 p.m. Neemu was attempting scheduled radio contact with W1AW in Washington, D.C. to check their status. He had already succeeded in contacting the U.S. Air Force colony in Cheyenne Mountain only to find that they were running out of supplies and fuel. Word was, they would probably last only another week or so before the deadly cold outside crept in the mountain chamber.

"W1AW . . . this is Darkstar. Are you there?" Neemu called. Galley was sweeping the night sky with the radio telescope trying to find the source of a strange signal he had just found. It was very similar to the pre-flash signals he found in Arecibo, and a very intense flash of light lasting several seconds had accompanied it. He fortunately had pointed the optical telescope away from the light source or it might have melted the image array again.

"W1AW . . . this is Darkstar. Are you there? Come in please," Neemu repeated.

"Darkstar . . . this is W1AW. Hello, Neemu. Cold here—how's it there?"

"Were hanging in here, Andrew. I think we've finally settled in for a cold winter's night . . . so to speak."

"Yeah, Neemu. We are too. The only problem we have is the damn bureaucrats here cut the war room budget many years ago. There are not many more supplies left. We're also being forced into daily blackouts to conserve power. It gets really dark and cold in here during that time, too. We can't use the telesco . . . what the hell is that—"

"*Neemu! Come here you've got to see this! You're not going to believe it!*" Galley screamed. Neemu dropped the microphone and ran from the radio console to the telescope video monitor. *The sky was ablaze with light!*

"How can that be? The Sun's on the other side of the Earth." Neemu murmured as he gazed into the monitor.

Galley reached over to the computer console and quickly keyed in WHOLE SKY SCAN /o / f=9000-10,000 MHz. The computer monitor showed a three-dimensional representation of the large dish above scanning the sky from horizon to horizon. As it scanned, the computer screen began to fill with received signals. After four minutes of collecting and processing data the computer beeped, signaling scan completion. The monitor glowed with the following readout:

SKY RADIO OPTICAL

SCAN DIRECTION FOUND	**SIGNAL FREQUENCY BRIGHTNESS**

NORTH QUADRANT   9000mHZ + DOPPLER
   3   24.22, -24.22, -24.22
   Azimuth (degrees): 0.00
   Elevations (degrees) #1= 65, #2= 75, #3= 85
   Data Stream Rate: NONE (CW)

EAST QUADRANT -   9090 MHz + DOPPLER
   2   24.22 24.22
   Azimuth (degrees): 90.0
   Elevations (degrees):#1= 75, #2= 85
   Data Stream Rate: NONE (CW)

SOUTH QUADRANT -   9180 MHz + DOPPLER
   3   -24.22, -24.22, -24.22
   Azimuth (degrees): 180.0
   Elevations (degrees):#1= 65, #2= 75, #3= 85
   Data Stream Rate: NONE (CW)

WEST QUADRANT -   9270 MHz + DOPPLER
   2   -24.22, -24.22

Azimuth (degrees): 270.0
Elevations (degrees):   #1= 75, #2= 85
Data Stream Rate: NONE (CW)

OVERHEAD -9911 MHZ + DOPPLER
1   DARK
Elevation (degrees): 90
Data Stream Rate: 411 MHz
Data Encryption:

UNKNOWN (APPARENTLY IMAGE)
Signal sync period: 41 bits
Signal string image:

START OF IMAGE:

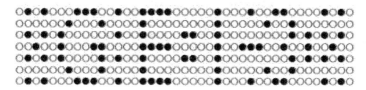

END OF IMAGE

"*The Darkstar signals!*" Galley yelled. "*That's them* . . . all together and they're moving! But there are more of them than we ever saw before! And there's one with no light. What's that?"

Neemu pointed to the BRIGHTNESS column and said, "Look how bright they are!" He grabbed a calculator from the desk and punched in a few numbers. "They're all exactly one-tenth as bright as our Sun. Isn't that strange?"

Galley pointed to the # FOUND column. "Neemu! Look how many illuminators there are!

Exactly ten . . . we have one-sun equivalent light out there!"

Neemu studied the screen again and said, "Wait . . . there are six in the North-South plane but only four in the East-West plane. That's really strange. What are these things, Galley? And look at that data stream image from the overhead signal."

"In Arecibo we thought the radio signals that accompanied the flashes were like some kind of homing or tracking signal. That must be exactly what they were. As we saw each flash, the homing signal was being tested . . . to see if it could lock onto Earth. Now they're all locked on . . . and we're rotating under some form of artificial daylight up there! They must be reflecting or tunneling our sunlight around the Cloud or something like that. It's crazy, Neemu. Someone out there is trying to help us! It also appears they're trying to tell us something, too."

Neemu was studying the repeating bit-mapped image coming in at a data rate of 411 megahertz. "Looks like letters and numbers if you squint your eyes."

"Could that be?" Galley squinted briefly at the flashing image. "Yes, Neemu, I see GE: 1-3. What does that mean?" He looked back at the coded image. "And why would it be in English? Isn't that a little egocentric?"

"Our SOS was sent from Arecibo, remember? It contained mostly English-language syntax and grammar. There was even a short tutorial on English and a few other World languages."

Galley agreed, "Oh, yeah . . . I forgot."

Neemu sat silently looking at the image for

several more seconds and then bowed his head. Slowly, he began to mutter something in Swedish under his breath.

"What's wrong, Neemu?

He looked up. "It's from the Bible."

"What do you mean, from the Bible? "

"You know, we use 411 — same number as the data rate — on Earth for our information number?"

"Yes, I understand that—it's a stretch though, but what about the Bible?"

"This is information for us."

"What kind of information?" Galley prodded, now showing impatience.

"Those things out there know a lot about us . . . and our God—maybe their God, too."

"Quit with the riddles, Neemu. *What does it mean*?"

Neemu quietly began, "Galley, the information from GE: 1-3?"

"Yes?"

"It's Genesis: 1-3 . . . *And God said, 'Let there be light,' and there was light . . .*"

Galley continued, "*God saw that the light was good, and he separated the light from the . . .*" He stared at Neemu for seconds. His mind was spinning. Suddenly he blurted out, *"My God, Neemu. What have we found?"*

Across the cavern hallway in the Medaid Center Janet Sherman and Geoff Chadwick converged in Jim Mason's office. Mason rose as they entered. "Well, what brings two of our finest scientists to my office?" His jovial mood immediately turned serious as he noticed Janet's reaction to his greeting. "Okay, what's wrong?"

Janet and Geoff quietly seated themselves in the two chairs opposite the desk. Mason sat back in his chair while Janet looked at her hands grasped together nervously in her lap. "Jim, I've just performed some tests on two of our sick animals. I originally thought they were being affected by the humidity and cold in the upper part of the cave . . . then I saw blood coming from the jaguar's nose. Jim . . . we have the hantavirus in the cave . . . two animals tested positive."

Mason sat silently twirling the pencil in his fingers for what seemed to Janet an eternity before he spoke. "What strain?" he asked quietly.

"Hantaan."

"Dr, Sherman, are you absolutely sure?"

"Jim, I would stake my life on it." Janet suddenly realized what she had said and looked back at her hands.

"I'm sorry to hear that Janet, but it does explain a baffling set of symptoms I've seen in a number of our Colonists, including the security chief, Steven Kane . . . I would never have suspected the hantavirus. But now the pieces of the puzzle fit together . . . it's not always fatal, you know? Over 40% of the population that contracts the virus lives through it."

Chadwick looked nervously between Janet and Jim Mason. "How would we know if we have it?"

"First, you may experience some mental confusion and a slight memory loss. This symptom can appear quite abruptly. Then, you'll develop a severe respiratory illness, like a bad flu. After that you'll fall into a state of malaise because of renal

311

failure. Past that point, every case is different. Let's just do a blood test on both of you and find out for sure." Mason rose from his desk and motioned for Janet and Geoff to follow him into the examining room.

Back in the Com Center, Galley and Neemu were still staring at the optical telescope monitor in amazement. The lights in the sky, of which they could see only one, were beginning to blind the image array once again. Suddenly the interoffice intercom squawked to life. "Is anyone in there?" the voice said. "This is Molly — in Control."

Galley rolled his chair to the intercom console and pushed the talk button. "Yes, Molly we're here . . . what's up?"

"I've just had an indication on the control panel of main elevator activation. I thought one of you might be heading to the surface. There's something very strange going on out there."

"Do you mean the light?"

"Yes. The surface surveillance cameras are showing the Hydrolox tanks in full daylight . . . how can that be? I thought one of you might be heading to the surface to check out what's going on."

"No, Molly we're both here, but that's not a bad idea. I think I'll go up," Galley said as he turned for the door.

"Wait, Galley. The monitor is picking up someone out there heading for the hydrogen tank."

Neemu punched the intercom switch and said, "Who is it, Molly?"

"I can't tell yet. Let me zoom in. Maybe I can get a closer look." As Molly pressed the zoom button and directed the remote control camera lens, she saw the clear image of a face she thought she recognized. "Neemu . . . Galley, can you come in here right now?"

Neemu and Galley ran down the hallway into the Control Room. As they neared the monitor, Neemu's eyes widened, not believing what he was seeing. *It was the security guard that shot him!* "I know him! He shot me! I thought Jackson fired him!" Neemu said unbelievingly. As he spoke, the main elevator light once again flickered to life, unseen by Molly and the group watching the monitor.

"He did," Molly said. "He must have stowed away in the cave after that . . . he knew everything about Antron. It was his job."

Galley looked closer at the monitor and pointed at something in the guard's hand. "What's that he's got with him?"

"Wait! What's he doing, now?" Molly asked.

They watched the guard running toward the white metal staircase spiraled around the large hydrogen tank. Galley yelled, "He's climbing the tank! I've got to stop him! He must be the one who sabotaged the tank earlier. I'm going up." Galley turned and raced for the door.

"Wait, Galley," Neemu said. "Look! There's someone after him."

Molly manipulated the remote camera joystick to zoom in on the second figure. As the image came into focus they all tensely watched Steven Kane gaining on the guard. He, too, was now climbing the ladder, only fifty feet back. Molly redirected the camera to the guard. He had reached the top of the tank, unaware of Kane closing in behind him.

Suddenly, the guard stopped, squinted up into the sky at the brightness then laid the small object he had been carrying at his feet.

Galley asked, "What's he doing now?"

The guard held out his arms, palms upward, toward the sky then fell to his knees with his hands clasped together.

"Looks like he's praying . . . strange," Molly answered.

Suddenly Kane was behind the guard. From the top stair he jumped through the air, landing squarely on the guard's back. The impact knocked both against the safety rail 100 feet above the frozen ground below. The guard struck back, kicking Kent across the platform into the opposing rail.

"*Oh no! He's going to fall!*" Molly screamed, putting her hands to her face. Kane, toppling backward, grabbed the railing with both hands and pulled himself back onto the platform.

Molly, Neemu and Galley, all frozen in disbelief, watched as the guard ran back to the center of the platform and pulled another small package from his parka. He held it in front of him, as if taunting Kane.

"What *is* that?" Galley asked as Janet tried to zoom in on the object.

"It appears to be a video cassette . . . *wait! That's the missing surveillance tape! I can tell by the label!*" Molly yelled.

They watched, their eyes affixed to the monitor screen, as the guard argued heatedly with Kane.

"What's he saying?" Neemu asked.

"It appears he's telling the Chief about that tape in his hand . . . .." Galley conjectured.

Kane once more sprung onto the guard, knocking the video tape cartridge from his hand and over the platform's edge. It fell slowly in fluttering free-fall to the ground near the Lockdown gate. Then they witnessed, in shocking slow motion, the guard fall upon the package he had placed at the center of the platform. Kane leapt upon him in continued struggle.

Frantically the guard reached his hand under his chest to the package and pulled out a small pin attached to a ring around his finger. *"Oh God! That thing is a grenade!"* Galley yelled.

The device's detonation knocked the guard and Kane at least thirty to forty feet into the air above the top of the tank. Suddenly, the hydrogen tank erupted into an explosive fireball as if all hell had opened up.

Molly, Neemu and Galley watched helplessly as the shock wave and heat from the blast approached and destroyed the remote surveillance camera. The monitor screen went dark as Molly started backing toward the wall, reaching backwards for support. *"Oh-h-h-h no! Get ready for the shock!"* she wailed.

In the Medaid Center Jim Mason had completed the viral tests and was returning to the examination room to discuss the test results with Geoff and Janet. As he entered the room, Janet, now quite nervous, looked up. "Jim, are we okay?"

Jim Mason looked between Geoff and Janet for a moment and began to speak. "Well, the tests—" He was interrupted as the examining room was once again plunged into a black, black darkness. The room's only sound was the slight hiss from the autoclave. Then the rumble and vibration started.

315

Vials and syringes on the counter flew across the room, narrowly missing Geoff in the darkness.

"What in the hell is going on?" Chadwick yelled. He reached into his pocket and pulled a small penlight out. As he switched it on, another shock came, knocking him to the ground.

"It's an earthquake!" Janet shouted. *"We're all going to die!"*

As abruptly as it started, the shaking stopped. Silence and darkness filled Antron. Children could be heard screaming in the distance with an occasional echoed trumpeting from the Rainforest elephants.

CHAPTER 14
GENESIS II

"All the people in my poems walk into the dark
All the animals walk up to the ark.
The people are deaf and limping like flies
Cunning shining soft sad as they walk,
And they do not know but they walk into the bad
dark.

All the animals in my poems walk into the sun
Blinking their eyes and licking their paws as they
go,
On and on up the proud procession of stairs
Up the proud stairs like a holy circus
And they do not know but they walk in the great
light.

JON SILKIN, from *Epilog*

Only moments had passed before the darkness was swept away by the reactivation of the Antron lighting system. Geoff grabbed his PCC and yelled into it, "Call Molly O'Quinn . . . Molly, is everything all right over there in Control?"

"In Antron Control . . . calling . . .."

"Yes, Geoff. I think we're okay . . . I'm here with Galley and Neemu . . . Geoff, that shock you just felt was *not* an earthquake, it was our hydrogen tank. We watched it on the surveillance camera. Oh, and remember our saboteur, supposedly Jon Morrow? Well, it wasn't a dead man who just blew away the hydrogen tank of our main power system—it was the security guard you fired after

317

he shot Neemu in the leg. Also, I think the second shock we felt was our oxygen tank going."

"Oh, crikey!" Chadwick said as he slammed his fist onto the examination table. "I'm coming over there . . . hang on." He ran into the cavernous hallway between the two buildings only to find hundreds of Colonists wandering about in confusion.

"Dr. Chadwick?" an elderly woman asked, grabbing his passing arm. "Are we all right? Is everything okay?" She pleaded for an answer.

"Yes, mum," he answered. "We've had a little accident on the surface with our power . . . but the emergency generators seem to be holding up well." As he pulled his arm free and continued across the crowded hallway, he suddenly remembered that the emergency generators had burned out and could not be repaired. "How *are* we getting power in here?" he muttered under his breath as he neared the Control Center.

"Hi Galley . . . Neemu. Molly, what's going on here? What's this about explosions?" Geoff asked as the vault door closed behind him. He walked to the security console where they were replaying the surveillance tape from the last few minutes.

"Look here, Geoff," Molly said, pointing to the kneeling figure on the monitor. "This is where he placed the grenade —"

"*Grenade?*" Chadwick yelled. "What in the hell is someone doing with a bloody grenade in here . . . and why is he kneeling . . . praying?"

"Never mind, Geoff. Watch this," Molly said as she pushed the fast forward cue control. They watched the video screen as the kneeling guard was attacked from his rear, thrown into the rail and rushed around at six times normal speed, fighting with a second super animated form. Molly released the cue button. Everything returned to normal speed just as Kane leapt onto the guard's back.

Chadwick watched the monitor in horror as the two bodies were thrown high into the air. His eyes widened further as he viewed the fiery eruption of the hydrogen fuel tank. Although the monitor screen immediately went dark, he continued to stare at the blank screen for several seconds. "But how are we getting power?" he asked numbly, still in an almost trance-like, unbelieving state.

"Emergency generators?" Neemu guessed.

Geoff pushed the rewind button to review the tape once more. "No. They were ruined during our last outage several weeks ago. We were never able to fix them. They were beyond—."

Chadwick was interrupted as the Control Center vault door opened once again. This time Janet Sherman entered. "I have an indication from Medusa of a breach in our Lockdown gate . . . the carnivore pens are dropping in temperature at a dangerous rate," she said rapidly as she rushed into the room. She looked directly into Chadwick's eyes. "Geoff, what in God's name happened out there?"

"All we know, Janet, is that the saboteur from several weeks ago was not Jon Morrow—it was the disgruntled security guard that I fired earlier. That same person just blew up our Hydrolox tanks. The explosions probably ruptured the Lockdown gate." He reached to the control panel and pushed the control button labeled ENTRANCE MONITOR CAMERA.

The screen flashed then slowly focused on what appeared to be a large white glowing disk with an extremely bright spot at its center. "This scene has always been dark because there are no lights shining on the Lockdown gate. Now we're seeing the outside light through the translucent ice. That bright spot in the center seems to be a rupture in the wall. It looks like the explosion did damage the wall."

Janet turned to leave. "I'm going up to the entrance to check the animals and the pens," she said as she grabbed her PCC and pressed the button. "See you guys later . . . send Hoxcart."

"I'm going with you," Chadwick said. "I've got to check the power station and the Lockdown gate."

"I'm going, too. I want to see what's up there in the sky giving us light," Neemu said quickly. "Care to go Galley? You and Molly are the only ones left."

"Of course, Neemu . . . and I think we should call CG, too. This has to be documented for the Colony records." Galley pushed the button on his PCC and spoke, "Call CG," as they left the Control Center.

"In living quarter . . . calling."

"*Ola*, Galley. *¿Que Pasa?*"

"CG, sorry to bother you so late. I assume you heard and felt the shocks."

"*Si*, they almost shook the living wall down . . . I'm glad it's attached at the top or we'd all be *muerto*. What happened? Was that an earthquake?"

"No, we had an explosion on the surface—our fuel tanks—caused by a saboteur. It turns out Jon Morrow was not the culprit in the earlier sabotage . . . it was a security guard out for revenge. And there's something else you need to document, CG. According to our surface surveillance camera—at least before it blew up—we have full sunlight in the middle of the night out there. We're going up to check it out. Want to go?"

"Sure. Give me time to throw on some warm clothes and I'll meet you in front of the cubicles."

Geoff Chadwick looked at Molly, still staring at the control console, and asked, "Molly, would you mind staying here and reporting any more unusual happenings to me by PCC?"

"No, of course not, Geoff." She looked at Chadwick briefly then turned her attention back to the computer console. "Actually, we seem to be having something unusual happening right now . . . we're experiencing a temperature increase of a fraction of a degree per minute on the surface thermometer."

The Hoxcart moved sluggishly up the winding steep cavern hallway with its five curious and crowded passengers struggling to stay aboard. Weaving slowly through the confused mass of Colonists in the hallway, Geoff tapped his hand impatiently on the Hoxcart steering column.

"Can't we go any faster, Geoff?" Janet asked impatiently as she grabbed his shoulder from behind.

"Janet, do you see any way to move along more quickly? I can't just run over people."

"Yes. On foot," she said jumping from the seat and starting to elbow through the crowd. "I've got to get to those animals."

The cart crept through the Big Room on a serpentine path, avoiding Colonists milling aimlessly along the way. As the increasingly impatient passengers watched Janet disappear from sight into the Temple of the Sun, CG broke the piercing tension, "I think she's right."

"*Who's* right?" Geoff queried.

"Janet. It will take us at least ten minutes to catch up with her at this rate. I'm going on foot, too." He stepped from the cart and started toward the upper rooms.

"Me, too," Galley said. "You game, Neemu? Can your leg take the walk?"

"Ya, who's thinking about pain at this time?"

Geoff stopped the Hoxcart and yelled, "Wait for us, CG . . . we're right behind you."

Passing from the Temple of the Sun into the Hall of Giants, the group began to gain on Janet. Soon they crossed the large dining room foyer, and saw its giant crystal chandelier had fallen. A motionless Colonist was pinned beneath it with delicate crystalline teardrops covering his twisted shape.

"We've got to keep moving," Geoff Chadwick said quickly. He grabbed his PCC and called for MEDAID assistance for the injured Colonist as they continued onward.

A short while later, the half-walking, half-running group anxiously neared the large concrete wall into the upper cave, only to find it mobbed by Colonists dressed in sub-zero clothing. Standing on tip-toes to see over the gathering, Geoff noticed

Janet at the small side door arguing with an irritable group of Colonists.

"We want to know what happened out there, too. Why *can't* we go with you?" one of them shouted indignantly. Another, standing several feet from Geoff and unaware of his approach, yelled, "I've got to get my babies out of here!" Several Colonists were standing, their face in tears, shaking with fear. Others were pushing forward through the crowd toward the large door to freedom—and the killing cold.

Realizing that something must be done to control the frenzied crowd, Geoff reached impulsively for his PCC and began to utilize a communication mode that no others possessed. Pushing the small red button, he said, "Call Colony emergency."

His PCC responded, "Please speak access password."

Chadwick paused momentarily, having some trouble remembering the cypher. He looked up from the ground and spoke rapidly into the device, "Armageddon."

The large entrance chamber shrieked with an ear-piercing whistle as the colonist's PCCs all sounded the incoming message alert simultaneously.

Geoff began to speak with an authoritative tone, his amplified words echoing through the chamber, "Er . . . may I have your attention please . . . this is Geoff Chadwick. We have had an explosion on the surface in our power system—it was not an earthquake. Please remain calm. I emphasize you *must* remain calm. Antron is in no immediate danger—"

One of the Colonists standing at the rear of the crowd heard Geoff's voice coming from behind him. He turned away from the door and, upon recognition of their Governor, shouted, "Here he is! Here's Chadwick!" The gathering of Colonists immediately turned toward the interrupting voice and began moving in its direction.

"I implore all Colonists to remain at ease. Some of the Colony Staff are presently going to the surface to investigate our damage up there," Chadwick continued.

The crowd became more agitated at his recent confirmation of danger.

"Please, *please* do not be concerned about the safety of Antron. On a hopeful note I want to relate another surface event we've just discovered: by some miraculous event, we have been given light again . . . in the middle of the night. The surface temperature is already beginning to warm. Please trust me, I will inform you as we gather more details." Chadwick completed his statement and began to lead his companions through the crowd.

Nearing the door, and Janet, Geoff and his associates turned back toward the crowd gathered round. Janet raised her arms and said, "We will be back in thirty minutes . . . wait here and we will return with news from the surface."

"The hell you will. You're deserting us and leaving us here to die," a terrified Colonist said accusingly.

"Shortly, we shall return to you with news of our investigation in the upper part of the caverns," Chadwick repeated, speaking loud enough to address the entire chamber. "Now we must go . . . there are freezing animals up there

324

that need our immediate attention." He moved to the small door at the side of the larger metallic double doors. A sign on the ground reading COLONISTS PROHIBITED BEYOND THIS POINT had been ripped from the wall.

As he reached for the cypher lock, Geoff realized that he was becoming extremely distraught with the situation. Much like during his final days at the Biosphere II where dissension was rampant and sabotage abounded he felt a gradual lessening of control over the Colony. He wiped the sweat from his forehead. His mind flashed back to the instructions Morrow had given him on opening the security doors to the upper cave. He punched the cypher code nine-nine-two into the lock. Nothing happened. Again he pushed the buttons with a different code. No results. The watching crowd murmured an audible gasp as Chadwick slammed his fist angrily into the cipher panel.

Seeing his frustration, Galley moved nearer to Chadwick and leaned close to his ear. "What's wrong? Won't it open?"

"No. I think I've forgotten the code. I thought it was nine—"

"Shhhh," Galley whispered. "Don't let them hear you, Geoff . . . move over. Are you all right?"

Chadwick looked obediently at Galley and moved aside to let him reach for the cipher lock panel. Galley keyed in the code nine-two-nine causing the handprint reader to activate. The silvery panel whished open to reveal a glass plate. "Put your hand there, Geoff—quickly!" Galley commanded.

Geoff stared blankly at Galley for a moment and then moved his attention slowly to the glass reader. "Why should I do that Galley?"

"To get us in, Geoff. Just do it!"

"Galley, I don't think I want to — you do it first."

Galley slapped his palm onto the glass reader and waited for the flash. A soft female message sounded from the nearby speaker, after which Galley responded, "Galley Pruitt." The small door clicked open allowing the staff members entrance.

Geoff, Neemu, Janet and CG proceeded singly through the narrow door into the chilly upper Main Corridor. As Galley began to move through the door, a large figure stepped forward from the crowd and grabbed his parka hood, letting the door slam behind CG. The jerking action twirled Galley around to face his captor. The bald huge caricature of a man, almost 6' 9" tall, must have weighed 350 pounds, all muscle. Galley immediately recognized him as the "Hulkman" from movies and professional wrestling. Hulkman lifted Galley off the ground by his parka, looked him directly in his eyes and asked in a loud deep voice, "You don't mind if we go with you, do you mister scientist?"

Galley swallowed audibly, and then responded in a slight choking voice, "I'm sorry but Colonists are not allowed up there . . . sir."

"We aren't? Why not?" Hulkman asked, looking toward the high-strung crowd.

A gentle sound murmured up from Galley's throat, "Antron rules."

"Screw the rules! We want out of here!" Hulkman growled as he released Pruitt's parka.

Galley stepped toward the small doorway,

followed closely by Hulkman and a few Colonists. "All right, but you're all going to freeze to death out there." He turned to face the door and placed his left hand on the cipher door lock as if he were unlocking it. With his right hand he unclipped his PCC from his collar. Galley watched over his shoulder as Hulkman turned to the crowd and smiled triumphantly. He silently pushed the button and whispered, "Call Antron Control." After speaking, Galley quickly clasped his hand over the PCC to muffle the expected response from being heard by the Colonists.

"Antron Control—Security . . . what can I do for you, Galley?" Molly's voice responded quietly behind Galley's palm.

"Send five strong armed guards up to the entrance to the upper part of the cave. A crowd of rowdy Colonists met our group at the upper door. They're holding me hostage until I let them out. I estimate there are about 70 to 80 of them. They're being led by a huge professional wrestler, the Hulkman."

"*Really?* I'd *love* to meet him!*"

"*Molly!*" Galley reprimanded, still whispering, "I'm seriously in danger; we'll have plenty of time for that after we get out of here. Now *please* get me those security men."

Molly typed: STAT: SEND FIVE GUARDS (>Strength 8) TO UPPER CAVERN-ARMED into the Medusa console. A message flashed on the screen:

COMMAND RECEIVED—DONE: <u>GUARDS</u>
    <u>ARMS</u>2@Strength 9
    TASER, AK-47, TMES-22

3@Strength 10
TASER, AK-47, TMES-45
RESPONDING STAT TO UPPER MAIN
CORRIDOR.

"Okay, Galley. The guards are on their way." Molly confirmed. "Anything else?"

"No, just hurry, damn it!" Galley whispered just before Hulkman grabbed his shoulder and whirled him around again.

"What's going on, little man? Can't you get the door open?"

"No, the computer thinks I already went through the door since I just unlocked it. Therefore it thinks it can't be me opening the door again. I've tried several times and it just doesn't believe it's me."

"Well then, who *can* open it?" Hulkman continued.

"Only staff members or security guards . . . I called a guard to come help me open it."

"Fine, we'll wait," Hulkman said, seating himself cross-legged on the floor near the door. He motioned with his hands palms-down for the crowd to sit.

Galley leaned against the cold metallic wall, trying to imagine what must be lying in wait for them outside.

Minutes later the crunching of footsteps on calcite crystals echoed up the Main Corridor toward the upper cave door. Five security guards dressed in black, looking like a metropolitan SWAT team, suddenly appeared in the corridor from the hallway below. Each was holding a small yellow Uzi-looking weapon at waist level pointed into the crowd of

Colonists. Laser beams spewed from their sights. The largest guard, slightly bigger than the wrestler, walked through the still-sitting assemblage to stand between Hulkman and Galley.

"Do you need assistance, Dr. Pruitt?" the deep-voiced guard asked with a chiding grin. The crowd stood and backed slowly from the door.

"Yes, I'm needed with Geoff Chadwick and the others up there," he motioned by nodding his head toward the upper cave. "Can you just help me get out of here safely? And by myself?"

"I think we can do that, yessir," the guard answered. "Go ahead."

As Medusa responded to Galley's spoken name, the motion of the door opening set Hulkman off. He screamed, "Noooooo! Not without uuuuuussss!" and began running toward Galley. The large guard gently squeezed the trigger on his weapon. A gentle pop sounded moments before Hulkman was slammed to the ground writhing in pain, screaming obscenities. The crowd continued to back from the door. Then Hulkman was silent.

Galley, surprised by the lack of noise and bloodshed from the evil looking weapon's discharge asked, "What happened?"

Smiling, the guard looked down and patted the weapon's breech. "It's called the Edge— Electronic-Drug Dart Gun. Works good, huh?"

Galley glanced at the weapon and noticed the small logo TMES stamped into the yellow metal breech. He smiled back, raised an eyebrow. "The Morrows strike again." Galley turned and left the chamber slamming the steel door solidly behind him.

Minutes later Galley caught up with Neemu, Chadwick and CG just as the upper-cave announcement warning beep burst from everyone's PCC simultaneously . . . again. Neemu put his hands over his ears and yelled, "Damn that Morrow." His cursing was not heard over the shrill canned security-warning statement: "You are entering a secured area. Please observe all instructions and warnings during your presence."

As the announcement echoes faded, the group of scientists continued to move deliberately uphill toward Antron's entrance with Janet still in the lead. Galley looked forward into the brightly illuminated Main Corridor. Ahead lay the steep trek to the Devil's Den and Whale's Mouth. Behind was a confused and nervous crowd of Colonists on the other side of the closed metal doors. Some were pounding with their fists to be freed.

Galley stepped quickly to catch up with Janet Sherman and match her pace. Neemu moved in smoothly beside them, also in lock-step. CG fell in behind. The prolonged uphill brisk-paced walking had winded the scientists beyond talking.

Galley noticed Janet look over to him expecting conversation. He held up his right index finger and waved it back and forth, then gasped, "Wait a minute." Janet smiled and kept her rapid pace for the carnivore pens.

Almost five minutes had passed before Galley caught his breath from the rapid trip up the steep corridor. They were now in the relatively flat chamber of the Devil's Den heading for the Whale's Mouth cavern. Galley, still breathing with rapid shallow gasps, looked toward Janet and asked, "Are you really worried about the animals?"

"Yes, of course I am. See how much colder it's getting as we approach the entrance?"

Neemu shivered involuntarily for an instant then looked at Chadwick, who was now stepping mechanically with sweat running down his face. "Are you all right, Geoff?"

"I'm okay. Just a little tired, Neemu," he answered. "I think . . . I need to rest for a moment."

Twenty minutes had passed before the group neared the carnivore pens. Janet left the group to enter the containment area surrounding the cages. Slowly pacing the long walkways between the cages she began to inspect, one-by-one, the animals confined there.

Galley, CG and Neemu continued onward toward the surface, helping Geoff stay on his feet as they went. He continued to exhibit a strange weakness and confusion, even after his two-minute rest.

As they neared the Bat Cave and Power Plant Complex, Galley looked up into the cavern entrance corridor—the Twilight Zone—and saw the light coming from behind the Lockdown Gate. As bright as daylight, with the same apparent color spectrum, the brilliance made him squint, even from this distant viewpoint. "Look guys," he said, "the light."

"Ya, I see." Neemu said quietly as he stared at the unbelievable sight.

"Wow!" CG agreed.

Geoff, looking toward the Power Plant asked, "Could one of you please help me into the Power Control Room?"

"Sure, Geoff. I will," Neemu said, lifting Geoff's arm over his shoulder. They moved toward the rumbling-humming concrete door of the Power

331

Plant as Galley and CG started up the Twilight Zone toward the entrance.

Noticing the temperature had dropped severely since he changed cavern corridors and was continuing to decrease as he neared the entrance, Galley once again pushed the PCC button, "Call Antron Control."

"Molly here, Galley. Did you make it past the upper-cave door safely? I saw my indicator light when you passed through it."

"Yes. Thank you, Molly, for sending the guards. I couldn't have made without them. Now, can you give me a temperature reading up here near the cave entrance? I think I'm in the Twilight Zone."

She keyed the request into Medusa and immediately saw the answer flash across the screen: -20 degrees F. "It's twenty below in there, Galley and still dropping. The heating system is having trouble battling the hole in the Gate . . . but what's really strange is that outside temperatures are warming up faster than your inside temperature is dropping."

Galley considered what Molly had said for several seconds before he responded. "Molly, could you work up an outside temperature versus time gradient for me over the next five-minute period. Then calculate from that the temperature increase per hour—and day. I want to get an idea of the warm-up rate out there."

"Sure, Galley. I'll have it to you shortly."

Galley proceeded carefully with CG toward the ice-wall Lockdown Gate, stepping over chunks of ice several feet in diameter that had blown out of the center of the Gate during the explosion. As they moved into the indirect light of the upper cave entrance, Galley saw that the Gate was fractured at a level some twenty feet above the ground. There was no possible way of leaving the cave through this hole in the ice . . . he estimated it to be only three to four feet in diameter. Moving to look up into the sky through the hole, he felt his foot step on a small hollow-sounding object.

"What's that?" CG asked, looking toward Galley's feet.

Galley said, "I don't know," and stooped to examine the rectangular black object, wiping away the dirt and dust with his glove. As the dust cleared, he saw on its face a torn black and yellow diagonally striped label reading: AN ON SE U IT A CH VES, AU U T 8, 2012. He rubbed the object's face again trying to uncover the missing letters but they wouldn't appear.

"What the hell is this?" he asked. He turned the partially damaged object in his hands. Then he recognized the familiar shape. "Wait. This must be the video tape the saboteur dropped from the top of the tank! It was probably blown into the cave by the explosion." He slowly realized that he was quite possibly holding the answer to the mysterious events leading to the Morrows' deaths.

"Let's go," he said as he shoved the tape into the side pocket of his parka. They sprinted—half hurdling ice boulders, half running—back to the Power Complex where Neemu and Geoff Chadwick were waiting.

"Well, what did you guys find up there?" Neemu asked eagerly, his eyes twinkling. "Did we grow a new Sun?"

Galley, again gasping in short breaths, shook

his head and answered, "Don't know. There *is* a hole in the Gate, but it's up too high to see out of. We're just going to have to wait until it thaws, if it ever—."

Almost as if on cue, Galley's PCC screeched with Molly's incoming message. "Galley, I have that warming trend data you wanted. I just don't know if you're ready for it — I wasn't."

"Try me."

"Over the past hour we've warmed almost eight degrees out there. That's about one-hundred degrees per day . . . assuming we get twelve hours of light per day."

"We'll be back to normal in less than three days at that rate!" Galley said quietly, not understanding what was happening. He looked unbelievingly at Neemu and CG. Geoff Chadwick was staring unemotionally up into the Twilight Zone. "Thanks, Molly. We'll have to let that news soak in a little while. Oh . . . and there is a hole in the Gate. It's just big enough to crawl through, but it's way over my head . . . about twenty feet up."

"Well, we'll just have to get a ladder. See when you get back, Galley. Hope you like the news . . . I'm packing my bags," Molly said preparing to sign off.

"Oh, Molly. I found something else up here that might interest you—a video tape that was apparently blown through the hole."

"*The missing archive tape?*" she responded, her voice distorting over the PCC.

"We think so. I'm bringing it in. Get the player ready."

"Hurry!"

As the group moved slowly back to the meat-eater cages, Neemu explained what he had managed to grasp from Geoff's confused rambling in the Power Complex. As Geoff examined the gauges and meters on the turbines, he vaguely remembered Morrow telling him to increase the efficiency of the Hydrolox liquefiers. He had initially questioned the request but then obediently followed orders. Although the giant storage tanks were, in fact, gone and their gauges read empty, the liquefiers were so efficient in the -200 degree outside temperature that they were providing full fuel flow for the main generators from the outside air.

"What's going to happen to the generators as we warm up out there?" CG asked.

Geoff looked blankly into CG's eyes and answered, "They quit . . . they just run out of gas and quit."

Galley thought momentarily as they walked. "Geoff, is there any way to store two days worth of fuel, if we cut back, now?" He was hoping there was something else Morrow might have planned for.

Geoff rubbed the sweat from his forehead and answered, "I think there are almost two days worth of liquefied gases stored in the transport pipes, alone. Those generators are very efficient. But don't worry . . . Jackson Morrow planned ahead, God rest his poor soul. There are diesel generators down the hill set to automatically start when the outside temperature reaches forty degrees. Those are supposed to keep us going until we all leave. I think there is about a week or two of fuel out there— when it thaws."

"Thank God," Galley exclaimed, "at least something's going right around here."

As they approached the cages, Janet walked out of the shadows into the Main Corridor. "The animals are very cold, but I turned up the heaters. If we don't do something else, they won't make it another week."

"Then quit worrying," Galley replied with a consoling smile. "Molly estimates the warming from that light outside will warm the Earth back to normal in less than three days."

The unexpected good news caused several minutes of gleeful cajoling among the scientists.

"What did it look like out there Galley? What's giving us light?" Neemu asked as the group moved downward with a quicker, more refreshed pace.

"Couldn't get out to see ... I'll explain it later."

The group returned to the Colony without disturbance, thanks to the guards waiting at the upper cavern entrance door. They dropped Geoff at the MEDAID center and headed directly for Antron Control.

"Molly, here's the tape," Galley said, entering the security monitoring room. She grabbed the tape and dropped it into the player.

"Now, let's see who really sabotaged the tanks," she said as she pushed PLAY.

The monitor flashed with light, showing a scene that surprised everyone in the room. It was not the illuminated Hydrolox tanks but a still, darkened view recorded at the carnivore pens. "What is this?" Molly asked, looking back to Galley.

He shrugged his shoulders. "I don't know. Let's watch."

Five minutes passed with no visual activity on the screen. The quiet was broken periodically by various animal roars and a pleading hollow voice screaming, "H-H-Help! P-P-Please get me out of h-h-here. I'm s-s-so cold."

Molly moved closer to the screen. "That's Jon Morrow yelling."

"Shhh," CG whispered.

As they continued to watch in silence, hushed footsteps echoed from the speaker. Seconds later a figure walked into view from the corridor. The dimly lit shape turned to look back. "It's that damn guard, again!" Neemu said, crowding Molly from the monitor.

As quickly as he appeared, he moved out of view into the cages. "Damn it," Neemu said, "he's gone . . . what's he going to —?"

Neemu's question was never finished. The security room again fell silent as a heated conversation began to flow from the console speaker. "Oh, t-t-thank God! Hey, c-c-can you get me out of h-h-here? I'm so c-c-cold . . . it's *y-y-you!* You're the g-g-guard I f-f-found messing with the h-h-hydrogen l-l-line. *You* s-s-sabotaged our p-p-power system!"

"Yes, it *was* me . . . but nobody else knows that. You're the only one who saw me. Why did you have to screw up my plan?"

"I-I-I was just f-f-following you, because I r-r-recognized you leaving the c-c-cave. You w-w-were the one who my b-b-brother and Geoff f-f-fired. I was j-j-just thought you f-f-forgot something and had c-c-come back to get it. T-T-Then I saw

337

you t-t-tamper with the f-f-fuel line and r-r-run back into cave. I f-f-followed you all th-th-the way. Why d-d-did you do th-th-that? Can you please l-l-let me out of h-h-ere? It's s-s-so cold."

"Don't worry jerk. You won't feel it much longer. With you out of the way, no one'll know about me and my plan. You people just can't do that to me. It was only an accident . . . and so will you be. You just got too close to the tiger and it mauled you."

"*N-n-nooo!* Please don't sh-sh-shoot! Please —." Jon's pleas were covered by an echoing gunshot. As the reverberations died an angry growl filled the chamber. Sounds of bones snapping . . . flesh tearing . . . a hungry mouth smacking on warm fresh meat drifted from the speaker.

Molly turned from the monitor and hit the STOP control. "My God, what a horrible way to die," she said mournfully, walking to the center of the room.

They all stood staring at the blank screen for moments. "I'm going home to get some sleep," Galley said obviously exhausted from the night's discoveries. "I think you all should, too."

Neemu, with reddening eyes, turned to leave. "Ya. Me too. See you all in the morning. At least I think we've finally seen the light at the end of the tunnel." As he turned back, a forced smile belied his emotions.

Molly walked to him and with a warm hug said, "Everything's going to be all right, Neemu . . . get some rest.

"Okay, guys. Goodnight. See you tomorrow."

X X X X X

"Good morning, Antronians," over 1000 PCC's blasted in unison. The voice of Geoff Chadwick echoed cheerfully through the cavern. The time was 7:22 p.m. "As you all know I have been ill for the past three days. It was not, as suspected, the Hantavirus but a combination of a simple influenza and exhaustion. I'm pleased to announce that I'm now quite well and ready to lead those of you that wish to venture out into the warm light. The temperature outside is now fifty-two degrees—above zero—and warming rapidly. It's so warm out there our power system switched automatically to diesel power last night. It should keep us in operation for another several weeks."

A cheer roared throughout the Colony. Expectations of the welcomed but still confusing revelation had been circulating among the Colonists since the return of the surface scouting team, three days earlier. People, upon hearing rumors, had started getting their belongings in order. Contingent existence in Antron had begun to take on an excitement never before felt.

Geoff's announcement continued, "Those Colonists that choose to march with us to the surface should be warned that we don't really know what to expect out there. This is because no one has been able to exit through the Ice Gate before now . . . it's now melted, as of an hour ago. Our elevator was destroyed in the explosion . . . that wasn't told to you because of the fear of panic. Now we're free to exit. Those that wish to explore our new beginning are welcome to join the staff at the upper cave doors in one hour.

"If you plan to leave permanently on this first trip-and I don't recommend it—please bring your children, pets and belongings. Those that do will be placed at the rear of the group allowing the unencumbered Colonists to pace readily ahead. Your vehicles should be warmed to the point of operation by our new light. If you have any problems with damaged vehicles from the explosion, we have over fifty buses parked down at the bottom of the canyon, waiting to take you home.

"All of you leaving Antron will find living with a twelve-hour reversal in daylight hours confusing at first. If you'll simply trade a.m. with p.m. the time shift should be easier to tolerate. Another difficulty you will find out there is a noticeable lack of humanity . . . and food. This is most unfortunate for everyone—but expected. Neemu Hatlem, our communications officer, has been on the shortwave radio talking to those that made it through. There are quite a few survivors out there that sought underground shelter like us—obviously without the opulence of our surroundings. But they are alive. Power is returning to some of the larger cities and even a few utilities are expected to resume service in a week or two.

"On a final note, I would like to invite all who wish to stay longer to join us in our topside Colony, New Antron, that will break ground next week. Jackson Morrow also planned for that before his death. It will be a self-sustaining colony with simple habitats, gardens and a very large zoo. Its purpose will be to gradually repopulate the Earth with humans, flora and fauna. Our workers and maintenance staff have agreed to stay with us and help bring the various biospheres to the surface.

"If you do return home and find it difficult to survive, please join us back here. Your initial initiation fee paid for it all, so there will be no further charges . . . but we do expect everyone to work.

"In closing it has been my pleasure serving as your Governor for the past few weeks. I feel I know each of you personally. I hope to continue serving on your behalf in New Antron. Please join me at the upper cave door in one hour— excuse me, fifty-six minutes, now—to venture forth and witness and be part of the Earth's second Genesis. Thanks to Jackson and some benevolent entity up there this mighty ark has landed safely ashore. What happens next is up to us. Thank you . . . and Godspeed."

In their cubicle, Jalisa smiled at Galley as Geoff completed his salutation. "What do you want to do, Galley?"

Galley looked over to Neemu and Rutha. "Neemu, what are you and Rutha going to do?

"I think we'll take the kids home and gather a few more belongings. I don't really think the VLA will open for business anytime soon, so I'd like to return here. That's a pretty nice telescope Morrow built for us up there . . . probably going to need some expert rebuilding after that explosion. We'll need to report on the remainder of Endlight, you know. Maybe we can even find out what those things in the sky are."

"Yeah, you're right," Galley agreed. "You and I still have a mystery to solve."

Jalisa and Rutha stood and hugged their husbands as the kids gathered around and began to shout, "We don't wanna leave! We don't wanna leave!"

"Done! Let's go back to Socorro, get some stuff and your car and we'll meet back here to start anew."

"Ya. Okey dokey with us, Galley," Neemu said letting a huge smile cover his face. The families stood together for several minutes, hugging and choking back the emotion built up during the past months.

"We love you guys—and this place," Galley said, "We're staying." Neemu and Rutha hugged, then kissed and responded in unison, "Us, too."

After carefully bundling the children in their cool winter wear, the two couples explained their decisions to them. The kids howled with joy as they left their cubicles for the large door.

Geoff Chadwick pressed the large red button with pride, parting the massive steel doors for the first time since Lockdown. With a crowd of over a thousand people behind him, he began to move up the Main Corridor toward the surface. The pace was brisk, resembling the start of a large marathon race, as everyone moved forward together. Minutes later they neared the Twilight Zone and apprehensions audibly rose. The mass of people were moving and chattering about their experiences in the cave. Some were looking to their future; some were reliving their past.

As Geoff reached the entrance he stopped and raised his hands, halting his followers. He turned toward the quieted mass and jubilantly commanded, "Talley ho! Onward the Light

Brigade!" jamming his right arm toward the light outside. Galley muttered quietly, "Oh brother, hope we don't end up like they did." Neemu rolled his eyes in response.

The mass moved slowly out into the new light, squinting as their eyes adjusted to the brightness of their new world. Some stopped to look mournfully at their barren surroundings. Everything was steaming in the strangely surrealistic landscape.

Others walked straight into the brilliant desert light outside the caverns where large gray thunderheads were building all around. All eventually overcame their daylight blindness and looked up into the new light. They fell to their knees, one by one, at what they saw. There, up above them, were the ten brilliant suns spanning most of the sky. The points of light were arranged in a perfect illuminating cross in the heavens. It's arms spread across the east-west sky, with the base pointing south. The people of Antron prayed. The Earth was saved.

Minutes later, after standing with his family arm-in-arm, Neemu smiled through watery eyes at Galley and Jalisa. "Okay, folks," he called. "Let's call it a day."

Galley and Jalisa laughed. "Neemu, you're so corny. Let's get back to the cave, man."

THE BEGINNING